Requiem in Vienna

This Large Print Book carries the
Seal of Approval of N.A.V.H.

REQUIEM IN VIENNA

A VIENNESE MYSTERY

J. SYDNEY JONES

THORNDIKE PRESS

A part of Gale, Cengage Learning

GALE
CENGAGE Learning

Detroit • New York • San Francisco • New Haven, Conn • Waterville, Maine • London

LIBRARY OF CONGRESS CATALOGING-IN-PUBLICATION DATA

Jones, J. Sydney.
    Requiem in Vienna : a Viennese mystery / by J. Sydney Jones.
        p. cm. — (Thorndike Press large print reviewers' choice)
    ISBN-13: 978-1-4104-2570-6 (alk. paper)
    ISBN-10: 1-4104-2570-3 (alk. paper)
    1. Mahler, Gustav, 1860–1911—Fiction. 2. Opera—Austria—
Vienna—Fiction. 3. Gross, Hans, 1847–1915—Fiction.
4. Criminologists—Fiction. 5. Vienna (Austria)—Fiction. 6. Large
type books. I. Title.
PS3610.O62553R47 2010b
813'.6—dc22   2010001875

Published in 2010 by arrangement with St. Martin's Press, LLC.

For the sibs, Gwen and Lowell

ACKNOWLEDGMENTS

Once again, thanks go out to the usual suspects. To Alexandra Machinist, for being the kind of supportive yet straight-talking agent every writer hopes for. To Peter Joseph, an editor of sagacity and wit and steadfast co-conspirator in the Viennese Mystery series. To Hector DeJean, publicity manager extraordinaire, whose personal enthusiasm and tireless efforts are greatly appreciated. To Margaret Smith, an editorial assistant who is always on top of things and always there with an answer. A round of thanks also to the art department, copy editors, and production folks for their creative labors on behalf of this book. And, to my wife, Kelly, and son, Evan, who have lived a good deal of time with these characters in our midst and who, like good hosts, have always been polite to them, a final thanks for your patience and love.

PROLOGUE

Observers afterward noted nothing different about the day. Just another typical rehearsal under the new Court Opera Director Gustav Mahler. "The drill sergeant," the singers called him.

They were preparing for a performance of *Lohengrin* and Mahler was particularly fussy about Wagner. A Jew — though he had converted to Christianity before being offered his new position — Mahler walked on Tiffany eggs whenever preparing for one of the Master of Bayreuth's works, for Wagner was still the darling of the German nationalist press. Upset one of those critics with a single note out of place, a slight misstep in staging, and Mahler would bear the brunt of their "What can you expect from a Jew" level of criticism.

So, today, hectoring, hectoring. And there would be a good eight hours of it if the Herr Director's usual routine was followed.

The object of his strident complaints this morning was Fräulein Margarethe Kaspar, a young mezzo from the back of beyond in the Austrian region of the Waldviertel, the most unlikely place for a singer to hail from. A pig farmer was more likely the product of that region; a slightly moon-faced, inbred specimen of the human race. Not a soprano at Vienna's Court Opera!

Yet here she was, Fräulein Kaspar from Krumau (not even an inhabitant of the so-called city of Zwettl!) in full regalia for her role as one of the four pages in Wagner's adaptation of the medieval German romance. Her heavily rouged lips were trembling; she was near tears.

"You're singing like you're calling in the pigs for slops," Mahler shouted at her. "Please do not make me regret my decision to sign you."

It was later reported that at that point the poor girl broke into the tears that had been accumulating, waiting for egress; that her otherwise creamy complexion turned a quite unattractive blotchy, mottled red at the cheeks, and she cupped her rather tiny hands over her face in shame.

"My God, woman," Mahler thundered on. "Do compose yourself. This a profession, you know. If you haven't the skin for it, go back to your rustic simplicity and the local boys with their thick hands."

This last was said with Mahler standing not a hand's length from the young girl, yet his comments carried to the last row of the balcony.

A sudden hush went over the entire cast; even the cacophonous tuning of the orchestra in the pit and last-minute backstage hammerings were stilled. This was too much, and even Mahler seemed to realize he had overstepped the bounds of propriety.

He drew closer and wrapped a protective arm around the girl — who was rumored to be his mistress, of course. She was of no great size; still, she stood half a head over the diminutive director, who was five feet and four inches in his scuffed leather boots.

"There, there, Grethe." He patted her shoulder, attempting rather unconvincingly to console the young girl. "I am sorry to shout at you so. But the high C must be hit, not simply approached. Essential, quite essential."

Then he left her, still sobbing, turning back to the rest of the opera chorus.

"What are you all gaping at? Back to work." He clapped his hands, an insistent schoolmaster.

At that very instant came a shout from

11

behind the partially curtained stage.

"Watch out!"

It was too late, however, for the heavy asbestos fire curtain, its hem filled with lead weights, came crashing down. It hurtled onto the unfortunate Fräulein Kaspar, who was still weeping into her cupped hands. The curtain narrowly missed Mahler, who dove out of the way.

The curtain hit the stage with a fearful crashing, after which there was a moment of stunned silence. Only the black patent leather shoes of the fallen soprano were to be seen from under the curtain. Then came shouted voices from the stagehands behind the curtain, one carried above the others: "She's dead. By God, the little songbird's dead and gone."

ONE

Tuesday, June 6, 1899
Vienna, Austria

Werthen refused to walk to the cemetery. He would show his respect to the dead by his presence at the grave site, but his damaged right knee, the result of a duel, kept him from making the two-mile pilgrimage by foot from the center of Vienna out to the Central Cemetery in Simmering, the recently incorporated Eleventh District, as hundreds of other dignitaries were doing.

A duel! My Lord, how blithely it played through his mind, but how improbable it would have seemed mere months before. As foreign to him as Swahili; as much an aberration to his staid existence as polite parlor conversation would be to a bushman.

A duel of words perhaps, verbal pyrotechnics before an easily amused judge; that had been his métier. But not a duel to the death; not the too-intimate warmth of an opponent's back against his before beginning the mandatory fifteen paces. Not the cold feel of metal in his hand from a pistol. Not such an eccentricity for Karl Werthen, *advokat* superior of wills and trusts!

But he had done it, and done it well enough to explode his opponent's cranium like a smashed pumpkin, spilling crimson blood and pinkish gray brains onto the green lawns of the Prater one chilly autumn morning. It had been a life-and-death struggle to rid himself, his friends, and his beloved wife Berthe of a man who quite simply wanted to kill them all one fine day.

Werthen shook the evil memory of that brutal killing out of his mind, taking up position as closely as he could to the freshly dug grave site in Group 32A, plot number 27, just between the final resting places of Franz Schubert and Johannes Brahms. In operation for only a quarter of century, the Central Cemetery was already filling up. Five hundred acres, and soon the place would be a high-rent district, Werthen mused. Half the size of Zürich, as the Viennese quipped, and twice the fun.

Here at Group 32A were all the notables of musical history: those that had died since the cemetery's opening in 1875, such as Brahms and Anton Bruckner, and those

dead from an earlier epoch — Gluck, Beethoven, Schubert — their remains dug up
and reinterred here in the 1880s. Missing,
of course, were Papa Haydn, buried in
Eisenstadt, and Mozart, and who knew
where that poor wretch's bones were.

No final resting place for Werthen in this
group. No, his bones would molder in the
Jewish plot near Gate 1.

Werthen had been dutifully at his office in
the Habsburgergasse this morning when the
crowds of mourners thronging the nearby
Episcopalian Church had reminded him
that this was the great one's funeral. What
the hell, he had thought. An outing. A show
of respect for a true master. He told his assistant, Doktor Wilfried Ungar, that he
would be back after lunch, and left before
the priggish young man could make a comment. Ungar was the sort to flaunt his
double degree in law and economics; even
his intimates called him Doktor Doktor Ungar. Werthen could not complain, however.
The junior lawyer had kept his firm going
for the last few months with Werthen's
extended healing from his dueling injury
and his subsequent reconsideration of what
he wanted to do with his life. Lying in his
recovery bed, he had felt like an adolescent
again, facing the great questions of career

15

and the meaning of life. A bullet in the flesh focuses one's mind wonderfully on what is most important in life. Actually, there had not been a lot of soul-searching involved: he'd begun his career in criminal law before turning to the more benign field of wills and trusts; he knew now he must return to his first calling in one form or another.

The crowds of mourners were only now reaching the cemetery after their long walk. Their route had been marked by gas street-lamps burning at midday. Businesses and schools had closed in order that the populace might pay their last respects as the funeral cortege passed by, the hearse drawn by four gray Lippizaners and accompanied by eight carriages full of flowers through the crowd-choked streets of Vienna.

It was unseasonably warm for early June. Werthen's black serge suit soaked in the sun's rays like a sponge. Sweat formed at his tight starched collar. He could imagine how uncomfortable those pilgrims were who had made the journey on foot; bad enough for him after a pleasant *fiaker* ride. Every able-bodied official, artist, musician, intellectual, and even a critic or two, had trudged along behind the coaches.

The sight of the funeral cortege approaching down the long lanes of the Central

Cemetery reminded him of another funeral just last September; that of the Empress Elisabeth, so cruelly assassinated in Geneva. He felt a twinge in his knee at the thought, for her death and the wound were inextricably linked.

He brought his mind back to today's events. People were jostling about him now, trying to get a good position to see the proceedings at graveside. An old and very diminutive gentleman who clearly had not made the trip on foot now crowded directly in front of Werthen, his rather unorthodox and impossibly high top hat completely blocking the lawyer's view.

Pinned in on both sides with newly arrived mourners, Werthen had no choice but to tap the old man on the shoulder.

A red face punctuated by a heavily veined nose turned to confront him.

"Sorry. Perhaps you could remove your hat so I could see."

"Nonsense," the man spluttered and turned back to the grave.

The mayor had now arrived. Werthen strained to see around the shiny black hat as Karl Lueger, already a Viennese legend for his good looks as much as for his demagoguery, scrambled atop a makeshift platform. Werthen had a momentary impulse to squash the damnable stovepipe in front of him, for he wanted to get a good look at the mayor as he spoke. He could hardly understand his fascination with this Jew-baiting mayor, but there it was: Werthen like most of Vienna had been mesmerized with the man's oratorical skill, his magnetism and charisma. Since taking office, Lueger, to his credit, had toned down his rhetoric, no longer blaming the Jews of the empire for every woe. He had initiated urban renewal projects, saw to the regulation of the Danube Canal and the completion of the *Stadtbahn,* the interurban rail, and initiated a form of welfarism for the citizens of the capital.

A hush fell over the gathered crowd as the mayor prepared to speak. At the same moment, Werthen, peering around the black column of hat in front of him, caught the eye of his old friend and client, the painter Gustav Klimt, standing on the opposite side of the grave from him. Klimt gave him a wink.

The painter, no giant himself — as broad as he was tall — towered over the man who stood next to him. Werthen recognized this smaller man as the director of the Hofoper, or Court Opera, Gustav Mahler, the youngest man to ever take the helm there, just thirty-seven when he arrived in Vienna two years earlier. They must have made the journey together on foot; Klimt, an eager walker, looked none the worse for wear. As he gazed at the pair of men, Werthen wondered when Klimt was ever going to pay his long overdue bill. Werthen now looked for the family members close by the graveside, but there were only distant members in attendance. Conspicuously missing was the man's widow, Adele, and his brother, Eduard. Werthen found that decidedly odd.

"My friends," Mayor Lueger began in booming tones guaranteed to reach the last rows, "we are gathered here today for a most solemn occasion. On the long mourning journey to this final resting place for our beloved maestro, thousands upon thousands gathered to bid a final farewell. Those Viennese citizens who took time off from their work, schools, and homes feel in their hearts the same as we all do who are gathered here — a heavy and heart-wrenching sadness at the loss of such a great man."

Werthen's attention was distracted from the speech by a thin wraith of a man who was attempting the impossible: to insert himself between Werthen and the old man with the top hat.

". . . to be honored by his beloved city,

buried between two other masters of music, Schubert and his beloved friend, Brahms. . . ."

He caught bits and pieces of the speech, focusing instead on the thin man who now edged effortlessly in front of him.

". . . We Viennese promise here on his grave never to forget this man or his music. . . ."

Werthen quickly saw the reason for the man's crowding. The fellow was obviously waiting for a high point in the speech to make his move.

"And so I say to you, my dear friends, that so long as a Viennese lives, he will never forget you, dear maestro. We have chosen your final resting place here amidst the greatest composers the world has ever known. We testify therewith, that whenever Vienna is spoken of, then also will come the name Johann Strauss. We take leave of you now, dear Waltz King, leaving you to make your way on your final voyage, promising to forever keep the flame of your triumphant spirit alive in our hearts and souls."

At this there was general applause, despite the solemn occasion, and it was then the thin man struck.

Werthen was familiar with the technique from his early days defending such miscreants. The man's wiry hand slipped neatly into the old man's jacket pocket, deftly extracting a change purse of alarming proportions. As the gathered mourners continued to applaud Mayor Lueger's speech, to be replaced on the platform by the director of the Vienna Friends of Music, the ghostlike creature in front of Werthen proceeded to edge away.

"Not so fast," Werthen said, grabbing the man's neck in a vicelike grip. The man's head turned to him, startled eyes glared at him.

"What do you want?" the man fairly hissed at him.

"Hand over the money or it's the Liesel for you."

The nickname for the city's main prison did the trick; the man dropped the bag of coins and Werthen released his grip. The wraith melted away into the crowds. All of this transpired with such speed that those around him had been unaware of the altercation.

Werthen bent to pick up the old man's purse. As he stood upright again, the old man turned, saw the purse in his hand, and began shouting.

"Thief! Thief! The bounder is stealing my purse."

Before Werthen could attempt an explanation, he was quickly pinioned at either arm by the men around him and hustled to the back of the crowd. The old man trundled along behind him making occasional outbursts. At the edge of the crowd, a gendarme in blue jacket and red pants clamped a heavy hand on his shoulder.

"Now, then," the gendarme said. "What's all this about?"

Werthen spent the next fifteen minutes explaining what had happened, interrupted repeatedly by the blustery old man.

"And where is this pickpocket now?" the policeman asked.

But Werthen could not spot the man among the crowd of mourners. He'd most likely made a run for it after hearing the commotion.

"I assure you, Officer, I do not come to funerals on the off chance of picking some man's pocket. I am a lawyer, after all, an officer of the court."

The crowds of people were beginning to trail away from the grave site now. Workers were busy unloading the flowers from the coaches, making hillocks of the heavily scented blooms. Other workers were spading dirt onto the coffin; the official gravestone would not be erected until later.

"Officer of the court or no," the policeman said, "there's a complaint against you . . ."

"May I be of service?"

Werthen had not noticed Klimt's approach. The usually gruff painter was all sweetness as he doffed his hat to the policeman and the old man alike. Those who had helped to take Werthen into "custody" had long since departed the scene, testifying only that they had seen the lawyer with the coin purse in his hand.

"That depends on the service you're offering," the policeman replied. Klimt did not blink at this, however, maintaining his sweetness-and-light demeanor. Werthen was about to greet his old friend when Klimt gave an abrupt, though surreptitious, shake of the head.

The painter pulled a card out of his vest pocket and handed it to the policeman.

"Herr Gustav Klimt, at your service." He tipped his hat again, smiling unctuously. "Painter to his majesty's court."

Stretching it a bit, thought Werthen. Sometimes painter of the ceilings of various public buildings, more like it. And full-time disruptor of the public sense of decency and morality with his nudes.

The policeman eyed the proffered card

suspiciously, rubbing a thick thumb over the embossed lettering.

. "I was standing across from these gentlemen and I saw everything that transpired. This gentleman here" — he indicated Werthen — "was simply acting the Good Samaritan, stopping a theft in progress. He was attempting to return a coin purse to this gentleman" — indicating the old man — "and there arose a subsequent misunderstanding."

"The man is a bounder," the old one all but shouted. It was unclear whom he meant by this admonition, Werthen or Klimt.

"I'll swear to it," Klimt plunged on. "You may take my testimony here and now if you like."

"Well," the policeman said.

"You're not taking his word for it. They're obviously in cahoots."

The policeman rolled his eyes at this statement from the elderly gent; a good sign, thought Werthen, who also realized any further protestations on his part would be counterproductive. The embossed lettering on Klimt's card had done the trick: IMPERIAL ROYAL COURT PAINTER, GUSTAV KLIMT.

The policeman plopped the coin purse back in the old man's hands.

"I think we can say that justice has been done. It would seem there was a simple misunderstanding."

"Why, you blithering idiot," the old man spluttered.

Werthen left the man to his explanations. But the officer no longer looked in the mood for discussion.

They found a corner seat in the Café Feldman, directly across the street. It was a cavernous establishment, catering to funeral parties. Nothing cosy or *gemütlich* about it. But it was handy to the cemetery.

"Many thanks," Werthen said as they sat.

"Nothing more or less than you've done for me. Glad to return the favor. And I am especially happy that these cards I had printed have finally come to some use."

"It was fortunate you saw what had transpired," Werthen said, eying the menu on the table.

"Didn't see a thing," Klimt said, not bothering to inspect his menu. "The duffer's hat blocked my view. But I heard the old fool blustering on and figured out what had transpired. Serves him right for being such a stick-in-the-mud."

"You know him?" Werthen asked.

"Of him. I recognized him straight off.

Surprised you didn't, as well. That was Eduard Hanslick, Vienna's self-styled musical dictator."

So that was Hanslick, Werthen thought. The man had ruled the musical scene for a generation; his critical opinions could still make or break a composer and performer. A great opponent to the Romantic music of Wagner and Bruckner, Hanslick supported the formal music of classicism, as represented by Brahms. What was his line about Johann Strauss? Something about the fact that Strauss's tunes made the listener unfit for serious music. The pompous old buzzard; Werthen hoped the policeman fined him for being rude.

The waitress arrived and Klimt ordered coffee with *schlag obers* — "A mountain of whipped cream," he said to the young woman. "Burying a man gives a fellow an appetite." This to be accompanied by a linzer torte.

Werthen had his usual *kleine braune;* he hoped to be home in time for lunch. Frau Blatschky had promised *zwiebelrostbraten* today. He could almost taste the succulent fried bits of onion and beef.

"A coincidence running into you like this," Klimt said. "I've been meaning to see you."

"Not another missing model, I hope," Werthen said, for it was the death of one of Klimt's models that had initiated Werthen's first case. He was beginning to think of his extralegal activities like that now: as cases. Just yesterday he had had his brass plaque at the entrance to Habsburgergasse changed. No longer did it read merely AD-VOKAT KARL WERTHEN, WILLS AND TRUSTS. Now it was: ADVOKAT KARL WER-THEN: WILLS AND TRUSTS, CRIMINAL LAW, PRIVATE INQUIRIES.

Klimt shook his head. "Nothing so serious I should think, though there does seem to be a hint of the dramatic to it. A possible case."

Werthen perked up.

"You know of the young Schindler girl, I expect?" Klimt asked.

"Schindler? You mean the landscape painter?"

"Emil Schindler. Yes. His daughter, Alma. Poor Emil, died of a ruptured appendix."

"That's right," Werthen recalled. "And his widow married your partner at the Secession, Moll."

"Carl Moll," Klimt said. "I am glad to see you keep up with art world gossip." He nodded knowingly at Werthen, as if he should now comprehend the full story.

He did not. "Obviously not all the gossip," Werthen admitted.

"Well, you see, the young lady and I are often thrown together both professionally and privately —"

"Tell me no more. Another conquest."

Klimt had the good grace to redden at this. "Hardly. Though I confess that I am, like many another man, rather smitten with the young thing. So beautiful. And a head full of brains to go with it. She fancies herself a musician."

Another pause as the coffees and pastry were delivered. Klimt's cup was a miniature Matterhorn of whipped cream. He looked pleased, gazing fondly at the waitress's behind as she departed.

"Such a sweet young thing," he said, turning back to his coffee and cake, and digging in.

Werthen allowed him five minutes of uninterrupted eating and drinking, by which time Klimt had made large inroads to both coffee and cake.

"Alma Schindler," Werthen prompted.

"Yes, yes. Marvelous girl, and I rather think she is besotted of me, as well. I traveled with her and her family to Italy this spring and there was chemistry between us to be sure. Walking in Venice's Piazza San

Marco. . . . But difficulties, as well. Carl . . . Moll, I mean, not you —"

"The stepfather does not approve."

Klimt shook his head sadly. "Bourgeois conventions. Alma knows her own mind and body, I can tell you. Any other sweet young thing would have shared my bed by now." He sighed deeply and sadly.

Werthen pulled out his pocket watch: eleven fifty-five. He could still make it home in time for lunch.

"What was it you wanted to tell me about Fräulein Schindler?"

"Yes, that. She has a penchant for older men, it would seem. Her latest pet project is Mahler."

"I noticed you with him. A new friend?"

"Not really my cup of tea, if you know what I mean."

"No. Actually, I don't."

"We ended up walking out here together. All the way to the cemetery he was complaining of how unctuous Reverend Zimmerman's eulogy was at the Episcopal Church, how the a cappella choir of the Männergesangverein finished a tone and a half lower at the end than at the beginning. As if it was his funeral. That sort of chap."

Werthen was still not sure what Klimt meant, but pushed on. "Are they close, then, Mahler and Alma Schindler?"

"Hardly. She's only seen him from afar, but swears he is the one for her. And what Alma wants, Alma gets."

"Sounds like a force to be reckoned with. But how does this pertain to me?"

"Here is the drama. She wants a private inquiry agent to make 'certain investigations,' as she so mysteriously puts it. She will tell me no more, but has listened to my tales extolling your brilliance in such matters and is desperate to meet with you."

Werthen thought for a moment. It sounded all very unpromising; sordid, as if the young girl wanted someone to follow Mahler about to see if he were carrying on an affair. Domestic work of the least interesting sort.

"I would consider it a personal favor," Klimt said.

The painter looked so eager that Werthen gave in.

"Well, I suppose you can tell her to arrange an appointment at my office. I'll see if there is any assistance I can offer."

"Bravo for you, Werthen. Giving up the old wills and trusts, are we then?"

"More like putting them in abeyance."

"And how is that excellent wife of yours? So sorry I could not be at the wedding. You see, that was when I was in Italy."

"It was a quiet affair," he said. So quiet his own parents had not deigned to make an appearance, protesting that it was a civil rather than a church affair.

"Do give her my best. A spirited filly, that one."

Werthen was not sure Berthe would care for the horse analogy, but understood Klimt's sentiment.

"Yes, she is. I'm a lucky man."

Werthen made to pay for his coffee, but Klimt stopped his hand. "Please, Werthen. Don't insult me."

Klimt turned back to the remaining crumbs of cake as Werthen gathered his hat and gloves.

About to leave, he said, "Oh, and Klimt —"

"I know. I know, old friend. It's in the mail. Or will be by tomorrow."

Two

Klimt was right, Werthen thought. A beauty.

Alma Schindler sat across the desk from him in his office. His wife, Berthe, now acting as part-time secretary at the firm, was seated in the corner behind the young lady and to his right, ready to take notes.

Fräulein Schindler wore a feathered hat that was much too old for a nineteen-year-old, obviously from the noble firm of Habig on the Wiedner Hauptstrasse. Her hair, one could see once she'd removed the hat, was done up in the popular fashion of the day, piled luxuriantly on top of the head, and full of waves and curls. She had on a white dress, embellished with appliqué, lace, and embroidery, with a high collar and puffed sleeves. Over this, she wore a tight-fitting vest of a cream color striped in dark silk. Werthen was not certain about such things, but thought he had seen a similar outfit in the exclusive dress shop Fournier on the

Graben.

Overall, Fräulein Schindler gave the appearance of a smartly dressed woman about town. Yet when she spoke, it was like conversing with an overly precocious adolescent. She was knowledgeable, but too eager to show her knowledge. Too enthusiastic in general for an era that prized reserve and a kind of bored satiety in its society ladies.

Looking at Fräulein Schindler and then at his wife, Werthen marveled at how different the two women were. Berthe was only a few years older than the Schindler girl, but there was a solidity as well as originality to his wife that was intoxicating. Where Alma Schindler wanted to shine and thereby gloat in her own reflected glory, Berthe was entirely within herself: poised, quietly confident, calm. Just the trace of a sardonic grin on her fine mouth, as if she always found the world slightly amusing. Berthe drew you in not by the separate strength of her features, nor by an animalistic force, but by her overall appeal. Hers was a quiet, domestic beauty, a warm jumble of womanhood that was not on display for the entire world.

Of course Werthen was not to be trusted for objectivity regarding his wife.

"It was good of you to see me on such

33

short notice, Advokat Werthen."

What *does* one say to that besides the obvious? he wondered. "Not at all."

"I don't know how much Gustav . . . Herr Klimt might have told you. . . ."

"Very little. Just that you had a concern you wished to discuss with me."

"You'll think I'm a silly little girl." She blushed on cue.

Werthen raised his eyes, glancing at Berthe. She did not alter the faintly amused expression on her face, busy with her shorthand.

Fräulein Schindler now leaned across the narrow desk to speak directly into Werthen's face, just a foot away. He could smell strawberries on her breath, the first of the season.

"You see, it is about Herr Mahler, the composer."

"The Court Opera director," Werthen added.

"That, too, but have you not heard his music? Sublime. If I could one day compose like that, my life would indeed have meaning."

She smiled sweetly at him as she spoke, still invading his side of the desk. Her dress had a sheer piece of lace for the uppermost half of the bodice; he studiously kept his eyes from her décolletage.

"No, I have not yet had the pleasure. He is most formidable at the podium, however."

"Sleight of hand." She said it dismissively. "But that is not why I am here. Dear, it sounds so silly now."

"Please," he said, being drawn to her obvious charms now in spite of himself. "Our conversation does not go beyond these walls."

"Someone is trying to hurt him, kill him perhaps. There. I've said it."

She sat back in her chair, folding her arms at her chest like a reprimanded, stubborn child.

Werthen took a breath. This was hardly what he was expecting. Berthe cast him a quick glance.

"What makes you say that?"

"Incidents."

"Plural."

"Yes."

"I have read, of course, of the unfortunate accident last week. The death of the young soprano."

"It was no accident."

He again looked at his wife; Berthe raised her eyebrows now.

"Could you elaborate?"

"Fire curtains do not simply fall by accident. They are double roped. The asbestos safety curtain at the Court Opera hangs directly behind the proscenium and has its own dedicated winch. It does not come down unless it is meant to."

Werthen was impressed. She had been doing her homework. Of course, all of Vienna was theater mad, himself a qualified inclusion therein. Fire curtains were a relatively new innovation in theaters, their worldwide spread the result of the tragic Ringstrasse Theater fire in this very city in December of 1881. Hundreds had been killed when a backstage blaze spread through the auditorium; the charred skeleton of the theater was later torn down, to be replaced by an apartment house called appropriately the House of Atonement.

"And what does the stage manager have to say of this?" Werthen questioned, coming back to the task at hand.

Fräulein Schindler now did something Werthen found quite uncharacteristic: she wrinkled up her pretty nose as if smelling horse droppings under the hot summer sun.

"The man is an idiot. He has no explanation other than that the ropes must have come untied somehow. These are not simply pretty bows tied in the hemp, Advokat Werthen, but quite ornate knots meant to hold. And two of them, remember."

"You mentioned other incidents."

"A scenery flat that fell perilously close to Herr Mahler. If you can believe it, the Court Opera is still primarily a hemp house."

She smiled at her use of the technical term, most likely expecting Werthen to be puzzled. Instead, he nodded. He, too, had a knowledge of stagecraft, a holdover from a case in Graz when he was practicing criminal law. It had involved an action against a stagehand accused of vandalism after being fired from his position at the Grazer Stadttheater. In Graz, as in Vienna, tradition was a strong influence; the oldest way was often considered the best. Thus, much of the scenery at the Court Opera was still hoisted by sheer human muscle power, with several men flying the scenery flats by use of hemp ropes. A "hemp house," in fact.

"Counterweight flying is, I understand, being introduced," Werthen responded. "Herr Mahler is no fan of tradition, so I hear."

A different sort of smile showed on her lips now, a rueful acceptance of the lawyer's knowledge; a realization that he would not be impressed by her obvious encyclopedia cramming.

" 'Tradition is laziness.' I have heard

Mahler say that a hundred times." Another coquettish smile from her. He noticed that she used the man's last name with no "Herr" before it; already a self-appointed intimate. "You see, I have taken to attending rehearsals. Mahler knows nothing of it, of course. A friend of Carl's . . . my step-father's, sees that I come in a side door and that I sit very quietly in the fourth balcony."

She let a moment of silence pass for this to sink in.

"His morning cup of chamomile tea was also once seemingly inadvertently used to mix paint. Mahler was fortunate not to drink from it."

"The opera direction has not seen fit to investigate these?"

"They are a pack of old ladies."

"And what about Mahler himself? Has he made no complaints of these incidents?"

"He is too involved in his music to see anything more than coincidence."

"But, Fräulein Schindler, why should anyone want to harm Mahler? He is, according to the press, quite transforming the musical scene in Vienna."

"There are winners and losers in any such transformation."

She was right, of course, but all of this sounded a bit too melodramatic. Kill a man because he wants to get rid of the claque or paid applauders? Because he turns the houselights down before performances and allows no latecomers in until pauses?

"And what is it you would like me to do?"

"Investigate. See who is responsible for these outrages. Stop him . . . or her before Mahler is seriously hurt. Or worse."

"I see." He said it flatly, without emotion.

"I am willing to pay. I have a secret bank account from my father. My real father, that is."

Werthen waved a hand at the suggestion. "Let us see where things stand first."

"Then you will take my case." For the first time, her face showed honest emotion, a childlike glee.

"I will talk with Herr Mahler."

"You mustn't tell him it was I who commissioned you."

"Strictest privacy, I assure you."

She stood suddenly, thrusting her hand forward.

"Klimt was right about you. He said you were marvelous. I think so, too."

He was surprised by the strength in her tiny hand when he shook it.

Alma Schindler nodded to Berthe on the way out, but otherwise made no acknowledgment of her presence.

They waited for a moment, listening for the exterior office door to close.

"Well?" he said.

"She's hard of hearing."

"What?"

"Don't tell me you are, too."

"Why do you say that?"

"That little act of leaning across the desk as if to become more intimate with you. Not the reason at all. She just has trouble hearing. I had a friend from school who did the same thing and with the same effect on the boys."

"I assure you —" he began.

"Oh, not to worry, Karl. She is an attractive thing, I will give her that. And smart. A difficult combination for a woman."

"What do you think of her story?"

Berthe gathered her notebook and pencil. "She has an active imagination, to be sure. But then, there is a dead soprano, no?"

"So, you think it is worth following up?"

"It doesn't matter what I think, does it? You've as much as promised the girl. And pro bono to boot."

He felt like a fool. "Yes, I suppose I have."

She came across the room to him, placing her warm, soft palm against his cheek.

"Don't worry, Karl. I am sure she has gotten the better of many other men, as well."

■ ■ ■ ■

Werthen and his wife took lunch out today, dining at one of their favorite *beisln* just two doors from the office. The Alte Schmiede was a simple and cozy place with a luncheon menu that changed daily. Today there was *leberknödel suppe* followed by a spicy goulash served with steamed new potatoes. They drank a red wine from Burgenland with lunch; neither had dessert. They sat for a time over small cups of coffee instead, talking of the morning and planning the afternoon.

Werthen, after the departure of Fräulein Schindler, had decided to push forward with things, and had placed a telephone call to the Court Opera attempting to get in touch with the director. Mahler, he was told, was at home today, suffering from a severe sore throat. He asked for, and, due to his title of lawyer, was given Mahler's home telephone number. A call there was answered by a female, who turned out to be one of the musician's sisters, Justine Mahler. She was chief housekeeper and, it would seem, bodyguard, by the manner in which she so closely questioned Werthen about the purpose of his proposed interview. He had pleaded the importance and privacy of his proposed meeting — and ultimately was able to secure an appointment for two this afternoon.

"Gustav should be up from his nap by then," the sharp voice on the other end said. "Otherwise, you will have to wait."

He took leave of Berthe, who was off to her afternoon work at the children's care center in Ottakring. The day was perfect for walking: a light breeze with high scudding clouds in a robin's-egg blue sky, like something out of a Bellotto view of the city. Strolling through the peaceful cobbled lanes of the Inner City, Werthen felt well with himself and the world. It was all he needed for now: the love of a good woman, a fine lunch under his belt, a day made for walking, and at the end of the stroll, a possible case.

Mahler's apartment was just outside the Ringstrasse on Auenbruggerstrasse, a short lane that led into Rennweg, the diplomatic quarter near the Belvedere. As he made his way up the Schwarzenbergplatz, he was reminded of the morning he and his old friend, the criminologist Hanns Gross, had left that same palace, the uninvited guests for the night of Archduke Franz Ferdinand.

Mahler's apartment, in fact, stood on the

corner of Rennweg, a few paces from the Lower Belvedere. It had been built by Otto Wagner, and this apartment block bore the architect's signature early style of recessed decorative panels at the corners and lines of similar friezelike ornaments underlying the windows of the third and fourth floors.

A modern building, this one had a lift, which Werthen decided to take, as his leg was acting up after the walk here. He rubbed his stiff knee as the lift carried him to Mahler's fourth-floor home. The door was opened at the second knock by a female version of the composer himself. Her hair was equally unruly and rather thin, the nose was hawklike, eyes lightly veiled and somehow predatory. She wore a broad tie on her off-white blouse, a wide white belt, and a full skirt that looked as if it were constructed of canvas.

"You'll be Herr Werthen," she said.

"Yes." He was unsure how to address her: *Gnädige Frau?* Unwritten rules turned a *fräulein* into a *frau* if they were still unmarried after the age of thirty or so. It was the "or so" that always confused him. He opted for a brief handshake instead of verbal salutations.

"I suppose you'll want to come in."

With that, she turned, leaving the door for

43

him to close after entering. Short, dark corridors led off in both directions from the entry with several rooms attached. Justine Mahler proceeded through mahogany double doors directly in front. These opened, Werthen soon discovered, into an inner hallway that was much longer and brighter, giving off to a second section of rooms. The Court Opera director was obviously doing very well for himself to be able to afford such a suite of rooms for just himself and his sister.

He continued to follow Justine Mahler as she turned left. He passed an open door to his right, and looked in as he walked by. A formal dining room with a quite elegant and very modern geometrical-styled dining table and chair. Obviously designed by the Werkstätte, the fine arts wing of the Jugendstil and Secessionist artists gathered around Klimt. Light spilled from the large streetside windows into the room.

She opened double doors to the next room and they entered a spacious sitting room, a glorious Bösendorfer grand piano gracing the middle of the parquet, its enamel freshly waxed and shining. In a far corner he thought he saw a pile of blankets on a settee; he soon saw that Mahler himself was huddled beneath this mountain of eiderdown, a white sticking plaster at his neck, and a thermometer in his mouth. Werthen had to suppress a laugh; it was like a cartoon out of *Der Floh* or some other comic illustrated weekly.

Next to the settee was a small enameled table on top of which lay a carton of *loukoumi,* or Turkish delight as the British called these sweets to which Mahler was addicted, according to the popular press. One journalistic account Werthen had read explained that the composer had a steady supply sent directly from the Ali Muhiddin Haci Bekir Company of Istanbul; a guilty domestic pleasure that made Mahler seem more human to Werthen. The little cubes of jellylike candy were richly powdered with sugar and smelled strongly of cinnamon and mint.

Justine Mahler halted abruptly in front of the settee, leaned over and extracted the thermometer from Mahler's mouth, squinted at it, uttered a humming sound at the results, then tucked the glass tube in her blouse pocket.

"Please do not tire him. He still has to prepare for the final opera of the season."

And she left them. Werthen felt the relief a person experiences when storm clouds blow over. He handed Mahler one of his new business cards. Mahler took it and also swept up a piece of Turkish delight now his sister was gone.

"Sit down, sit down," he said, popping the sweet into his mouth, not bothering to offer Werthen one.

Mahler's voice, sore throat or no, held authority and was much lower than one would expect, given his size. He reached for the pince-nez at his side, adjusted them on the bridge of his sharp nose, and appraised Werthen, then his card. He chewed the candy thoroughly before recommencing.

"A trio of personalities," Mahler said, tapping the card. "Which one visits me today?"

"Inquiries," Werthen replied vaguely.

"So what is this vitally important information you have for me?" Mahler asked as Werthen drew a rather uncomfortable armchair to the settee. Lovely designs, the Werkstätte, but made for looking at rather than sitting on.

The musician's dark eyes sparkled. A ghost of a smile appeared on his thin lips. His shock of uncontrollable hair atop his head looked not so out of place here in a sick bed as it did seeing Mahler hatless making his way along the Kärntnerstrasse, his characteristic uneven gait often bringing jeers from children. Even now as he lay under the eiderdown, Mahler's nervous energy caused the fingers of his left hand to tick out a rhythm against the comforter.

Werthen cleared his throat and began. "There have been certain incidents at the Court Opera, as I understand. Culminating with the death of Fräulein Kaspar."

Mahler said nothing, continuing to hold Werthen in his steely gaze.

"There was also the instance of a dropped scenery flat, of a poisonous substance in your teacup."

"My lord, Herr" — he examined the card again — "Herr Werthen. Had you told me you were coming with a new and quite melodramatic libretto, I would have dressed for the occasion."

Werthen felt himself redden, then decided to hell with politesse.

"I've been commissioned to investigate attempts against your life."

This clear summation took the supercilious smile from Mahler's lips.

"And who might your commissioner be?"

"I am not at liberty to divulge that."

"Yes, of course. It would be Prince Montenuovo. Protecting his investment."

Mahler was indicating the feared assistant court chamberlain and supreme administrator of the Court Opera, answerable only to

Kaiser Franz Josef.

"As I said, I am not at liberty to divulge that person's identity. I have come to ascertain if you agree with such an assumption."

"What? That someone is out to kill me? Ridiculous. Grethe, perhaps. Fräulein Kaspar, that is. You can tell your unnamed client to investigate that, instead. Tell him to look at the opera cats who might have had their fangs out for the young soprano. Everyone knew she was my lover. It was an open secret. Plenty of those cats had it in for her, I'm sure."

"By cats I assume you mean other female singers."

"You are being too kind; many of them call themselves singers. I will soon clean the stables of those untalented old maids in search of a pension. Meanwhile, I merely put up with them."

"So you see no threat to yourself?"

"Only to my ears, having to listen to some of them."

If someone actually were trying to kill Mahler, Werthen thought he could understand their motive.

"Seriously, I may have ruffled some feathers, but I have neither the time nor the patience to worry about popularity. It's the music. It's all about the music. Those who do not understand that must go. But a matter of murder? I think not."

"And the scenery flat? The tainted teacup?"

"Accidents. We have more than a hundred people working on both sides of the proscenium. One comes to expect such things."

"Yes." Werthen was putting on his best lawyerlike countenance now, not giving anything away. But suddenly he felt rather a fool. Mahler was obviously right. Accident. Coincidence. Perhaps the death of the Kaspar woman was more than that. But if so, that was a matter for the police. Fräulein Schindler had obviously been allowing her over eager imagination to run away with itself.

"Well, then . . ." Werthen rose, ready to make adieus.

"Your card. It says 'Wills and Trusts.' Is that true?"

Werthen was taken aback by the question. "Of course it is. I do not misrepresent myself."

"Relax. No insult intended. But I'm in need of someone to write my new will. Certain amendments to be made in light of altered circumstances. When can we begin?"

No niceties about requesting service for

49

Mahler. He was too used to giving commands for such things.

"You wish to engage my services."

Mahler sat up on the settee now, looking revived and ready for action. He pulled the plaster away from his throat.

"Herr Werthen, you must forgive my brusqueness. It comes from having to deal with stubborn singers day in and day out. Yes, I wish to engage you."

Despite his demeanor, there was something about Mahler that appealed to Werthen. Here was a man who lived life on his own terms.

"You are Jewish," Mahler suddenly said. Not a question.

"I'm not sure how that enters the matter."

"Though clearly baptized. Assimilated as it were. As am I."

"Yes."

"And from Moravia originally, as, again, am I."

"You checked on me," Werthen said.

"Wouldn't you in my place? A discreet telephone call to a friend in a high place. No more."

"And you were satisfied with what you heard?"

"Or else my sister would not have allowed you in." Another tight-lipped smile; irregular but very white teeth showed. "So, what do you say? Am I to be your new client?"

"Certainly. It would be an honor, Herr Mahler."

Mahler's sister was waiting on the other side of the door to show Werthen out. Good timing or had she been eavesdropping?

At the front door she tapped his arm lightly, her eyes squinting at him. She had about her the look of a woman about to go to confession.

"Gustl needs protection. Whether he knows it or not. I, for one, am glad you came."

Before Werthen had a chance to ask what she meant, Justine Mahler politely but firmly showed him out.

THREE

Werthen and Berthe had begun to grow into a steady yet unstructured domesticity. Their household was run, not by the perceived aristocratic notions — breakfast in the morning room, visitors' cards laid out neatly on a high table by the entry door, *jause* of poppy seed cake and coffee promptly at four thirty, endless and rather pointless at-homes — nor was it run to the stricter tempo of an Orthodox household with its kosher kitchen and strictly observed Friday Shabbat and Torah readings. Instead, Werthen and Berthe were slowly developing their own rhythm and their own rituals.

Breakfast, for example. This morning — the sacred Sunday when all offices and schools were closed — they lounged in the study, each engrossed in a favorite occupation, reading. They had discovered that reading at table had been forbidden in both their families. To be exact, they were not at table now, but bookends at opposite ends of an immense leather sofa that Berthe had insisted they purchase.

Not at table, but at breakfast, the food laid out on a low table in front of the sofa. For Werthen this meal still consisted of Frau Blatschky's aromatic and powerful coffee and a kipfel from the bakery in the bottom of their apartment building. Werthen would awaken at five to the first tantalizing whiffs of those rolls as the sweet and yeasty aromas wafted upward in the apartment house. For Berthe, who had been converted to the habit after a brief stay in London, breakfast meant a pot of Ceylon tea and crisps of toast spread with Frank Cooper's Oxford marmalade. Both tea and marmalade came from Schönbichler's on the Wollzeile. Berthe had introduced Werthen to the shop's wonders one rainy March day, tucked away in a *durchhaus* off the noble Wollzeile. Werthen had never smelled such spicy aromas gathered together in one place before.

She was reading the *Neue Freie Presse* before turning to Hermann Bahr's new book of essays on the Viennese theater, while Werthen was immersed in Engelbert Bauer's new book, *The Practical Uses of Electricity.* He loved gaining new knowledge, forcing his mind out of old ways of thinking and learning new and wonderful things about a world that was changing daily.

This was their Sunday morning ritual even though their marriage was only a pair of months old.

Frau Blatschky, however, bore an air of aggrieved distaste at the new informal arrangement. It was quite all right for Werthen, a bachelor, to take his breakfast in the study, but now that he was a married man, the cook had higher expectations for the new lady of the house.

After the wedding, Frau Blatschky had come to him, offering her resignation, saying that surely the young lady had her own staff she would want to install. Both Werthen and Berthe assured her they would be pleased if she stayed on. Yet it was difficult for her at times. It was not only the informality of the newlyweds that bothered her. The Ericsson phone that Berthe had installed was also a constant source of befuddlement to Frau Blatschky. He would see her standing stock-still in front of the apparatus when it jangled to life, fearful of touching it. No amount of soothing explanation could convince her that she would not be electrocuted if she answered the call. And the fact that Werthen and Berthe shared a bedroom rather than kept separate sleeping arrangements seemed to shock Frau Blatschky in an entirely different manner.

But Werthen had grown accustomed to her over the years and Berthe put up with her because of the woman's wonderful *zwiebelrostbraten.*

And so they had ignored her look of distaste as she had set down the breakfast tray and left them there, comfortable and cozy.

"My God," Berthe suddenly said from behind her paper.

Werthen looked up from his book. "What is it?" Werthen asked with feigned horror. "Parliamentarians brawling again?" The Viennese parliament was known for its rather rambunctious debates that at times turned physical.

"No." Berthe looked at him and Werthen realized it was serious.

"It's Mahler. He's had an accident at the Court Opera."

Werthen was halfway out the front door by the time he finally heard Berthe's suggestion.

"Wouldn't it be prudent to telephone ahead first?"

In his haste, he had completely forgotten

about the luxury of the telephone in their foyer.

"Right," he said, still flustered.

"You're not going to be much of a help to anybody like this. Deep breaths now, five of them."

To his surprise he obeyed, and did feel better at the end of the fifth.

He called the Mahler residence and reached the composer's sister, Justine. After learning that Mahler's injuries were not life threatening and that Mahler wished to see him later today, Werthen rang off, placing the receiver in its Bakelite cradle. The instrument made a jingling sound as he did so to announce the breaking of the connection.

"Better?" she asked.

"Decidedly. Will you accompany me?"

"To Mahler's?"

"I thought we might pay a visit to the Hofoper first."

"But my *friseur* is closed today." She made comical patting motions at her hair.

"The building, not a performance."

This silly bantering normalized things for Werthen, who was still amazed by his response to Berthe's announcement of Mahler's injury. Truth be told, Mahler as a human meant little to him. However, Wer-

56

then had offered his services to the Schindler girl and felt pain and embarrassment that he had done nothing to protect the composer. In fact he had notified Fräulein Schindler just yesterday that her fears regarding Mahler's safety were unfounded. She, of course, had argued to the contrary, and he had played the wiser, older man, assuring her that everything was under control. Now he was regretting his words and his tone of smug complacency over the telephone to that young woman.

Berthe's level-headed approach to things was exactly what was needed now; hence his invitation to join him in the investigation. She tried not to show it, but Werthen could tell that she was pleased to be included.

Five minutes later, after a further quick call to the opera administration, they were outside and walking at a brisk pace toward the Ringstrasse.

The Royal Court Opera was just thirty years old, but had the appearance and gravity of great age. Its sandstone already bore a reddish brown patina, the copper of the roof was oxidized to pastel green. Constructed in a mélange of historical styles typical of other Ringstrasse buildings, the Renaissance style held sway, especially in the loggias and porticoes jutting out the side walls. An immense building, it was built on a site of at least 150,000 square feet bordering the Ringstrasse and the fashionable Kärntnerstrasse. For Werthen, however, the one drawback of the Court Opera was the fact that it was too huddled amidst other buildings to get a full view; no broad boulevard led up to it as with the Paris Opera.

The Hofoper's six-million-gulden price tag had been enough at the time to build at least six working-class apartment buildings, Berthe never tired of telling Werthen. Such apartment buildings would have given shelter to a few hundreds of the thousands of working poor who either rented bed space — *bettgehers* — when the rightful owners were otherwise engaged, or who were dependent on public charities and warming rooms for their shelter. Worse off still were the thousands more who, as a result of the fourfold increase in population in Vienna in less than a generation, had to lay their heads down on park benches or who lived like rats in the vast underground network of sewers.

Werthen, however, was not considering the perennial argument between the needs of art versus the needs of society when he and Berthe went to the ticketing window on the Kärntnerstrasse side of the building. Happily there were yet no crowds gathered at this arcaded window. A few hours from now, though, men, women, and children would be thronging the ticket office, pleading for the best seats; scalpers in patched greatcoats would be offering their tickets at exorbitant rates and would always find a fan desperate enough to pay the price.

Herr Regierungsrath Leitner, the third in command at the Vienna Court Opera behind the assistant lord chamberlain, Prince Montenuovo, and the intendant, Baron Wilhelm von Menkl, was waiting at this entrance as arranged. It had taken Werthen only a moment on the telephone before leaving his apartment to indicate that he was Mahler's attorney and to let Herr Regierungsrath's mind run wild with that information. An injury suit, perhaps? Werthen did nothing to disabuse the man of such an assumption.

Leitner, a senior civil servant, was, after proper introductions had been made, all smiles and condescending chatter as he led the way up the grand staircase to the main auditorium. He was a man of medium height and dressed in a black, double-breasted worsted suit and a high starched collar on this warm day. Just looking at him made Werthen, who had chosen a green linen *trachten* country suit, break out in a sympathetic sweat. Though it was still early June, the heat was already upon the city.

Leitner, however, showed no sign of heat sensitivity. His salt-and-pepper hair was rather short cut and looked as though he might have neglected brushing it thoroughly this morning. He wore a beard, also showing flecks of gray at the cheeks and chin, that was, like his hair, cut close. The eyes were brown, Werthen noticed once they entered the auditorium, and held one fast in their glance. Overall, he gave the appearance of one accustomed to command.

"And as I was indicating, the incident transpired in the blinking of an eye. But I assure you, medical attention was summoned immediately. . . ."

The words, calculated, fawning almost, struck a distinct discord with Leitner's appearance. Werthen glanced at Berthe to see if she observed it, as well. However, her eyes had trailed upward, looking at the enormous space into which they had entered. Werthen's view followed hers. He had never been in the Court Opera during the daytime before, not that any daylight reached this vast gilded hall. However, electrically lighted for the past decade, the theater came alive under the gleam of hundreds of lights in the central chandelier high overhead. A ghost light, only barely visible amidst the overhead illumination, still burned downstage center to ward off any evil spirits.

The space was indeed vast: almost three thousand seats. The central orchestra seating was surrounded by a horse shoe of boxes and galleries. The uppermost, the fourth gallery where the cheapest seats were and where the music-hungry yet impoverished aficionados were relegated, was so distant from the stage as to make the singers appear dwarflike without the aid of opera glasses. The royal box took up two levels directly opposite the stage and was infrequently at best attended by the emperor. Especially so now that the empress was dead.

Everywhere the gilt decoration sparkled and made the view even more resplendent. Werthen, who liked a rather more understated presentation, still found himself deeply moved.

"Yes," Leitner said. "It is glorious."

The comment called for no response, yet served to bridge an unspoken gap between them.

"Magnificent," Werthen murmured.

Leitner nodded then rubbed his hands together.

"This way." And he led them down the aisle between the silent ranks of orchestra seats toward the pit and stage.

"Herr Mahler was very specific about the placement of his podium. We raised and lowered the entire orchestra pit several times to get the proper elevation."

Werthen and Berthe looked into the pit, but saw no podium, either raised or lowered.

"Herr Mahler is a great innovator," Leitner went on. "Before his time the conductor would stand right up by the footlights. Jahn" — meaning Mahler's direct predecessor — "was content to direct from a cane chair placed in the midst of the orchestra. But for Herr Mahler the need for precision was utmost."

To Werthen's ears this sounded like a complaint rather than praise.

"Finally he opted for the podium to be slightly raised and placed close to the strings. He insisted that he was conducting an orchestra and singers, not merely singers on the stage."

"And what exactly transpired?" Werthen said, tiring of Leitner's asides.

"It was yesterday at afternoon rehearsal. Everything was going quite smoothly. I was watching from the second box in the second tier, the administrative box — Mahler has even had a telephone installed there for communication with the stage and the pit —"

"Yes," Werthen persisted.

"Well." Leitner spread his hands in front of him. "Then it happened. Quite out of the blue."

"It?" Berthe asked, then smiled at Werthen who had been about to make the same comment.

"Yes. The, well, the accident."

"Did you witness it?" This from Werthen.

"I am afraid I did not. At that very moment my attention was fixed on the new soubrette we employed after the unfortunate death of Fräulein Kaspar. I heard a thumping sound and then loud gasps and shouting from the pit. I naturally ran down as quickly as I could. Herr Mahler was still on his back when I arrived."

"The podium simply collapsed?" Werthen said.

"Apparently. At least that is the explanation Herr Blauer gave."

"And Herr Blauer would be?"

"Siegfried Blauer, our stage manager. He is responsible for everything on the other side of the curtain."

Werthen again looked into the pit, seeing only a vacant spot next to the strings where the podium should have been.

"Is it being repaired?"

Leitner looked perplexed at the question.

"The podium, I mean," Werthen continued.

Leitner gave a sigh of comprehension. "No, no. Not yet, at any rate. You'll have to ask Blauer. But Herr Richter has taken over conducting duties while Herr Mahler is indisposed. He prefers the chair amid the orchestra. And our season ends tomorrow —"

"Yes, but where is the podium now?"

Once again the outspread hands from Leitner. Werthen finally decided that outward appearances were indeed deceiving. Leitner was a bureaucrat practiced at all forms of bureaucratic deception, such as fobbing off responsibilities on others.

"Herr Blauer again?" Berthe asked, her voice had a sarcastic overtone.

"To be sure," Leitner replied, flashing them a smile that came from the mouth only. "The other side of the curtain and all that."

Leitner led them on a miniature tour of the building in his circuitous route to get backstage. They exited the main auditorium

64

by a side door and took the stairs to the second tier where he showed them the administrative box where he, Leitner, was seated when the accident took place.

He looked sheepish for a moment, and then said, "I would appreciate it if you did not mention to Mahler that I was sitting up here."

Werthen found the request odd, but was about to reply in the affirmative when Leitner charged on.

"Herr Mahler is rather peculiar about its use. We might call it the administrative box, but he takes it as his private fiefdom. If he is not using it, the box remains empty." He pursed his lips and blinked hard at them. "I am sure you understand."

Then he led them back to the corridor where he turned left, heading toward what appeared to be a dead end at a wall.

"A bit of secret here," he said, attempting a winning smile. "Not to be shared with others?"

"Of course," Werthen said.

There was a well-concealed door handle in the wall that Leitner released and with a jerk opened a small door that was otherwise quite unnoticeable. The door led directly backstage, onto a metal platform some twenty feet above the stage.

"It provides quick access to the stage and also a bit of a balcony for shouting out orders," Leitner explained.

Beneath the platform, metals stairs zigzagged down to the stage.

Descending these, Werthen and Berthe were again confronted with a monumental space, actually larger even than the auditorium on the other side of the curtain. The backstage was several stories high and so deep they could barely see to the far end of it. Everywhere was activity: men hauling large flats by hemp ropes; others crawling about high overhead like sailors in a rigging, tying off ropes; still others were calling out where to set two-dimensional and three-dimensional scenic pieces.

"Behold the revolving stage," Leitner said, sweeping his hand in front of him.

Only then did Werthen notice a huge circular portion cut out of the stage, at least twenty meters in diameter. One section of it jutted out beyond the proscenium, the rest was concealed backstage.

"It is mounted on an iron shaft below the stage," Leitner explained, though there was an edge to his voice that made Werthen think he did not approve of such innovations. "The shaft in turn rests on well-oiled ball bearings, making it almost silent in operation. Electrically driven, of course. Everything must be up-to-date for Herr Mahler."

It was clever, Werthen had to admit. He had read about the pioneering revolving stage built in Munich in 1896. The idea was that several scene changes could be mounted on the stage well before the performance, and with a simple flick of a switch the stage could revolve to expose a new scene beyond the proscenium while the other scenes remained hidden in back.

"Of course such a device is better suited to a small repertory house than to an institution like the Hofoper," Leitner said. "The cost is prohibitive, as you can imagine. Complete sets must be built for each production if they are to fit the Chinese puzzle of the revolving stage. But cost is no problem for Herr Mahler, it seems. He simply goes over my head to Montenuovo and pleads artistic necessity."

Werthen caught the malice in Leitner's voice, and so, it seemed, did Herr Regierungsrath himself, for he abruptly halted his critique and cast Werthen and Berthe a cheery smile.

"But that is not your interest today, is it?"

It took them another ten minutes to find Blauer backstage. Unlike other Viennese whose workweek extended from Monday to half-day Saturday, employees at the Royal Court Opera regularly worked both days of the weekend, for performances knew no days off. Blauer was discussing the finer points of fly loft operation with a new stagehand when Leitner pointed him out.

"I will take my leave now," Leitner said. "I assure you, the unfortunate accident was not a matter of malfeasance on the part of the Court Opera direction. If you have further questions, I shall be in my office."

He was gone before Werthen had a chance to ask a question, let alone raise a complaint.

"No malfeasance?" Berthe whispered as the man made a hasty departure. "Perhaps Mahler simply threw himself off the podium in a fit of pique at a missed note."

Exactly Werthen's thoughts; he smiled at his wife, then turned to Blauer and the stagehand once again, waiting politely for their discussion to finish before making introductions. Leitner, in his haste, had neglected even that common civility.

Blauer was a compact man with spectacles, listening patiently to the stagehand, a large, florid sort with muttonchops. No one in Vienna, save the emperor, still wore such whiskers. By the sound of the large man's accent, he was a denizen of Ottakring, a working-class district known for its beer and impenetrable dialect. The perfect sort, Werthen thought, for the mulelike work of hoisting scenery flats with rope.

As the conversation finished, Werthen and Berthe approached the two.

"Herr Blauer," Werthen said.

"Yes."

Werthen stopped in his tracks when he realized it was the large man who responded.

"How may I help you?" Blauer nodded for the smaller man to be about his business.

Suddenly the man's accent was diminished, assuming more of a neutral Viennese tone, still singsong, but not as harsh or guttural as before.

"Herr Regierungsrath Leitner suggested I, we, speak with you." Werthen made quick introductions. The mention of his professional association with Mahler made the man noticeably stiffen.

"Yes?"

"It is about the unfortunate accident with the podium. I wonder if it would be possible to take a look at it."

Blauer looked from Werthen to Berthe and back to the lawyer, folded his massive arms over his barrel chest, and slowly shook his head.

"Afraid not," he said.

"You refuse to allow an inspection?" Werthen said.

Another brusque shake of the man's head. "No, not like that at all. But it's impossible, you see. We tossed the podium yesterday. It'll be wood chips by now in our set factory. We're constructing a new one."

"Unfortunate," Werthen muttered.

"How's that?" Blauer cupped his ear toward Werthen; the commotion all around them had made his comment unintelligible.

"Nothing," Werthen said. "Simply that it would have been advantageous to examine the old podium for design flaws."

"Well, we did that, didn't we? Nothing we could see but the usual wear and tear. I think Herr Mahler slipped off, becoming rather agitated during rehearsals."

Not so far off the mark of Berthe's earlier sarcastic remark.

"If that'll be all?" Blauer said, his body already in motion. "Lots to see to this afternoon."

"There was an earlier accident, as well," Werthen said, ignoring the man's question.

Blauer sighed. "Fräulein Kaspar, you mean?"

"Yes," Werthen responded. "Fräulein Kaspar and the fire curtain. Herr Mahler came close to injury in that matter, did he not?"

"The young singer fared rather worse, I should think." Blauer inadvertently strayed into his Ottakring accent as he said this.

"Nonetheless, two such accidents should raise concern."

"We got rid of the stagehand responsible for that," Blauer explained. "I was forever telling the man not to saddle a dead horse, but would he listen?"

"By that, I assume you mean one should not clamp the nonload-bearing end of a rope?"

Blauer looked impressed. "Exactly so. Have you worked as a stagehand?"

Werthen felt himself redden at the question. He caught Berthe hiding a smile behind her hand.

"No," he curtly answered. "I am merely well read."

Blauer ignored this. "Redl was his name. He could never get the basic concepts in his head. After the incident with the fire curtain, I let him go."

"You're saying that this Herr Redl was responsible for the fire curtain falling."

"He denied it, of course. But I took a look at the cables afterward. Clamped all wrong. The man was a fool."

"And where might one contact Herr Redl?"

Blauer blew his lips in disgust. "Nowhere near here, that is for sure. Couldn't find a job anywhere in the empire after that. Stage gossip is the fellow made off for America where they won't know about his work record. Worse luck for them."

The day was still fine, so they decided to walk to Mahler's apartment. First, however, was the matter of food. This morning's kipferl was now just a distant memory, and he was feeling and hearing a distinct rumbling that demanded attention.

"You must be hungry, darling," he said as they departed the Court Opera.

She cocked her head at him, smiling. "Which means you must be."

"Yes, well, one tries to be a gentleman about such things."

"About hunger? I did not realize the rules of decorum pertained."

"What we both need is a snug little booth, a plate of schnitzel, and a chilled glass of Vetliner. Agreed?"

She nodded vigorously, taking his arm. "Lead on, hungry one."

And he did, taking them to the Opera Café where they indeed found a snug little booth out of the foot traffic, and were soon treated to plates upon which generous slices of breaded veal overlapped the edges. This was accompanied by a cabbage salad with cumin seeds and tart vinegar dressing. The Vetliner was of a coolness as if the bottle had been stored in an alpine brook.

They ate in silence for a time, both of them hungry and giving their sensations over to tastes and aromas for the time being.

"What did you think of him?" Werthen finally asked.

"Him? Leitner or Blauer?"

"Leitner is a self-server." Werthen waved his fork at the idea. "Blauer is the trickier one."

"A modern man," Berthe pronounced.

"Blauer? With those muttonchops?"

She nodded, placing fork and knife on her plate for the moment.

"A self-made man, obviously. Connections did not win him a job as stage manager at the Royal Court Opera. Most likely the product of night school, hard work, and ambition. You heard how he could modulate his accent."

"But is he honest?"

"That, my dear, is harder to discern."

"No podium to examine, no stagehand to

question about the earlier accident. A bit too convenient, I would say."

"For whom?"

"For whoever is trying to kill Mahler."

If she had been wearing reading glasses, she would have looked over the rims at him doubtingly.

"So now you are taking Fräulein Schindler's story at face value?"

"No," he answered. "I'm taking the facts at face value."

They arrived at Mahler's apartment in the afternoon, as arranged. The composer's sister obviously did not feel compelled to answer the door herself this time. Instead, the maid, a wiry little woman in a freshly starched blue uniform and apron, opened the door. He had not seen the woman on his previous visit, but clearly she had been notified of his imminent arrival. Just as clearly, no one had apprised her of the fact that he might be arriving in company. She looked from Werthen to Berthe and allowed a tiny gasp from her birdlike mouth.

"Herr Werthen and his wife to see Herr Mahler," he announced loudly enough, he hoped, for his voice to carry to the inner rooms thereby allaying any further surprise caused by Berthe. It had been Werthen's experience that a household run by a sister was generally one where other females were not welcome. Justine Mahler had given the impression upon first meeting of a most protective and territorial sort of woman. In part, that is why he insisted Berthe accompany him to Mahler's this afternoon; he wanted the sister discomfited, put off her guard. If there were deeper truths to be gotten at, then comfortable was not how Werthen wanted the sister, or brother for that matter.

His volume did the trick, for the maid was quickly relieved of her duties by Justine Mahler, who arrived in a swoosh of heavy skirt and a clacking of heels. She wore — was it the same one? — a broad dove-gray tie with her blouse as before, tucked into the waist of her white belted skirt.

"Herr Werthen." She pronounced it as if it were a question.

"Fräulein Mahler." He nodded. "May I present my wife, Berthe Meisner."

Justine Mahler quickly appraised Berthe, measuring her as if for a coffin, then slowly outstretched her hand.

"A pleasure, Frau Werthen."

Berthe shook the proffered hand. "Frau Meisner, actually. I have kept my family name for professional reasons."

Justine Mahler squinted her eyes at Berthe. This information was obviously as little welcome as another woman in the apartment was.

"But forgive me," the composer's sister finally said. "I am so little accustomed to society caring for the needs of my brother. I forget the amenities. Please do come in, and welcome, both of you."

Once again Werthen followed the sister into the cavernous flat, crossing the outer hall to the inner rooms. A violin sounded; something by Bach, Werthen thought, and the tone quality was quite good. He and Berthe were led to the same sitting room where he had earlier met with Mahler. As before, the composer was installed in a daybed, but now his left arm was in a sling. The violin was being played by a tall, one might say statuesque, woman in a long white gown that draped in folds about her feet. She played without the benefit of music and now Werthen placed the selection: the chaconne for violin from the *Solo Violin Partita 2*. He had first heard the piece as a young boy at his family's estate when, for a dinner party, a young Viennese violinist, a protégé not much older than Werthen himself still in knee pants, was brought in to entertain the guests. Werthen well remembered the heat of embarrassment he felt as the guests seated at dinner paid the young musician little heed, instead laughing and drinking and clinking their silverware as they continued to consume the dinner of wild boar and red currant sauce. But for Werthen, seated at the far end of the table from his parents and from their strained joviality, the music hit a profound chord. He lost himself in it as he had never before done with any piece of music. Only written words — the poetry of Schiller, for example — had heretofore been able to take him so outside of himself. But that evening, with the young violinist from Vienna playing so passionately the notes written one hundred and fifty years earlier, he was shocked to find tears at his eyes, realizing he was crying only when one tear splashed the edge of his plate of untouched food.

Now, many years later, he once again felt that same profound stirring at this music as they entered the salon. The woman, eyes closed, seemed to sense rather than hear their presence and abruptly broke off the music, dramatically removing the violin from under her chin, and resting it in the crook of her right arm. She peered at Werthen and Berthe with her head cocked like a bemused pigeon.

"Please, Natalie," Justine Mahler said. "Not on our account. It was quite lovely."

The woman named Natalie merely smiled at Justine, making no overture toward recommencing.

"Werthen," Mahler called out from his sickbed. "We must stop meeting like this. You are going to take me for an invalid, while I am, despite my slightness, a rather robust individual. And who might this charming young woman be?"

Noting a look of disapproval from both the other women at Mahler's remark, Werthen made introductions and was introduced in turn to the violinist, Natalie Bauer-Lechner, an old family friend. A friend, that is, of Mahler's since the days when he was a poor music student in Vienna.

Mahler did not bother with common civilities; not waiting for small talk, he immediately said, "Now, ladies, I am sure you will forgive Herr Werthen and myself for secreting ourselves for a small business conference."

His sister and Frau Bauer-Lechner were immune to Mahler's abruptness, clearly having suffered it, perhaps even encouraging it as a sign of his artistic genius, for long years. Berthe, however, noticeably bristled at the remark, but said nothing. Instead, she repaired with the other women to the kitchen for a cup of tea.

Mahler waited for the double doors to shut behind them, then breathed a sigh of relief.

"Sometimes a chap needs to be on his own."

Werthen smiled at the comment, having felt the same way at times.

"Sit, sit." Mahler waved his good arm at a nearby armchair. "By your concerned demeanor, Werthen, I assume you believe this latest fiasco is a further attempt on my life."

"The thought had crossed my mind."

"Poppycock. Though it is interesting. I suppose you are a student of musical history, no?"

"Of a sort."

"Of course you recall the sad events of 1870? This was five years before I entered the conservatory here, but even in the backwater of Iglau where I grew up we heard of the tragedy to befall Josef Strauss, the talented brother of Johann and Eduard."

Werthen did recall the incident now. Strauss, on a tour of Poland, had fallen from his podium and died not long after. There was a deal of mystery surrounding the death, for his widow would not allow an autopsy. It was not known whether the composer died of injuries suffered from his fall, or if he had injuries or an illness prior to that.

"Surely you are not comparing the two?" Werthen objected. "There was no indication the podium in that instance was at fault."

"Is there in this instance?" Mahler responded. "I have been known to experience vertigo. Sometimes in the high mountain peaks I am so overcome with passion for the scenery that I quite forget myself."

"You're saying that you may simply have fallen from the podium. That it did not, in fact, crumble beneath you."

"One moment I was conducting Wagner, the next I was flat on my back in the orchestra pit gazing up at the rather shiny white shins of Arnold Rosé, my first violinist, as he hovered over me, his trousers billowing at the ankle."

"He was the first to reach you?"

"Please, Werthen. The man hopes to be my brother-in-law. Murdering me would hardly win him a warm place in Justine's heart."

Werthen felt himself growing annoyed at Mahler's cavalier response to this latest outrage.

"There is indeed a long history of odd

musical deaths, Werthen, none of which were necessarily attributed to nefarious plots. Take the unfortunate Jean-Baptiste Lully, for instance. You think my fall from a podium was dire? Monsieur Lully, in the French style of the day, pounded out the rhythm of his music from the wings, using a large staff. One night the poor man impaled his own foot while thus conducting and died of gangrene not long thereafter."

Mahler chuckled to himself.

Werthen had had enough.

"It is missing. That is one problem."

Mahler drew himself out of his humorous reverie.

"What is missing?"

"The podium. The stage manager says it is wood chips by now, so there is no way to ascertain whether or not it had been tampered with."

Mahler considered this for a moment. Then, "You say that is *one* problem. Implying others."

"The stagehand supposedly responsible for the dropped fire curtain is no longer at the Hofoper."

"Nor would I want the blighter to be."

"Nor is he in Austria, it would seem. Rumor has it he has emigrated to America."

A further silence from Mahler.

"Was he also the one responsible for the dropped scenery flat?"

Werthen had not questioned the stage manager about that, he now realized.

"Possibly," he said, to cover up his own error.

"And the tainted chamomile tea?"

Werthen simply shrugged at this. "You yourself enumerate four dangerous, possibly life-threatening incidents, yet you continue to joke about it," he said instead. "Do you think that is the appropriate response? Why have you summoned me today?"

Mahler smiled broadly. "My revised will, or have you forgotten?"

"On a Sunday?"

Mahler nodded his head against the white expanse of pillow. "All right. Yes, I do feel some concern. Especially now you mention the podium has so handily disappeared."

Werthen said nothing, forcing Mahler himself to say it.

"Fine, then. Investigate away, damn you."

"Why so stubborn?" Berthe asked as they strolled back toward the Josefstädterstrasse and their home.

"He simply refuses to believe he works alongside someone who wants him dead. I can imagine it is a rather chilling thought, not something you want to contemplate."

"Why limit the investigation?"

"How do you mean?" Werthen asked. They were approaching the Ringstrasse once again. A streetcar passed, newly electrified, sparks flying from its overhead arm. "You say that Mahler might be working alongside someone who wants him dead. Is it not possible there are domestic possibilities, as well?"

"You mean his sister?"

"Why not? Or the jilted lover?"

"And who might that be?"

"It took less than a half cup of tea for me to see that Natalie Bauer-Lechner is hopelessly in love with Mahler. And for me to understand from Justine Mahler's comments that she stands no chance of ever becoming his wife."

"Quite a happy little domicile."

She raised her eyebrows. "They hover over him like wasps." Then she tucked her arm more tightly in his.

They reached their apartment a quarter hour later, tired after a full day. Werthen thought fondly of a hot bath, perhaps some sherry before dinner, and a chance to read a bit more. Then a cozy night at home with his wife and early to bed. The thought of that filled him with a sudden warmth beneath his stomach. He was a happy man.

As they let themselves in, Frau Blatschky was quick to meet them at the door, her voice almost a whisper.

"I told him you were out, but he insisted on waiting for you. He's been here several hours. And eaten twice, I might add."

Werthen was about to ask her who their mysterious guest might be, when a familiar voice thundered at them from the sitting room:

"Werthen, my good man, where the devil have you been all day?"

The stentorian tones of none other than Dr. Hanns Gross, Werthen's old friend and colleague, and the foremost "criminalist" — as Gross fashioned himself — in the empire.

FOUR

"I don't care if I never see another beech tree," Gross said as he cut into the boiled beef and horseradish sauce Frau Blatschky had set before them. "That's what the region's name comes from, Buchenland, land of the beeches."

Last year Gross had been posted to the Franz Josef University in Bukovina's capital, Czernowitz, to open the first department of criminology in Austro-Hungary, final recognition of his years of research and writing in what he liked to call criminalistics. With the university closed for the summer, Gross had come to Vienna for a conference at the university, while his wife, Adele, was in Paris visiting friends.

"My lord," he spluttered through bites of beef, "even the streets of the so-called capital are lined with those beastly arboreal intrusions."

"But I've heard it is quite a lovely city,"

Werthen said, winking at Berthe as he did so.

Gross laid down fork and knife, casting a withering look at the lawyer.

"My dear Werthen. I have known you for years and will therefore not be drawn out by that faux innocent remark. Suffice to say, calling the place a city is a disservice to the language. It is a dusty and dirty claptrap of dodgy buildings, many of them gussied up to look like the Austrian homeland, but largely a Potemkin village. Their façades may indicate several stories, but the dark and impoverished interiors are one or two levels at best. Catherine the Great herself would be impressed by the deception."

Berthe now raised her brows at her husband.

"I saw that gesture, my good lady," Gross went on. "You think I exaggerate. Far from it. Czernowitz boasts a population of a hundred thousand, but you have to go long and far to find a German. The place is an overgrown Jewish shtetl, no insult intended."

Werthen and Berthe, both of Jewish background, were too accustomed to Gross's unconscious anti-Semitic comments to even attempt a response. Oddly enough, he meant no harm by such comments; for him they were merely statements of fact.

"I have heard they have a lively musical scene there," Berthe said.

"If you enjoy the rather overheated melodrama of *zigeuner* music."

"There is nothing to recommend the place?" Werthen asked.

"I am told the mathematician Leopold Gegenbauer hailed from there," Gross said, taking up knife and fork again. "It is, in short, dear friends, a backwater. My poor lady-wife, Adele, is perishing for want of companionship and culture. She slips off to visit her cousin in Paris or to fuss over our empty apartment in Graz whenever she has the chance. As for me, I have one or two bright pupils. The rest would better serve the empire in the army."

"I am sure you do not really believe that, Dr. Gross," Berthe said brightly.

"And I am sure I do, dear lady. If not cannon fodder, then perhaps milkers and stable hands. Czernowitz is a dreadful place. However, those in power have finally decided to recognize my work by giving me the chair in criminology, and that is the only reason I languish there. If criminalistics is ever to be considered a true science, then I need to build my department into a top-flight research and training center equal to

Paris or Scotland Yard."

They ate in silence for a time, the standard clock on the wall behind Werthen making a pleasant tocking noise to punctuate the clink of cutlery against porcelain.

Finally Gross looked up from his meal. "You must pardon my execrable manners," he said. "Prattling on about my own situation and not bothering to find out what you two have been up to."

"Well," Werthen began, "we have been a bit busy."

Gross rubbed his hands together. "Do tell."

"Redecorating, buying new furniture. The sorts of things newlyweds do."

Gross twitched his salt-and-pepper mustache. "You know very well that is not the sort of busy-ness I was inquiring after."

"Oh, tell him," Berthe said.

Werthen smiled at this; she had a kinder heart than he did.

"We are working on a new investigation."

"That is more like it," Gross said. "I knew that once you got your teeth into the criminal world again, you would be hooked. Who is involved?"

"Mahler."

"The composer? Whatever has he done other than assault our eardrums with his

88

music?"

"Not what he has done," Werthen explained, "but rather what someone is trying to do to him. It appears he is the target of a killer."

"Marvelous." This time Gross clapped his hands in delight. "By the way," he said in an aside to Berthe, "do you think we might move on to dessert?" Then beaming again at Werthen, he said, "Explain away."

Over coffee and strudel, Werthen detailed the investigation thus far: what appeared to be individual accidents, but which, when put together could suggest several failed attempts on Mahler's life.

"I take it you have somehow investigated this Schindler girl?" Gross suddenly interrupted.

"Investigated?" Werthen asked.

"Checked on her particulars," Gross explained.

"I know what the blasted word means, Gross. But investigate her to what purpose?"

"To ascertain that she is, in fact, not the perpetrator."

"Don't be ridiculous, man," Werthen exploded.

"No. Dr. Gross makes a valid point," Berthe joined in. "After all, what more do we know of her than that Klimt was pursuing her, just as he pursues anyone in skirts. But if she is so smitten with Mahler, then she might be trying to gain his attention, win his goodwill."

"By trying to kill him?" Werthen replied.

"Quite the contrary, old man," Gross said. "By seeming to come to his rescue. By raising the alarm in the first place."

"She has made it quite clear that I am not to divulge her identity to Mahler."

Gross nodded. "Yes . . ."

"But there is nothing to stop *her* from doing so," Berthe said.

"Exactly my point," Gross said, nodding appreciatively at Berthe.

Werthen was beginning to feel outnumbered and outflanked.

"It is essential," Gross announced, "as your wife suggests, that we take all possibilities into account."

"We?" Werthen blurted out. "Hold on now, Gross. What about your conference?"

Gross made a dismissive "pahh" sound. "The matter of a few hours here or there. While this case poses tantalizing possibilities."

"It's hardly a case yet," Werthen countered. "And I doubt the Schindler girl will be able to produce a fee."

"Yes, but you say Mahler has given you

the go-ahead. And you *are* his lawyer."

Werthen felt suddenly very protective of his investigation. He was not sure he wanted Gross nudging his way into it and, of course, attempting to lead it. This was his investigation; Mahler was his client.

As if reading his thoughts, Gross took a final sip of his coffee, daubed at his bristling mustache with the linen napkin and said, "Of course, it is *your* case, Werthen. I shall merely provide ancillary support, as it were. A consultant, I believe it is called."

"Paid or unpaid?" Berthe wisely asked.

Gross feigned shock. "You do me a disservice, my good woman. Unpaid, naturally. Or should I say that I shall thereby repay your kindness and generosity in inviting me to stay with you rather than book a room at the Bristol. Taking that into account, I will be well remunerated for any services I shall be able to provide you."

Werthen and Berthe looked at each other for a moment.

"Deal?" Gross finally asked.

Werthen slowly nodded. But he had to admit to a twinge of disappointment that Gross had so neatly maneuvered his way onto the case.

It was one thing for Gross to say he would

simply consult, but quite a different matter for him to actually take second chair in any investigation.

The next morning at breakfast they began mapping out a course of action. Berthe wisely remained silent while the men conferred. They quickly agreed on the first order of business. Alma Schindler and her motives would come later. For now, the initial step was to check into the life of the unfortunate Fräulein Kaspar, who died under the fire curtain. If she were not the intended victim of that "accident," then it would go a long way toward indicating that Mahler was.

As luck had it, Gross knew the examining magistrate of the Waldviertel region from which the young soprano hailed. A call to him could begin the process of gathering information about her: had she left behind a jealous or rejected lover? Perhaps a voice teacher that she had outgrown? Was there someone, anyone, who might have a motive for killing Fräulein Kaspar? Interviews would also have to be conducted at the Hofoper to see if there were other singers who might see the girl as a threat to their career.

"Professional jealousy can prove a powerful motive," Gross intoned. "The theater is a most dangerous place to work."

Werthen nodded. "And let us not forget that there may have simply been a baser form of jealousy at play. Mahler did say he and Fräulein Kaspar had been lovers. Who knows how many other singers the man has wooed and which of those might not appreciate having a new paramour paraded in front of her?"

"Anna von Mildenburg for one," Berthe suddenly said. She was speaking of the Austrian Wagnerian soprano who had recently been brought to the Hofoper from Hamburg, where Mahler himself had previously conducted.

"How do you know that?" Werthen wondered aloud.

"By reading the *lowbrow* papers, as you call them. One can discover all sorts of valuable information. The papers were full of the affair when von Mildenburg was hired. It seems she and Mahler had a relationship for quite some time in Hamburg."

"There you have it then, Werthen," Gross said. "A starting point."

Once such preliminary measures were settled, however, the two immediately hit a stumbling block on how next best to proceed.

"The list of Mahler's enemies could be quite extensive," Gross said. "I have heard he is a stern taskmaster. A perfectionist. Not the sort of personality to hit it off with certain Viennese, I should think."

Gross was referring to the Viennese, if not Austrian, custom of *schlamperei,* or sloppiness or laziness in one's job or profession. Mahler required more of a singer than a mere performance; he demanded the best from his performers, or they were asked to find employment elsewhere. Werthen imagined there were many at the Hofoper who had been rubbed the wrong way by Mahler's perfectionism, but at the same time he did not want to encourage Gross with a reply. He knew where the criminologist was going with this line of reasoning.

"First we need to assemble a list of possible suspects," Gross said, confirming Werthen's suspicion. "I highly doubt, however, that we will get much cooperation from the opera administration. After all, it is their task to assure the world that everything is just fine at the Court Opera."

Gross waited a moment for some reply, but when none was offered, he went on unconcerned. "No, what we need is more good, old-fashioned gossip from someone who knows where the bodies are buried. Perhaps even a journalist of some sort."

Gross pronounced the word "journalist"

with such distaste that Werthen could not help but smile. Indeed, Werthen knew the very man for the role of informer, the young writer Karl Kraus, for he had made Kraus's acquaintance when submitting one of his short stories to the literary journals. Despite his youth (he was only twenty-five), Kraus had already assumed a prominent role in the Vienna literary scene, serving on the editorial boards of several of those journals. Initially joining the Jung-Wien literary movement peopled by the likes of Bahr, the vagabond, sandal-wearing Peter Altenberg, Richard Beer-Hofmann, Hugo von Hofmannstahl, and Felix Salten, Kraus had ultimately broken with those men, writing a scathing satire of the destruction of their favorite coffeehouse. He had also taken on the Zionist leader Theodor Herzl in another satirical article, decrying such separatist views. Like Werthen, Kraus was a Jew who believed in assimilation.

Earlier this year, Kraus had begun his own journal, *Die Fackel,* or *The Torch,* which he wrote almost single-handedly, attacking Habsburg hypocrisy and corruption, and poking fun at movements from psychoanalysis to German nationalism. Kraus most assuredly knew, as Gross had said, where the bodies were buried in Vienna. And best of all, he was a supporter of Mahler, applauding his work at the Hofoper of "cleaning the stables," as he had termed it in one article.

But this too could wait. First Werthen needed to make a point, and make it strongly.

"I believe, Gross, that we diverge here. You may seek to find the perpetrator or perpetrators, thus halting further attempts on Mahler's life. In effect, to 'cure' the malady. I, however, see another option — prevention."

"You're not proposing a bodyguard, are you, Werthen?" Gross said.

"Karl, Mahler would never put up with that," added Berthe.

Werthen tapped his nose. "What he doesn't know. An ounce of prevention is worth a pound of cure any day."

"And who do you propose for such a role?" Gross asked. "Surely not yourself."

Werthen shook his head.

"And not one of Klimt's thugs, I hope." Gross was referring to several criminal characters with whom the painter Klimt was acquainted. Klimt, had, in point of fact, established those men as bodyguards for Werthen and Gross when it was clear that their labors in Klimt's defense had put their lives in danger.

Werthen did not reply to Gross's suggestion.

Berthe let out a low laugh. "Karl, you are incorrigible. Have you already contracted those men?"

"The idea only came to me last night. I've hardly had time to implement it."

"*Yet,* you mean?" she said.

"So we are at an impasse, then," Gross said. "You propose one course of action, I another."

"Is there a reason we cannot follow both courses simultaneously?" Berthe reasonably suggested.

Werthen, still smarting from the fact that Gross had made himself part of the investigation, was not feeling reasonable at the moment; nonetheless, a truce was called.

Later that morning, Werthen managed to contact Klimt, who in turn, put Werthen into contact with two of the fellows who had helped them out the year before. Herr Prokop and Herr Meier were their names, and Werthen had a speedy and rather clandestine meeting with them at their favorite local — a wine bar near the Margarethen Gürtel underneath the tracks of the new *Stadtbahn.* Werthen, not a small man, felt like a pygmy amidst the hulking men gathered at this bar, playing cards and laughing at stories of battered skulls and stolen carriage horses. Prokop and Meier were as bulky and ominous-looking as Werthen remembered them from their previous encounters, but even they looked like meek friars as compared to some of the other bowler-wearing toughs gathered there.

Prokop was missing a tooth since their last meeting; Meier wore a soiled bandage on his left little finger, whose final joint appeared to be missing. Prokop, who did most of the talking, had a choirboy's voice to counter his boxer's demeanor. Their discussion was continually interrupted by the rattle of trains overhead. Each time one passed, their wineglasses danced about the chipped table. After taking a sampling of the wine, Werthen left his glass on the table to dance.

A fee and plan of action were agreed upon: the two would maintain a half-day surveillance each on Mahler. Leitner at the Court Opera indicated that tonight's performance would be the final one of the season, to be conducted by Hans Richter as Mahler was still recovering from his injury. Thus the services of Prokop and Meier would, at first, be restricted to watching the composer's flat. Werthen wisely brought a recent news photo of the composer with him, for these two would surely never have heard of the man. Another surprise, however, for Meier turned out to be a great fan of operetta; Strauss's *Die Fledermaus* had played at the Hofoper in honor of the man's passing, and Meier had been in attendance, seeing Mahler conduct the performance himself.

The agreement was marked by handshakes and a large swig of the rancid wine.

Two hours later, Werthen was still suffering from that ritual. He and Gross were on their way to an appointment with Anna von Mildenburg at her Ringstrasse apartment. Von Mildenburg lived in the Sühnhaus, at Schotten Ring 7, the northwestern section of that boulevard. The address seemed ominous, for the apartment was built on the ruins of the Ring Theater, which had burned to the ground in 1881, killing hundreds of those attending the night's performance. Werthen remembered that incident only too vividly. A teenager, he and his family were in Vienna for the Christmas season and had tickets to that evening's performance of Offenbach's *Tales of Hoffman.* But his maman had come down with a bout of intestinal influenza and their father decided that it would be ungentlemanly for the rest of the family — his younger brother, Max, had still been alive at that time — to be enjoying themselves while his wife was bedridden. For once, his father's "gentlemanly" code — forever aping what he thought to be the mannerisms of the titled classes — served them well.

The emperor himself had ordered the building of this "House of Atonement," a magnificent structure combining elements of Gothic and Renaissance styles, surmounted by churchlike spires. The building contained apartments, commercial properties, and a memorial chapel as a remembrance to those who had died. Despite its elegance and its quality address, the Sühnhaus was always a safe bet for a quick rental, for the Viennese were a superstitious lot, and the address was not a favored one. But for someone who had the cash and was in urgent need of upscale lodgings, the Sühnhaus was a popular short-term address. The singer surely had enough for the monthly rent: Berthe had informed him that von Mildenburg had been hired at the unheard of sum of 14,000 gulden, as much as some advisors to the emperor earned.

Their appointment had been arranged through the singer's agent. Berthe had easily found the man's name in the annual agent's list and had made the call while Werthen had been engaging Prokop and Meier. As far as the agent or the singer knew, Werthen, accompanied by his "assistant" Gross, had a commission from Mahler. Berthe had wisely left the nature of the commission up in the air.

("A fine addition, that wife of yours," Gross had muttered as they had earlier left the Josefstadt to walk to their appointment. For Gross, that was high praise indeed.)

Von Mildenburg lived on the top floor, overlooking the broad Ring. The Stock Exchange was just across the street, while a close neighbor on the same side of the boulevard was the Police Praesidium.

They stood in front of the door to the singer's apartment and Werthen touched the bronze clapper that was shaped like a Dutch clog against the doorplate. The singer herself answered the door a moment later: Werthen recognized her, for he had seen her in the role of Brünnhilde at the Hofoper. Usually stars of the stage are much smaller when encountered outside the theater. However, Anna von Mildenburg was actually bigger in life; not a heavy woman for a Wagnerian soprano, but substantial, like the building she lived in. She was tall and thick-boned and wore a flow-ing wrap, half kimono and half robe. A shock of dark brown hair was held aloft with pins and combs; her face was punctuated by a broad Roman nose. She gazed at them curiously.

"You would be Herr Werthen," she said, extending her hand.

Werthen took the warm hand in his, feeling an electric pulse from her. Actresses and singers always had this effect on him: he blushed up to his hair roots and had trouble finding his voice as she led them into a sitting room. Everything here was right angles and geometric designs as if a decorator from the Werkstätte had been given free rein, just as at Mahler's apartment. Werthen finally stammered introductions all around and found a seat next to Gross on a settee covered in a fine byzantine, mosaiclike design that Klimt himself could have painted.

"So you are investigating these attempts on Mahler's life."

Werthen was caught off guard. He looked at Gross, who simply nodded an assent to her.

"But of course I called Mahler after your assistant made such a mysterious appointment. We have nothing to hide from each other."

"It would appear so," Werthen finally said.

"And you, sir," she said, turning to Gross, "are not the nameless assistant Herr Werthen makes you out to be, are you?"

"Well —" Gross began.

She cut him off. "Of course you're not. I may be merely a performing artist, but I am no fool. I have seen your photo before. The criminologist, Dr. Hanns Gross, if I am not mistaken."

"You are not," Gross allowed.

"Then this is serious," she said. "Not merely one of Gustav's flights of fancy."

"He is subject to such things?" Gross inquired.

A sly smile from von Mildenburg as she settled back in her Hoffmann chair, drawing the Japanese robe demurely over an exposed ankle.

"He is a creative genius. The world reveres him for his flights of fancy."

"At the podium or piano, however," Gross added.

"One cannot compartmentalize one's life," she said. "Or can one?"

Werthen had by now lost any and all awe of the singer; in fact, he was becoming increasingly irritated by her manner. And Mahler. What was the man thinking of to blurt out the nature of their mission to his former lover? He was hoping to catch the woman off guard or at least off balance. Now, however, she was in control of the interview. They might just as well call it a day.

"Why so perturbed, Counselor?" she said. "As I said, Mahler and I share no secrets. We may no longer be engaged, but the spiritual connection remains."

"To be sure," Werthen said, eager to move on to another subject. "You knew the young Kaspar girl, did you not?"

"Of course. She was a singer at the Hof-oper, as am I. Were we friends? Intimates? Hardly. She was far too jejune a creature for me. But for Mahler, oh, she was just right. Malleable. Someone to form, to build."

"As he did with you?" Werthen bluntly asked.

She nodded. "As he did with me. But then, I had already had the wonderful coaching of Rosa Papier at the konservato-rium at the beginning of my career, and later the invaluable help of Cosima Wagner herself in interpreting her husband's works. Whereas Fräulein Kaspar . . . well, she had Mahler."

"And native talent?"

"No end of that. Quite a lovely little

soubrette and a perfect mezzo. Mahler, however, had plans to turn her into a coloratura."

"Were you present at the rehearsal where the unfortunate young woman died?" Gross asked.

"No, thank God. That would have been more than my nerves could have taken. To see poor Mahler so close to injury, perhaps death!"

"There was of course the death of Fräulein Kaspar, as well," Werthen said, an edge to his voice.

Anna von Mildenburg pulled herself out of her melodramatic swoon, and fixed him with a fish-cold stare.

"Tragic, of course. But merely an unfortunate by-product."

"By-product?" Werthen said.

"Of the attempt on Mahler's life. That is why you are here, no? You surely cannot think that Kaspar was the intended victim. Who would care enough about the mousy little creature to send a fire curtain hurtling down on her?"

"She was a promising talent, is that not so?" Gross said.

"Promising, but not yet actualized. Besides, she was no threat to other singers. Mitzi had already left the company."

"That would be Mitzi Brauner?" Werthen said.

She smiled appreciatively. "I see we have an opera fan present."

Werthen ignored this remark, staring instead directly into the singer's face, herding her like a sheepdog back onto the track she perpetually desired to stray from.

"Yes, Mitzi Brauner," von Mildenburg continued. "She left for Aachen. Not a great house, but then her time was *vorbei,* past. She no longer had the looks to carry the soubrette roles. So the Kaspar girl had a clear field."

"And what about Fräulein Kaspar's affair with Mahler?" Werthen asked. "Were there —"

"Angry, jealous, and spurned lovers ready to scratch her eyes out?" she finished for him. Then she let out a low laugh. "Hardly. Though he has been here less than two years, Mahler has, I understand, made several conquests. But there were no bad feelings afterward with them, just as there are none with Mahler and me. You cannot put light in a bottle. We fellow artists recognize that."

"Nothing so base as jealousy afoot then." Werthen said.

"Be skeptical if it suits you," she said, suddenly bristling.

Now we are getting somewhere, Werthen thought.

"Are artists above normal human emotions?" he pressed on.

"How can I begin to explain to someone not involved in the arts?"

"Oh, please, madam," Gross interjected. "Werthen here is a published writer, in point of fact. His short stories have been highly lauded."

Werthen cut his eyes at Gross, but the criminologist was having too much fun to pay him any attention.

"I had no idea," she said, looking at Werthen.

"Part of the reason Herr Mahler hired him. Because he understands the artistic temperament. He is one of you."

As usual, Gross liked to pile it on thick, but it amused Werthen to see how von Mildenburg changed her attitude.

"You *will* understand then," she said, shifting in her chair, and leaning toward Werthen as if to impart a secret. "You see there could not possibly be that sort of jealousy. I mean Mahler, he wants to possess a woman, but not in the physical way. He wants her soul, not her body. His conquests were of the spirit, not the flesh."

107

"You mean, you and he . . ."

"Exactly. As if a sword were placed between us in the bed. There were thus no spurned lovers. There were no lovers at all."

FIVE

Death forged a truce between Werthen and Gross.

Detective Inspector Bernhard Drechsler, a razor-thin man, directed the foot traffic inside the small First District flat. Three beefy constables stood at ease by the door, waiting while Werthen and Gross got about their business. The largest of the three, a man with a nose so veined and scarlet as to suggest he had poured most of the annual wine harvest of Burgenland into his body, wore a bemused expression. His thick arms were folded across his chest like a challenge.

Werthen was unsure what they were looking for, but Gross insisted they should investigate, and they had arrived at the scene just in time to forestall any initial police examination. A personal favor from Drechsler, whom Werthen had never before met. Sent to Czernowitz for a crash course in the spring, the Viennese inspector and

Gross had formed a collegial relationship. Far from friendship, their connection was professional and highly competitive.

Yesterday, Gross had apprised the inspector of the Mahler affair, but Drechsler quite appropriately indicated that until there was a crime, there could be no investigation. The death of Fräulein Kaspar had been put down to accident. Gross, of course, had known this. He had approached Drechsler not assuming the police would take part in the case. Instead, he wanted a conduit to the inside; if any other opera-related incidents were to take place, Gross wanted to know of them.

The death of Friedrich Gunther was such an incident. Gunther, a member of the Vienna Philharmonic, was also part of the Hofoper orchestra, third violinist.

Discovered by his cleaning lady at nine this morning, Gunther was hanging by his neck from a tasseled length of chartreuse green curtain cord attached to the brass chandelier in his sitting room. Under the body was a faux Jacobean dining chair, tipped on its side. Werthen and Gross had arrived while the body was still suspended; Werthen caught sight of the swollen, reddish blue face and came close to being ill.

Gross, however, was fascinated by the

dangling body, approaching it from all angles, closely examining the carpeting underfoot with a strong, handheld magnifier plucked from out of his ever-present crime-scene bag. He muttered to himself, examined the carpet more closely, and then glanced quickly at the largest of the constables, his arms still crossed in front of him.

"I assume you wear a size forty-seven boot, Officer."

It was not a question.

The constable nodded his head, suspicion now replacing bemusement.

"And that you have also violated the most basic of crime-scene principles. Do not trample the evidence." Gross's voice raised in volume.

"Didn't know it was a crime to kill yourself . . . sir." Insolence gleamed in the constable's eye.

"That'll do, Schmidt," Drechsler cautioned. Then to Gross: "They were summoned from the local police station. I arrived in time to stop them cutting the man down."

"We thought the chandelier would come falling down any minute," Constable Schmidt said by way of self-defense.

Gross appraised the condition of the chandelier. "If it withstood the initial drop, then it will hold." He glanced from the chair to the boots of the victim, dangling in front of him. "Did you touch anything? Rearrange anything? The chair, for instance."

Schmidt shook his head. The other constables stood mute beside him.

"Officers?" Gross indicated the other two.

"No, sir," they chimed in unison.

While Gross produced a tape measure and chalk from his crime-scene bag, Werthen took in the ambience of the room.

Gunther had obviously been a bachelor. The size of the flat and its appointments would have told him that if the cleaning lady, still sobbing in the kitchen, had not already done so. No wife, for example, would have tolerated the cheap reproduction furniture with which Gunther had littered his flat. Through a small archway to the left was a dining area. Darkly painted chairs in medieval design were clustered around a dining table that was at least two shades lighter and of Renaissance design. The chair Gunther had used to stand on before hanging himself was from the dining area. In the sitting room a solitary and massive armchair of execrable taste was placed quite near the middle of the room, a marquetry table at its side. On the walls hung prints of fine artworks: Vermeer, Hals, Brueghel. Gunther's taste veered toward the Dutch and Flemish schools; toward the trappings of culture, but with no coherence, no taste. Werthen did not need to go to the small back bedroom in order to know that there would most likely be a single bed and cavernous wardrobe, both in the heavy Alt Deutsch style. Or perhaps more of the faux Jacobean.

Gross still busied himself beneath Gunther's body. Now he was photographing the scene from several different angles, a spark of flash illuminating the room from time to time.

What little other light there was came from two gas lamps on the sitting room wall. The chandelier was a gesture, merely. Non-functioning. Werthen marveled that it could actually hold the weight of the dead violinist, though Gunther was a slight man. He went to the only window in the sitting room; it let out onto a light shaft. Gunther's address was noble enough, the Herrengasse. However, the cramped apartment was at the back of the building, which had once been a city palace for the Lobkowitz family. Perhaps then it housed domestics, but with the conversion of the old *palais* in the last decade, it had become a freestanding apartment.

Musicians earned little enough, Werthen knew. The job was a sinecure — at least it had been before Mahler's reign of terror at the Court Opera and Philharmonic — but such security came at a high price. Herr Gunther clearly had made barely enough for a single man to subside on; whether by design or necessity, his violin had also become his wife. A sad sort of life, Werthen thought. Devoted to art, yes. But then to come home from the lofty world of music to such a depressing environment. Once again, Werthen marveled that a sense of beauty was not something that was generalized to all aspects of one's life. That is, he was amazed that a man such as Gunther who, one assumed, had been filled with the beauty inherent in music, could still live in such unaesthetic surroundings. Or, like much of Vienna, perhaps Herr Gunther had spent his free time in his favorite coffee house and not in the restricted confines of his unwelcoming apartment.

Werthen's ruminations were cut short by a snort from Gross.

"Suicide. Utter nonsense."

Drechsler also perked up at this comment.

"Well, I admit that the lack of any suicide note looks suspicious. But what makes you say so without even examining the body?"

To which comment Gross simply righted the dining chair, placing it under the dangling feet of Gunther. The tips of the dead man's boots were suspended two inches above the chair seat.

"I'll be damned," Drechsler said. "Cut him down." He motioned to the constables who now finished the work they had earlier begun.

They laid the body gently onto the floor, and Gross leaned down to make a quick examination. Drechsler, his hawklike face marred by a rather unattractive overbite, squatted next to him.

The inspector assumed control now, slipping a forefinger under the front of the noose. The skin underneath was neither bruised nor rope-burned. He worked around to the back of the man's head, feeling for broken vertebrae with his eyes closed. He shook his head.

"Amateur," Gross spluttered, as if it was the worst offense he could imagine. "As if he didn't care enough to even try to deceive us."

Werthen assumed Gross was not referring to the dead man but rather to some unknown assailant.

"Perhaps he had no idea *you* would be investigating, Dr. Gross." Drechsler said this, so Werthen thought, with no little degree of irony.

"Had your constables had their way," Gross replied with equanimity, "this may very well have passed muster as a suicide. Or perhaps he was relying on the elevated suicide rate of Vienna to cover the true crime."

"He?" Werthen said. Of course he knew what Gross meant. But it was as if he was denied the power of deduction when the master criminalist was in attendance.

"Find me the woman who could have hoisted Herr Gunther up there and I shall be happy to arrest her."

"Arresting, I believe, still comes under my purview," Drechsler said, suddenly taking offense.

"A manner of speaking only," Gross allowed.

This seemed to mollify Drechsler, who continued his examination. "The absence of ligature marks on the neck is also consistent with the obvious interpretation," Drechsler added.

The words were out before Werthen could stop them: "What interpretation?" Which comment allowed Gross and Drechsler to share commiserating looks.

This was really too much. On his own, he

was quick to grasp all implications. However, the very presence of Gross seemed to unman him, to sap him of all intellectual initiative. Werthen was quick to cover up his question. "I mean, I assume you hypothesize that Herr Gunther was killed and then hung up here to make it look like suicide."

"Bravo, Werthen," Gross said. "That is precisely what we believe. Though I note that your mouth still works more quickly than your mind."

Which brought a low chuckle from Constable Schmidt, silenced immediately by a glare from Drechsler.

Werthen needed badly to rehabilitate himself. Though forensic pathology was not his strong suit, he ventured on.

"The aspect of the man's face would, however, suggest death by strangulation, would it not?"

Gross, still leaning over the body, now looked to Drechsler for permission, and moved the noose to reveal bruising on each side of the neck.

"As you say, Werthen, death by strangulation. The blood spots on the cheeks from burst ocular capillaries, as well as the cyanotic, engorged aspect of the face itself all indicate that. Manual strangulation. You can see the clear outline of fingers here and here." He pressed his thumb into the small triangle formed by the junction of the dead man's collarbones. "And a ruptured larynx, if I am not mistaken. We will know more with the full autopsy."

Drechsler stood now, flexing his back. "Motive," he said. "A musician seems a harmless enough sort. Who would want to kill him?"

"That, my dear inspector, is what we intend to discover."

Herr Regierungsrath Leitner was not overjoyed to see Werthen again.

"I don't see how the unfortunate death of Herr Gunther has anything to do with your investigations on Herr Mahler's behalf."

"Humor us," Gross said. "We are inordinately curious where violent death is concerned."

The addition of Gross to the investigation seemed to discomfit Leitner. The criminologist's reputation preceded him; Leitner reddened at Gross's comment, wringing his hands and attempting with little success to control an eye twitch.

"Most irregular," he muttered.

They said nothing and finally Leitner rose from his desk in the opera offices, and led their way via a series of mazelike stairways to the main auditorium.

As they approached the orchestra pit, Leitner pointed to a chair on the left side.

"There. That was Herr Gunther's position as third violinist. He sat in that very chair for the final performance of the season last night."

Without asking permission, Gross suddenly dropped down into the slightly depressed pit, sat on the chair in question, and peered at the stage.

"I will need the curtain opened, if you don't mind, Herr Regierungsrath Leitner."

When Leitner hesitated, Gross added, "A simple enough matter, no?" The criminologist grinned at Leitner with false bonhomie.

"It will take a moment," Leitner replied, leaving Werthen and Gross to summon a stagehand.

"Examining the sight lines, Gross?" Werthen asked, now they were alone. "It would be better if you slouched down some in the chair. Gunther was a smaller man than you."

Gross was about to make a comment, but thought better of it. Instead, he took Werthen's advice.

"Yes," he said, once the curtains were opened. "As I thought." He sprang out of the chair and reached up to Werthen. "A hand, Werthen, if you please."

Werthen was surprised at the strength of his friend's grip as he helped to tug Gross out of the orchestra pit.

"I must thank our mutual friend Klimt," the criminologist said, brushing at imaginary dust on his dark gray trousers. "He recommended a course of training with dumbbells, though I personally employ the Indian club. It's done wonders for my stamina and mobility. Time was I would never have dreamed of jumping down into that pit."

"Damn the exercise, Gross. Did you find what I assume you were looking for?"

At which moment Leitner returned.

"Satisfied, gentlemen?"

"Inordinately," Gross said.

Leitner did not like the sound of this. "If there is any other assistance I can be . . ."

But this was said with tepid indifference.

"I assume you keep records of attendance by orchestra members. I mean, specifically, at rehearsals."

"Yes." A measured nod of the head from Leitner.

"Then, perhaps?" Gross swept his arm in invitation.

Back in Leitner's office they were shown an enormous ledger recording the schedules of each musician and singer. Gross stabbed the sheet with a large forefinger, following it down the page and through the dates of late May and June. He gave a large sigh.

"Thank you, Herr Regierungsrath Leitner. You have been most helpful."

Leitner cast Werthen a pleading look to which Werthen merely raised his eyebrows, as if to say he was as much in the dark as the assistant director was. Partly true; just partly.

Once outside, Werthen halted Gross with a hand to his arm.

"I assume you were checking for Herr Gunther's whereabouts on the days of other incidents."

"Yes, Werthen. Indeed I was. And he was present and accounted for in each circumstance."

Werthen shook his head. "And that proves . . . ?"

"Very little, without the added information of his view."

"From Herr Gunther's third violin chair, you mean?"

"Correct again. Gunther would clearly have been a witness."

"As I thought," Werthen said, and was pleased to see the anticipatory smirk forming on Gross's face disappear.

"Witness, that is, to the death of Fräulein

Kaspar," Gross said importantly.

But Werthen simply nodded. "Yes, of course. From his position, Gunther most probably had a perfect view of who might have been in the rigging, who, indeed, might have let the fire curtain loose."

Gross nodded appreciatively. "Well done, Werthen. I believe you are truly becoming a master of criminal investigation."

"Which means," Werthen went on, ignoring him, "that our villain is now intent in concealing his earlier attempts. If that is so, a further implication is clear. He intends to strike again. Mahler is in grave danger."

It was so like men to charge ahead, leaving the women to take care of such silly and mundane things as making sure a legal practice runs smoothly. Berthe held regard for Dr. Gross, but at the same time wished that he had chosen another moment to make his appearance. She and Karl were just beginning to work as a sort of team in this investigation lark. Now, however, the great criminologist was on the scene, and Karl was once again tagging after him like a puppy.

And here she was, stuck in the office making sure bills were paid and appointments kept.

She wondered if this was the beginning of what they called the slippery slope. After all, she had her own career as an educator and writer. Since her marriage, however, she had written but one article — on the Austrian peace movement and its female leaders. She had also reduced her time with the settlement house in Ottakring. Modeled on the English settlement movement begun by Mary Ward, the Vienna Settlement house reached out to the underprivileged children of the city, offering education and specialized play centers. She had helped guide the settlement, opening it to children with disabilities and using the center at night to host cultural opportunities for the working-class parents of Ottakring.

Yet this work, too, had suffered since her marriage. She now spent fewer hours at the Settlement, the better to help out at Karl's law firm. Her clients were not suffering, however, for she had recruited talented volunteers. Yet she missed her children. Missed her independent accomplishments.

Karl had not requested such sacrifices. Far from it. He praised her endlessly for her achievements. Yet she felt that somehow she needed to contribute to their life together, that they could not forever live parallel lives.

Enough of the self-pity, she told herself,

filing the last of the paperwork on the von Bülow probate.

Thank God for Ungar, she thought. Dr. Wilfried Ungar, Karl's assistant at the firm. Arrogant the young man might be, but he had been a mainstay for the firm, especially with Karl's injury last year, and then with the new direction her husband had decided to take in both criminal law and investigations.

A light tap sounded at the doorjamb. The door was open.

"Yes?"

Dr. Ungar stepped into the room. "If I am not interrupting," he said.

"No, not at all," she said. "Please do come in."

He attempted to look older than his twenty-eight years by wearing pince-nez and a mustache that turned up at the ends. His light gray suit fitted him well, not too ostentatious, not too humble. Guaranteed to put his clients at ease. His hair was already thinning; he combed it from one side to conceal this.

He sat in the client's chair across the desk from her in Karl's office. She did not like the look on his face; Ungar appeared to be attending a funeral.

"What is it?"

"I regret to inform you, Frau Meisner, that I can no longer practice my profession at this firm."

"But why ever not?"

"It's the new sign, you see."

"Sign? What sign?"

" 'Advokat Karl Werthen: Wills and Trusts, Criminal Law, Private Inquiries.' "

"Ah, yes," she said. "That sign."

"The criminal law I could tolerate. After all, Herr Werthen is a practiced hand at those from his days in Graz. But inquiries? Madam, do I look like a private inspector? I can no longer hold my head up amongst my peers. I find it necessary, in short, madam, to search for a position at a more respectable legal firm."

She was torn between an urge to slap the insolent young man and to get on her knees and beg him to stay.

"I am sorry to hear that," she said, settling for the middle way.

He put up a hand as if to halt her supplications, though she had made no such overture.

"I assure you, madam, I shall not be dissuaded from my decision. I have written Herr Werthen the same. I felt it incumbent upon my own integrity, however, to apprise you of my decision personally."

"That is good of you, Dr. Ungar."

"But again, I shall not be dissuaded from my course of action. Were the sign, however, to be abridged . . ."

"Yes," she said, now giving vent to pique, "that is a shame. But we shall have to somehow struggle on without you. When will your last day be?"

His pince-nez became disarranged at this, she was pleased to notice.

Seated in the Café Museum, which the firebrand architect Adolf Loos had just designed, Werthen and Gross were finally having an interview with the young journalist, Karl Kraus, attempting to pick his brain of any gossip relevant to Gustav Mahler.

The establishment they were seated in was nicknamed the "Café Nihilism" by one journalistic wag, for the interior embodied Loos's renunciation of ornamentation for modern, unadorned design. Strips of brass running across the vaulted ceiling were the sole pieces of near ornamentation, but these actually served to cover the electric wires. Bare lightbulbs hung from these brass railings overhead. Light green walls were set in contrast to the red bentwood chairs, which Loos himself had designed.

Gross looked uncomfortable in the minimalist surroundings, opting in personal taste for potted palms and caryatids supporting interior columns. Werthen, however, felt quite at home in this modern ambience.

"Of course you realize that journalism is the goiter of the world," Kraus said with affable conviction.

What is one to do with such a comment, Werthen thought, other than nod one's head sagely in agreement? It was Kraus's specialty, the aphorism that shocked.

A "goiter" industry or not, journalism was still the profession Kraus partook of. Satirist and self-appointed policeman in charge of patrolling sloppy language, bad grammar, poor word choice, and the misplaced comma, Kraus despised the languorous and breezy long newspaper essay, the feuilleton, with which many newspapers filled the bottom of their front pages.

"To write a feuilleton is to curl locks on a bald head," Kraus continued. "But the public likes such curls better than a lion's mane of thought." He smiled at this quip, thin lips revealing crooked teeth.

So young to be so full of himself, Werthen thought, but nodded in appreciation at the saying which, he imagined, he would soon be reading in the pages of the thrice-monthly *The Torch*. A slight man with a curly head of hair and tiny oval wire-rim glasses that reflected the overhead lights, Kraus dressed like a banker. One of nine children of a Bohemian Jew who had made his money in paper bags, Kraus lived on a family allowance that allowed him to poke fun at everyone in the pages of his journal.

Werthen had been trying for the last half hour to steer the conversation to its destination — Mahler and his possible enemies — but Kraus was having none of it.

"Herr Kraus," Gross finally interrupted. "I have no doubt of your intellectual qualities, nor of your wide and eclectic group of acquaintances, but can we please return to the point in hand?"

Kraus sat up in his chair as if his manufacturer father had upbraided him at dinner.

"I apologize, gentlemen. My pet peeves, you know."

Despite his slightness of bearing, Kraus had a fine speaking voice. He had tried for a career as an actor as a younger man, but stage fright had intervened. He was said to be experimenting with a new form of entertainment, however, much like the American, Mark Twain, and his famous one-person shows. At fashionable salons, Kraus was already entertaining the cognoscenti with his interpretations of Shakespeare and with readings from his own writings. Another of his aphorisms Werthen had heard: "When I read, it is not acted literature; but what I write is written acting."

"And yes, I believe I can aid you in your inquiries. I do not overstate the case, I think, to say that I am a focal point in the city. Vienna is an onion. We see that in the ring upon ring nature of the very city planning. The noble Inner City encircled by the Ringstrasse; the middle-class suburbs ringed by the Gürtel boulevard; and then the poorer outer districts where the workers live their forgotten, neglected lives."

Gross was about to interrupt again, but Werthen tapped his foot under the table, sensing that Kraus was finally coming to the point.

"I am part of this great smelly onion, gentlemen, perhaps even at the very heart of it. I hear things as a publisher. People write to me, stop me on the street to share secrets, leave messages with the *herr ober* at my favorite coffeehouses. I also hear things through my intellectual contacts. A few friends and I have a regular table at the Café Central where we meet weekly to discuss — well, to discuss the world in the crucible that is Vienna. These friends in turn belong to other circles, to that of Freud, or Schnitzler, or Klimt, or Loos, Victor Adler, Mach. Even, and most important for you two, Mahler."

He cast them another of his tight-lipped, reptilian smiles, eyes flashing behind his tiny spectacles.

"The long and short of it, Herr Kraus?" Gross said, losing patience now.

"Dr. Gross, I am sure you could not bear the long version. Apoplexy might result."

"The short of it then," Gross said.

"The list is extensive," Kraus said. "Off the top of my head, I can think of several possibilities. It is too bad you exempt women . . ."

Werthen had taken Kraus into their confidence enough to explain the broad outlines of the possible threat to Mahler. Would this threat find its way into print in Kraus's journal? Kraus had given his word of honor that it would not, but Werthen would put no money on that.

". . . For I personally know Gerta Rheingold would delight in Mahler's demise."

"The Mozart soprano at the Hofoper?" Werthen said.

"Yes, and her complaint is really quite delightful. At rehearsal last month for *The Magic Flute,* she was made to sing the lines, 'Die, horrid monster!' thirty times in succession, as Mahler was unsatisfied with her performance. Finally, she simply shrieked the lines at Mahler himself, bringing the entire rehearsal to a standstill. But then, she is a woman. However, today's modern, liberated woman should, I feel, be included in one's list of possible miscreants. Yet what is a liberated woman, but a fish that has fought its way to shore."

Another witticism that would soon spice the pages of *The Torch,* Werthen thought.

"Perhaps we can turn to the male candidates?" Gross prompted, looking awfully uncomfortable in the delicate contours of his bentwood chair. His coffee had long since been finished, the spoon upended in the cup.

"Well, I should question Herr Hans Richter, if I were you. He was one of the conductors under the former director, Jahn, and had reason to suspect that he himself would be named successor. Then Mahler arrives, a usurper to his crown, as it were. Touchy business, that. Leitner, of course, figures highly on such a list."

"Why so?" Werthen asked.

"He was an early supporter when Mahler first arrived from Hamburg. But Mahler has proved to be his own man. He will not allow Leitner to have the final say on finances, on hiring and firing policies, or any of the day-to-day management policies of the Court Opera. Mahler has gone over Leitner's head several times to Prince Montenuovo to get his own way. Then, of course, there is the stage manager, that Blauer chap. Cut from rough cloth. Mahler and he do not get along; opposite sides of the coin. Blauer makes no secret of the fact that Mahler's staging demands are too ambitious. Mahler is, in fact, a follower of Appia's principles, you know," Kraus said, indicating the Swiss pioneer in stage design. "A stickler for realism, three-dimensionality, and authentic lighting. While our friends behind the curtain at the Hofoper are quite content to continue with the scenic principles and traditions of long centuries."

"But would either of those complaints, Leitner's or Blauer's, be of such magnitude as to —"

"Warrant killing Mahler?" Kraus finished for Werthen. "Not in a sane society. But the theater is not sane; Vienna is not sane."

"You see the enemies as only within the Court Opera?" Gross asked, keeping the focus.

"What is it you criminologists say?" Kraus looked into the vaulted ceiling as if searching for the answer there. "Motive and opportunity. The second is strong for these men. But there are, of course, others who might have fewer opportunities. Eberhard Hassler, the music critic for the *Deutsches Volksblatt,* has been an outspoken critic of Mahler. His critique is largely based on the fact that Mahler is of Jewish origin. Hassler is a rabid anti-Semite; he thinks Mahler is destroying the Viennese musical tradition with his 'oriental' theories, whatever that may mean. Motive, but perhaps little opportunity. And one other that comes immediately to mind. The head of the claque, Peter Schreier, has screamed foul play that Mahler has banned him and his cohort from performances. Mahler wants no undue applause to break the momentum of his conducting. But Schreier and his friends make their living from their applause, paid for by well-established and younger singers alike. Schreier, as he wrote in a letter he hoped I would publish, believes the matter is a 'life-and-death affair.' I should say there is motive there, and perhaps, knowing his access to the stage, opportunity, as well."

"The same could be said for Hassler," Gross added. "After all, a music critic surely could gain access to rehearsals."

The three sat in silence for a time; all about them was a constant hum of conversation; waiters, attired in tuxedoes, brought trays of coffee and water to customers with elegant, quiet dispatch.

"The list is indeed long," Gross finally said. "And these are only the obvious choices. This is a desperate business. I must admit I do not care for the odds against us."

Six

The next evening Werthen received a call at his flat from Mahler. The composer's voice sounded strong if not strident; he was seemingly recovered from his latest "accident." He informed Werthen that he was off in the morning to the village of Altaussee in the western Salzkammergut region for his annual summer holidays. He and his sister, in the company of their friend Natalie, had taken a remote house for six weeks, the Villa Kerry, about a half hour from the village. There Mahler would continue work on his new symphony.

He spoke eloquently of the rustic wonders of Altaussee and its magical surroundings: the clear, deep blue-black waters of the alpine lake ringed by peaks of the Loser mountain and others; the quiet and hidden charm of the village with its few hundred inhabitants; the excellence of hiking and bicycling paths.

"Sounds idyllic," Werthen managed to say between Mahler's gushing pronouncements.

"You think so? Yes, I believe you will like it."

Werthen waited a moment to make sure he understood.

"You want me to accompany you?"

"Not accompany. Shadow, perhaps, would be a better description. Of course there is no spare room at our villa, but in the village there are excellent accommodations at the Hotel am See. I hope you do not mind that I have taken the liberty of booking you a room. One cannot be too cautious about such matters this time of year."

"Herr Mahler —" Werthen began.

Mahler, however, interrupted: "Your two simianlike employees would stand out much too much in such bucolic surroundings, Werthen. No, I believe you will do, if you feel I need personal protection."

So Mahler had discovered his bodyguards, Werthen thought. Of course, it had only been a matter of time before he would. But this was news to him that Mahler was moving house for the summer. Perhaps it was for the best; after all, what could happen to him in the country? Their nameless adversary would be loath to strike in such surroundings, where any outsider would be instantly noticeable.

"Herr Werthen? Are you still there?"

Werthen looked over his shoulder and into the sitting room where Berthe sat reading, a splash of gaslight casting a halo of warm orange-yellow light over her face, her lips squeezed tight in concentration. He felt a sudden and overwhelming love for her.

"Yes."

"Shall we see you in the country then?"

"Yes. Fine."

"Excellent," Mahler said, though with little enthusiasm. "We shall see you tomorrow then."

Werthen felt rotten to be leaving Berthe in Vienna, but someone had to find a new junior member for the firm. Berthe assured him that she could see to that, and Gross for his part was quite content to continue their investigation and interviews in Vienna. The lawyer suspected Gross was secretly relieved to be on his own with the investigation; there was nothing for it, however, but to follow Mahler to the country. Surely he would not be needed the entire six weeks of the composer's stay. He intended to take stock of the situation and then return to Vienna at the earliest possible opportunity.

Werthen boarded the Salzburg express on Thursday with a guilty joy at his upcoming time in the country, for Vienna was stifling under a hazy blue sky and a humidity.

However, he met with the direct opposite in terms of meteorological conditions once he had set down from the narrow single-gauge train in Altaussee.

It rained for the next two days. A slow, persistent rain that made the hedgerows of lilac bushes, long since out of bloom, hang like weeping willows.

Werthen was installed in the Hotel am See, an immense alpine building positively bristling with stag horns and oozing *gemütlich* touches, such as Tyrolean curtains, foot-thick eiderdown comforters on the beds, and freshly churned butter for the homemade rolls at morning coffee. Were Werthen's favorite boulevardier character from his short stories, Count Joachim von Hildesheim, to describe the hotel, he would characterize it as "aggressively charming."

Werthen himself, however, was warily seduced by the actual charm of the place and of the friendly *gastgebers,* or proprietors, the family Woolf. They were too good to be true: friendly, full of bonhomie, brimming over with solicitousness and concern for the comfort of their guests. However, sometimes things are just what they seem, he told himself, and one should damn well enjoy oneself. The Woolfs were indeed almost too good to be true: three towheaded young dirndl-clad daughters served in the dining room, their rosy cheeks a constant reminder to Werthen to get more fresh air and exercise, even as he feasted on fresh venison steak or a goulash made of mountain goat lung. The older sons, equally blond and alarmingly blue-eyed, resplendent in lederhosen and sparkling white shirts, served as attendants in the hotel, working the desk, carrying luggage, helping as guides for adventurous wanderers. And Frau Woolf supervised the kitchen while Herr Woolf was the organizing spirit and genial host of the establishment.

Both parents were dark-haired, which made Werthen wonder at their progeny; such wonderment and his subsequent jottings regarding the family were the first inklings of a return of his creative energies, creating mood pictures of Austria and the Austrians in short stories. Perhaps, though, he thought, such creativity would be better channeled into recording the minutiae of the cases he had become involved in rather than in the goings-on of such characters as the foppish Count von Hildesheim.

At night the Woolf family charmed their guests with musical evenings following dinner. They sang alpine melodies to the accompaniment of Herr Woolf's guitar and Frau Woolf's accordion. Werthen was usually no great fan of this wheezing and often skirling instrument, but in the hands of Frau Woolf it was turned into a plaintive and melodic joy.

Now, however, it was Saturday, and the dreary alpine weather had finally broken. Steam rose from the damp earth under a high, warm sun. Werthen determined to set out for Mahler's. He had been there only once, the very afternoon he had arrived, and managed to get soaked to the skin on his return journey to the hotel, barely escaping the dangers of an electrical storm that sent huge jagged daggers of wild energy slanting into the very lake bottom it had seemed.

What a difference two days had made, for now the weather was clear and fine. Songbirds accompanied him on his way along the sodden dirt path leading out of the village. An occasional oxen-drawn cart passed, its owner casting a suspicious glance his way, eyes half-hidden under a green alpine hat with a brush of oxen tail hair sprouting from its side. However, suspicion would turn to warm greeting when Werthen offered the traditional, *"Grüss Gott,"* God's greeting. It was a salutation he studiously avoided in Vienna, opting instead always for the more formal and neutral *"Guten tag"* or *"Guten abend."* Rejecting his own Judaism, he wanted his greetings to be as secular as possible.

He was just approaching the Villa Kerry when he heard the faint melody of the village band wafting from the village, the tuba carrying the melodic line along with clarinets and horns. He was unsure of the tune. As he came in sight of Mahler's rented house, he noted a small group of three men and two women gathered on the road in front, conversing and looking up at the Villa Kerry as if expecting a changing of the guard. They were obviously city dwellers — the women wore long white dresses and impossibly floppy hats that no sensible villager would ever don; the men were bowler-clad and their city suits looked foreign amidst the greenery and flowers of the front park to the Villa Kerry. As he passed them, Werthen overheard a distinctive Schönbrunner German accent that marked them as upper-class Viennese. One man, who wore dramatically curling mustaches, told the others: "He'll be at his piano now, composing. But later he likes to take a stroll. Perhaps then . . ."

Werthen did not linger to find out what

the man expected. Clearly they were no threat to Mahler, just music-mad and devoted fans of the Hofoper director and conductor. Had they planned their holiday to coincide with Mahler's? But then Werthen reminded himself that the fashionable *kurort* of Bad Aussee was nearby; they were most likely staying there and taking the waters.

At the house, Werthen was greeted by Mahler himself, who quickly drew the lawyer in before closing the front door behind them.

"Did you see them?"

He sounded in a panic.

"Who?" Werthen asked.

"Those." He swept his right hand in the direction of his front park. "Those parasites gathered outside. My God, they even send me letters asking for an autographed portrait. Soon they will take to spying on me through opera glasses."

"They mean no harm —" Werthen began.

"No harm! They are insufferable. Can they not simply let me be and get on with my work? And that infernal racket from the village. Every day now they will begin their blasted hooting and trumpeting before lunch and go on into the afternoon. One prays for rain to dampen their spirits."

Mahler, agitated, went to one of the

windows set on either side of the front door and peeked through lace curtains at his unwelcome visitors.

He turned back to address Werthen. "Be a good chap and send them on their way."

"Don't be absurd, Mahler. I am here to protect you from deadly intent, not from your fans."

"But they *are* killing me." His voice was desperate. "Killing my creativity, which is the same thing. I have but six weeks each year in which to compose. But how can I be expected to concentrate on my Fourth Symphony with those interlopers gaping up at my windows? With that hideous noise seeping through the woodwork?"

Werthen went to the other window and found that the little group had moved on. He was blessedly saved from such an onerous task.

Two days later, Gross, in Vienna, smiled amiably at the young woman seated across the desk from him. Quite a fetching young thing, he thought. Normally the charms of the fairer sex had little appeal for him. Adele and he had been married for decades now; he was settled into a quiescent domestic complacency where matters of the flesh were concerned. Theirs had never been a deeply physical union; Gross in fact found such couplings rather laborious as well as interfering with his main concern in life — devising a system of detection and analysis that would revolutionize the science of criminology. He imagined Adele probably felt the same; after all, women — except for the occasional nymphomaniac — were not intended to enjoy the acts of the bedroom. Following the birth of their only child, Otto, they had largely foregone those supposed pleasures. Staying with Werthen and his wife, he was startled to discover that they shared a bedroom. A rather messy state of affairs, as far as Gross was concerned.

No. Gross had adapted a Socratic attitude where sex was concerned, reaching the age of reason wherein he was no longer controlled or even affected by such impulses.

Or so he had thought.

However, the presence of this young Schindler woman across the desk this Monday morning caught him off guard, quite unnerved him, and had set off some long dormant feelings. He felt himself wanting to please her; he found himself needing to avert his eyes from her, as if she were casting some spell on him; her scent pleasurably engulfed him, much as a well-baked *guglhupf* cake might.

She had called earlier in the day, telling Berthe that she had new information for Advokat Werthen. However, learning that the lawyer was otherwise disposed, Fräulein Schindler had agreed to meet with Werthen's colleague at the law offices. As before, Berthe was seated near the door taking notes as Gross began to conduct the interview.

"So, young lady, how may I be of assistance?"

"I had hoped to speak with Advokat Werthen," she said, smiling coyly at Gross.

"Yes. As Frau Werthen told you, he is not at this time available." Gross ignored the fiery look Berthe cast him at his mistake in her name.

"No, no," Alma went on. "Do not misunderstand me. I meant to say that I hardly expected to be speaking with the distinguished Dr. Hanns Gross in his stead."

Gross manufactured a rictus of a smile at this comment. "At your service, Fräulein." He seemed not to hear the sigh that came from Berthe. "I know that Advokat Werthen was interested in people who might, for some reason or another, have reason to wish Herr Mahler ill."

Just as in her first interview, Fräulein Schindler now leaned across the desk, as if confiding in the bulky criminologist. Gross instinctively retreated at this advance; the springs of his desk chair groaned as he leaned backward.

"There is someone you should know about," she continued in a breathless fashion.

Slowly Gross was unwrapping himself from the young woman's blanket of charms, so obvious were her techniques of entrapment.

"Please elaborate," he said now with neutral authority.

It was as if she had caught the subtle shift in power and relaxed in her own chair once again.

"I have — and I do not mean to sound full of myself — numerous admirers. Among them I count one Heinricus von Tratten. He is of an old German family. In his case the 'von' is hereditary and not purchased. He insists I call him Heini, but that is rather too much. He is, in fact, a great deal older than I. We have been much thrown together of late, sitting next to each other at dinner parties, accidentally meeting at art openings. He is a bit of a philistine, but he is also a generous sponsor of the Secession. Carl, my stepfather that is, values Herr von Tratten in that regard."

She smiled winningly at Gross, but by now he had steeled himself against Fräulein Schindler's seductive powers and was concentrating solely on the information at hand.

"Yes, yes," he said impatiently.

"Herr von Tratten is, as I said, of German origin. As are you, I imagine, Dr. Gross."

When he did not respond, she continued her tale. "For Herr von Tratten, such origins are not simply a matter of pride, but are something to protect, if you follow me."

"That is to say that Herr von Tratten has certain leanings, certain preferences?" Gross delicately offered, not wishing to flush the bird before she had laid her golden egg.

"Exactly."

Berthe interrupted. "Sorry, but just so that I can get the word correct for the files. We are speaking of anti-Semitism here, yes?"

"Yes," Gross said, casting a disparaging look Berthe's way. "I believe that is what Fräulein Schindler is implying."

"Mind you," Alma quickly added, "that in and of itself is not something to raise suspicion. Many hold the view that Vienna is too much under the sway of Jewish ownership, from manufacture to newspapers."

"And the legal profession as well," Berthe said, sotto voce, but she was again ignored.

"However, in Herr von Tratten's case?" Gross prompted her.

"Well, you see, he discovered a silly photograph I carry with me. Some friends, knowing of my deep respect for Herr Mahler, went to pains to obtain for me a signed portrait of him. Several weeks ago, while seated next to him at a dinner party at the Zuckerkandls, I had occasion to open my handbag and he caught sight of the picture of Mahler. Naturally we began speaking about the maestro's reorganization of the Hofoper and of his genius. Well, I began extolling his genius, that is. I am sure Herr von Tratten was able to read my emotions accurately, to comprehend my devotion to Mahler's art, perhaps even to the man himself, though I have never met him. Herr von Tratten suddenly began the most frightening tirade about the anathema of the Jewish race and how any Jew who ever thought of despoiling a fair Aryan maid should be destroyed. That was the exact expression he used: *vernichtet werden.* It was quite chilling, really."

"And why did you not mention this at your first interview with Advokat Werthen?" Gross asked.

"People say things in the heat of the moment. I was unsure of his actual intent. But you see, since that evening, Herr von Tratten has continued to seek me out. I believe he is actively courting me, though I have given him no cause for optimism in that regard. He is an absolute toad of a man, regardless of his 'von' or family money. And he continues to pester me about my regard for Mahler, always asking me how my 'Jewish song master' is faring. Quite frankly, I do not care for his insinuations. Additionally, if I may be honest, he has the most horrid breath."

"I am not sure that is actionable, Fräulein," Gross said.

But she was all earnestness. "Nor did I mean to imply it was."

"It is good you have come to us with this added information, Fräulein Schindler. We have a list of persons we intend to interview; Herr von Tratten's name shall be added thereto."

"So you do believe Mahler to be in danger?" Her eyes sparkled at the thought.

"We are taking this quite seriously," Gross said.

"Marvelous." She suddenly stood, extending her hand to Gross. "I am so excited you have been included in this matter, Dr. Gross. I know you will put things right."

And she was gone, in a swirl of skirts and

a whirlwind of scent, not bothering to discuss such mundane matters as fees to be paid.

"Quite a force to be reckoned with," Gross said, after the outer door shut.

Berthe nodded her head.

"I should not like to be the man she sets her sights on," Gross further pronounced. "He will stand little chance of escape."

Later that same day Berthe sat alone in her husband's office examining replies she had received to an advertisement inserted in the *Austrian Legal Journal,* seeking a new member of chambers specializing in wills and trusts. There were four promising candidates, though all but one were unavailable for the next several weeks. The one available immediately was a lawyer from Linz, one Wilhelm Tor, forty, with a degree from Berlin. A native of Vienna, it seemed he greatly desired to return to his birthplace and was most eager to join a firm with the reputation of Advokat Werthen's.

That Tor's bona fides were in order, his résumé impressive, and his availability immediate all conspired to make Berthe pick up her pen and write to him a letter to be sent by afternoon post. Advokat Werthen would be pleased to offer Herr Tor an interview, she related. Never mind that Karl would not be present; she knew the sort of man they needed for the firm.

Let us hope that Herr Tor is as good in the flesh as he is on paper, she thought, signing the letter for her husband with a flourish.

She looked at the embossed letterhead, liking the solid, no-frills strength conveyed by the modern lettering; no Old German or Gothic styling for Karl. Admittedly, there was a baroque nature to her husband, a sensitive soul too often hidden by overly ornate verbiage; how to avoid such a thing if born in Austria? But her gentle teasing about his stuffy language, her barbs at his ambivalence vis-à-vis the monarchy, and above all her encouragement of his return to criminal law and to pursue his newfound love of investigations had all served to bring him out of his formal shell and make their union stronger, deeper.

Now, however, there might soon be need of a reckoning. It was all very well for Karl to branch out while he was still able to devote energy to the clients he already had. Yet now, with his absence in the Salzkammergut, things were coming to a head. The law firm could not simply run itself, nor could it rely on an assistant, no matter how talented and ambitious. After all, such ambition would lead any normal man to set off on his own eventually, to establish his own firm.

She dreaded the reality that was setting in on them, and at the same time longed for it. It was all very well for Karl to change his business sign: ADVOKAT KARL WERTHEN: WILLS AND TRUSTS, CRIMINAL LAW, PRIVATE INQUIRIES. However, it was the wills and trusts that were making their living. Private inquiries had yet to earn a florin for the firm; Klimt had not even paid for Karl's services from the previous year and Fräulein Schindler was obviously not quite so eager as she had been upon first meeting to dip into her inheritance from her father to pay for such investigations. Granted, Mahler had retained Karl, but one fee would hardly compensate for the others lost while her husband devoted all his energies on the case, neglecting other clients.

When Karl returned, they would have to have a serious discussion about all this. Circumstances had changed after the visit to her doctor last Friday. Now she was filled not only with a new sense of purpose, but also with a more urgent sense of responsibility. She dreaded such a discussion, for Karl had come alive with his newfound career in inquiries; still, neither of them were in a financial position where they could afford to play sleuth.

Karl's parents could surely provide a larger allowance for their sole living heir, but they disapproved of his match. They made no secret of that, pointedly not attending Berthe and Werthen's brief civil ceremony. Relations with her in-laws had continued to be decidedly cool since the marriage. And her own father was of the school that says money spoils. He was a successful, self-made man, and he had wanted his daughter to make her own way in the world, too, not to be considered a fine catch for some greedy suitor. Thus, he had not settled any money on her.

So, the reality was obvious, the new reality as revealed to her by Doktor Franck. She wished Karl were here now. Perhaps she should telegram him?

No. Instead she took five deep breaths — her usual remedy for any panic — and settled back in the chair. Things would work out. Oh, how she hoped they would.

Werthen was beginning to regret taking on this case. Here he was installed in the foyer of Villa Kerry like a butler waiting upon his master's wishes rather than a lawyer or

153

inquiry agent going about his professional work. Of course it was not stated in so many words, but it was increasingly clear Mahler had determined that Werthen's task should be to protect him from any and all obstacles to his composition. Thus, from early morning to late afternoon, Werthen was seated in his "office" in the foyer on a hard-backed chair, in attendance when either Justine or Natalie answered the door, ready to send autograph hounds on their way or to fend off advances of besotted young women and addled middle-aged men who wanted to share a melodic passage with the maestro. It also became clear that Mahler wished him to keep his sister, Justine, and his old friend, Natalie, at bay. This task had proved the most difficult, for it was obvious they both felt Werthen was usurping their own roles in Mahler's life. They cast him evil glances throughout the long and tiresome days. Whenever food was served, Werthen's portion was sure to be cold.

Yet occasionally Werthen felt it might be worth it, for he would hear bits and pieces of Mahler's work, as pecked out on a piano in the third-floor room he had claimed as a music studio. Mahler had little piano technique; still the snatches Werthen overheard quite moved him. There was a simple lyricism to the melodic lines he heard; a sort of subtle majesty. Walking with Mahler in the afternoons after the composing work had been finished for the day, Werthen had been appraised of other aspects of this work. Unlike his earlier symphonies, Mahler would use no tubas or trombones in the Fourth Symphony. It was clear to Werthen why this should be so, for there were already far too many tubas and trombones in the umpapa band music wafting across the lake from Altaussee. It was also planned to be the composer's shortest symphony to date, lasting perhaps just under an hour. Divided into the usual four movements, the last would be a song for soprano taken from the German collection of folk poems, *Des knaben Wunderhorn,* or *The Youth's Magic Horn,* from which Mahler had taken earlier inspiration for songs. In this case, he would employ a poem that deals with a young boy's idea of what heaven might be like.

"There is just no music on earth, That can compare to ours," the youth sings at one point, and Werthen had to admit that some of the passages he had overheard were heavenly, indeed.

Yet, did his involvement in such artistic pursuits really warrant his absence from Vienna? He missed Berthe and felt guiltier every day he was away from her. This was not the professional working holiday he had hoped for. In his imagination, he would be half sleuth and half stoic protector, not a functionary whose task it was to send unwanted visitors on their way or to be a sounding board for Gustav Mahler's artistic musings as they tramped across the countryside in the afternoons, the brilliant composer munching continually on the Turkish delights he'd stuffed into his pocket.

No. Sublime though the music might be, it was not his objective nor duty to create an atmosphere conducive to artistic creation. It was his job to prevent Mahler from being killed, and quite frankly, Werthen could see no possible danger to the composer in Altaussee. His sister, Justine, and friend, Natalie, were the only watchdogs the man needed. While he, Werthen, was surely more in need in Vienna.

He stood now, flexing his back. His right knee hurt and his rear end had gone to sleep seated too long on the hard chair. Werthen decided at that moment that he would leave the next day or perhaps the day after. It was unfair of him to thrust the duty of finding a substitute for Ungar on Berthe. And thinking of Gross, he was also reminded that the criminologist was most likely usurping the case from him, following the more promising trail in Vienna while he languished in the rustic outback of Altaussee.

Indeed, he would have to return at any rate, for he had neglected to bring Mahler's paperwork with him, the revision of his will. Yesterday Mahler had asked about it, wanting to sign it and be done with the process of writing his newly married sister, Emma, out of his will.

The previous year, this sister had married Eduard Rosé, founder of the renowned Rosé Quartet. Gossip had it that Eduard, a cellist, had hoped for some advantage from this marriage to the sister of the new Hofoper conductor, but in the event, Mahler had, in a flight of pique that the man had taken his sister and helpmate from him, declared that he would never employ Eduard at the Hofoper. Thus, the couple emigrated to the United States, where Eduard was engaged with the Boston Symphony.

Eduard Rosé was the brother of Arnold Rosé, concertmaster of the Vienna Philharmonic and suitor to Mahler's other sister, Justine. Werthen wondered if Arnold would fare any better than his brother once married. Of course, from what Werthen could judge, Arnold Rosé was going about things less precipitously than his older brother.

At any rate, the exclusion of Emma from his will had occasioned the rewriting. Werthen decided to send a telegram to Berthe, explaining that he would need to return to fetch the Mahler file. He did not want to simply tell the truth: that he missed her and was damned tired of being treated like a servant by Mahler. It seemed too much like returning home with one's tail between one's legs. Yes. He would send the telegram off this very evening.

"Herr Werthen."

He brought himself out of his private thoughts, focusing on Justine, who had spoken his name.

"Gustav is ready for his afternoon walk."

"Yes," he said. "Fine. Fresh air is the very thing we all need." He did not, however, feel too enthusiastic about the coming cross-country tramp, trying to keep up with Mahler's presto walking tempo or his never-ending musical discussions.

"He so looks forward to these outings," Justine said.

Werthen willed himself out of his lassitude and ill feeling toward Mahler. After all, he reminded himself, he was in the man's employ and had promised to watch over the composer. He knew that someone had tried to kill Mahler before and most likely would attempt it again. Thus, he, Werthen, would perform his duties to the utmost while at the Villa Kerry. Yes, Justine, and their friend, Natalie, were able watchers, but their care did not extend to that of bodyguards. He had conjured up a picture of Mahler's seeming domestic security in part to rationalize his own departure.

Werthen would return to Vienna, kiss his wife and tell her how much he loved her, fetch the will, and hasten back to this vigil. This was no time to let one's guard down.

"You look lost in thought, Advokat Werthen," Justine said.

"Not lost," he said. "I know my way."

SEVEN

The offices of Alfred, Prince of Montenuovo, were located in the Imperial Palace,
across from the Reichskanzlei, the Imperial
Chancellery, where the emperor had his
apartments. Gross looked through the fine
lace curtains covering the floor-to-ceiling
windows, through the embroidered Habsburg eagle in the center of the curtain, and
felt a shudder pass over his body. His and
Werthen's last investigation had led them to
the very doors of the emperor; he was not
overly pleased to be once again treading so
close to that seat of power.

Officially, Montenuovo, the grandson of
the Empress Marie Louise, second wife to
Napoleon Bonaparte, was the assistant to
the current grand master of the court,
Prince Rudolf Liechtenstein. However,
horses figured higher in Liechtenstein's
regard than opera singers, and the ultimate
duties of the administration of the Hofoper

fell on the rather narrow shoulders of his assistant, Prince Montenuovo.

A hidden door in a wall of bookshelves suddenly opened behind Gross and Montenuovo, dressed in the quasimilitary style of his office with embroidered blue tunic and sword at his side supported by a broad red sash from right shoulder to left hip, made a rather dramatic entrance.

Montenuovo was a small man with an immense amount of power and bore himself regally, for he had been brought up close to the crown. He was known for his unflinching stubbornness and his complete and utter loyalty to the traditions of the Habsburg Empire, to which he owed everything, including his title. It was widely speculated that upon Liechtenstein's retirement or death, Montenuovo would become the new court chamberlain, responsible for access to the emperor, for the upkeep of imperial libraries and museums, for the determination of marriageable lineages for young Habsburgs, for everything in the running of the imperial-royal household from horse breeding to matters at the court theaters, including the Hofoper.

Kraus had proven himself useful. According to him this diminutive ringmaster was a staunch supporter of Mahler. As Kraus had it, the prince believed not only in Mahler's genius, but also in his inherent honesty and integrity. Already Mahler had successfully gone over the head of the assistant intendant, Leitner, on several matters of budget and personnel.

So, wanting to bolster legitimacy, Gross had decided to go to Montenuovo this morning. He thought it was time that the prince be advised of his and Werthen's efforts on Mahler's behalf.

Gross rose as Montenuovo crossed to his rosewood desk.

"No, please, Dr. Gross. Remain seated. You are not in the presence of royalty."

The voice was surprisingly low and virile for such a small man. Montenuovo's closely cropped gray hair and beard added to his imposing appearance; he seated himself gingerly, as one who is accustomed to having his chair nudged in under him.

"We are pleased to finally meet the great criminologist."

The use of the royal "we" was not lost on Gross.

"It was good of you to make time for me at such short notice."

"Nonsense. Your fine work in Czernowitz has not gone unobserved."

No mention of his good works in Vienna

162

of last year, he noticed. No bravura applause for his and Werthen's uncovering of a heinous crime in high places.

Gross merely nodded at the compliment.

"How may I be of assistance?" Montenuovo folded his well-manicured hands in front of him on the massive desk.

"I felt it incumbent upon me to inform you, sir, of an investigation I and my assistant are conducting at the Hofoper."

"That would be Advokat Werthen, would it not?"

What was it his critics said of Montenuovo? *He is everywhere.* Something to that effect, Gross thought. And Montenuovo was proving them correct. He was all-seeing and all-knowing about matters to do with the court.

"Yes. Advokat Werthen," Gross said.

Montenuovo's cordially neutral expression did not change as he spoke: "What sort of investigation might that be, Dr. Gross?"

"We are under the employ of Herr Mahler."

This comment brought a semblance of animation to the prince's face.

"Our esteemed director. Don't tell me you are assigning meaning to a random series of accidents we have recently experienced?"

"Neither so random nor so accidental, in

my opinion, Prince."

"You believe Mahler to be in real danger?"
He attempted to keep his neutral expression, but a whiteness showed at his knuckles
as his hands clenched spasmodically.

Gross brought the prince up to date with
the investigation, reviewing the incidents
under scrutiny and the meager progress
achieved since they had come into Mahler's
employ, including the murder of Friedrich
Gunther and the possibility of that man being a witness to the killing of Fräulein Kaspar.

There had been nothing new to be learned
from the postmortem of Herr Gunther, late
of the Hofoper orchestra. Detective Inspector Drechsler had notified Gross that, as
surmised at the scene of the crime, the
man's larynx had been manually ruptured.
Indeed, it was incontestable that Gunther
had been strangled by an unknown assailant and then strung up to appear a suicide.
The approximate time of death had been
some ten hours before the discovery of the
body, which meant that the violinist had
been killed not long after returning from
what was not only the end of the season at
the Hofoper but from what also turned out
to be Herr Gunther's final performance.
Detective Inspector Drechsler and his men

had interviewed other residents and neighbors, but no one had noticed any strange comings and goings. Thus far, the police investigation had come to a complete dead end.

Gross had, however, piqued the interest of Drechsler in the death of the soprano, Fräulein Kaspar, opening that incident to police scrutiny for the first time. That in itself was proving to be a tremendous aid, for the police had better access to opera staff than he or Werthen could ever hope for. Gross had still not convinced the inspector of the danger to Mahler's life, but at least there appeared to be doubts now.

Gross now took out a large folded paper from the inside pocket of his morning coat. It was a charted schedule of names with columns for motive, means, and opportunity, with a baseline that collated their whereabouts at the time of what could have been various attempts on Mahler's life. With Drechsler's information thus far he had already been able to provisionally exclude the stage manager, Blauer, from the list, for that man had been absent from rehearsals the day of Kaspar's death.

Montenuovo listened closely, read the proffered chart, and shook his head.

"Quite detailed. And complex."

"To be honest, Prince, this is perhaps the oddest case I have yet been involved in, for on one level we are not investigating a crime at all. Rather we are attempting to prevent a crime from taking place. However, two people have already died, and in my mind those two were victims of the person who was trying to kill Mahler. Thus the investigation should focus on those deaths, and on incidents such as the collapse of the conductor's podium."

"I quite agree," Prince Montenuovo said. "Now that you present it like this, I find it disgraceful nothing has been done earlier. Mahler. Good God, man, he has gone to the country. We must dispatch someone."

"Not to worry. My colleague Werthen is in attendance."

"But this should be a police matter. You speak of trying to convince this Inspector Drechsler of the danger. That is absurd. There is no further question of convincing. The police are, after all, via the Ministry of the Interior, under the control of his majesty. I shall have a word with the emperor this very morning."

This was more than Gross had expected, but for an instant he felt rather downcast. With the police officially taking over the investigation, he and Werthen would be shoved aside. He had got his teeth into this case now and did not want that to happen. And what would it mean if in fact the case were taken from him? A hasty return to Czernowitz, sweltering in summer heat and humidity? Not a pleasant thought.

"Of course you and your colleague must continue with your investigation quite independently of the police. They can be awful plodders at times and you, Dr. Gross, well, your reputation speaks for you. This is, however, no longer a private matter between you and Herr Mahler. Were the newspapers to discover such an arrangement, there would be one awful scandal. No, the Hofoper itself shall employ your services."

Gross smiled politely at the prince, inwardly shouting a hurrah.

Herr Tor was an amiable enough man, as it turned out. Berthe found him both intelligent and amenable. He was rather larger than she had imagined he would be, a thickset man of middle age with somber eyes and a broad, almost bulbous nose. He had none of the social graces of Wilfried Ungar, but neither did he appear to have that man's overweening ego. Herr Tor was, in fact, rather a hopeless case in terms of social conventions, tending even to a stutter when asked a direct question. He also had a continual sniff, the result, she soon discovered, of a most outdated habit of taking snuff.

She was abashed to note that all this almost endeared him to her. A man so artless and defenseless in terms of etiquette, yet quite obviously brimming over with innate intelligence. He would not, she consoled herself, be taking cases to trial. Rather, he would be doing the dogsbody work of drawing up contracts and wills, a job still done largely in handwritten documents despite the advent of typewriters. The legal profession was slow in making such changes; clients trusted the steady and rather artistic look of handwriting over the aridly mechanical typewriter. And Herr Tor, by the looks of his cover letter and résumé, had an impeccable hand.

"Your résumé speaks for itself, Herr Tor," she told him, and this seemed to put him somewhat at ease.

"I am glad you think so, Frau Meisner."

He had not so much as blinked earlier when she had excused her husband's absence and introduced herself, using her maiden name. This also served to put him in her good stead; she was tired of forever reminding Gross of her legal name. The stuffy old criminologist, of course, misused her name on purpose. His way of showing disapproval of such modern conventions. Herr Wilhelm Tor, however, showed no discomfort, as if he were oblivious of such matters.

"I do not mean to pry," she went on, "but I do find it curious that a man of such obvious qualifications should need apply for a post as a junior member of chambers."

She left it at that, not wishing to overexplain her query.

He stumbled for a moment, then seemed to visibly gird himself, taking a deep breath.

"Yes. I understand your concern. There is of course my strong desire to return to my *heimat,* my hometown. I have been for too long a stranger in strange lands. An Austrian by birth, I earned my degree in Germany. Then I spent many years living abroad. I was searching. I think you can say I was in search of my life. I know that is considered neither fashionable nor wise as regards one's career, but there you have it. The years immediately following my degree were ones of travel and seeking. I did not practice law in America. Instead, I followed my instincts, mining in Nevada, selling musical instruments in Ohio, working for a German-language newspaper in New York. Ten years ago, I decided that whatever it was I was seeking was not to be found in the New World. Thus, I returned to Europe, taking a position at a law firm in Frankfurt. I left that firm last year, moving to Linz, getting that much closer to my real goal, Vienna. And then I saw your advertisement, Frau Meisner. It seemed a dream come true."

It was a long speech for Tor and he appeared almost fatigued by it, but suddenly decided to add more. When he spoke, his body remained absolutely still, his hands held placidly in his lap.

"I am not an ambitious man, Frau Meisner. I do not seek fame or fortune. I have learned not to fly too closely to the sun. Some of those nearest and dearest to me have, with tragic results. No. Give me a steady job of work where I can use my education and intelligence, and I am a happy man. I have no desire to open my own legal offices nor to impress my colleagues. I see by your husband's very nameplate on the street door that you are a diverse firm, pursuing several legal avenues. That must stretch the resources of one lawyer. I thus deduce that you are seeking someone solid and steady. Someone to take care of the day-to-day details of wills and trusts, leaving Advokat Werthen to pursue the criminal side of things. But of course, if I am wrong, if you are seeking someone for criminal law, I regretfully inform you that I am not your man."

"No. No. Herr Tor, you have it exactly correct. Someone for wills and trusts. And I greatly value your candor."

She valued it, in fact, quite enough to offer him the job then and there. Tor agreed to begin the next day.

Suddenly she thought of her husband's telegram, delivered late last evening. Karl was obviously disappointed at having to interrupt his surveillance simply to return to Vienna to fetch the Mahler papers. And here was Herr Tor traveling in that general direction anyway, for he would have to go back to Linz to gather his things.

"This may seem an odd request," she began.

"What is it?" he asked pleasantly.

She explained the situation briefly, and Herr Tor announced himself more than willing and eager to serve as messenger to Herr Werthen in Altaussee. "It will also give me the opportunity to introduce myself to your esteemed husband," he added.

They arranged it quickly: Tor would leave immediately for the Salzkammergut. Karl had written that he would return tomorrow.

Thus she could save him the trouble of the journey. She would need to telegram him immediately at his hotel to forestall his departure. As much as she wanted to see Karl again, she knew he must feel torn in his duties, and wished to make things as easy as possible for him. There would be time later to inform him of their gladsome news. And now with Herr Tor joining the firm it seemed she might not have to have her little talk with Karl about the profitability of private inquiries after all.

It had been, as she reflected on it later that evening, dining at the Alte Schmiede with her friend Rosa Mayreder, a good day's work. Their conversation quickly turned to the feminist league that Mayreder was then organizing.

All the while, however, Berthe kept in mind the tiny life now forming in her, nearly oblivious of the food in front of her: a succulent mound of *germknödl,* a great white puff of a dumpling filled with plum jam and topped with ground poppy seeds, melted butter, and sugar icing. Its yeasty fragrance, once so appealing to her, now set Berthe's teeth on edge, and she moved the plate away, an action not unnoticed by her friend.

"I've put on a kilo or two since the marriage," she said by way of explanation.

Though hardly a devotee of the physical cult as had been the late empress who traveled nowhere without her exercise machines, Berthe prided herself on maintaining a healthy physical condition.

Rosa smiled at the explanation, but Berthe felt she was not fooled.

Rosa Mayreder was an imposing figure in Vienna, and Berthe felt fortunate to count her among her friends. Author, painter, musician, and feminist, she was a Renaissance woman who was connected to many of the new movements in art and thought in Vienna both through her own work and through that of her husband, the architect Karl Mayreder. It was Rosa's husband, in fact, who had given the architect and designer Adolf Loos his first job after the young man returned from his American sojourn.

Berthe had met Rosa through her Settlement work; Rosa volunteered to help the children with art projects. Watching her with the children, Berthe had been impressed by how warm and playful she was. She had no children of her own, and now in her forties, it was doubtful she ever would. Partly for that reason Berthe did not mention her own condition; she did not know if her lack of children was a regret or not for Rosa. She never mentioned it and Berthe followed this lead.

"Is that husband of yours involved in anything of interest?" Rosa suddenly asked, as if changing a subject that had remained unspoken.

Berthe brightened. "As a matter of fact, he is."

She lowered her voice, leaning over the table toward Rosa. The two looked like conspirators as Berthe described their efforts at protecting Mahler.

"My Lord," Rosa said once Berthe had finished her précis. "One has heard the man's a martinet at the Hofoper, of course, but to try and do away with him?"

"It could be unrelated to his music," Berthe said, "but neither Karl nor Dr. Gross believes so."

"And there's another martinet, to be sure," Rosa said, meaning Gross.

Berthe lifted her eyebrows in agreement. "But he can also be a funny old bear."

"I should like to see that." Rosa finished her meal, setting the fork and knife together on the plate. "Come to think of it, though, perhaps Mahler's professional personality is sufficient motive for murder. Think of his shameful treatment of Hugo Wolf."

Berthe made a tsking sound with her

tongue. "That poor man."

Wolf, a musical genius whose *lieder* compositions alone had ensured his lasting fame, had gone mad in 1897 at the age of only thirty-seven, and was now lodged at the Lower Austrian Landesirrenanstalt, an asylum in the Alsergrund district.

"He visited Mahler just before going into his mental twilight," Rosa said. "Mahler had promised to produce our opera, but then he went back on his pledge."

Berthe remembered now: Rosa had written the libretto for Wolf's opera, *Der Corregidor.* She and Wolf had in fact become fast friends during this collaboration. And when Mahler refused to produce the opera, Wolf became totally unbalanced, declaiming for all to hear in front of the Hofoper that Mahler had been dismissed and that he, Hugo Wolf, was the newly appointed director. Wolf was thereafter confined to a mental asylum by his friends.

"An awful time," Rosa said, reliving those moments in her mind as well. "It was the sense of betrayal. That is what finally pushed him over the edge. He and Mahler had been such close friends, and then that refusal."

Berthe did not know of this friendship. "When did they meet?"

"At the conservatory. They were poor

struggling students together, even shared a flat for a time. One wonders what other former friends Mahler has angered."

The off hand comment from Rosa struck home for Berthe. Neither she nor her husband, not even Gross, had considered this possibility before. Despite the presence of the old friend Natalie Bauer-Lechner, they had all overlooked the fact that Mahler had spent the years of 1875 to 1880 in Vienna, training under teachers such as Anton Bruckner and earning an impecunious living as a music teacher to young pupils.

Thus far Karl and Dr. Gross had been focusing on those people in Mahler's current life who might have a grudge against him. But what if this was about the past, not the present? Who else had Mahler been friends with during those years?

Hugo Wolf, according to Rosa's account of the tale, had motive enough to want to do away with Mahler. However, incarcerated in an asylum, he was clearly not a suspect. But who else might bear Mahler a grudge from those years? What other betrayals might earlier acquaintances have experienced, nurturing their hatred for a score of years? After all, one did not become director of the prestigious Hofoper at the tender age of thirty-seven without having stepped on toes or perhaps even dislodging other climbers from the ladder of success.

It was most definitely a new direction for their investigation, and Berthe was anxious to share it with her husband.

"Thank you, Rosa," she said, reaching across the table and patting her friend's hand.

Rosa did not ask what the thanks were for; she simply smiled in return.

The next morning Gross reached the newspaper offices of the *Deutsches Volksblatt* at Bäckerstrasse 20, in the First District, eager to move forward with the investigation. Eberhard Hassler was, as the journalist Kraus had opined, a possible suspect because of his vituperative critiques of Mahler.

Gross had had an opportunity to read some of these notices, and had to admit that they went well beyond the bounds of musical criticism, attacking the man himself and his putative religion-race: "Herr Mahler, it would seem, intends to turn the Hofoper into the Jewish Opera, ridding our fine institution of such voices as Marie Renard and the conductor Hans Richter, and replacing them with Jews, such as the feeble soprano Selma Kurz and the untested conductor Franz Schalk. Where will this end? Is there no man among us who will stop Herr Mahler before he completely disgraces the most noble institution in the empire?"

The last sentence in particular had made Gross ponder; it was as if Hassler were inciting violence upon Mahler. Though he thought little of the malformed journalist Kraus — much too fond of his own voice — Gross did have to allow that he was a keen witness of the Viennese scene. Hassler indeed was a man warranting an interview.

The man's office was on the third floor of the neoclassical building housing the newspaper, controlled by the anti-Semitic Christian Democratic Party, whose leader, Karl Lueger, had been mayor of Vienna for the past two years. Inside the double doors, Gross pointedly ignored the newly installed electric elevator, opting instead for the stairs that took him up five flights to Hassler's office. There was no indication of shortness of breath by the time the criminologist — no longer a young man at fifty-two — reached the desired office door.

He had called ahead for an appointment, but Hassler's secretary told him there were none available.

"Herr Hassler," the man told him in a rather high and imperious voice, "is not in the habit of being interviewed. Rather, he is the one to conduct such interviews."

Gross thought of himself as a force of nature. He simply assumed that his fame preceded him wherever he went; that individuals would be eager to help him in whatever investigation he might currently be involved. Thus this callow private secretary's rebuke came as something of a shock to him. He would, however, not let it impede his investigation.

Gross was, in addition to being supremely self-confident, also a realist. He did not take the secretary's reproof personally; it was only an indication of the young man's impoverished intellect. But it had prompted him, in part, to seek out Prince Montenuovo. Now, armed with a letter from the prince, Gross felt no door would be barred to him in Vienna.

The journalist was guarded, Gross assumed, by the same young private secretary he had spoken to on the telephone. He looked no older than a *matura* student, but then Gross found himself, as he grew older, to be a poor judge of age in others. Gross did not bother addressing the young man; instead he simply handed over his letter from Prince Montenuovo. This had the intended result, for the young man immediately got out of his chair and disappeared into an inner office. Less than a minute later, he returned.

"Herr Hassler will see you now." It was the same high voice from the phone.

Gross still did not bother exchanging the barest pleasantry with the young man as he was ushered into a large corner office, its walls overflowing with all manner of odd symbolism: a stuffed stag's head overlooked a diploma from the University of Vienna; English prints of hunting scenes were framed by crossed sabers; the red, gold, and black of the flag of a united Germany was a prominent color scheme in both curtains and wall hangings. Gross thought the decoration was excessive, but that hardly made the man a potential killer.

"Dr. Gross. A pleasure to meet you."

The man addressing him neatly fit into the excessively symbolic surroundings: a dueling scar etched the left side of his face from eyebrow to chin, his short black hair was all but glued to his head by heavy pomade, while a stub of a mustache bristled underneath his ample nose. In contrast, his subtle brown suit was well tailored, and partially concealed the paunch forming at his midriff.

Gross sat in the leather upholstered

straight-back chair Hassler motioned him to. A cumbersome typewriter resided on the desk between them, so that Gross had to adjust his chair to have a clear view of his interlocutor.

"You have powerful friends," Hassler began.

"An employer rather than a personal friend. But yes, powerful," Gross allowed.

"Then it is court business you have come about? I am not sure how I can be of help in that regard." Hassler smiled amiably, rippling the scar at the side of his face.

"Court Opera business, in specific," Gross said.

Hassler's amiability quickly disappeared. "And they've sent a criminologist to discuss that. What crime have I committed then?"

Before Gross had a chance to reply, Hassler surged on: "They have sent their polite requests on the emperor's embossed stationery no less. As if that should impress me. As if that will still my pen. And now they presume to frighten me off with a criminologist. Outrageous!" He slammed his meaty fist on the desk, shaking the keys of his typewriter.

"Herr Hassler, I haven't the least idea of what you are talking about."

"I am talking about nothing less than

freedom of the press. I know that may ring hollow in this land of open governmental censorship, when white space occurs daily in front-page stories suppressed at the last moment because the authorities deem them too sensitive. But to take such censorship to the cultural pages is an outrage. Blasphemy."

Gross began to understand the lay of the land. Apparently Montenuovo's office had attempted to tone down Hassler's criticism of Mahler, and thus the journalist took him, Gross, for one more envoy from the count. He decided not to disabuse the blustery reporter of this assumption. The longer he could keep his actual purpose hidden, the more information he might be able to squeeze out of the volatile man.

"You must admit, Herr Hassler, that some of your columns have sailed rather close to the wind. There are libel laws in effect, after all."

As Gross hoped, this intensified Hassler's ire.

"Libel! Every word I print is the truth. You prove otherwise. Mahler is destroying the Hofoper, and that is attested to by any number of musicians and singers."

"It is one thing to critique his musicality, quite another to impugn his race."

"But he is a Jew. No matter that he converted just so he could be appointed to the position. Once a Jew always a Jew."

"If not libel, defamation, then," Gross said.

"You are saying he is not a Jew?" Hassler smiled cunningly, as if he had just scored a point in a trial.

Gross allowed him this small victory, indeed made a gift of it in order to make Hassler feel in control of the conversation. He thereby might become reckless.

"You do not like Herr Mahler on a personal basis, is that so?" Gross asked.

"I do not know him on such a basis, nor would I care to."

"You've never met him? Never been to a rehearsal then?"

"I see what you're about," Hassler said, leaning back in his chair and nodding his head at Gross. "Trying to make it appear I have no inside knowledge about Mahler and his regime. That I am writing a pack of innuendo and opinion. But let me tell you, Dr. Gross, I have my sources. I also attend numerous rehearsals, so that I know what goes on behind the scenes. I have witnessed Mahler browbeating his singers, his musicians."

"As with the unfortunate Fräulein Kaspar? I assume you must have been at the rehearsal where she was accidentally killed. Your subsequent article supplied so much information that I imagine you witnessed the incident yourself."

Hassler ran a forefinger down his scar. "A most unfortunate affair, to be sure. But no, I was not personally present. My information came from one of my opera sources, himself an eyewitness to the tragedy. But that does not mean my information is not one hundred percent accurate. I cannot be in all places at once. That day I had a meeting to attend in Graz."

Gross said nothing, hoping Hassler would offer more information, something that would verify his absence.

"So get on with it," Hassler said. "Give me your dire warning from the lord chamberlain and let me proceed with my work. Or is that why you've come at all? What really is your business, Dr. Gross? Why the curiosity about my attendance at rehearsals?"

"I merely hope to ascertain the truth."

"About what?"

Instead of answering the man's questions, Gross merely rose and nodded politely. "I thank you for your time, Herr Hassler. As you say, I shall let you get on with your work now."

"You can tell Montenuovo and his crowd that I am one journalist who won't be cowed. I will keep printing the truth until Mahler is sent packing."

The final words were spoken to Gross's back as he passed the surprised face of the secretary in the outer office.

In Altaussee the next day, Thursday, Werthen was struggling with a recalcitrant bicycle. He had not ridden a bicycle since he had grown out of knee pants. It was hardly his idea of a good time, but here he was pumping with alacrity to simply keep up with Mahler, an experienced cyclist. They had set out an hour ago from the Villa Kerry. Made aware of Werthen's decision to return to Vienna, Mahler decided their farewell outing should be memorable. It was as if the composer were punishing Werthen for his imminent departure. Mahler was the sort of man, Werthen had decided, who interpreted the slightest change of plans that might cause him any inconvenience as a sign of betrayal. The world revolved around him. Anything disturbing the orderly rotation of his one-man solar system was anathema.

The leather saddle bit into Werthen's scrotum painfully; his thighs were beginning to cramp from the long uphill climb —

they were following an oxen trail that traversed the southern base of the Loser mountain. The trail switched back and forth in endless zigzags, but the gradient was still arduous. Mahler reveled in the exercise. Werthen felt sweaty and miserable, but he plowed on, not one to give up or to be outdone.

Mahler continued to pull farther and farther ahead. Werthen soon lost sight of the black-clad musician, who had gained enough distance to be on the far end of each turn, already around the western corner when Werthen appeared around the eastern and vice versa.

With Mahler out of sight, Werthen tried to divert himself from the unpleasant task at hand by reviewing the events of the past days. He stopped the bike, dismounted, and began walking with the cycle at his side, maintaining a brisk pace despite an ache in his damaged knee.

He had received Berthe's answering telegram on Tuesday evening, and was deeply disappointed that he no longer had a ready excuse for returning to Vienna earlier than planned. However, he had put his best face on and met the new employee, Wilhelm Tor, at the train station in Altaussee, and received the Mahler file from him. It took Werthen only a few minutes to understand why Berthe had settled on this fellow, the polar opposite of Ungar. She would have felt compassion for his rather shy demeanor, Werthen knew. But speaking with him, Werthen decided that Tor seemed a solid enough man. Not someone you would want to share a bottle of wine with, but then he was meant as an employee, not an intimate.

It was much too late on Tuesday for Tor to attempt returning to his home in Linz. Instead, Werthen booked him a room at his hotel, though one not quite so regal as his own. In the morning Tor volunteered to copy over some of the materials, for he had reviewed the file on his lengthy train trip. Werthen was more than happy for the assistance, as he needed to be in attendance at the Villa Kerry first thing in the morning. He gave Tor directions; the man would later deliver his copies to the villa before catching the noon train.

Then, approaching the Villa Kerry on Wednesday morning, Werthen had noticed several bicycles, recent purchases, lined up against the wall of the building. Mahler was obviously planning on more brisk physical exercise than he had heretofore been taking.

Inside the villa that morning, Werthen was

surprised at its transformation. Suddenly the place was filled with visitors, all descending on Mahler and his family at once. Arnold Rosé, suitor to Mahler's sister, Justine. He was a handsome, solidly built man and with his neatly trimmed Vandyke beard looked more like a doctor than a musician.

Seated across from him were Regierungsrath Leitner, the conductor Hans Richter, his enormous beard the repository of *semmel* crumbs, and a fourth man, the famous tenor Baltazar Franacek. Coffee cups in the rustic Gmunden pattern littered the dining table.

This gathering pleased Werthen, for he thought it might provide him the possibility of interviewing Richter and Franacek, both of whose names had been mentioned in connection with disputes with Mahler. Leitner, though the only one of the men at the table to know Werthen, studiously avoided acknowledging him. There seemed no question of introductions, so Werthen was about to take up his post at the door with barely a nod at the quartet of men when Mahler himself appeared at the top of the stairs, his suit rumpled and hair looking as if it had not seen a brush in days.

"Oh, good, Werthen. You've arrived. You know these chaps, I assume." He waved a bored right hand at the four men. In his fingers he held a half-consumed piece of Turkish delight.

"No, not actually," Werthen replied, casting a sly smile at Leitner, who should now have to suffer for his bad manners.

Mahler had made the introductions himself, careful to refer to Werthen simply as his lawyer.

While Rosé was there to spend holiday time with the family Mahler, the other men, it turned out, had come on business.

As the day progressed, one after the other of these three men had private meetings with Mahler. The volubility of the exchanges grew in intensity from Richter, who had come to formally announce his departure from the Hofoper and whom Mahler vociferously accused of betrayal, to Leitner, who came to argue a matter of too much sick leave granted to one of the sopranos, and finally to Franacek, whose demands for an increase in salary turned into a shouting match, clearly heard throughout the house.

As each in turn made their departure, Werthen attempted a brief word. Richter turned out to be the biggest surprise, for when Werthen made a discreet query as to their argument, the burly conductor had broken into a wide smile.

"Well, there was no cause for harsh words on my part, I can assure you. Herr Mahler has done me the supreme favor of first of all becoming director of the Hofoper, a position they were hoping to saddle me with. I hasten to add, Advokat, that the political wrangling accompanying such a position is neither to my liking nor to my talent. Thus the good Herr Mahler saved me from a miserable fate. And now he has made my conducting position rather untenable as well, for he has assumed most of the Wagnerian material, my forte."

Richter cast another broad grin at Werthen, and then tapped his nose conspiratorially. "But again, he has been at my service, for I have long desired to leave Vienna for the more welcoming climes of London, where I am in great demand. Mahler has thus given me the excuse I have needed to break my contract. There are those who might say I wish Herr Mahler ill, but why I ask, when he has been such a boon to me?"

And with that the portly gentleman left, laughter trailing behind him.

Leitner was hardly so cheerful, merely shooting Werthen a tight-lipped nod and saying a curt good day to him, and Franacek, too, displayed great displeasure at his meeting, being in such a hurry that Werthen had no time for a brief conference.

"The man is impossible," the tenor said, as he swept his Panama hat from the elk horn hat rack and made his departure, almost knocking down Wilhelm Tor, who was at that very moment making his entrance to the villa.

Mahler had been a mess the rest of the day, for the village band had begun by the time his visitors had departed and any thought of composing was lost for the rest of the day. Tor made his departure quickly, presumably to take the same train the other three were going to catch at midday.

Werthen had spent a restless night Wednesday, but by the next morning he had finally made his decision: it was a return to Vienna for him. Especially so since the arrival of the telegram from Gross telling him of the meeting with Prince Montenuovo and the fact that the gendarmerie would be taking over the duties of protecting Mahler soon.

Of course such information did not settle well with Mahler, especially following so closely upon his other contentious interviews. He had taken Werthen's news this morning as an act of treachery. Thus the punishment of this grueling bicycle ride.

It had begun to mist now. So engrossed

had Werthen been in his own thoughts that he had not even noticed the change in the weather. Their sunny day had been quickly replaced by mountain fog followed by a mist so dense that it soaked through their clothing. Werthen increased his walking pace, but did not bother remounting the bicycle. He expected Mahler to be on the return run of his journey at any moment.

Instead he heard faint noises ahead of him. It sounded like a man's voice, but he was not sure. There was, however, a distinct sound of panic in it. He tried to move more quickly, but it was awkward walking with the bicycle, its pedals forever knocking against his shins. Then he heard the voice clearly.

"Help! Help!"

It was Mahler. He dropped the bicycle and began running up the track to the sound of the calls. His foot caught a large stone in the path and he fell to his hands and knees, scraping his palm on an exposed root. He got to his feet and once again began running toward the shouts.

Finally, coming round a western bend in the switchbacks, he caught sight of Mahler, or rather of the man's bike. It was wrapped around a tree trunk at the very edge of the trail, dangling over a precipice. He charged on to the bicycle and there was Mahler, several meters below the bicycle, clinging to a cluster of branches of alpine blueberry, his oval glasses askew and a look of panic on his face.

"Thank God you finally got here, Werthen. I don't know how much longer I can hang on."

Werthen said nothing as he quickly surveyed the scene. The edge of the trail was scree and provided little good footing. Below Mahler was a drop of several hundred meters; the accident could not have happened at a worse section of the trail.

"Don't just stand there, man. Help me."

Werthen moved back up onto the track.

"Where are you going? Stop. Help me."

He was concentrating too hard to bother responding to Mahler. Instead, he went back to the bicycle and wrapped it more tightly around the trunk of the white fir, then tested it. It held. He quickly unbuttoned his leather suspenders, tying the two straps together in a square knot, and then tying one end to the bicycle frame. He jerked on what was now a life rope several times to make sure it was steady, then made his way back down to where Mahler dangled.

Werthen wrapped the leather end of his

braces around his left hand several times, inching toward the blueberry bush that was providing Mahler with his support. Loose rock spilled downward beneath his feet, falling over Mahler, but now the composer saw what Werthen was attempting and remained quiet, clutching at the branches for all he was worth. Werthen could see that the low bush was beginning to come out by the roots.

Slowly he inched his way toward Mahler, not wanting to loosen more rock. Each step became an agony of caution. Suddenly he could go no farther, for the assembled line of suspenders had played out its length. Yet he was still just out of reach of Mahler.

He rapidly unwrapped one loop of the suspender from his left hand, gripping it now solely in his palm. He reached his right hand out for Mahler, touching the sharp angles of the blueberry brush and finally grasping a wrist.

"When I say go, you try to thrust upward. Understand?"

Mahler, his eyes wide, nodded.

Werthen made sure his left hand had a good grip on the suspender. He spread his legs wide to get as solid a base as he could, hoping only that his bad right leg would not give out on him. Then, tightening his grip on Mahler's wrist, he shouted, "Go!"

He gave a mighty tug and at the same time felt Mahler attempting to shove upward, but not letting go of the bush.

"I've got you," Werthen hissed. "Let go of the bush. Try to find a foothold."

He tugged and struggled to pull Mahler up. For an instant, his right knee failed him, almost buckling. Then he shifted weight to his left, uphill leg, bracing himself.

The composer gave a mighty grunt as he began to claw his way up from the overhang. Finally he was able to swing a leg over the ledge and Werthen knew they had won. But Mahler did not rest until he had crawled his way up to the path again. Then he rolled over on his back and began to laugh hysterically.

Werthen was panting. He sat in the mist by the trunk of the tree and began inspecting Mahler's bike.

"This was no accident," he suddenly said.

Mahler ceased his laughter, rolled over onto his belly, righted his glasses, and looked up at Werthen.

"I was coming back down for you. Coming around that corner. I couldn't brake."

"No wonder," Werthen said, holding up the severed end of one of the brake cables. "It's been cut almost clean through. It would not withstand more than a few attempts at braking."

"But who — ?" Mahler began, then thought better of the question.

Who indeed? Werthen asked himself. They were not lacking for suspects now after the houseful of visitors.

Walking their bikes back down the mountainside, the mist ceased as quickly as it had begun and the sun once again came out. Toward the bottom of the switchbacks they passed another bicycling party, a gaggle of laughing young men and women.

Werthen was startled to see among them none other than Alma Schindler. She looked as surprised as Werthen, and when he was about to call out to her, she shook her head, then began laughing overloud at some comment one of her male companions made.

No, Werthen thought as they continued walking. They were most definitely not lacking in suspects.

EIGHT

"Any one of them had the opportunity," Werthen said. "The bicycles were lined up outside the villa."

"But how to know which one to tamper with?" Gross said. "That was either devilishly clever or very lucky."

"Mahler is not a tall man. Anyone with basic knowledge of bicycling could determine which bicycle was intended for him."

Werthen had returned to Vienna on the early morning train, once it was determined that a member of the gendarmerie was to be installed at the Villa Kerry on a regular basis. Mahler, of course, would not hear of returning to Vienna. His summer weeks for composition remained sacred, even if they were also life threatening.

Werthen, Berthe, and Gross were now seated around the dining table, enjoying a peaceful lunch together. Werthen found it difficult to take his eyes off his wife, who wore a lovely shade of pale blue that contrasted well with her eyes. Her face was long, but not overlong, chin strong, nose slightly curved at the tip. A trace of freckles appeared in summer; she hid them with face powder — her one vanity. Hers was a quiet, domestic beauty, a warm jumble of womanhood that was not on display for the entire world.

He did not want to be going over these matters with Gross right now; he would much rather be ensconced in the privacy of the bedroom with Berthe, telling her how much he had missed her.

He knew this was not the sort of thing proper husbands do in the middle of the day. He was not, however, feeling very proper at the moment.

Frau Blatschky had graced their table with stuffed green peppers and boiled potatoes. The minced pork stuffing was liberally dosed with Hungarian paprika and capers, her secret ingredients. Berthe seemed to be off her food today, Werthen noticed, as he half-listened to Gross explaining what he had been up to during Werthen's absence.

"Our Herr Schreier, leader of the claque, proved to be an irascible character, as promised. I met him in an impossibly shabby café in a godforsaken outer district."

There was palpable distaste in Gross's voice, making Werthen and Berthe smile at each other.

"Yes, that is correct," he said, attuned to their amusement. "Godforsaken is the only word that can be used to describe such places. Bleak rows of blackened worker flats thrown up every which way. Here and there a remnant of older village life, a charming baroque building dwarfed by hulking tenements. And they call it progress. It was as if you could chew the very air of the place."

"Herr Schreier?" Werthen prompted.

"Yes, indeed. An apt name, *schreier,* the 'screamer.' Even in conversation his voice was amplified and excoriating. Hairs growing out of his ears, no less. It is amazing they even allow him into the Hofoper. He as good as admitted he would like to see Mahler dead. Anything it took, just to be rid of his direction at the Hofoper. Seemed a desperate sort to me. But" — and here he paused for emphasis — "he was not in attendance at the rehearsal the day of Fräulein Kaspar's death. Three regulars at the café attested to this along with the proprietor himself. I spoke with that man, Herr Radetzky, privately after my interview with Schreier. No mistaking it. He said Schreier was at his regular table, *stammtisch,* all day, demanding cloudburst after cloudburst after his sole coffee had been imbibed."

Werthen was impressed with the manner in which Gross had picked up Viennese slang, but then remembered he had an entire section on criminal argot in his groundbreaking tome, *Criminal Investigation.* "Cloudburst" was slang for gratis glasses of water a waiter would bring customers at a café, allowing them to keep their table at no extra cost.

"How can Herr Radetzky be so sure of the day?" Berthe sensibly asked.

Gross nodded, as if to indicate he had already thought of that. "It was his daughter's twelfth birthday and he had been hoping to close in the middle of the day to buy her a present. But Schreier would not budge from his seat, so the present went unpurchased."

"Civil of him," Werthen noted, with no little amazement, for he, like all Viennese, had met his fair share of *uncivil* waiters. Such men were laws unto themselves, reigning emperors in Lilliputian café empires. If you were a favored client, there could be no greater ally, but if for some reason the *herr ober* took a dislike to you, it was best to simply find a new café, for you would always be last served and least cared for. Herr Radetzky seemed to be the exception to the rule of the imperious waiter.

Gross quickly filled them in on his further research, including his interview with Montenuovo and his visiting both the anti-Semitic journalist Hassler and Alma's admirer, von Tratten. The latter voiced similar distaste for Mahler but had strong alibis for two of the incidents in question.

"Of course," said Werthen, "such alibis prove nothing. Not if there is an accomplice involved."

Another understanding nod from Gross. "But of course. It is simply a means for narrowing the initial field. It hardly disqualifies one from suspicion. Unfortunate you had no opportunity to interview Richter at greater length," Gross added.

"What I heard convinced me of his innocence, however," Werthen replied. "It is true that Richter might, of all our suspects, have the strongest motive. After all, he was the obvious candidate to become the new director. Then Mahler usurped his position, even to the point of taking over direction of Wagner operas, Richter's specialty. In a manner of speaking he did force Richter to resign. But the man was genuinely glad of that at Altaussee. His jubilation was not feigned. He is happy to be departing for London. Of the tenor Franacek I am less certain."

Werthen's further information that Alma Schindler had also been in attendance in the vicinity of Altaussee the day of the near tragedy brought a sigh from Gross.

"I was hoping we were narrowing the list of suspects rather than broadening it."

"In ways, we have," Werthen replied. "Barring the use of an accomplice, this most recent attack does limit the list to those in and around Altaussee at the time."

"Barring accomplices," Berthe repeated.

"And barring the tampering of the brakes at the bicycle factory or shop," Gross added.

Werthen sighed. There seemed to be no narrowing of this case, only an ever-widening pool of suspects.

They finished the luncheon, and Frau Blatschky delivered a welcome pot of her aromatic and strong coffee.

"I am sorry to be the bearer of more bad news," Berthe suddenly said, "but the list may be even longer than we initially thought." She described her dinner conversation with Rosa Mayreder and the possibility that Mahler's enemy might actually be someone from his past, as demonstrated by the example of Hugo Wolf. Berthe had saved this information until she could share it in the presence of her husband.

"Excellent." Gross beamed at her. "Something that we have completely ignored, Mahler's early years in Vienna. Compliments, Frau . . . Meisner."

Now it was her turn to blush. Gross had even gotten the name correct, Werthen noted.

"But this is not all bad news," Gross said. "No. With this latest attempt on Mahler's life we approach a psychological profile of our man. I posit a romantic by nature. One who is hypersensitive and with an acute sense of persecution. A youngish man of action — witness the ruthless killing of Herr Gunther — yet one who mounts elaborate and rather absurd plans to do away with Mahler. He does not take the direct route. How simple to use a pistol; how much more efficient. Shoot Mahler and have done with it. But no, our man plans symbolic attacks: a fire curtain drops, a podium crumbles underfoot, a bicycle brake is severed. Such are the convoluted strategies of our man. It is obvious then that for Mahler he holds a special loathing, a special grudge. He is extracting vengeance, not merely trying to kill a man. We are getting close to him. Yes, closer and closer."

"I am glad you think so at least," Werthen said.

"You weren't very hungry today," Werthen said as he and Berthe walked to the law offices.

The Josefstädterstrasse was a hectic thoroughfare this afternoon with horse-drawn carts and streetcars tumbling over cobbles and along metal rails, metal shutters rattling open after the midday closing, and shoppers bustling here and there with wicker baskets already filled with fruit and bread. After the chill of the Salzkammergut, the summertime warmth of Vienna was comforting to him; a perfect day for a postprandial stroll.

"No," she said, suddenly gripping his hand more tightly. Then, "Karl?"

"Yes, my dear." He loved the lilting way in which she said his name.

"I have something to tell you, and this is hardly the way I imagined it would occur, walking down a busy avenue."

Indeed, "What is it?" He felt sudden alarm. Was she ill? But she was so young and hearty.

"Well, I suppose the best way is the most direct. I . . . I mean we, well, we are going to have a baby. I am pregnant."

This news filled him with sudden elation; he felt his chest swell. A child. Their child. But at the same time he felt a sudden sadness that his parents, who had rejected his marriage, should not be a part of this happiness. Would they reject their grandchild, as well?

"That is wonderful news," he said flatly.

"What's wrong. You do want a child, don't you?"

They had stopped in the middle of the busy sidewalk and pedestrians grumbled as they had to maneuver around them.

"Of course, dear." He weighed telling her of his concern, deciding against it. Now was not a time to burden her. She needed to focus on the tiny life inside of her. "It is just such a surprise." He willed a smile onto his face. "A glorious surprise. And you shall be the most beautiful mother in all of Vienna."

But his false bonhomie served only to chill her.

"I am afraid Gross will be losing his pied-à-terre in Vienna," Werthen laughed. "Soon it will become a nursery."

She made no attempt to join in the forced laughter. It should be the happiest day of our lives, she thought.

Instead, they walked the rest of the way into the First District in silence, each deep in his or her own thoughts.

Herr Tor was busy at his desk when they arrived. Werthen was glad for his presence, as he could feel Berthe readying herself to probe him more deeply about his response to her news. Why not just tell her the truth, he thought. She is my wife, she has a right to know my concerns. But a misguided sense of male protection kept him from burdening her, and thus the misunderstanding was allowed to grow.

They each went about their own tasks the rest of the afternoon, Berthe taking care of billings that were long overdue — Klimt's among them — and Werthen retiring to his office to deal with the difficulties presented by a trust being set up by Count Lasko, certain intricacies of which Tor did not feel competent to handle. Yet when Werthen took a look at what Tor had accomplished with the trust, he thought it fine. Which left him with free time to ruminate more over the Mahler matter.

He took out a piece of foolscap, dipped his pen in the inkwell on his desk, and made three columns, one for suspects at the Hofoper, one for those at the Villa Kerry, and one for those out of Mahler's past, particularly his early days in Vienna. The first column, of course, was the longest, despite the fact that several of these people had supplied alibis. Leitner, Blauer, Schreier, and Hassler topped the list. But there were also Richter (a distant possibility) and the tenor Franacek, both of whom had also been in attendance at the Villa Kerry, as was Leitner. These he scrawled into the second column. Additionally, on that second list was Mahler's prospective brother-in-law, Rosé, and then his sister Justine, and thwarted lover, Natalie. And Alma Schindler, though this seemed rather far-fetched to Werthen, as he had subsequently learned that she had been in the company of her sister and several cousins that day in the mountains. Highly unlikely that she could escape their companionship long enough to adulterate Mahler's brakes; equally unlikely that all of them were guilty of the deed. But he could not totally dismiss Alma or her companions from his list. The women, of course, would necessarily need an accomplice.

Werthen then added Alma's name to the first list, as well, for she had admitted to attending Mahler's rehearsals at the Hofoper.

The third list, Mahler's past, was the shortest, just Hugo Wolf's name. But that was where the investigation now needed to focus, he thought. What other names could be included in that last column? He made several question marks where there might be new names to be discovered.

So many possibilities. At least there was one positive thing that had come from their efforts thus far. As Gross reported, through their investigation, Montenuovo had been enlisted and now the police were also involved. Mahler would at least be under police protection as they sifted the evidence for the killer of Fräulein Kaspar and Herr Gunther.

A light rapping on his door roused him.

"Yes?"

Tor entered, carrying the rest of the Count Lasko file with him.

"I think that about accomplishes the other matters," he said, placing the file on the desk next to Werthen's list of suspects.

"Fine," Werthen said, quickly glancing through the file, admiring Tor's penmanship as well as the wording.

Tor lingered for a moment close by the desk, scanning, Werthen thought, the three columns of his list of suspects.

"Is there something else I can do for you?"

"If it wouldn't be an inconvenience, might I leave a bit early today, Advokat Werthen? I am still getting settled, and there are several things I need for my rooms."

"Of course, Herr Tor. You've more than earned the time with your ramble to Altaussee on our behalf. Take the time you need to get settled in. I shall not be leaving town again this summer."

Tor attempted a smile, Werthen thought. But it came across more like the show of sympathy one might cast a family member at a funeral.

Poor man, Werthen thought. He really is painfully shy. But he had a first-class legal mind and they were lucky to have him. Good for Berthe, he thought after Tor had made his departure, for seeing this jewel in the rough.

Thinking of his wife, he decided to go to her then, to explain himself. But when he went to the outer office, there was a note on her desk:

Karl,
I need to pick up a few things at Gerngross. See you at home later.

B

He read the note twice. Berthe had never, to his knowledge, set foot in the new emporium of Gerngross on the Mariahilferstrasse. Such a self-styled "department

209

store" on the American model was an abomination to her, a spearhead of a kind of capitalism run amok that she warned would ruin the very fabric of Viennese society, forcing family-run businesses to stay open during lunch, perhaps even on weekends. Unthinkable.

He found himself smiling at her imagined diatribe. But the fact was, she would never "pick up a few things at Gerngross," and she also knew that he was aware of that.

Her coded message was a rebuke to him.

Hofrat Richard Freiherr von Krafft-Ebing, chair of the psychiatry department of the University of Vienna, had a corner office on the third floor of the new Ringstrasse University building. It was every centimeter a working space: glass-fronted lawyer's bookcases lined the walls and framed large windows overlooked the Ringstrasse. His smallish desk was piled high with notebooks, paperbound journals, and thick books, many of which lay open, and others generously bookmarked with slips of blue paper.

Of medium height, Krafft-Ebing dressed conservatively and wore his graying hair short. His beard was trimmed to a sharp V under his chin, and his eyes, as Werthen had noted at their initial meeting last year, were a gray-green that seemed to spill light.

Gross and Werthen had consulted the neuropsychiatrist on their previous case, and his researches into the etiology of syphilis had proven invaluable in that matter. Gross and he were old friends from Graz, where together they helped pioneer the field of forensic psychopathology, the study of mental disorders as put to the use of criminology.

Now, on Saturday morning, they had come to him on a different errand. In his role as hofrat, Krafft-Ebing also oversaw the direction of one of the primary mental clinics in Vienna, the Lower Austrian State Lunatic Asylum, where the composer Hugo Wolf was now housed.

After social pleasantries were dispensed with, Krafft-Ebing got to the point.

"Your message mentioned Hugo Wolf. I must admit he is one of our more renowned guests. I am not, however, sure that he is compos mentis any longer. He is in the final stage of syphilis, as I suppose you know."

"I had no idea," Gross said.

"Tragic case," Krafft-Ebing said, shaking his head. "Contracted the disease as a young man. His initiation into the wonderful world of sexuality at the hands of one of this city's legion of prostitutes. A great pity. You are familiar with his music?"

He addressed the question to Werthen, being only too well aware of his friend Gross's taste in music — nothing later than Haydn for him.

"I've attended several of his *lieder* evenings at the Musikverein," Werthen responded. "There is genius in him."

"Was," Krafft-Ebing corrected. "His friends and sponsors still insist on paying for an expensive room with a view of the Stephansdom. A grand piano also graces the room. All to no avail. For him, music is now 'loathsome.' The view out his window he thinks is a mural."

"Nonetheless," Gross said, "we would like to speak with him if at all possible. We shall not overexcite him."

"Forewarned," Krafft-Ebing told them. "Do not expect much. I will call to the administration. By the time you arrive, it should be arranged."

The State Lunatic Asylum was located at Lazarretgasse 14, near the General Hospital in the Ninth District, Alsergrund. It was a fine day and they decided to walk there, turning off the Ring at Universitätsstrasse and passing the General Hospital first. It was there, in the Narrenturm, the fool's tower or madhouse tower, where the insane had been "treated" until only four decades before. Such treatment included chaining the poor souls to the walls, throwing them in ice baths, and making them wear leather masks to supposedly reduce their anxiety.

The nearby State Lunatic Asylum, opened in 1853, improved the lot of these sufferers, but still scandalous occurrences took place even there. In 1865 the great physician Ignaz Semmelweis, whose discovery that simple hand washing provided valuable antisepsis in the prevention of puerperal fever or childbirth fever, was confined to the asylum after suffering a nervous breakdown. He died two weeks after being admitted, supposedly from a sepsis caused, ironically, by a surgically infected finger. Werthen, however, knew the truth from a lawyer representing the family, who had unsuccessfully attempted to sue the facility: Semmelweis had, in fact, died of injuries suffered at the hands of asylum personnel who had beaten him violently.

Passing the General Hospital, they neared the intersection with Spitalgasse, where they turned right.

Until now they had walked in silence, but suddenly Gross cleared his throat.

"Tell me, Werthen," he said. "Am I causing undue strain by my presence in your home?"

"Whatever do you mean, Gross?"

"It is just that I sensed a certain, how shall I put it, glacial ambience last evening. Your lady-wife was not her usual self at dinner. There was no spark to her conversation. Indeed, she managed to rearrange the peas on her plate several times. You can be honest with me. I know I am an old curmudgeon at times. The wonder is that Adele still puts up with me. But then she has to, doesn't she? But I would understand if my presence is off-putting to your wife."

"Trust me, Gross, it has nothing to do with you."

"Ah, your trip to the Salzkammergut, then? She does not like to be abandoned."

"And not that, either."

Gross stopped walking. "Well, what is it, then? I do not mean to pry into your private business, but something is obviously bothering the both of you. If something causes you to give less than full concentration to our case, then it *is* my concern."

"*Our* case!" Werthen felt his temper flash. "This is *my* case, Gross. I invited your co-operation, but have not relinquished control."

"There, you see. How unlike you to lose

your temper. Something is preying upon you. It affects your judgment, your usual good nature."

Confound the man, Werthen thought. He would keep picking and prying until he had his answer. Werthen was about to charge into a further tirade, but suddenly saw the sense of what Gross was saying. He was allowing this absurd misunderstanding between him and Berthe to continue too long.

Thus he found himself confiding in Gross, telling him of Berthe's wonderful news and the strange manner in which he had reacted to it.

"But that is only natural," Gross said after listening patiently. "Of course you are concerned about your parents' reaction to the news. Of course you want them to accept your wife and offspring. And I think I might have a way to ensure that. Just leave that to me, old friend. And when we return for lunch, no, when you return for lunch sans the baleful Dr. Gross, then take your young wife in your arms and tell her the truth. Tell her your hesitation was caused not by the blessed news of the baby, but by considerations about your parents. Share your burdens, man. Marriage is about sharing."

Werthen could not imagine Gross living

in accord with such prescriptions. In fact, an intimate to the Gross ménage from his years earlier in Graz, Werthen could guarantee that Gross was the autocratic paterfamilias in his household, every bit as tyrannical in its operation as Mahler was in his. Werthen did, however, make no mention of this.

"Thank you, Gross. That is fine advice, indeed."

"And not to worry about my missed lunch," the criminologist said. "I am sure to find a bite somewhere."

As if he were an urchin seeking handouts on the street. Werthen had to smile at this bid for sympathy.

"I am sure you will."

They continued on their way, and Werthen did feel a new lightness to his spirit as a result of their little talk. He could, in fact, concentrate more fully on the matter at hand.

Spitalgasse soon intersected with Lazarettgasse and they stood in front of the imposing gray walls of the State Lunatic Asylum.

"Shoot me first, old friend," Gross muttered as they mounted the steps to the front door. "If I go barking mad, never let them lock me up in such a place."

A day of revelations, Werthen thought, as they entered through the large front doors past the uniformed doorman and headed for the inquiries desk.

The fat, florid official there was dressed in a dark blue and red uniform that appeared to be a bizarre blend of Hussar and train conductor.

"What is it?" he asked before either Gross or Werthen had a chance to make an inquiry. On the small desk in front of him lay the most recent copy of the *Reichspost*.

Krafft-Ebing's message had obviously arrived, for the man quickly changed his aggressively unhelpful demeanor once Gross had introduced themselves.

"This way, gentlemen. Why didn't you say so at first? The Herr Hofrath called specially in this regard."

They followed the rotund man up the central staircase and then down a corridor marked Abteilung 2A. Muffled sounds reached them from behind closed doors. The official moved surprisingly quickly for such a large man, obviously in a hurry to get back to his edifying reading on the Jewish problem in Austria, thought Werthen.

"Here it is," he finally said, stopping in front of a door with number thirteen stenciled over it. He did not bother knocking;

instead he slipped his master key into the lock and opened it, sticking his head in the room.

"Visitors for you, Herr Wolf. You be nice now, or no strudel for you tonight."

The man drew his head out and winked at them conspiratorially as one might after chastising a naughty child.

"He should be cooperative now. If not, I can have a stronger talk with him. . . ."

"That won't be necessary," Gross said. "You may leave now."

"Most irregular," the man said.

His official pique, however, subsided, when Werthen offered him three florins.

"Well, the Herr Hofrath himself allowed the visit, so I suppose it is all right."

"Indeed," Gross said, sidling past him and into the room. Werthen followed, closing the door behind him.

On the bed a slip of a man stared at them with the largest and most distant eyes Werthen had ever seen. Wolf was lean and with a brooding face that appeared more chiseled than molded. He had violet smudges under his deep-set eyes and deep lines drawing the flesh in under his cheekbones as if scarred. His beard, sparse because of a nervous tick that forced him to continually pick the whiskers out, was reduced to a faint blur of a mustache and goatee.

The room, as promised, had a view of the tower of St. Stephen's cathedral, Werthen noted, though it was fragmented in quadrants by the barred windows; a dusty Bösendorfer grand took up most of the floor space.

"I knew you would come." Wolf's voice was powerful, booming, in complete contrast to his appearance. It made Werthen jump.

"Is he gone now? Do people finally understand?"

Gross, well versed in psychology, did not miss a beat.

"Yes," he said. "All is as it should be."

Wolf seemed almost to brighten at this statement, wrapping his arms around his knees and pulling them under his chin. He began rocking on the bed.

"At last," he uttered.

It was almost more than Werthen could bear to see the man so reduced. This was the great torchbearer of Richard Wagner, composer of the *Möriker Lieder*, the *Eichendorff Lieder*, the *Goethe Lieder*, the *Italian Serenade*, and the opera *Der Corregidor*, all noted for their depth of feeling, for their groundbreaking tonality. And now he was but a shell of a man.

"They can perform my opera. Now that I am director."

His mind was obviously still on the Mahler dispute, Werthen thought, which was, he realized guiltily, to their advantage.

"Yes," Gross agreed. "At long last."

"He is a devil, you know." His voice rose to almost a cry with the word "devil." Wolf turned to stare directly at Werthen rather than Gross.

The words chilled the lawyer, but he summoned a response.

"In what way?"

"He stole my idea for a libretto. Oh, yes, stole it word for word. And I was not the only one. No. The other. The genius. The devil stole from him, too. And he ended his days here. Just like me. Oh, he is a devil, to be sure."

"Mahler?" Gross said. "Is he the devil?"

Suddenly Wolf threw himself off the bed, crashing into one of the walls headfirst and opening a deep gash on his forehead. Blood streamed down his skeletal face and he began laughing hysterically.

Werthen raced to the door, opened it, and called for an attendant. Heavy boots pounded along the corridor. Two burly men in long white smocks came bursting into the room, grabbed Wolf by the arms, and slammed him down on the bed. The biggest applied pressure with his knee on the composer's frail chest to restrain him.

"Is that quite necessary?" Werthen said.

The other attendant glared at him. "You two should leave now. You've created enough trouble."

Gross took Werthen's arm. "Come. The man is right."

True to his word, Gross left Werthen and Berthe alone for lunch, taking himself off to a local *gasthaus.* As it was Frau Blatschky's free half day, husband and wife found themselves alone for once, and Werthen quickly told Berthe why he had reacted to the joyful news of her pregnancy with less than elation.

She took him in her arms. "Karl, Karl. Such a bright man to be so silly."

And she led him down the hallway to their bedroom. He was amazed and somewhat bemused to see her begin to disrobe.

"Hurry," she said. "Before Frau Blatschky returns and is scandalized."

He joined her in the bed, holding her gently in his arms like a fragile doll. Then she rolled onto her back, pulling Werthen on top.

"I'm pregnant, not sick," Berthe said, pressing down on the small of his back with her cool hands. "I won't break." She wrapped her legs around his, digging into the backs of his thighs with her heels and lifting into him.

He soon forgot to be a gentleman, lost in the movement of his hips.

Later they lay tangled under the thin cotton summer comforter, her head nestled into his left shoulder.

"You didn't really imagine men and women stopped wanting one another for nine months, did you?"

He hadn't thought about it. It was not something his parents ever talked about, not something one learned at school.

Now she lifted herself up on her elbow to look him directly in the eye.

"Never be so stupid again," she said fiercely. "Talk to me. Believe in me. Promise?"

"I promise."

"I am just amazed that stodgy Dr. Gross was the one to make the suggestion," she said as she dished two omelets onto plates for their late lunch.

"He did not exactly say 'bed your wife.' Rather it was 'take her in your arms' or something to that effect."

As they repaired to the dining room, they heard the metal clack of the mail slot on their door. The second post.

Werthen placed the dishes on the table and went to the foyer to collect the mail. He examined the letters, placing bills and business communications on the hall table for later perusal. One had no return address and was thus less easily categorized. He took it with him back to the dining room.

Berthe had begun without him, looking somewhat abashed as he entered.

"I'm famished. Sorry. Omelets are about the only food I can abide these days."

He sat and joined her, setting the envelope next to his plate. He had a bad feeling, for it was not usual for a letter to arrive without a return address.

"Are you going to open it or admire it?"

She was quite lively after their lovemaking, he noted. And her appetite had picked up.

"Perhaps we should take a siesta more often."

But this did not embarrass her nor dampen her high spirits.

"In the back there is a portion called the flap," she said. "It is customary to tear that."

He did as he was told, digging out a single

piece of paper from the envelope. He could tell by the feel of it that the paper was cheap stuff, coarse and without a finish. Opening it he was confronted with a short message written in what appeared to be a schoolboy scrawl of printing. The bottom half of the letter held a musical notation. He placed the missive on the table between them.

"Strange," Berthe muttered between bites of her meal.

Werthen quickly perused it, then read it a second time just to be certain.

"More than strange," he said. "Downright bizarre. If this is true . . ."

"If this is true," Gross said later that afternoon upon returning to the flat, "then we have a case of historic dimensions on our hands."

"The disguised handwriting might lend credence to it," Werthen observed.

"True," Gross said. "The writer did take the time to disguise his or her handwriting. Which attests to one of two things: either he has an extremely unique handwriting that would give him away, or his handwriting is known to us, individually or collectively."

"A practical joke," Berthe said. "Someone has gotten word of our investigation and is having fun at our expense."

Neither Gross nor Werthen responded to this.

Gross read the letter out loud again:

"Dear Advokat Werthen,
You and your friends should take a wider worldview. Herr Mahler is not and has not been the only composer under threat in Vienna. Others have died for their profligacy. Other so-called great musicians. Need I name names? But I do not want to give too much away. Where would be the fun in that? Just know, that I have struck before and I shall strike again for the sake of art!"

"What do you make of the musical notation?" Werthen asked.

"I am no musician," Gross said, holding the paper up to the light, searching in vain for any telltale manufacturing marks.

"May I?" Berthe held out her hand, took the letter, and led the way into the small music room she had created out of an unused maid's quarters. There was just enough space for an upright piano. She sat at the keyboard, the letter in front of her, and played the notes once, then twice.

"Familiar somehow," she said. "Almost

like the melody from a late Beethoven quartet. But I think it's an original melody line. I think the person who wrote the letter also wrote this fragment."

"Curious," Gross said.

"Other composers," Werthen mused. "Well, we have had a rash of deaths lately. Strauss earlier this month."

"Brahms two years ago," added Berthe.

"And Bruckner died the year before that." Werthen shook his head. "But they all died natural deaths."

"This way lies madness," Gross muttered. "Are we to question every musical death of the last decade? Rubbish."

But Werthen knew that Gross's interest had been well and truly piqued.

NINE

Over the course of the next day, Gross became increasingly consumed with the possibility that Vienna had a madman in its midst who was, one by one, killing the great musicians of the age. All day Sunday he paced his room, for unseasonable rain kept him inside. Berthe and Werthen could clearly hear the rhythmic steps, a maddening tattoo that finally drove them out into the rain, umbrellas in hand.

On their walk they made no mention of the mysterious letter. Instead they enjoyed the fresh smells of the city in the rain, strolling along the Ringstrasse with the plane trees dripping onto their black umbrellas. A few other intrepid walkers had come out as well, but the city, usually quiet on Sundays, was doubly so today.

Back at the flat Gross had finally left the precincts of his room. Now, clothed in a silk dressing gown over his trousers, white shirt, tie, and waistcoat, he was ensconced in the sitting room, sprawled out on the leather couch like a pasha.

"Where have you two been?" he said as they entered the room. "It is imperative that we talk of the new direction our investigation is headed." With this he rose from the couch and began pacing the sitting room.

"Gross —" Werthen began but was immediately interrupted.

"I know that tone of voice," the criminologist said, stopping midstep. "You are now going to attempt to bring me back down to earth. That is the sensible Karl Werthen speaking. I am much too familiar with that modulation."

"Obviously somebody needs to reintroduce you to reality," Werthen said. "How can you have been so convinced by a solitary anonymous letter?"

"It speaks of the crime of the ages."

"Is fame all that important to you?" Werthen said, amazed at the admission. "One would think you had quite enough notoriety already."

"It is not a matter of fame, my dear Werthen. You totally misread me. No. It is the hideousness of the crimes. To deprive the world of the wonders of such music, and all for what? A moment of pique? What does the blighter mean by 'profligacy'? His or theirs?"

"But, Gross, surely you have considered the obvious. That the letter is false in content and intent."

"To be sure," he said, waving the suggestion away as if swatting at a mildly irritating fly. "It could of course be, as your lady-wife suggests, a mere practical joke. Perhaps one of our interviewees from the Hofoper or elsewhere became perturbed with our questions and wished to cause us a bit of discomfort with a leg-pull. Or perhaps one of our interviewees *is* the culprit and feels our investigation is coming rather too close for comfort. Thus a ruse, as it were."

"And there is always the possibility of some unbalanced correspondent," Berthe offered. "Someone whose feeling of self-importance is enhanced by such inventions. Someone better off in an asylum."

"Or perhaps somebody who already is in an asylum," Gross said pointedly, as if suggesting Hugo Wolf could have somehow gotten this missive sent. "And yes, I have considered these possibilities. I am not a fool, after all."

Werthen agreed with that self-evaluation. However, he was not buying Gross's explanation for his interest.

"I had not realized you were such a lover of modern music, Gross. I thought that Haydn demarked the limits of musical achievement for you."

Gross shot him a venomous look, and returned to his pacing, hands clasped behind his back. Werthen had had a law professor at the University of Vienna who assumed this exact posture when lecturing, pacing back and forth behind the lectern, making the floorboards creak as a punctuation to his monotone voice.

"It is impossible to speak with you if you insist on this continual moving about," Werthen finally said.

"I need an appetite for lunch. Frau Blatschky informs me she will be serving her excellent *palatschinken,* and promises a drizzle of chocolate sauce."

So they left Gross to his "exercise" and later met for lunch, the men at least doing justice to Frau Blatschky's delicate crêpes stuffed with apricot jam and served with a bright and sparkling Moselle.

Over coffee they were finally able to discuss the new developments. The food had a palliative effect on Gross.

"I admit," he said, "to being somewhat bedazzled by the possible enormity of such a proposition. That someone is killing off the great musicians of Vienna is an event, yes, that grabs the imagination. I would be less than candid were I not to admit to certain baser impulses. Were I . . . we to solve such a crime, then my criminalistic principles would become known worldwide and virtually overnight. I suppose that such a motivation in part spurs me on. However, let me quickly add, that such a crime, if true, also fires my desire for justice, for retribution. That such a blackguard could perpetrate these crimes and not be held accountable. Well, that is unthinkable, for then we might as well be living in the deepest jungle despite our civilized trappings."

There was no response necessary to this little speech. It had the ring of truth, for Gross had always been concerned as much for the pursuit of justice as he had been for celebrity.

"Am I absolutely convinced by this anonymous letter?" Gross said. "No. Of course not. Do I believe that it is possible? Yes. Is it a direction worthy of investigation? Again, yes. To discount it out of hand would be a matter of criminal negligence in my opinion."

"I would imagine then," Berthe said, "that we should begin with the death of Johann Strauss. The most recent, the easiest to investigate."

"My thoughts exactly," Gross said, tipping his coffee cup toward her.

The next morning, Werthen and Gross acted upon this suggestion.

For Werthen it was as if the case were coming full turn, as it had all begun with the funeral of Johann Strauss. Was that only a few short weeks before? So much had passed between then and now that it seemed months had gone by.

Strauss's *palais* was located in the Fourth District, at Igelgasse 4, where his widow Adele still lived. Vienna's Waltz King had been a complicated man, Werthen knew. The disseminator of music that some called terribly sweet and others sweetly terrible, Strauss was not an overtly happy man. His first marriage, to a former opera singer, Henriette Treffz-Chalupetzky, whom Strauss called his Jetty, had been a turning point in his life. The mistress of the banker Baron Todesco when Strauss met her, Jetty was seven years his senior and the mother of seven illegitimate children. Their unlikely liaison was solemnized by marriage in 1862, a ceremony performed at St. Stephen's. Setting up house in the Second District, Jetty dispatched her children to their various fathers and thenceforth took the career of Johann Strauss as her primary mission in life. She proved to be the perfect manager, secretary, and Hausfrau, pushing the tune-master Strauss to write operettas. Indeed, Strauss, soon after the marriage, began envisioning the waltz nor merely as a dance, but as the kernel of great symphonic works. The first of his popular operettas, *Die Fledermaus,* appeared in 1874. He would compose more than a dozen more as well as an opera, *Ritter Pasman.*

Jetty died in 1878 of a stroke, and Strauss, never one to be alone, married just fifty days later, but this time disastrously. Angelica "Lili" Dittrich was twenty-five years Strauss's junior and another singer. She had cultivated Strauss in hopes of winning an appointment to the Theater an der Wien. Strauss, however, had been looking not for a mentoring relationship, but for a bit of dalliance with a younger woman. The two had begun their affair well before Jetty's death. Thus, the lonely and newly widowed Strauss naturally turned to her. Married at the Karlskirche, the couple moved into the *palais* on Igelgasse; the building had been drawn to plans suggested and inspired by Jetty.

It was not a happy marriage. Lili carried

on an affair with the director of the Theater an der Wien, an open secret in Vienna at the time, which caused Strauss great anguish. She finally ran off with the director after four years of turbulent marriage to Strauss (and was in turn deserted by the director not long after), and it was said she was now living in Berlin, operating a hat shop, living on the edge of poverty, and taking every opportunity to disparage her former husband in the press.

Not long after the breakup of this marriage, Strauss met Adele Deutsch Strauss, thirty-one years his junior, and the widow of a banker, also named Strauss. It was as if their union was meant to be. The two quickly found solace in each other, and with Adele's support, Strauss once again got back on his feet creatively, turning out masterpieces such as the operetta *Der Zigeunerbaron*. Marriage to her in Vienna, however, was impossible, as the Catholic Church did not recognize his divorce nor did it offer the sanctity of marriage to those who had thus ended their marriages.

Strauss and Adele simply lived together for a time, until they desperately desired to have their union legalized. To do so, Strauss renounced his Austrian citizenship, took up residence in Saxony-Coburg for a time to gain citizenship where divorce was legal, and also gave up his Catholic faith for Protestantism, which allowed for the marriage of divorced people. It must be said, that such a conversion should not have been all that difficult for Strauss, for he was Jewish by origin, Catholicism an assumed trapping to allow the family upward mobility in the empire. In 1887 Strauss and Adele were finally married and thereafter returned to Vienna. Adele proved to be as able a manager as Jetty had been, and the last years of Strauss's life had been productive and content. Indeed, Adele had demonstrated herself so able in the administration of Strauss's affairs that some were already referring to her as "Cosima in waltztime," comparing her to the aggressively proprietary widow of Richard Wagner.

As their *fiaker* turned off the busy Wiedner Hauptstrasse onto the more elegantly quiet Igelgasse, Werthen found himself actually looking forward to their interview with the widow. One thing he hoped to discover was why she had not attended the funeral of her husband, something that had caused quite a scandal at the time.

Drawing up to the door of Igelgasse 4, an imposing building with a façade of Schönbrunn yellow decorated with a plentiful number of caryatids, Gross was first out of the cab. As usual, he left such mundane matters as the payment of the driver to Werthen. Today, however, this did not irk the lawyer as it usually did.

They were expected, and shown into a drawing room of rather daunting proportions. A marble floor was covered in fine carpets; embroidered silk cushions adorned the large sofas placed parallel to each other in front of a massive fireplace whose mantel appeared to be in the Venetian-Moorish style. Crystal chandeliers overhead caught and refracted the sun's rays from the large east-facing windows; lozenges of red, blue, and yellow light danced around the ceiling and walls.

Frau Strauss's private secretary bad been reached by phone this morning, and Werthen had explained that he and his colleague were eager to discuss her late husband's relationship with the Hofoper director, Gustav Mahler. The very mention of the name Prince Montenuovo as their sponsor in this endeavor had silenced any further questions from the secretary. Now, shown into this overtly ostentatious room, they imagined that Adele Strauss had also been impressed.

"Please, gentlemen, sit." The voice came

from a small, mousy-looking woman who suddenly swept into the room from a side door. Adorned in black from head to foot, she moved with a certain elegance, her silk skirts making a sound like wind through autumn leaves.

She waved at the sofa near which they were standing, while she sat opposite them.

"It was good of you to see us on such short notice, Frau Strauss," Werthen said. They had agreed that he would lead this interview.

"Not at all," she said, sitting primly on the edge of the sofa like a bird about to take flight. "I must admit, however, that your purpose quite eludes me. Schani, I mean Johann, had very little to do with Herr Mahler. I believe they exchanged polite letters last year when Mahler conducted *Die Fledermaus* at the Hofoper. They were also briefly in contact in May when Johann conducted the overture to that operetta at the Hofoper. But they were hardly intimates."

"Herr Mahler is a great fan of your husband's work," Werthen said. "He is desirous of making a tribute to him." It was the story they had agreed upon, though Werthen still found it a rather limp entrée. However, they could hardly come to Frau Strauss and ask her if she suspected foul play in her husband's death.

"What an extraordinary statement," she said, her voice filled with pique. "After what Mahler said about my Johann's *Aschenbrödel.*"

"I was unaware of any comments, Frau Strauss," Werthen said. She looked at both of them in surprise. "Emissaries of Herr Mahler and you do not know that he rejected out of hand a performance of my husband's final and perhaps greatest work? A ballet, dealing with the story of Cinderella. Johann wrote the last notes to it on his deathbed. It was a labor of love for him, and it cost him dearly to focus on music at such a time. His mind was much troubled in his final days, but he stayed with music until the very end. His final words, in fact, were from the popular song, *"Brüderlein fein,"* written by his old music teacher Joseph Drechsler: *'es muss geschieden sein,'* it is time to part. Such agony it cost dear Johann to continue with his ballet up to the last minute of his life, and Herr Mahler has the nerve to refer to this final labor as an assemblage of 'asthmatic melodies.' "

Werthen raised his eyebrows at the term. It sounded only too much like Mahler, tactless when it came to his artistic judgments.

"We are not exactly direct emissaries of Herr Mahler," Werthen quickly put in, making it up as he went along. "Rather, I should have explained, the Hofoper direction has sent us to determine a fitting tribute."

This seemed to mollify her; she let out a sigh. "Well, you know now what I find a fitting tribute. A performance of *Aschenbrödel*. Though I assume my dear husband's conducting of *Die Fledermaus* was meant as a sort of honor. A tragedy, as it turned out."

"How so?" Gross now asked.

She turned her attention to him. She appeared to like Gross's demeanor better, for her pinched mouth relaxed somewhat. Werthen let the criminologist now take the lead.

"Well, that is where he caught his chill, isn't it? Whit Monday, May 22. I told him not to go to that chilly old barn of an opera house, for the weather had turned quite inclement as it can in late spring. Or at the very least, I demanded that he wear long underwear. But Johann would not hear of such blasphemy. He was a very vain man; he wanted to cut a trim and dashing figure in his tailcoat. But it was then and there that his health was destroyed. The chill turned into pneumonia and carried him off not two weeks later."

She sniffed at this, digging out a silk handkerchief from her left sleeve and dabbing at her nose.

Werthen, like the rest of Vienna, of course knew of this tragic ending. Now he suddenly saw it as yet another connection between the Hofoper and death. But one could hardly search for a culprit in that. No one could plan for the death of another by catching a chill.

Suddenly she turned her gaze back to Werthen. "I believe you mentioned that you are a lawyer. Is that so?"

Werthen nodded.

"Perhaps you can advise me about something."

"I am sure your usual counsel provides excellent advice."

"They are a bunch of old women. And this is something novel, something revolutionary I am proposing. Currently the copyright for musical works is only thirty years. I find that grossly unfair. I want to have a law written that would extend that period to fifty years. After all, I am a young woman, and with most of my husband's estate going to the Society of Music, I shall have to live off the royalties from his compositions."

Werthen looked at this small woman with

something like respect. She was made of steel at the core, he realized, to be so concerned about such matters this soon after her husband's death. Perhaps that explained her mysterious absence at the funeral in the Zentralfriedhof: she had no need of such public displays. She was the widow; she would carry on the name of Strauss into the new century. It was her duty. Werthen had little doubt that she would outstrip even Cosima Wagner in creating a cult of genius around her dead husband.

"We could discuss this matter further if you continue to be interested," he said.

"Naturally I shall remain interested. Perhaps you can leave your professional card."

She rose, indicating that the interview, for her purposes, was completed.

"You can tell the prince then about my wishes."

"Yes, of course," Gross said with real earnestness in his voice.

Again she cast the burly criminologist a look that could only be called approving.

"One thing still puzzles me," she said, as she proffered her delicate hand to be kissed.

"And what might that be, dear lady," Gross said, bending over the hand and making a discreet smacking noise a centimeter above the flesh.

"How there could have been such a mix-up. I assume it occurred in the prince's very office. And I must admit, gentlemen, I also assumed that was why you had come today. To explain."

"Explain what?" Gross asked.

"How such an invitation could be sent by accident. Johann was already at death's door; then came the summons from the Hofburg. Johann got up out of his sickbed, would not be deterred. And off he went only to discover that no one at the Hofburg had summoned him. Returning home, he took to his bed, never more to rise."

"You are saying the your husband received a summons from the Hofburg, perhaps from Prince Montenuovo's very office, in the midst of his final illness." Gross said. "But when he arrived at the Hofburg, he discovered that no one had sent for him. That in fact, such a missive was erroneous?"

She nodded.

"Do you still have this letter?"

"No. I am afraid Johann burned it in disgust after returning home. But that letter killed him as surely as if someone had pointed a gun at his head and pulled the trigger."

■ ■ ■ ■

Once outside, Werthen and Gross could only shake their heads.

"So, it could be true after all," Werthen said. "Strauss's death could be considered murder, if indeed somebody falsified a letter from the Hofburg with the purpose of drawing a very sick man out of his bed. After all, no one refuses an invitation from the emperor."

"Yes," Gross said, beginning to walk to the major thoroughfare where they could more easily hail a passing *fiaker*. "That is my understanding, as well. There was, however, another point of interest to be gained from our interview."

Werthen thought back to the conversation. "The connection to the Hofoper? But no one can plan for another to catch a chill."

Gross shook his head. "No. Something else Frau Strauss mentioned. Her husband's last words: *'es muss geschieden sein.'* Couldn't they just have easily been, *'es muss die Geschiedene sein'*?"

Werthen stopped in the middle of the sidewalk, staring at his colleague.

"By God, Gross, I think you might have something there. Not, 'we must be parted,' but 'it must be the ex-wife.' Meaning his second wife, Lili. Did he suspect her of sending him the false summons from the Hofburg? She might be up for such maliciousness, for from what I hear she has not done well after the divorce from Strauss, and she holds him responsible for her plight."

"It is, my friend, another avenue of thought, to be sure," Gross said.

Meanwhile, Berthe had spent the morning at the Settlement house in Ottakring, her first visit there in too long. The house was closing up for the rest of June, July, and August and she helped store books and writing utensils for the upcoming autumn term.

She was not alone in her endeavors. Frau Emma Adler was also helping out today. Theirs was not a coincidental meeting: Berthe knew that Emma was scheduled for today at the Settlement house, and thought she would be a likely source to query regarding those who knew Mahler during his student days in Vienna. For if Berthe remembered correctly, Emma's husband had been a friend to Mahler at the time.

Emma, the daughter of a Jewish railway engineer, met a young physician, Victor

Adler, son of a well-to-do businessman from Prague. They married in 1878 and had a son together, Friedrich, the following year. After several more years of practicing medicine, Adler had given it up altogether to follow his true calling, International Socialism. He was at the very heart of the Austrian socialist movement, had been instrumental in inaugurating the first of the May Day parades for workers, and he had put his considerable personal fortune behind *Die Arbeiter Zeitung.*

Berthe and Emma had met at the offices of the leftist newspaper, for Emma worked there as journalist and translator, while Berthe had placed numerous freelance articles with the paper. Emma was a handsome woman sixteen years Berthe's senior, and had served as a model for more than one painter, rather famously for a picture of the Virgin Mary for the altar of a church at Attersee, a lakeland resort where the Adlers vacationed. Emma loved to tell the humorous tale of how, when the finished painting was finally placed on the altar, one old rustic from the village was heard complaining: "But that's the Adler woman, not the Mother of God at all!" Two years later the church burned to the ground after being struck by lightning and the only thing saved from it was this painting, which had since become a sort of holy relic for the villagers, prayed to for miraculous intercession.

But there was nothing miraculous or fabulist about Emma. She was one of the most profoundly down-to-earth women Berthe knew.

"We have missed your contributions of late," Emma said, after they had caught up on recent news and Berthe had shared the glad tidings of her pregnancy. They continued packing school primers into a wooden crate as they conversed.

"I've been helping out at Karl's office more," Berthe said.

"Not at the expense of your own career, I hope."

"It's not like that," Berthe assured her, yet she was not so certain herself. "It's not all paperwork. Karl has branched out into criminal law again and investigations."

"So we gathered." Emma made no further explanation, but Berthe assumed that she had somehow gotten word of Karl's investigations the previous year into the serial killings in Vienna. "Any wonderful case at the moment?"

Berthe had hoped for just such curiosity in her old friend.

"Mahler," Emma whispered once Berthe

had finished her explanations. "Such an odd wee man."

"Yes, isn't he? You were friends of his once, as I recall."

"Victor was. I only met him a few times. But Victor was full of tales about Mahler." Emma smiled. "Of course this was donkey's years ago, when we were all young and bohemian. It was about the time Victor and I first met, in 1878. He had established the Vegetarian Society — we were all great advocates of Wagner and his claim that vegetarianism could save the world. We wanted so desperately to save the world then, by the most direct means available." She shook her head, dusting the back of one book before placing it in the crate. "We've since learned that the world is a bit more complicated than that. Sometimes it doesn't even want saving. Impertinent world." She laughed lightly.

"I was hoping you or Victor could tell me about Mahler's friends from that time."

"Ah, collecting a lot of suspects from his past?" Emma said. "But there's really not much to tell. They would meet at a miserable dingy little cellar restaurant at the corner of Wallnerstrasse and Fahnengasse . . . the Ramharter. Yes, that was the name. Lord, I have not thought of that dim cold place in years. I accompanied Victor to a few unappetizing dinners there, but it was quickly obvious that those oh-so-advanced males did not want a woman in attendance. Yet it was there I first met Mahler. He was sporting a beard in those days, a big, furry mess of a thing. He must have thought it made him look older than his age. He was only eighteen, nineteen at the time. But already so full of himself."

"The eternal artist," Berthe said, almost a sigh.

"Eternal bore, more like it. I mean how can you be eighteen, in the bloom of youth and fine health, and be forever going on about a *sehnsucht,* longing, for death? But the others were little better. There was Hermann Bahr as well, a young rather bovine-looking writer hoping to make his way. Which in fact he has done. And Engelbert Pernerstorfer. You know him, he is still at the center of our socialist movement. At the time, he edited their little paper, *Deutsche Wort.* Oh, yes. In addition to being socialists and vegetarians, they were all great German nationalists. What a laugh. A gaggle of Jewish intellectuals all cozying up to those anti-Semites. Victor left German nationalism behind when its Jew hatred had become all too obvious. My brothers, Heinrich and

Otto, were also part of the group, and the journalist Richard von Kralik. Hugo Wolf sometimes made an appearance, as well, but he was more likely to be found at the Café Griensteidl, where all the young would-be artists of the time gathered. The Café Megalomania, I liked to call it. And then there was that poor boy Rott."

"Him I do not know," Berthe said.

"A great tragedy, to be sure. Hans Rott. He was at the conservatory with Mahler and Wolf. A great genius, by all accounts. But he went completely mad in 1880, died in a sanatorium four years later. Such a pity. They all laid it to Brahms."

"Brahms was responsible for this musician going insane?"

"Clearly he already had the propensity. Victor worked with Freud for a time, you know. He was very interested in psychology. He said young Rott was a fragile sort, full of nervous energy that needed channeling."

"Sounds rather like my own husband," Berthe joked.

"And mine. But this young man was walking a tightrope emotionally. Then, when Brahms destroyed his chances for a state fellowship, Rott simply snapped. Riding on a train for a possible position in Alsace, he pulled a revolver on a fellow passenger who was about to light a cigar. Claimed that Brahms had filled the train with dynamite and he was not to strike his match. They disarmed Rott finally, and put him in the Psychiatric Clinic here. And it was all about the damned politics of music, not about Rott's music at all."

Berthe began to feel as if she and Emma had been living on different planets for the past years, for she was privy to none of this information.

"I am afraid you need to explain that one."

"The Wagner-Brahms battle, I mean. You supported one or the other of them as a young musician, and woe unto you if you fell under the control of the opposite camp. Rott, like Mahler and Wolf, was a great lover of Wagner and a disciple of Bruckner at the conservatory. Brahms thought Bruckner was a sham, that his music would be forgotten in a few years. . . . But if your husband is working for Mahler now he should ask him. Or better yet, ask Natalie Bauer-Lechner. I am sure she is still in attendance to her one and only."

"She is," Berthe replied. "I didn't realize you knew her, too."

"They all met at the conservatory, you see," Emma said. "And then I met them through Victor and his society. I would hardly say I *knew* any of them. At any rate, she is a great source of information about those years. Knows where the bodies are hidden. Sometime have her tell you about Mahler's falling-out with Wolf over an early libretto. The stuff of tragedy and comedy."

"Wolf went insane, too," Berthe muttered. "An awful lot of that going about, it seems."

TEN

Werthen had a strange sense of déjà vu, seated in a chair, along with Gross, in the office of Police Praesidium Inspector Meindl. They had had occasion to deal with this man on their previous case. Werthen noted that there was an oil painting missing from the wall in back of the inspector that had been there on their last visit. Now the mandatory muttonchopped framed visage of the emperor hung alone and lonely where once two portraits had resided. The other portrait had been of a man whom Werthen had killed in a duel, the very man who had threatened him, Berthe, and all those close to him. He took a deep breath at the thought.

They were surprised to discover that the hawk-nosed and gaunt Detective Inspector Bernhard Drechsler had also been invited to this meeting. They had received their summons via telegram first thing this morning.

"A pleasure to see you gentlemen again," Meindl said, his eyes, behind his pince-nez, fixed solely on Gross. He was turned out well; his lightweight charcoal suit looked as if Knize himself had tailored it. Despite his words, Meindl did not appear, in any way, pleased. Clean-shaven and red-cheeked, Meindl appeared almost cherubic sitting behind his gargantuan cherrywood desk. An angry cherub, by the look of his pinched lips.

He had reason to be, Werthen suspected, for the man whom Werthen had dueled had been Meindl's protector, his mentor, his benefactor. Since that powerful man's death, Meindl's career had stalled; he had been passed over for chief inspector earlier in the year. But Werthen sensed there was more to it than that.

"It appears you fellows are once again coming to the aid of the Vienna police." Meindl's voice was so heavy with irony that it grated. "I refer, of course," Meindl continued, "to the affair of Herr Mahler. Prince Montenuovo wants us to see to the Hofoper director's continued safety and good health."

"I felt it incumbent upon myself to apprise the prince of our investigations," Gross said, as if to mollify the elfish man. It did not work.

"Quite," Meindl said through pursed lips. "It would, however, have been good of you, considering our past history, to have come to me first."

Werthen could feel Gross stirring in the chair next to him. He was not one to suffer fools gladly.

"And what would you have done, Inspector?" Gross asked. "Told me that the death of Fräulein Kaspar was accidental and to come back when there was more positive evidence of a direct attack upon Mahler?"

Detective Inspector Drechsler cleared his throat, an unconscious admission that that was exactly what he had done when confronted with Gross's information.

"I doubt even the death of the unfortunate violinist, Friedrich Gunther, would have stirred your interest, Inspector," Gross continued.

"We shall never know now, shall we?" Meindl rejoined. "But let us not accuse one another. We obviously have a difficult task ahead of us. Drechsler here has acquainted me with the facts of the case to date."

"Including the attempt on Mahler's life last week?" Werthen said.

Meindl's eyes remained fixed on Gross,

pointedly ignoring Werthen. "Yes, we have had word of that accident from our Bad Aussee colleagues."

"The brakes had obviously been cut," Werthen continued. "It was no accident."

Meindl finally turned his eyes to Werthen. "My misstatement. Not an accident."

He managed to invest those five words with a level of hatred Werthen had never before felt directed at him. It was chilling yet it also angered Werthen. He decided, however, to hold his tongue. Though deprived of his major sponsor, Meindl still had some friends in high places. Word had reached Werthen last year that he had only narrowly missed being prosecuted for murder as a result of his duel. Against the law, dueling was nonetheless a crime seldom prosecuted. But Meindl had, so Werthen learned, struggled so mightily to have him arrested that he was saved only by imperial intercession. The emperor had no wish for certain facts to be broadcast.

Thus, though Meindl was annoying, he could also be a dangerous enemy. Werthen wisely decided to keep silent, letting Gross take the lead.

"So we will let you get about your work, then," Gross said, attempting to cut the proceedings short.

But Meindl had his own agenda for this meeting. "What does Frau Strauss have to do with these investigations?" he suddenly asked.

So that was it, Werthen thought. The good widow had gotten the wind up after they had left, pulling a few of her own powerful strings to find out exactly what they had really been after on their visit to her.

"We like to be thorough," Gross said. "Strauss and Mahler had connections of a sort with each other."

"Of a sort," Meindl repeated, adjusting his pince-nez and nodding. "I believe Herr Mahler conducted Strauss's operetta —"

"*Die Fledermaus,*" Drechsler read from a notebook he had now produced.

"Yes," Meindl agreed. "And Strauss contracted his final illness while conducting at the Hofoper. Not much of a connection, I would say. Nothing there to bother a grieving widow with."

Gross had finally reached his boiling point. "Inspector Meindl, may I remind you that I and Advokat Werthen are employed by Prince Montenuovo. We are answerable to him. Whom we choose to interview and not interview is thus not a police matter."

"I beg to differ. It is now very much a police matter."

Meindl's voice raised a full half tone as he said this. He took a deep breath.

"Look," he said, calming himself. "We are former colleagues. There is no need for rancor between us. I admit to a certain amount of professional pique. However, when one of the most important people in our cultural life makes a complaint —"

"Frau Strauss complained of our visit?" Gross asked.

"Well" — Meindl clasped his hands together on the desk in front of him — "not so much a complaint as an official inquiry. She was bothered by the visit, confused as to your actual intent."

"As I said," Gross noted, "we like to be thorough. Follow all possible leads. Someone is trying to kill Herr Mahler, and we would like to find that person before he, or she, is successful."

"I had rather thought we narrowed down the list of suspects to a man," Meindl said, glancing at Detective Inspector Drechsler. "There was the matter of hoisting Herr Gunther up into a noose."

"Yes," Gross allowed. "But then there is always the possibility of accomplices."

"I for one can hardly see a woman seeking such revenge, especially on Herr Mahler. For what? A love affair gone badly? A word of criticism at a rehearsal?"

None of the other three responded to this. That Meindl was so blind to human motivation was an indication of just how far out of his depth he was as an inspector. He was simply a self-serving bureaucrat eager for advancement, not a policeman at all, Werthen thought. It amazed him to realize that a man could be so shrewd in the byzantine matters of court politics, yet remain so ignorant of the basic workings of the human psyche.

"What I have called you in for is not to argue, but rather to ensure that we are on the same side of things here," Meindl said, attempting a gracious manner. "I would like to know what direction your investigations are taking you, whom you will be interviewing. It should save both of us time. We do not wish, after all, to duplicate services."

Gross sighed. There was nothing for it but to attempt at least a show of cooperation with Meindl.

"Well, it is a somewhat complex matter," Gross began.

Twenty minutes later the criminologist finished with a concise overview of the case to date, including a brief list of possible suspects and what possible alibis they had for various dates in question. He also noted the direction their inquiries were now heading, looking into friends and enemies from Mahler's past as a student in Vienna. However, Gross did not even hint at the bigger investigation at hand now — the possible serial murders of some of Vienna's greatest musicians.

Meindl nodded his head sagely throughout this recitation, but Werthen doubted he was taking much of it in. Instead, he relied on Drechsler to take close notes.

"We should focus on those gathered in Altaussee," Meindl said as they were adjourning. "After all, it would seem we have a more finite cast of suspects in that incident."

"As long as you do not allow for someone cutting the brakes before the bicycle was even delivered." Werthen could not help himself; he wanted to wipe the self-satisfied grin off of Meindl's face. "Or for a visitor who might have arrived unnoticed in the middle of the night. The bicycles were kept outside and left unattended."

"To be sure," the inspector said, but without conviction. Addressing Gross he said, "It is fortunate you thought to have a man on the scene in the country."

Gross simply shook his head at this comment.

As they were leaving, Meindl addressed one further comment their direction:

"Time is of the utmost importance, gentlemen. I have thus far managed to keep any speculation about attempts on Mahler's life out of the newspapers. But I can not be expected to keep this hidden and secret for much longer. It is only a matter of time before some enterprising, or shall I say scandalmongering journalist discovers the facts and splashes them across the front page of one of Vienna's dailies. Then our quarry shall go to ground, or worse, choose to strike quickly and be done with it."

Werthen did not like doing so, but did have to admit that Meindl had a valid point. Time was also playing against them.

He and Gross were accompanied by Drechsler out of the Praesidium office on Schottenring. The day was warming. Gross suggested a bite to eat, but Drechsler pleaded other urgent business.

Before taking his leave, however, he said, "There's been a development in the Gunther case. We've finally found a witness, a young woman of somewhat dubious profession, if you understand, who was occupying a street corner not far from Gunther's flat the night he died. One of my bright young sergeants decided to survey the nighttime scene on nearby streets to see if some woman plied her trade nearby. It took time, but we finally found this working girl."

Gross was less interested in the means it took to find the witness than in what she had to say. "Out with it, man."

"She mentions a man leaving the building in the wee hours of the night. A largish man who left on foot. The gas lamp nearest Gunther's building was not working, though, so she could give us little more. Age, facial characteristics, dress. Nothing there, though she seemed to think he might be middle-aged rather than younger by the way he moved. But when she realized he wasn't going to be giving her any business, she lost interest."

"And there was no carriage waiting for him, no *fiaker?*" Gross asked.

"She reports that he left on foot. Headed down the Herrengasse toward the Hofburg and not in her direction."

"Can she be more specific about the time than the 'wee' hours?" Werthen asked.

Drechsler shrugged to the lawyer. "She remembers the bell of the Minoriten Church going two, but was unsure how long that was before she saw the man."

"So somewhere between two and three in the morning?" Gross said.

"That would seem reasonable," Drechsler said.

Werthen was about to make the obvious conclusion when Gross spoke up, quite literally taking the words out of his mouth.

"And I suppose you have this same bright young sergeant investigating the nighttime scene along the farther stretches of Herrengasse in the hopes of finding another witness?"

Drechsler smiled. "It is a pleasure working with you, Dr. Gross. One need not overexplain."

Gross nodded at the compliment.

"And one other thing," Drechsler said. "He's not a man to cross."

"Meindl, you mean?" Werthen said.

Drechsler nodded. "He doesn't much like you."

"That was made abundantly apparent," Werthen replied.

"He is hoping you make a misstep in this investigation. That he can somehow destroy your career, your reputation."

Werthen took this in, wondering why Drechsler would be so candid.

"And he thinks you're a bag of gas," Drechsler said to Gross.

This brought the red to Gross's cheeks, but he said nothing.

"You are being rather frank, Detective Inspector," Werthen said.

"Truth is, I don't like the man. He knows bugger all about policing. His fancy friends secured him his position on the Praesidium. He treats his men like retrieving dogs, takes all the credit for any convictions and none of the blame for those cases we cannot close."

"And you think you would be a better choice as inspector of the Police Praesidium," Gross said.

"Even my aunt Gretl would be," Drechsler said. "But they'll never pick a man like me. I didn't go to the university, don't have the right friends. No, I'm not that kind of ambitious, but I would like to see a better man as my boss."

"I believe, Detective Inspector," Gross said, "that is a wish shared by others, as well."

"Well, maybe we can help each other, then," Drechsler said, somewhat ambiguously, and left, turning into the First District, headed toward Freyung.

Werthen and Gross strolled along the Ring.

"I really wouldn't mind a spot to eat," Gross finally said.

But before looking for a likely restaurant,

Werthen had to know.

"Drechsler was quite candid with us. But you did not reciprocate. You made no mention of our anonymous letter or of a possible link to Mahler's past."

"Is that a question?" Gross asked.

"I suppose so."

"My answer then is that neither did you."

"I am sure you were not waiting for my lead in the matter."

"Actually I was, my dear Werthen. This is, after all, as you are wont to remind me, your case. Ergo, your decision whom to take into your confidence."

"I am not sure it was a conscious decision. I just —"

"Exactly," Gross said. "You went by instincts, by feelings. And they are perfectly sound. At this point in our new investigations, the fewer people who know the better. So, how about that plate of wurst?"

Werthen looked around him, remembering a *gemütlich* locale nearby just off the Ring. He led Gross to the Black Swann, an inn near the Rathaus that had just the sort of rustic ambience Gross enjoyed.

Once seated snugly in a solid oak corner booth, Gross ordered his plate of sliced wurst with onions, and Werthen settled for a midmorning glass of slivowitz and a *kleine braune.*

"There are too many trails to follow," Werthen said as he watched Gross dig into the food.

"In which case it is recommended that the wise investigator narrow his options to a more manageable amount," Gross said, through his final bites. "I recommend that, for the time being, we put Herr Mahler on the back burner." He patted his oily lips with a linen napkin. "To use a culinary metaphor."

"Berthe will be disappointed," Werthen said. "She has developed the lead to Mahler's past quite extensively, especially with the information yesterday from Frau Adler."

"Such information has lingered for decades," Gross said. "It can wait a few more days or weeks while we investigate the deaths of Brahms and Bruckner. Just as my return to Czernowitz can be delayed. After all, the term is over and Adele is still in Paris."

Which, Werthen assumed, was Gross's way of requesting further lodgings so that he could continue with the investigation. Werthen did not bother responding to that comment. Instead he asked, "And how do you mean to go about that investigation?"

"Well, an obvious starting point would be your friend, Herr Kraus. He seems to know all the chitchat that passes for news in this fair city."

"What sort of 'ponderables' are we speaking of?" Karl Kraus asked later that day.

They were seated in the office of *Die Fackel* at Maximiliantstrasse 13, one street in from the Ring and just across from the Hofoper. Kraus was thus at the very geo graphical center of Vienna culture. Despite the imposing address, the journalist oper- ated out of a cramped and cluttered corner office, which contained a small desk and a battered leather sofa along one wall that was currently filled with back copies of the *Wiener Zeitung, Neue Freie Presse, Frem- denblatt, Wiener Mode,* and the *Deutsche Zeitung.* Werthen and Gross occupied two rather unstable straight-back chairs. In front of them, Kraus's desk was a mess of paper. He wrote the entire content of his magazine himself and in longhand, a tight scrawl as Werthen could observe on the pages of foolscap strewn about the desktop.

"Ponderables such as the nature of Bruck- ner's and Brahms's deaths." Gross smiled at Kraus insouciantly.

"My, but you two are heading for heavy water."

"In what way?" asked Gross.

Now it was Kraus's turn to return an innocent smile. "Why not include the death of dear Herr Strauss, as well?" he asked. "We make such business of death in Vienna."

"Is that what you are working on now?" Werthen asked.

"For my late June issue," Kraus said, tapping the page in front of him. "The 'Mercantile Mourning of Johann Strauss.' Has a nice ring to it, don't you think? His death has given rise to a flood of new productions in every theater in the land. Even the amusement park in the Prater has joined it with a 'Venice in Vienna Death Celebration.' I assume they will have some dark-haired southerner crooning Strauss melodies from a gondola afloat on one of those ludicrously artificial canals. Tastelessness knows no bounds."

"We have already made certain inquiries regarding Herr Strauss," Gross allowed. "Good of you to advise it, though. Herr Brahms and Herr Bruckner will suffice for now, thank you."

Kraus was a quick study, Werthen knew. No need to explain things to him; no sense in trying to obfuscate the matter, either, for he was sure to understand the implications of their new inquiries.

"Well," Kraus began, leaning back in his chair, "I am sure you are aware of the basic facts. Bruckner died on October 11, 1896. He was seventy-two, had just moved into a small apartment in the Upper Belvedere Palace, and was trying furiously to finish the final movement of his Ninth Symphony. He had been in poor health for several years, but it was still quite a shock when his housekeeper discovered his body. Of course he never married. He died quite alone."

"Was there a will?" Gross asked.

Kraus cast a bemused glanced at the criminologist. This query evidently confirmed Kraus's suspicions about their line of questioning.

"Oh, yes. Everything proper and above-board there. Signed it in 1893, leaving all his autograph manuscripts to the imperial library. Other than that, there was little of worth to bequeath. He had a rough road, did poor Bruckner."

"His support of Wagner cost him dearly," Werthen said.

"Yes," Kraus allowed. "That surely set the musical establishment against him. Hanslick and his minions. They called his music wild and incomprehensible."

By whom he meant Eduard Hanslick, doyen of Vienna's music critics and a staunch enemy of the music of Wagner and any other proponent of the new music.

" 'Music has no subject beyond the combinations of notes we hear, for music speaks not only by means of sounds, it speaks nothing but sound.' I believe that is a fair recitation of Hanslick's central thesis," Kraus said, pleased with himself. "Thus, Romanticism with its emphasis on feelings was his sworn enemy. Wagner's dramatics and use of music to further such drama fell afoul of the critic's theories. But Wagner got back at Hanslick, you know, with the buffoonish and pedantic critic Beckmesser in *Die Meistersinger von Nürnberg.* Wagner had wanted to call the character Hans Lick, but his lawyers changed his mind for him. Of course, Wagner was not the only target of Hanslick's barbs. Bruckner, who supported Wagner, and who committed the great sin of deviating from the classical mode also became anathema. Hanslick went so far as to block performances of Bruckner's music and to use all his influence to keep that simple country organist even from teaching. But in that respect, Hanslick was not totally successful. Though Hanslick managed to prevent him from being appointed a professor at the University of Vienna, Bruckner did teach organ and counterpoint at the conservatory. I believe your friend Mahler was a student and early devotee, as was Hugo Wolf, another special target for Hanslick's critical venom."

Werthen made the sudden connection: Hanslick had been the man in the top hat obstructing his view at Strauss's funeral, the one who accused him of picking his pocket.

"I believe we had an informal meeting once," Werthen blurted out, and then explained the odd circumstances of that meeting.

"Watch yourself, or you will end up skewered in his column one fine day," Kraus said. "Though he is in semiretirement, he still casts the odd poison dart from time to time. Strange he was at Strauss's funeral at all. He had no love for the man's music."

Gross had sat quietly through this seeming aside, but now interrupted.

"Was there a cause of death mentioned?"

"No, nothing of that sort. Though, as I said, Bruckner had been ill the final years of his life. An odd sort of man. Dressed abominably, like a schoolmaster from the country. Which in fact his father was. All Bruckner really cared about was his music. Playing the organ and composing. Quite helpless in the ways of the big city. There is the very charming story of Bruckner once pressing a tip into the palm of Hans Richter after that man successfully conducted his Fourth Symphony."

"And Brahms?" Gross prompted.

"That was a bit more straightforward. He died of liver cancer, the same complaint that took his father. That was in April, I believe, two years ago. And if you ask me about *his* will, there you will have a story of human deceit, concupiscence, and greed. In short, Herr Brahms died without a will and that set everyone from his landlady to his music publisher to distant German cousins snarling at one another over the quite substantial wealth the man left. The matter is still working its way through the courts. But then, Advokat Werthen, I assume you would be only too aware of the case. Like something out of Dickens."

"To be sure," Werthen said, happy that he had nothing to do with it, for the proceedings were sure to go on for another decade and suck dry the bank accounts of the litigants. "Brahms will certainly make his way into textbook lore as a prime example for writing one's will in a timely fashion."

"Brahms, of course, was on the other side

of the divide in the War of the Romantics," Gross said.

Kraus nodded his head emphatically. "He and Hanslick were a pair. Brahms even let him see his compositions before they were performed. Together they conspired to create the musical culture of Vienna. They sat on prize committees, passing judgment on the works of young conservatory musicians. There was one poor unfortunate . . . I forget his name now, but it will come to me. One student, at any rate, said to have real musical genius. Brahms declared that the youth's composition, a symphony, had simply not been written by him. Too good to be the work of a simple conservatory student. It destroyed the student's career. He was taken off a train not long after, delirious and babbling on about Brahms having set a bomb on the train. He later died in an asylum."

Kraus broke off, looking upward to a swath of spiderwebbing hanging from the ceiling like a tattered pennon, seemingly attempting to retrieve the missing name.

"Do you mean a fellow named Rott?" Werthen offered, for Berthe had informed him of that young man mentioned by Emma Adler.

"That's the very one," Kraus said. "Hans Rott. How clever of you, Advokat."

Werthen nodded at this, somewhat surprised at the mention of the young musician in these two different contexts.

"At any rate," Kraus continued, "Brahms was not simply or solely a stuffed shirt. He was a great friend of Strauss, did you know that?"

Both Werthen and Gross allowed that they did not.

"Yes, despite Hanslick's contempt for Strauss's music, Brahms was a real devotee. He even wrote an inscription on Adele Strauss's fan. Under the opening notes of the *Blue Danube* he noted, 'Alas, not by Brahms.' He had a sense of playfulness. There was all that business about musical coding."

Kraus looked to them for a sign of recognition, but again Werthen and Gross were quite in the dark as to his references.

"I refer, in the first instance, to the piece he wrote with Schumann, the *F–A–E Sonata,* dedicated to a violinist whose motto was *Frei aber einsam,* free but alone. They used the musical notes of F, A, and E to play with that theme. Brahms later modified that to F–A–F, *frei aber froh,* free but happy. He also included sweet references to the ladies in his life in such codes. Clara Schumann, for example, with musical themes using C and an E-flat standing for S. The same for Adele Strauss, so they say. The A–E-flat combination is everywhere in his later music."

"Are you saying that Brahms and Frau Strauss were —"

"Hardly," Kraus said. "Actually, I quite believe great composers to be like eunuchs or Catholic priests. Married to a higher art or god. Even with Clara Schumann, who was, after all, widowed, Brahms conducted to all accounts a sexless affair. But he was *true* to her to the very end, one of the chief mourners at her funeral. Which came, by the way, less than a year before Brahms's own death."

Kraus smiled at them, as much amused at his uncanny ability of recall as at Werthen's and Gross's interest in his tales.

"And speaking of Clara Schumann, there is one more interesting bit about Brahms. She was his one true confidante. Max Kalbeck himself told me this story."

Meaning, Werthen registered, the well-known music critic and longtime friend of Brahms who was busy writing a monumental life of the composer.

"Kalbeck told me of a private communication sent to Frau Schumann regarding Hanslick's magnum opus, *The Beautiful in*

Music. To Hanslick's face, Brahms was all praise, but to Clara Schumann he confessed he found the work so stupid that he had to give up reading it and only hoped Hanslick would not quiz him on it."

Another moment of silence as the import of this story settled in.

"You have certainly given us some things to think about, Herr Kraus."

Gross rose from his chair with effort. They had been sitting for some time, and Werthen too could feel a twinge in his right knee as he stood.

"Thanks, Kraus," Werthen said with sincerity.

"Not to mention," the journalist said, now rising from behind his desk, too. "Gives the gray cells a chance to perform. But, if you ever do get to the bottom of all this, you must promise to inform me."

"That we shall do, Herr Kraus," Gross said, donning his bowler and making his way briskly out of the office.

At the office on Habsburgergasse, Berthe was just finishing with the afternoon mail. The letter from Mahler had been hidden by larger envelopes, or else she would have opened it first. The man's handwriting was neat and precise, so different from his ruffled physical appearance. She read quickly through it, discovering that the composer had yet more alterations he wanted made to his will and requested that Karl come as soon as possible.

Not likely, she thought. She would dispatch Tor instead, and this weekend, no sooner. After all, Mahler was not their only client, though he acted as if he were. It was patently obvious to her that Mahler was becoming far too dependent on her husband. She even wondered at the reality of this sudden change for his will. It was more probable that he was using it as an excuse just to get Karl in his orbit again.

No, this weekend was soon enough. She needed Tor here for the rest of the week to take care of the backlog of other paying clients while Karl was off with Gross chasing ghosts.

Unkind thought, but true. Figments. Spirits. Fabrications of some deluded mind. That is how she saw the anonymous letter. And meanwhile she had developed, through her conversations with Rosa Mayreder and Emma Adler, a perfectly viable line of investigation.

Put it on hold, darling, Karl had counseled her at lunch today. *Gross and I may be onto something.*

Well, she was not going to put it on hold. She was assuredly not going to become the office mule while her husband and Gross were off having a fine time tilting at windmills. She knew who she needed to talk to next: Natalie Bauer-Lechner. The lady who knew all about Mahler from his conservatory days. But she was with Mahler in Altaussee.

Perhaps *she* should go to Mahler instead of Tor. Two birds with one stone.

Suddenly an acid taste made her wince. No, she thought. Not now. Not here.

But she had no choice.

She barely made it to the communal washroom in the hallway before disgorging most of Frau Blatschky's wonderful lunch.

My dear child, she thought as she looked at her disheveled hair in the mirror, wiping her mouth with alpine cold water. I hope you will be worth it.

But then it was as if she could feel the tiny, precious life inside of her, and knew that it would be worth any effort.

ELEVEN

Soft rosy light leaked through a crack in the heavy drapes. Werthen had just awoken from a dream of his childhood on the family estate in Lower Austria. He and Stein, the gamekeeper and general factotum for the Werthen estate, were indulging in one of the "Master's" (Stein's label for the young Karl Werthen) favorite pastimes: blowing up beaver dams in the brooks that fed the large ponds dotting the estate. Karl's father, Herr Werthen, loved to watch the birds of passage that would settle on those ponds for a few hours, days, or months. But the beaver dams kept fresh water from feeding and filtering those ponds. If left unattended, the ponds would turn fetid in a matter of weeks. Thus, periodically old Stein would break out the sticks of dynamite he kept stored in the toolshed under lock and key and explode the larger dams. The smaller ones, he would tackle by hand.

The gamekeeper knew his way around dynamite, knew how to set a charge and detonate it from a distance. In his dream, Werthen watched Stein's calloused fingers attaching red and blue wires with the efficient dexterity of a fine violinist. Stein, despite his age, eschewed the old-fashioned fuse, which one lit with a safety match; opting instead for a battery-operated detonator. Wonder of wonders, Stein then allowed Werthen to push the plunger on the detonator, setting off an immense roar and a spray of water and broken sticks. And there the dream broke off.

Werthen felt alert and expectant this morning, filled with a sort of buoyant optimism that he carried around with him like a talisman. It was a sort of puppyish joy that irritated Berthe on the best of days first thing in the morning.

She was still sleeping, though somewhat fitfully. Uncommon for her not to sleep deeply, but perhaps it was the baby, he thought. He rolled to his side and looked at her as she slept on her back, her hair splayed out on the damask pillow slip. A twitch at her left eye. The steady thrum of blood pulsed in a vein just under her ear. A scatter of freckles played across the bridge of her nose and upper cheeks. Her steady breathing was suddenly broken; she breathed deeply then opened an eye, saw him gazing at her and smiled.

"Morning, darling," he said.

Her response came out a muted "hmmm."

"Looks like another beautiful day."

Another muttered groan as she rolled on her side, turning away from him.

He spooned his body around hers, hugging her tightly with his right arm.

"So cheerful so early," she whispered.

"Reason to be."

Another noncommittal "hmmm" from her.

He smelled her hair and felt a smile settle over his entire face.

"I am sorry about sticking you with all the business," he said, returning to the conversation they had had at bedtime last night. "Gross is fixated on these new leads and I must admit he has kindled my interest, as well."

She rolled over onto her back again, opening one eye at him. "*Kindled* your interest? There goes the pompous lawyer again."

He kissed her cheek. "All right. I've got a feeling about this, that it might actually lead to much larger things."

"Larger than someone trying to kill the director of the Hofoper?" Both eyes now open. "Karl, not every case involves high-level conspiracies and killings."

"Right."

"Meaning *wrong*." She sighed. "Are you forgetting that Brahms died of cancer?"

"I am not a doctor, but I intend to consult one. For now let us assume that someone might be able to replicate the symptoms of liver cancer with some poison or drug."

Berthe made no reply to this. Instead, she said, "I can't sleep on my side anymore."

"Nausea?"

"Oh, yes. And heartburn. Why do they call it morning sickness? I get it all day and night."

"Poor darling." He ran a sympathetic hand through her hair but she shrugged it away.

"I am not a poor anything. But my body has never let me down before."

"It's not letting you down, just preparing for the new life."

"By making me so sick I can't eat? If you subscribe to Mr. Darwin's principles, then you must admit there is a wrinkle in the evolutionary process that needs to be ironed out."

They lay together a few more moments in silence.

"I am going to proceed with the conservatory leads to Mahler," she finally said.

"Yes, do. I think that is a good idea."

"I wasn't asking for permission."

When he did not reply, she added, "Sorry. They say you get bad-tempered the first few months. Another evolutionary advance, I suppose."

At breakfast they learned that Gross had already risen, eaten — two eggs, a sweet bun, and two cups of coffee, according to a mightily put-upon Frau Blatschky — and was off for his morning stroll.

"He said he would return by nine," the cook said as she brought in the Augarten porcelain pot, filling the room with the rich aroma of fresh coffee.

Berthe waited for Frau Blatschky to close the door behind her before crying out, "Even the *smell* of it makes me sick."

Werthen put his napkin over the pot, attempting to quell the spread of coffee aroma. After a few moments, she was better and they were able to discuss the day's schedule.

He and Gross had scheduled an interview with the critic Hanslick. Many roads seemed to lead to him. According to Kraus's information, the man was a staunch enemy of both Bruckner and Strauss. Could musical dislikes actually lead to murder? Werthen did not know, but his brief encounter with the critic at Strauss's funeral demonstrated an active temper in the man. But how to link Hanslick to Brahms's death? After all, they had been intimates.

Werthen, however, had done his homework yesterday afternoon at the Imperial Library following their meeting with Kraus. He had gone through the past decade of reviews by Hanslick in the *Neue Freie Presse* and had discovered that, shortly before Brahms's death, Hanslick had written a series of reviews of the master's final clarinet quintets, noting that Brahms had betrayed classical ideals with such emotional music. Add to this the story Kraus had related yesterday of Brahms's disparaging comments about Hanslick's book — after all, if Kraus had got wind of the story, why not Hanslick himself — and there might well be sufficient motive to link Hanslick to the deaths of all three composers.

Neither was Hanslick a champion of Mahler. Surprisingly, given Mahler's position in the earlier Wagner-Brahms divide, Hanslick had initially welcomed Mahler to Vienna in 1897. His first reviews had even praised the composer-conductor's devotion to texts, whether they were by Wagner or

Mozart. But such enthusiasm soon turned to vitriol; more recent notices, Werthen discovered yesterday, disparaged Mahler's work at the Hofoper, worrying that the man was ruining centuries of tradition in a headlong and rather ill-advised attempt at modernity.

Thus, there were many reasons to interview Hanslick, not least of which that he might prove to be their major suspect. Werthen wondered if the man would remember him; after all, Hanslick's anger at the funeral had got the better of the older man, even with the policeman involved in that altercation. However, if Hanslick did recognize him, it could, as Gross had pointed out, be all to the good, discomfiting the critic and putting him off balance. Their bona fides, as attested to by Prince Montenuovo, made them above reproach for a man of the establishment such as Hanslick. Thus, it would be a confusing situation for the critic to discover that a man whom you had accused of being a common thief turns out to be a top-level emissary for the lord chamberlain.

"I thought of paying a visit to the offices of the *Arbeiter Zeitung*," Berthe in turn explained. "If I get this nausea under control. I have not spoken to Victor Adler in months. He was a personal friend of Mahler's once."

Werthen nodded. "And you still think it is best to make the trip to Altaussee?" he asked.

She was about to erupt, but took a moment and understood that he was only showing his concern for her, not attempting to control her movements.

"It perhaps can wait. After all, they'll all be coming back to Vienna next month. I can talk to Natalie then."

"And Tor?" Werthen asked. "I think you are absolutely correct about Mahler growing a bit too needy and dependent on me. After all, what can happen with the police guarding him day and night?"

They decided to dispatch Tor sooner rather than later. Berthe would see to it this morning. Tor could thus be in Altaussee in the late afternoon and be able to return to Vienna on Thursday. Werthen could go to the office and pick up some of the loose threads of the practice in the afternoon. Gross had talked about speaking with cleaning ladies who had served Bruckner and Brahms; Werthen thought the criminologist could deal with that task on his own.

"So," he said, drinking off the last of his coffee, "settled."

She swallowed hard, putting down the crisp of toast she was about to eat.

"Not quite," she said, rising and making her way quickly toward the bathroom.

Eduard Hanslick met them at the Café Frauenhuber on the Himmelpfortgasse in the Inner City. One of the city's newest cafés, it had begun life as a bath house, but after five hundred years of keeping the population clean, it became, in 1795, a restaurant run by the former pastry chef to Empress Maria Theresa. During that incarnation, Mozart and Beethoven had conducted their works in a specially built concert hall in the building. It was not until 1891 that the present café was established, but in less than a decade the Frauenhuber had become a Viennese institution, its bank of windows on the narrow cobbled street providing a welcome dose of natural light.

It was a bit of a haven in the Inner City, Werthen thought, the very spirit of Viennese *gemütlichkeit.* As they entered the café, he was greeted by the beckoning aroma of *zwetschkenstrudel* — the unmistakable smell of freshly baked plums. The marble tables, red velvet benches, and bentwood Thonet chairs fit well with the low, corbelled ceiling and parquet floor. An array of small oil paintings — landscapes, portraits — hung on the mortared walls, a rack of well-thumbed newspapers stood by the door, and the waiters in their black tuxedoes and white ties moved unobtrusively with their heavily laden silver trays held shoulder height on upraised palms. One such waiter was just making presentation of a coffee to Hanslick, who was seated in the far corner, near the recently installed telephone.

Werthen recognized this *herr ober*. Herr Otto, he was called, a former waiter at the Café Landtmann. It had been some time since Werthen had last seen the man.

Herr Otto, once he had finished serving Hanslick, also recognized Werthen and nodded politely at him as he and Gross approached Hanslick's table.

"Good day to you, Advokat," the waiter said, a slight — some might say mischievous — grin on his face.

"And how are you, Herr Otto? Changed locales, I see."

There was no winter coat for the waiter to hump off his shoulders; instead he waited for Werthen and Gross to dislodge their summer hats, and swept them up in his right hand with a certain reverence.

"Thanks to you, Herr Advokat. Thanks to you."

"Not returning to the Landtmann, then?"

Herr Otto shook his head vehemently. "Never in this life. No trust, sir. A terrible thing that. As terrible as was the deed you did me good."

A small thing, actually, Werthen reflected. Herr Otto, the former headwaiter at the Café Landtmann, and something of a local legend, had lost his position, accused of theft. Another waiter, Herr Turnig, had gone to the management claiming that he had seen Otto, on several occasions, taking money out of the till as he did the closing. As Turnig was a cousin of the owner's wife, his word was respected in the matter. Herr Otto was fired and subsequently, Herr Turnig himself became headwaiter.

Werthen had known Otto for years and when informed of his troubles and assured of the man's innocence, he had taken it upon himself to clear up matters. This was during the time he was still convalescing from his leg wound and had wanted to keep his hand in with investigations. A simple enough matter, really, for if Herr Otto were innocent of the charges, that meant that Herr Turnig had fabricated them and had stolen the money himself, for indeed the accounts were off by several thousand crowns. The motive, beyond the money, was obvious: ambition. Herr Otto's disgrace allowed Turnig to take over his position at the noble Café Landtmann.

Werthen began by investigating the private life of Herr Turnig, and quickly discovered the man was living well beyond his means, residing in a spacious apartment in the First District and keeping a summer chalet in Carinthia.

Confronted with these facts, Herr Turnig quickly folded under Werthen's questioning. He absconded rather than waiting for the police to arrive at his door, and was reportedly now working as a waiter in Florence, beyond the reach of Austrian authorities.

Herr Otto's good name was restored and he had become headwaiter at the Frauenhuber, another good reason for Werthen to change his café preferences from the Landtmann to the Frauenhuber.

Herr Otto took Werthen's hand now, shaking it firmly.

"If you do not mind, sir, a million thanks to you. And from my wife. The usual, I assume, for both you and your friend?"

Werthen nodded.

The exchange had been the matter of but a few instants, yet it had caught the attention of several of the customers, Hanslick among them. Gross, who already knew of Werthen's assistance to the waiter, focused his attention on the music critic, and Werthen now eyed the man, too.

There was no hint of recognition in Hanslick's eyes.

"Herr Hanslick?" Gross inquired.

The smallish man half stood, nodding at them.

"At your service, gentlemen. Dr. Gross and Advokat Werthen is it?"

He nodded at them as he spoke their names, indicating them wrongly, but Werthen quickly corrected the confusion as they joined him at table.

Gross then set right to the task at hand.

"I imagine you are wondering at the purpose of our interview, Herr Hanslick."

The critic allowed a slight smile to cross his lips; he gestured with a small hand — a wave of assent.

"I admit to curiosity. As a functionary of his majesty's government, however, I bow to official requests."

"Yes," Gross said. "The prince said you were a most forthcoming and cooperative servant."

Werthen knew the criminologist had chosen the word "servant" carefully — its resonance was broad and powerful. Hanslick was the sort of man who needed reminding of his official status.

Herr Otto delivered two coffees for Werthen and Gross, appearing and disappearing with barely a notice.

"I and my colleague, Advokat Werthen, have had a chance to peruse your work," Gross went on, "especially your informed and excellent *The Beautiful in Music,* and I can say we both think you are the perfect man for the job."

Hanslick beamed at the praise, but also squinted his eyes in incomprehension.

"Which job would that be, gentlemen?"

"Prince Montenuovo has conceived of a project to educate the young of our empire in its cultural assets. To that end, he wishes to prepare several school primers in the arts, from music to painting to sculpture and design. Each tome shall be written by the absolute authority in the field. When it came to music, your name, Herr Hanslick, was, of course, at the very top of the list."

"A primer?"

Gross shook his head. "An ill-chosen term, perhaps. A book, indeed, to share the musical wealth of this great land of ours. To fill the young with the wonders of our composers. And who better situated than you to do so?"

Gross smiled unctuously at the critic. It really was a good performance, Werthen had to admit. He almost believed that such a project actually existed. This time, however, unlike their supposed commission from Mahler to Frau Strauss, Werthen and Gross had cleared the ruse with Prince Montenuovo first. If Hanslick were to check on the authenticity of this supposed primer at the office of the lord chamberlain, he would be reassured. Then, of course, after the passage of some time, the same office would regretfully announce that the project had been postponed.

"Well, I am pleased," Hanslick began.

"Excellent, excellent," Gross enthused. "We have come, however, to ensure that the full breadth of compositional skills will be included in such a work. We are, naturally, aware of your position in the so-called War of the Romantics."

Hanslick raised a hand at this; his small, blunt fingers tapped at them, as if playing the piano.

"Please, not that old baggage."

"Old baggage, sir?" Gross said.

Hanslick took a sip from is coffee. "The musical quibbles of decades ago. High time to let all that matter rest."

"We had rather thought that you had

strong opinions regarding certain of our composers," Werthen said delicately.

"Strong opinions, to be sure. I assume you are fearful that I shall give short shrift to those such as Bruckner or Strauss who veered too much to the emotional in music?"

"Well," Werthen went on, "it had crossed our minds. I believe you referred to the 'muddled hangover style' of Bruckner's Eighth Symphony in your notice of its premiere."

"My critics, I fear, do not always understand me. Or perhaps they do and simply misrepresent what I really say. Some would indicate that I have drawn the line in the sand: whether a musical composition can be regarded as an intellectual or emotional content embodied in tones, or can be regarded as nothing but a contentless tonal structure. My critics — some might say enemies — claim I do the latter to the detriment of the former. However, I believe I have built a rational argument in my tract, *The Beautiful in Music,* between these two extremes. It is true I found and continue to find Bruckner's work tedious. The Eighth, as other Bruckner symphonies, was interesting in detail but strange as a whole and even repugnant. The nature of the work consists basically in applying Wagner's dramatic style to the symphonic form."

"And Wagner's work is . . ." Gross searched for the proper word.

"Overly dramatic?" Hanslick supplied for him. "Do not misunderstand me. I was quite a fan of Wagner in my youth, and I still enjoy much of his music. However, it is the theory behind it to which I take exception. Yes, I once wrote that the prelude to *Tristan und Isolde* reminds me of an old Italian painting of a martyr whose intestines are slowly unwound from his body on a reel. But that is not the entire oeuvre of the man, nor my entire estimation. For Wagner, music was a means for presenting drama, for evoking emotion. But music should not be understood in terms of emotion. It is not essential to music to possess emotions, arouse emotions, express emotions, or even represent emotions. No, gentlemen, the true value of music lies within the formal aesthetics of music itself, not in the expression of extramusical feelings."

Werthen watched Hanslick closely as he spoke with what Werthen could only describe as restrained enthusiasm or muted emotion. Such must be his lectures at the university. From what Mahler had told him (for Mahler, as a student at the university had taken Hanslick's class), the critic stood at a lectern and read into his moustache from scripted notes, in a nearly inaudible, high-pitched monotone, "soporific but not displeasing" as Mahler put it. At the piano, his small hands and fingers moved quickly and economically over the keys while he swayed to the music and kept time with a tapping foot, playing always from memory. Mahler felt these lectures were comical to behold, but not unmusical.

Werthen also remembered that Hanslick was, first of all, a trained lawyer. He did present a convincing argument.

"If you have read my eulogy to Strauss, then you could hardly count me an enemy to his music, either," Hanslick said. "My notice in the *Neue Freie Presse* grieved his death as the loss of our most original musical talent."

Both Gross and Werthen showed even more amazement at this.

"Oh, I know," Hanslick said, seeing their astonishment. "Everyone likes to quote me about how his melodies made people unfit for serious music. What they seem to be unaware of is that admonition was made against his father, and was said when I was a very young and irascible sort of critic, out to make a name for myself. But I mourned the death of Johan Strauss the Elder as well, writing that Vienna had lost its most talented composer with his death. For the son, Johann the Younger, I had great admiration. His rhythms pulsated with animated variety, the sources of his melodic invention were as fine as they were inexhaustible. He was a noble gentleman. One of the last great symbols of a pleasant time now coming abruptly to an end. We are, I am sure you are aware, on the very cusp of the twentieth century. Only months left to this elegant century to which we all belong. And who knows what horrors await us on the other side of midnight, December 31, 1899?"

"What indeed?" Gross agreed.

"But I am not trying to 'sell myself' as the Americans say," Hanslick continued. "I should indeed be honored to add my thoughts to the prince's project. Yet I tell you all this not out of a desire to curry favor; instead, I dislike intensely being misunderstood and misquoted."

He drained his coffee cup, then adjusted the bottom edges of his mustache with his right forefinger.

"And now, gentlemen, I must take my leave of you. I have a lecture to prepare for this afternoon."

As he left, Hanslick looked Werthen closely

in the eye.

"A pleasure to make your acquaintance again, sir, under more favorable circumstances."

He left before the shocked Werthen had a chance to reply.

"You know, Gross," Werthen said after Hanslick had left the café. "I do not believe that fellow was one bit taken in by our little tale of a school primer."

"I agree, Werthen. A very astute judge of character, I should say."

"Then why continue with the farce?"

"Hardly a farce, dear Werthen. Our story may have been fabricated, but there is nothing false about our credentials from Prince Montenuovo. One can be sure that he checked our bona fides before agreeing to this little talk. No, Herr Hanslick is not a fool. He clearly saw our real intentions — gathering information about his relations with Bruckner and Strauss — and wisely delivered the information we were seeking."

"But can we believe him?"

"Your investigation, Werthen."

"Damn, Gross, must you be forever contentious?"

The criminologist merely raised his eyebrows.

"All right," Werthen said. "Yes, I think we can trust him. Partisan he may be, but I also felt a note of sincerity in how he felt, above all, about Strauss."

Gross nodded. "And we can also check his obituary notice in the *Neue Freie Presse.* But I do not sense that he was lying."

"We may, in fact, be able to check him off our list of suspects," Werthen added. "Provisionally."

Herr Otto delivered a pair of glasses of water, nodding solemnly as he did so.

"Herr Hanslick is something of a legend," Otto offered.

"He comes in here regularly?" Werthen asked.

Herr Otto slightly nodded his head. "Generally at this table. And often in the company of his colleague, Herr Kalbeck."

Meaning Max Kalbeck, Werthen thought. The music critic for the *Neues Wiener Tagblatt* and the friend of Brahms whom Kraus had mentioned as the source of his story about how Brahms had disliked Hanslick's musical tract.

"Colleagues, you say?"

Another slight nod from Herr Otto. "They meet at least three or four times each week here. Often they share remarks on texts they have written. Herr Kalbeck was here in fact just minutes before you gentlemen arrived. No texts today, though. The two of them were sat hunched together speaking in whispers like conspirators. When I delivered their coffee, they broke off the conversation and only started again once I was out of earshot."

Which might or might not have something to do with their meeting with Hanslick, Werthen thought.

"Tell me, Advokat. Are you working on another case? Is that what brings you here? Something involving Herr Hanslick, perhaps?"

Werthen was amazed at the seeming pleasure Herr Otto took in such questions.

"Just like that English gentleman, eh?" Otto said. "Always smoking his pipe, playing his violin, and catching the culprit."

Which comment brought an angry clearing of the throat from Gross, who continued to claim that Arthur Conan Doyle had stolen from his own early writings in the creation of his character, Sherlock Holmes.

"Not a bit like the English gentleman, I assure you," Werthen was quick to say.

Herr Otto waited a moment, as if in hopes that Werthen might answer his other question, as well. But Werthen merely smiled.

"What is the expression?" the waiter said

before moving off to another customer. "Thick as thieves. That's what Herr Hanslick and Kalbeck looked like before you gentlemen arrived."

So much for his plans to put in an afternoon of work back at the office. Instead, Werthen felt compelled to follow up the lead from Herr Otto and speak with Max Kalbeck.

But Kalbeck was not at his office at the *Neues Wiener Tagblatt,* nor did his editor know when he might return.

"Max makes his own schedules," the man told Werthen, looking not the least bit abashed at such an admission, for it seemed Kalbeck had powerful *beziehungen,* connections, with the publisher of the paper — his mother had been the publisher's mother's best friend in school — and could indeed set the times of his coming and going.

The editor, Herr Pfingsten, had a head as round as a wheel of farmer's rye bread. Stuck into it like buttons on a scarecrow were two eyes so dark they appeared black. A smudge of a mustache covered his long upper lip; heavily pomaded hair was combed forward giving him the aspect of a disreputable Roman senator.

"He has his contacts," Pfingsten added, putting heavy irony on the last word. "In my day, we went to the performance, listened carefully, took notes, and then wrote up a notice for the next day's paper. Now it's all contacts, inside information, Hofoper gossip. I ask you, is this music or military espionage we're covering?"

Werthen could not answer the question for the gray-faced Herr Pfingsten and took his leave. So, an afternoon at his own office, after all.

Herr Tor had been sent to Altaussee, and Berthe was supposedly visiting Viktor Adler, so Werthen thought he would not be distracted in any way from catching up on work. As he approached the doorway on the Habsburgergasse, Werthen noticed that it had been left ajar. He had complained of this several times to the *portier,* Frau Ignatz, an aging woman with a penchant for cats. One of the tenants on the upper floors consistently neglected to pull the street door completely shut. A nuisance, really, for anyone could enter the building.

Frau Ignatz was not in her lodge in the foyer, so Werthen filed his complaint for another time. He went to his office on the second floor, and thought for a moment that he saw a shadow pass in front of the frosted glass of the door. But then that was impossible.

301

Or perhaps Berthe had decided to help out at the office instead. He felt a sudden surge of pride at the fact that she should give up her own investigation to help out at the office. Especially in her condition.

The door was locked, but that did not mean she was not inside. After all, it was still officially lunchtime, and the office was closed from noon until two.

He slipped his key into the lock, twisted it, and opened the door.

"Berthe," he called out, for the reception was empty. "You here?"

There was no answer. He felt suddenly deflated. Well, nothing for it then but to get busy with paperwork.

He entered his office and was momentarily shocked to see drawers pulled out of the desk and papers strewn everywhere. He sensed a movement behind him, but before he could react, a sharp crack of pain tore into the back of his head. His knees gave out and he slumped to the floor, unconscious.

"My God, Werthen, you could have been killed." Gross dabbed at the wound with a wet compress. "This might need sutures."

Werthen's head pounded like a timpani. He raised himself on one elbow and could not resist the temptation to put his other hand to the wound. It felt wet and warm; taking his hand away he saw blood, but not quantities.

"Someone broke in," he said.

"Apparently," Gross agreed.

"How long have I been unconscious?"

"I am a criminalist, not a psychic, Werthen. When did you arrive?"

"A little after one."

Gross glanced at the standard clock on the wall behind them.

"Then about a half hour. The landladies to Brahms and Bruckner have both taken themselves off to the country for the month, so I decided to meet you back here."

Gross examined the mess of the office for a moment.

"Did you see who attacked you?"

"No. No time."

"What could he have been after?" Gross asked.

"You think it is our man?" Werthen was now sitting up and despite a momentary dizziness, he thought he would be all right. No concussion. No hospital. That was the last place he wanted to be today.

"I see no other conclusion possible. Unless you are currently engaged in some rather sensitive matter of a contentious will."

Werthen shook his head, a mistake that turned the timpani into a kettledrum. He closed his eyes and squeezed the bridge of his nose.

"No," he finally managed to say. "Nothing like that."

"Then it seems patently obvious to me. But what the devil could he have been searching for? Do you keep private papers here?"

"No," Werthen said again. And then a sudden fear tore at him. "My notes of the investigation are at home. My God, Gross. Might he have gone there? Berthe . . ."

"Quickly, man," Gross grabbed his left arm and helped him to stand. "Not a minute to lose."

After the first few steps he was able to control his nausea. The first flight of stairs down was an agony, but then he began to deal with the pain, the dizziness. As they passed Frau Ignatz's lodge, the *portier* saw his condition and came to the door.

"Advokat, what is it? Blood."

"Not to worry, madam," Gross said bluffly.

But her concern was not for Werthen.

"I knew it would mean trouble. That sign of yours. It attracts all the riff raff of Vienna. And now this. In my house!"

She turned and closed the door of the lodge behind her before either Gross or Werthen could reply.

They were in luck; a *fiaker* was just passing by outside. On the ride to the Josefstadt and his apartment, Werthen tried to console himself with the thought that Berthe had planned, after her brief morning at the office, to visit Victor Adler. She would not be home; she would be safe. He must believe that; he must.

But what of Frau Blatschky? Had he put her in danger's way?

The *fiaker* was held up for a time when one of the new electrified streetcars on the Josefstädterstrasse stalled, blocking the intersection at Langegasse and backing up traffic in four directions.

Gross pounded the roof with his fist. "Find a way around this, my good man. We have an emergency."

The driver grumbled something about pregnancy, Werthen thought, some typically droll Viennese rejoinder. He was not in the mood for drollness.

"Fifty kreutzer if you find a way around this mess!" Werthen shouted at the driver out the window.

No witty riposte this time; instead the driver reined his horses to the left. There was a scraping and jolt as the *fiaker* took over part of the sidewalk for half a block, then skidded on the cobbles down a side street to detour around the stopped traffic. The man drove his two horses like a jockey at the racecourse in the Prater's Freudenau track. In no time they had circled the bottleneck and were back onto the Josef-städterstrasse just at Werthen's apartment house.

He quickly leaped from the *fiaker,* leaving Gross for once to pick up the tab of his extravagantly guaranteed tip.

He did not bother with the elevator, but instead took the stairs two at a time, heedless of the pain in the back of his head, or of his damaged right knee. Up the stairs he flew with Gross now puffing behind him.

Reaching his door, he tried the latch, but it was, as it should be, locked. He quickly turned his key in the lock, threw the door open, and called out.

"Frau Blatschky!"

There was no sound and for a moment Werthen panicked, thinking the worst. But from the foyer, the apartment looked undisturbed.

Gross now joined him, breathing quite heavily, and they moved into the sitting room.

A sudden movement behind them put them both on guard.

"You simply must be more quiet, Advokat."

It was Frau Blatschky standing in the doorway to the sitting room.

"There you are," Werthen said.

"Well, of course I am here. And so is your poor dear wife. And future mother." She positively beamed as she spoke these words. "You should have told me. The poor woman cannot stand rich food now. It won't do. I have her in bed, where she should have been before. Yes, and some soothing chicken broth. We shall eat more simply now that I know of her condition."

"She's all right?"

"Of course. But she is with child." Another smile at this statement. "And we must all be considerate of that."

"Do I take that to mean no more *zwiebel-rostbraten?*" Gross asked.

"And no more *bauernschmaus* or *palatschinken* or other such rich foodstuffs that will unsettle the lady's stomach," Frau Blatschky declared.

Gross looked downcast.

"And morning coffee?"

"Herbal tea shall suffice," she sternly answered. "Now what sort of mischief have

307

you got into, Advokat? There is blood down the back of your collar."

TWELVE

Forty-eight hours later, Werthen was beginning to feel human again. He spent the rest of Wednesday and all of Thursday in bed, along with Berthe, Frau Blatschky fussing over the both of them, and no longer making eyes at them for sharing the same bed. At the end of it, he didn't care if he never saw another bowl of chicken soup again in his life.

One positive aspect of Berthe's morning sickness, however, was that it brought a rapprochement between the two women of the house. Now Frau Blatschky did not look upon Berthe as an uninvited guest, a modern woman who had no sense of domesticity; in short, as some sort of threat to her own position in the household. Berthe's pregnancy validated her in Frau Blatschky's eyes.

It was as if Frau Blatschky, the widow of a naval officer who had been killed only a week after their marriage, suddenly found in Berthe the daughter she had never had. And Werthen was not going to say one word that might upset this lovely new balance.

It had been Frau Blatschky, in fact, wisely enough, who made Werthen tell Berthe about the attack on him. He was at first reluctant, not wanting to burden or upset his wife, especially at this delicate time in her pregnancy. But Frau Blatschky convinced him that he must not lie to his wife, and Werthen was reminded of how earlier his failure to be honest about his parents had caused an unneeded rift between them.

In fact, Berthe took the news of the attack at the office quite well, telling him only that the back of his head had been rather too prominent anyway.

Gross and he had also had plenty of time to speculate about the attack over the past two days: the possible perpetrator and possible reasons. Still they came up with nothing plausible. Was it a message, then? A warning? For there was scant little to be learned about their investigation from any files in Werthen's office or home.

But if it were meant as a warning, then it was most unsuccessful, for it only made Werthen more determined than ever to get to the bottom of this case.

Thursday afternoon, after Gross had made inquiries and with Berthe up and out of bed for an afternoon stroll about the apartment, he and the criminologist conferred, Werthen still flat on his back in bed.

After questioning by Gross, Frau Ignatz could remember seeing no strangers in the building on Wednesday. Of course she had been absent when Werthen himself had entered the building.

"A most impertinent woman," Gross said in addition, but would not elaborate.

Gross also found it interesting that though the street door had been left open to the Habsburgergasse building that day, the door to Werthen's office had been locked.

"This could imply someone on the inside," Gross said.

Werthen had dissented at this suggestion. "The only person on the inside, as you say, is Tor. And he was off to Altaussee."

Gross nodded at this, pursing his lips, and had begun speaking of nibs, pin wrenches, edge levers, and all assortment of other tools of the breaking-and-entry trade.

"Someone skilled in the profession could open your lock from the outside, and in a matters of seconds, not minutes," Gross said with a faint hint of disapproval at the primitive state of the lock in question. "However, one wonders why he would lock the door behind him."

"Clearly the person wanted to make things appear normal," Werthen replied. "What if a client came early, and, ignorant of the midday closing, simply opened the door and stepped into a burglary in progress? Also, as was the case, the locked door bought the man time. Hearing me put my key in the lock, he was able to sequester himself and take me unawares when I entered the inner office."

"True," Gross said. "I have considered these things myself." However, he did not look convinced.

In the end, they decided not to inform the police of the break-in. There was no reason to clutter their investigation further.

Friday Werthen was able to return to the office by midmorning. Tor had already straightened up the place. Werthen, owing the man no marital loyalty, decided to not tell Tor the full story, merely that there had been an intruder who had gone through files and that, owing to a bit of bad fish he'd eaten, he had not been able to make it to the office for a couple of days.

Tor seemed genuinely alarmed at the fact someone had broken into the office, but Werthen quickly reassured him.

"We'll have Frau Ignatz on the lookout for any suspicious characters from now on."

Tor, however, took this bit of levity sincerely. "She is a cautious woman."

Werthen could only agree.

"And how was your little expedition to Altaussee, Herr Tor?"

"Uneventful, sir. But the sun was out for a change. And Herr Mahler's further inquiries were simple enough to deal with."

It seemed there was more to add, but that Tor was reluctant to proceed.

"But?" Werthen offered him an opening.

"Well, it is hardly for me to say, sir, but it seems he is being unduly harsh vis-à-vis his sister."

"But that has already been settled, I thought. Emma has been written out of the will."

"Not Emma, Advokat. It is Justine this time. If she marries Herr Rosé, then Mahler proposes to disinherit her, as well. That was what he wanted to add."

Werthen had expected as much. It seemed Arnold Rosé would fare no better than his brother Eduard if he married one of the Mahler girls. He wondered at what spite and animus could be involved in such a petty decision on Mahler's part, but it was hardly for him to judge. He and Tor were only the agents of such decisions, not the perpetrators.

He was about to make this case, when suddenly the outer office door burst open and in marched Alma Schindler in a state of high distress.

"My God, Advokat. It has happened again."

"Calm yourself, Fräulein," he said, taking her arm and ushering her into his office for privacy's sake.

He helped her take a seat by his desk.

"Now what is it. Another attack on Mahler? But that cannot be possible. The police —"

"No, not Mahler," she all but shrieked. "Zemlinsky this time. Every man I get close to is in danger, it seems."

She really was in a state; he feared that she might faint.

"Deep breaths, Fräulein Schindler," he advised, following Berthe's time-honored recipe. "Deep breaths. Follow my count."

By the time he reached ten, she had calmed herself enough to tell him what had happened.

The story sent shivers down his spine. Another composer. Another possible target.

Alexander Zemlinsky lived with his newly

widowed mother and sister Mathilde on Weissgerberstrasse, located in the Third District, but with a view over the canal to the Leopoldstadt, the Jewish quarter, from which they had recently resettled. The family represented the strange mélange of races and creeds that made up much of the population of Vienna. The father, Adolf, who had died earlier in the summer, was the son of Catholic parents but had fallen in love with Clara, the daughter of a Sephardic Jew and a Muslim woman. The entire family converted to Judaism, the religion in which Zemlinsky was raised.

Zemlinsky, so Kraus had once told Werthen, was a composer of promise. Three years Kraus's senior, he studied at the Vienna Conservatory, won prizes and accolades for his compositions, and this summer had been appointed music director at the Carl Theater, a stunning achievement for a man just turned twenty-eight. It was said that his opera, *Es War Einmal,* was to be staged by Mahler at the Hofoper next winter. Like Mahler, Zemlinsky renounced his Judaism in order to better assimilate.

As Werthen was led into the composer's room at the family dwelling he could see that the walls of this study-cum-bedroom were covered with all sorts of decorations.

Laurel wreaths adorned one entire wall; another was taken up with pictures of composers the young man obviously respected: Johannes Brahms had a place of prominence, for he had been an early champion of Zemlinsky's work, according to Kraus. Wagner was there as well, represented in a photogravure with a sprig of mistletoe lodged on the top of the frame as if the picture had been a Christmas gift. On the man's desk stood a bust of Brahms along with a picture of a young and very attractive woman.

Alma Schindler, in point of fact.

And the composer himself, all five feet two inches of him, lay on a daybed, a large plaster on his forehead. Kraus had delighted in shocking Werthen with rumors of this small man's gargantuan sexual adventures, for despite his stature and a face so ugly that it was vibrant, Zemlinsky seemed to attract beautiful or at least willing women like a toad draws princesses. His chin was almost nonexistent, his nose large and ungainly, and his eyes bulged so that it seemed they would pop out of his head at any instant.

Tending to him were several people: his sister, Mathilde; a young soprano who was introduced as Melanie Guttmann (whom

Werthen later learned was Zemlinsky's fiancée); and a rather portly young man with a receding hairline, a very intense gaze, and a soft collar — Herr Arnold Schoenberg, a former pupil of Zemlinsky's and a fellow member of Zemlinsky's small orchestra, Polyhymnia. By the manner in which Mathilde and Schoenberg exchanged looks during Werthen's visit, and their hands would inadvertently touch when pulling up the coverlet over the injured Zemlinsky or handing him a glass of water, Werthen assumed they were already courting.

The small, tangled world of Viennese music and musicians.

Fräulein Schindler made brief introductions, and as Zemlinsky was about to speak, Schoenberg cut him off.

"We told you this was unnecessary, Fräulein Schindler. It was merely a silly accident. Accidents do happen at theaters."

His voice was surprisingly high, but he spoke with vehemence.

"Poor Zem," Alma said. "It's all too dreadful. It was my fault for becoming your student. I am a curse to all those who get too close."

At this comment, Fräulein Guttmann visibly bristled.

"I am sure there is a logical explanation,"

she said. "We should not become overly melodramatic. It serves no purpose."

"Quiet, all of you," Zemlinsky said from his sickbed. "Just who is this fellow you have brought, Alma?"

Werthen spoke up before she had a chance to tell them too much about his investigations regarding Mahler.

"A family retainer who has lately taken to private inquiries, as well," he said. "Fräulein Schindler was fearful that something less, or rather more than accidental had happened to you. I agreed to accompany her. And I assure you, I do not tend toward melodrama."

"You speak like a lawyer," Zemlinsky said with obvious distaste. "Is that what you are?"

"Guilty," Werthen quipped.

Which brought the semblance of a smile to Zemlinsky's thin lips.

"Wonderful," Schoenberg whined. "Now the legal profession is involved. You *would* have to interfere."

This was directed at Alma Schindler, but she pointedly ignored the remark, instead getting onto her knees at the bedside, taking the composer's hand in hers, and kissing it.

"Please forgive me, Zem."

318

The room went deadly quiet at this performance. Even the volatile Schoenberg was at a loss for words.

Finally Zemlinsky broke the spell of communal embarrassment.

"Nonsense, girl. Up, up. Nothing to forgive. A cigar will set me right."

Werthen, whose own head still throbbed from his recent attack, doubted the veracity, but appreciated the bravado of this remark.

Alma did as she was told, standing again and looking at the others haughtily.

"And there is really no reason to waste your time, Advokat," the composer continued. "As Schoenberg here says, accidents do happen at theaters. I am overfond of leaning backward on the podium, that is the long and short of it. The guardrails were not meant to support a man's weight, merely to remind one of the confines of the space. That is what my stage manager tells me, at least."

"You mean you fell from your podium?"

Zemlinsky closed his eyes at this, almost ashamed.

"Yes," he said in a weak voice.

Alma Schindler looked at Werthen meaningfully, as if to remind him of Mahler's own fall from his conductor's podium.

"Now," Schoenberg said, "it really is time

for visitors to go. Alex needs his rest. I must insist."

He spread his thick arms out like a shepherd moving sheep.

As Zemlinsky himself made no counter-suggestion, Werthen hardly felt he could intrude longer. But Alma had other ideas.

"Who appointed you major domo, Herr Schoenberg? It is for Zem himself, or his sister, Fräulein Zemlinsky —"

But she was a poor observer of the human condition outside her own needy limits. She had not noticed the connection between Mathilde and Schoenberg, and now, at Alma's obvious rudeness, the sister came to her friend's defense.

"I really think it is time for you to leave, Fräulein Schindler, before some native truths are spoken which you would not care to hear."

Alma threw her shoulders back in defiance before Werthen could intervene.

"Such as?"

"Such as that your attempts at composition are feeble, derivative, and boorish," Schoenberg said. "Not my opinion, of course."

Alma looked at Zemlinsky.

"Is that what you think?" she all but cried out. "Is that what you told them? After all

320

we have meant to each other. After all I suffered from my family on your account."

My God, Werthen thought. The cheek of the girl. Here lay an injured man, and she was only concerned with her own hurt feelings. Were they actually lovers? The beautiful Alma Schindler and this gnome?

"It is time now that you leave," Fräulein Guttmann said in a measured voice.

Such restraint toward her obvious rival, however, was causing this young woman real pain, Werthen could see. She would much rather be scratching at Alma's eyes.

"Come," Werthen said to Fraulein Schindler. "This is to no avail."

He took her arm, but she shook his hand off, moving on her own toward the door.

"Typical," she spat out as they were leaving. "You all stick together. You and your kind. And then you wonder why people dislike you."

Werthen now had to control his own rage, getting the young woman out of the house and onto the street. But once under the warm summer sun, he could no longer hold himself in.

"Never, never speak like that in front of me again. Or do you forget that I am Jewish, too?"

She was about to strike out at him with

more vitriol, but suddenly stopped, assuming a contrite expression.

"No, you are right. I don't know what came over me. But that Schoenberg. He is such a sponge, such an old lady. Talk about feeble compositions, just listen to his *Verklaerte Nacht*."

Then she cast Werthen a winning smile as she put her arm through his.

"Please forgive me, say you do, please, please."

Like a schoolgirl instead of the femme fatale she normally liked to play. It was his turn now to shrug her arm off.

"Are you two lovers?"

The question did not seem to surprise her, though there was a slight reddening at her cheeks.

"Advokat, that is not a question one asks a young woman."

"Fräulein Schindler, you are a young woman in age only. I think there is very little innocent about you and my question is not a matter of prurient interest. Are you his lover?"

"We have had moments of intimacy, yes. Why is it important?"

"You answered that yourself earlier. Everyone close to you seems to be having accidents."

Which did not explain Bruckner, Brahms, or Strauss, but did serve to give her something to think about as they rode back into the Inner City via *fiaker*. He dropped her off at her dressmaker's on the Seilerstrasse and then continued on to his office at Habsburgergasse 4. The sturdy figures of Atlas decorating the first-story façade gave him a solid, secure feeling as he entered the street door.

Today that door was locked, as it was supposed to be.

Gross and he met for lunch, as planned. Frau Blatschky's sudden discovery of healthy cuisine had driven Gross from their table; Werthen was happy to join him today at Zum roten Igel, the Sign of the Red Hedgehog, in Wildpretmarkt. The eatery had been a favorite with Brahms, and for good reason: it had perhaps the best inexpensive food in Vienna, solid fare of meat and potatoes, both of which were now in short supply at Werthen's table. It was a fine day of mild, sunny weather, so Werthen looked for Gross in the garden, but he was sitting instead in the *stube* in the back of the restaurant, a large, dark room with barrel vaulting where the working-class eaters usually gathered at communal tables. Gross had claimed one of these large tables exclusively for himself and Werthen.

"It is where Brahms preferred to eat," Gross said by way of explanation when Werthen joined him.

Gross continued his homage to Brahms by having Hungarian Tokay with lunch, the very wine the gruff old composer had enjoyed. Werthen meanwhile occupied himself with a *viertel* of tart Nussberger from Krems. Both ordered lavishly as if to celebrate eating once again. For Gross that meant a wooden platter piled high with sausages and sauerkraut, while for Werthen such gustatory opulence included boiled beef with freshly ground horseradish. These were preceded by liver dumpling soup and followed by two plates of apple strudel, its crust flaky and golden.

They spoke little during the meal. Gross was usually talkative at any time, but now, after barely surviving the rigors of Frau Blatschky's table, he was reserving whatever sounds he could muster to sensual moans of pleasure at the first bite of each new dish.

"This calls for coffee," Gross managed after finishing the last of his strudel.

They sat over their mochas and Werthen shared his adventures this morning at Zemlinsky's. Gross listened carefully and when

Werthen had finished, nodded his big head.

"So our killer is moving on to other game? Mahler has proved too difficult a quarry. Instead he chooses this Zemlinsky. As a composer, is he actually of a status of Brahms and Strauss?"

Werthen shrugged. "Kraus seems to think so. He talked about the man once, before all this started. And Zemlinsky *has* been made music director of the Carl Theater."

"Not the most prestigious of engagements."

"No," Werthen allowed, "but he's not yet thirty. Impressive enough. Brahms thought he had talent. One of his operas won the Luitpold Prize in Munich, I believe."

Gross made a condescending humph through his nose to show how much he though of German taste in music.

"Well, I suppose this means that we shall have to follow the lead to the Carl Theater," he said.

Werthen was surprised. He thought Gross would be elated by this latest development. But he seemed almost put out that there was another potential victim — just as Werthen himself was feeling. This new line of investigation really was getting them nowhere, or to too many other destinations.

"Another set of suspects. More interviews.

Sometimes I feel we have stepped into a morass with this case."

"I can deal with the Carl Theater," Werthen halfheartedly offered.

"It's not a matter of *dealing* with something," Gross said, suddenly irritated. "Of course we can *deal* with the new lead. But we make no headway scurrying off this way and that in search of a new suspect, a new interview. Perhaps we are making things too complicated."

Exactly Werthen's thought, but he could not let the criminologist off so easily.

"You were the one so enthusiastic about the possibility of a serial killer murdering the great composers of Vienna," Werthen reminded him. "Something bigger than a simple assault on Mahler."

"I beg to differ. You have not bothered to ask me how I spent my morning."

"All right. How did you spend your morning?"

"At an eminent surgeon's, a disciple of the great Billroth himself, complaining of liver problems in hope of a diagnosis of liver cancer."

Werthen thought for a moment that Gross's judgment had become clouded by his lack of real food. Then the connection was made.

"You mean Brahms?"

"Yes. And I learned that there is no way to fabricate the symptoms of liver cancer. In addition to which, a brief autopsy was done before Brahms's interment in the Zentralfriedhof in the musician's grove. It was certain that he died of cancer, not some exotic poison."

"And Bruckner? Strauss?"

Gross held up his hands. "We shall see."

"What is it you are suggesting, then?"

Gross waited a moment, took a deep breath, and said, "Simplification."

Gross's desire for simplification had intensified by the time they returned to Werthen's office.

Tor greeted them as they entered. "Your wife called, Advokat. She said it was urgent."

Sudden panic gripped Werthen, fearing the worst regarding her pregnancy.

Gross noticed his change of color. "Easy, Werthen. It could mean anything."

In his office, Werthen hastily picked up the receiver and gave the operator his home number. It seemed to take forever for the woman to connect him. Then he could finally hear ringing on the other end of the line. Once, twice, three times.

Frau Blatschky could be standing there in

fear, trembling to pick up the contraption lest it electrocute her, while Berthe was lying somewhere unconscious or worse.

The receiver was lifted on the fifth ring.

"The Werthen-Meisner residence."

It was Berthe's voice.

"Are you all right?"

"Yes, darling. Sorry to worry you," she said. "It's not me."

"What is it then?"

"Mahler. Someone's poisoned him."

THIRTEEN

He looked like a wax effigy.

They carried Mahler off the special express from Salzburg on a stretcher with four bulky soldiers of the Alpin Korps on guard duty. Prince Montenuovo was sparing no expense, now that there had been yet another "assassination attempt," as the prince insisted on calling the poisoning.

Mahler's face was greenish yellow; his chest rose and fell with great difficulty. As they hustled the stretcher past Werthen at the Empress Elisabeth Bahnhof, the composer's eyelids fluttered open, and he recognized the lawyer.

He lifted a beckoning hand, and Werthen went to him, bending down over the stretcher.

Mahler whispered, but Werthen could not hear his words at first. Leaning down more closely so that Mahler's breath warmed his ear, Werthen was finally able to hear the message: "Find him, Werthen, before it is too late."

"He was a lucky man," Dr. Baumgartner, the attending physician at the General Hospital said. "Well, unlucky to have been poisoned in the first place, but fortunate in that he ate so little of the tainted sweet. I believe he will fully recover with no significant liver damage."

"You are certain it was the Turkish delight?" Werthen said.

"The laboratory tests have come back already. Positive for arsenic. And a very healthy dose, at that."

"We will need to see the box," Gross said.

"You'll have to speak with . . . I believe his name is Detective Inspector Drechsler, about that."

Gross emitted a vexed sigh. "May we speak with Herr Mahler?"

A curt shaking of the head from the doctor. "He is resting now. I would imagine by tomorrow morning —"

Gross did not wait for the medical man to finish, but wheeled around and stormed out of the waiting area.

Werthen reddened at Gross's bad behavior.

"I apologize for my colleague's curtness,

Dr. Baumgartner."

"You really should get your friend to calm down. He is headed for a myocardial infarction at this rate."

And the doctor departed as abruptly as Gross had, perhaps headed for his own bit of coronary difficulty.

Which left Werthen alone in the waiting room with Natalie Bauer-Lechner; Justine was keeping personal watch in her brother's room.

"Good news at last," she said, collapsing into a chair.

"May I get you something? Water?"

"No. I am fine. It has been such a terrifying experience. He was retching all afternoon, burning up, and drinking so much water, as if he were dying of thirst. Awful, awful. We were preparing to return to Vienna today anyway. Gustl needs to prepare for the *Tannhäuser* next week. And now this."

The Hofoper was closed during part of June and all of July, but this summer there was to be a special celebration in honor of Richard Wagner's widow, Cosima Wagner, founder of the Bayreuth Festival. This would include a performance of the opera *Tannhäuser* in her honor. The celebration, however, was not welcomed by all of Vienna's musical and artistic establishment, Werthen knew, for Wagner was still an object of controversy for musical purists.

He sat next to Frau Bauer-Lechner, patting her arm. "It's all right now. You heard the doctor. No permanent damage."

"Yes," she said without conviction. "She blames you. Justine, that is. For deserting her brother."

"Hardly deserted. The police took over the watch."

"He asked to see you, but you sent your assistant."

She was clearly distraught. But this was not the time for such a discussion. "If you don't mind, there are some questions I would like to ask."

"The police have already been over all of this. Can't you just speak with them?"

"It helps to have it firsthand. Herr Mahler pressed me to find the culprit. You saw him talk to me at the railroad station."

"Yes, you are right. We are a little overwhelmed by events of late. Go ahead. Anything to help Gustl."

"Let us begin with the most obvious." Werthen fished out his leather notebook from this inside jacket pocket. "Who was at the Villa Kerry recently?"

"You mean in addition to myself, Justine,

and Arnold?"

So Rosé had stayed on, Werthen thought. Written out of Mahler's will if he married Justine, but still a houseguest.

"Yes."

"Well, there was Herr Regierungsrath Leitner. He was at the villa yesterday. He had some important papers for Gustl to sign. They spoke together for some time. Herr Leitner returned to Vienna this morning, I believe."

"Did he bring anything with him to the meeting?"

"A box of Turkish delight, you mean?"

Werthen nodded.

"That box was delivered almost a week ago, directly from Istanbul. Gustl has eaten I do not know how many pieces of candy from it. I am sure they are mistaken about that being the source of the poison."

"But was their talk . . . congenial?"

She looked at him with gray, perceptive eyes. "Do you mean, could we hear shouting as at his last visit?"

"Did you?"

"No. In fact their dealings seemed rather cordial."

"Anyone else?"

"That soprano, Gerta Rheingold, showed up quite unexpectedly on Wednesday."

The one Mahler had made sing a Mozart aria thirty times in an attempt to get it right. The one who had finally screamed the message of the aria directly at Mahler: "Die, horrid monster!"

"I believe a rapprochement was achieved there, as well," Natalie said. "And neither did she appear to have sweets sequestered on her person. There were *bussis*, cheek kisses, left and right at her departure. Of course there were also the policeman on duty and your man, Herr Tor, who was there yesterday. Quite efficient, he seems, but painfully shy."

Werthen concurred.

"No, it simply must be that hideous little man the police took into custody lurking about the villa this afternoon."

It was the first Werthen had heard of this.

"Who?"

"I heard the name. What is it? I can't . . . such a disgusting little person. Saying that Gustl had sent for him. Nonsense. Why would he want to speak with such a man? Gustl is totally against the use of the claque."

Gross was waiting for him at the entrance to the hospital.

"I thought Frau Bauer-Lechner might be

more responsive to your questions without my presence. Was that the case?"

Werthen quickly told Gross what he had learned.

"Schreier," Gross surmised. "It has to be him. The head of the claque. He's in custody? But that is absurd."

Werthen hoped they could delay meeting Drechsler until the morning so he could get back to Berthe, but this new information made it more pressing that they speak with him this evening. It was still light, a soft evening with a sweet water smell coming off the Danube. As they walked toward the Police Praesidium, they further discussed these new developments.

"Who knew of Mahler's penchant for those hideous sweets?" Gross asked.

"Anyone who ever visited his premises. A box was always lying around somewhere close to hand. Or anyone who reads the gossip columns. Journalists love those sorts of telling private details."

"Telling of what?"

Werthen shrugged. "Well, that Mahler is human after all, I assume. That he has a sweet tooth. He had them sent from Istanbul."

"Apparently not this box," Gross said. "Or have the Turks decided on long overdue revenge for losing the siege of Vienna four hundred years ago?"

"Someone at the Villa Kerry must have placed some poisoned pieces in the box from Istanbul," Werthen thought out loud.

"Yes," Gross said. "The most logical conclusion. Beyond, that is, a renewal of the Islamic invasion of Europe."

Werthen thought it was probably a good sign that Gross was in a humorous mood, but he also found the remarks somehow irritating.

"Nervous tic," Gross admitted, as if reading his friend's mind. "Adele usually tells me to hold my fire. Always thought that was a damn fine way for a woman to tell a man to keep his mouth shut."

"Tactful woman, your wife," Werthen said as they reached Schottenring and headed for the police headquarters, the Praesidium, where Drechsler was still on duty when they checked in. Drechsler looked exhausted. He stood by a small open window in his office, breathing deeply of the pleasant evening air.

"Sit, gentlemen," he said. There was little choice offered: two old wooden chairs faced Drechsler's desk. Gross and Werthen took these.

"I was scheduled for vacation starting this week," the inspector said, throwing himself into his leather-padded chair, the only sign of self-indulgence in the small, spartan office. Werthen noticed a picture of a pigeon-bosomed woman and several boys in short pants. Drechsler's family? One assumed so, though the inspector hardly seemed the family man.

"Instead, my family is up in the Semmering without me. They were hoping I would at least be able to come up for this weekend, but now, with this Mahler poisoning, even that is out. Meindl wants this taken care of over the weekend."

"In other words, you are to squeeze a confession from Herr Schreier?"

"Confound you, Gross. How did you know about his arrest? Right. You went to the hospital. Saw the sister —"

"Frau Bauer-Lechner, in point of fact," Werthen said.

Drechsler nodded. "We caught the blighter dead to rights. Lurking about the grounds like a common burglar. Had a grudge, too. Mahler's new rules prohibiting the claque put him right out of a job."

"What does Schreier say?" Gross asked.

"What do you think he says? That he's innocent, of course. Framed by someone. That Mahler himself sent him a letter inviting him to the Villa Kerry to patch things up between them."

"And the letter?" Gross asked.

"Not the best of liars, is friend Schreier. He claims that Mahler requested, in the letter, that he destroy it lest it fall into the hands of journalists somehow and that word would get out of their secret meeting. According to Schreier, Mahler wanted to end their feud, but did not want the public to know he had capitulated to his singers."

"A perhaps not unreasonable request," Gross said.

"You don't believe the man, do you? He's a cad."

"I know. I have spoken to him. But that does not necessarily make him a murderer," Gross replied. "Besides, he has a solid alibi for earlier attempts on Mahler's life."

"There could be two perpetrators," Drechsler quickly countered. "Mahler is not everyone's friend, after all. Perhaps Schreier got wind of the investigation. Perhaps he hoped to fob off his murder onto whoever has been trying to kill Mahler. A murder of opportunity. Not unheard of. He does stand to gain by Mahler's death."

"Only if Mahler's successor at the Hofoper rescinded Mahler's new rules," Werthen reminded him.

Drechsler ignored this appeal to logic.

"Meindl wants closure," the inspector said again. "There are heavy pressures coming from the court as a result of this latest incident. After all, we had one of our men stationed inside the villa and still could not protect Mahler."

Neither Gross nor Werthen responded to this.

Drechsler slammed his fist onto the desktop.

"All right. I don't believe it either. The man seems too much of an idiot to be able to get his hands on arsenic, let alone doctor some pieces of Turkish delight with it and then manage to insert them into Mahler's box of sweets unnoticed. Besides, we have no evidence Schreier ever made it inside the house. He says that by the time he arrived at the Villa Kerry, it was fairly crawling with our boys. He was afraid to go inside, but also afraid to leave lest he miss his meeting with Mahler."

"What are you going to do, Drechsler?"

The inspector shook his head. "I don't really know. Easiest thing in the world to scare Schreier into a confession, I would think. It would buy me a weekend in the mountains. I could use the shut-eye, I tell you. I just cannot sleep when the family is away."

Werthen sympathized with him; his sojourn at Altaussee, away from Berthe, had given him sleepless nights, as well.

"What did Schreier do with the letter?" Gross asked.

"Burned it, as Mahler demanded. Or so he says. And then flushed the ashes down his toilet, also as the letter supposedly instructed."

"Let's assume he is telling the truth about the letter," Gross said. "Why so thorough? A simple demand to destroy the letter would have sufficed, one would think, to keep it out of the hands of journalists. *If* Mahler had actually written the letter. But if someone else had, posing as Mahler, then they might have reason to go to extraordinary lengths to ensure the letter was never examined. Even burnt paper can lend itself to examination, to handwriting analysis."

"Or let's assume the letter is Schreier's fabrication," Drechsler said. "In which case the fiction of its total and irrevocable disappearance ensures that Schreier's story cannot be contradicted."

"There were other visitors," Werthen offered. "Others with a possible motive and with foreknowledge of Mahler's love of Turkish delight."

Drechsler consulted a sheet of paper on his desk. "Right. Leitner and the soprano. They both seemed to be making it up with Mahler, though, by all accounts. Why bother to poison him then?" He glanced at the paper again. "And your man," he said, nodding at Werthen.

"Yes. Herr Tor. He had to make a change to Mahler's will."

"And what change would that be?" the inspector asked.

"I am not sure I am at liberty to tell you that, Detective Inspector. Herr Mahler is, after all, my client."

"Advokat, I needn't remind you that this is a murder investigation."

"Not Mahler's," Werthen said. "Not yet. Fräulein Kaspar and Herr Gunther, yes, but have we actually connected those to the attempts on Mahler's life beyond a doubt?"

"I say," Gross broke in, "are you not being a touch unreasonable here, Werthen? I mean, after all, we are all on the same side in this."

"It is not about sides, Gross. It is about principle. If a man cannot have a reasonable expectation of privacy with his attorney, then I don't know where we are."

"Civilization won't crumble, man," Gross thundered.

"Your objection has no basis in law, Werthen," Drechsler said. "No such privilege exists in Austria, but I duly note that you object to the sharing of such communications."

"I really should consult Mahler about this."

"Lord knows when he will be in any shape to talk," Gross said. "I think he would, at this point, be happy for any information leading to the person responsible for these attacks. He told you as much as he came off the train."

Drechsler was, of course, correct, Werthen knew. In Austrian law there was as yet no guarantee of privacy or secrecy between a client and his attorney as existed in England and other countries, but it was something the profession needed to see to in the future. In matters of criminal law, what client would fully divulge to his attorney if said attorney could be forced to share such information with the prosecution? None. At least not one in his right mind. So of course, an attorney could never be sure of his client's story, making a defense all that harder to mount. Gross, an investigating officer for years as well as a prosecutor, was hardly on the same side as Werthen, a defense attorney, in such matters. However, now was not the time or place to fight such a battle.

"In brief, Mahler wanted to stipulate that his sister Justine, were she to marry Herr Arnold Rosé, would be henceforth written out of his will."

Drechsler let out a low whistle. "And she knew of this?"

"That I could not say," Werthen responded.

"Could not or would not?" Drechsler pressed the point.

"I have no knowledge of it. The Villa Kerry is not a spacious domicile. She may have overheard the conference between Mahler and Tor. Check with your man posted there to see if he noticed the sister hovering outside doors."

"What about domestic staff?" Gross asked. "There must be a cook or a day maid."

Drechsler and Werthen both shook their heads.

"Mahler would not tolerate any servants in the country," Werthen explained. "He says they pollute the air and that he is unable to create with them around. Summers are his time for composing."

"The sister and Frau Bauer-Lechner took care of domestic responsibilities," Drechsler added. "Perhaps it is time we spoke more closely with this sister, and with her suitor."

"Delicately, Detective Inspector," Gross warned. "After all, her brother has just been poisoned."

"Yes, and she may have done the deed."

Werthen shook his head at this. "Before you run wild with the idea of the will as motive, Drechsler, I should tell you that Herr Mahler is not a wealthy man. He has what he makes as director of the Hofoper, but his living expenses are not meager. Neither did he save much money at his previous engagements in Hamburg and Budapest. And as a composer, he has earned very little from his symphonies and song cycles. Perhaps in the future, but not now. Thus, cutting his sister out of his will is more symbolic than consequential."

"Herr Rosé is another matter however, Werthen, right?"

Werthen was uncertain what Gross meant by this.

Gross went on: "As we see with the brother, Eduard, who married another Mahler sister, he was all but driven out of Vienna for lack of work. Jealous and vindictive is our Herr Mahler. Anything that upsets his schedule, his domestic and creative routine, is the enemy. Perhaps Arnold Rosé feared the same would happen with him and took measures to prevent such a turn of events?"

It was a possibility, Werthen thought, but definitely not a probability. The little he had seen of Arnold Rosé while staying at the Villa Kerry had made him sympathize with the man more than suspect him. Rosé seemed a good and loyal friend to both Mahler and Justine. Somehow he could not imagine this musician doctoring Mahler's Turkish delight with arsenic.

"If you do not mind, Drechsler," Werthen said, "perhaps we could conduct those interviews first. They know me and would not be unduly put on guard as they might were a member of the police to question them."

From what Natalie had told him, though, Justine might be less than amenable to such a tête-à-tête now, blaming him for "deserting" her brother. But he did not tell Drechsler of this possibility.

Drechsler thought for a moment. "Sounds reasonable enough. But I want a full transcript of the interview."

Werthen readily agreed to that, and then by way of an afterthought he asked, "Is there any way to trace the arsenic?"

"We're looking into that, as well," Drechsler said. "But there are major difficulties involved there, as I am sure *you* are well aware."

He nodded at Gross as he said this and the criminologists returned the nod. Gross had written widely on the subject. He now quickly explained to Werthen that arsenic was readily available from a number of sources. It was prescribed by doctors to treat ailments from eczema and rheumatism to syphilis. It was also used in industry, to cure hides and to work with gold. It was even mixed with tar and worked into cracks in roofs, floors, and walls to protect against rats and termites. Tracing it would prove difficult, especially so as there was probably only a small amount involved in this poisoning.

"Doesn't sound promising," Werthen allowed.

"No," Drechsler said evenly, "it does not. And now if you do not mind, gentlemen, I have a good deal on my plate for this evening."

"I want to speak with him," Gross said.

"Who? Schreier?"

Gross nodded.

"What could you hope to discover from the man. I've already questioned him thoroughly."

"A theory."

"You want to share this bright theory of yours?" the inspector said.

"I shall. Afterward."

"All right. I will call over to the Liesel and let them know you are coming."

On their way out Drechsler cocked his head at Werthen.

"I understand you had an intruder at your law offices, Advokat."

"How did you hear of that?"

"I believe her name is Frau Ignatz. She reported a disturbance to your Josefstadt station. Nothing is secret in Vienna with a *portier* in attendance. Were you planning on telling me about it?"

Werthen felt himself redden. "It was nothing, really."

"Sounds like police business to me. The lady says you had blood down the back of your neck. Assault, in fact."

Werthen had no answer for this.

"I assume you will inform the police in the future of such occurrences," Drechsler said.

"An accident, merely," Werthen offered, but Drechsler was clearly unconvinced. The inspector clucked his tongue at this explanation.

"We work together at times, Advokat, but you must remember there are some things an inquiries agent is not trained to deal with."

The Landesgericht prison, or Liesel in common parlance, was not far from the Police Praesidium, south around the Ring and in back of the Rathaus, or city hall. Again they walked, for the evening was so pleasant. The park being built around the neo-Gothic Rathaus was not quite finished: plane trees were still held in place by wooden braces, and fountains due to be finished a decade ago were only now beginning to spout water flumes into the gloaming. They stopped at a small *gasthaus* behind the glowering silhouette of the Rathaus, and ate a simple meal of smoked ham and sauerkraut, washed down by foaming *krügeln* of Styrian beer, the best that Austria had to offer. They sat in the garden of the inn, under a massive chestnut tree, and suddenly Werthen realized this was the very eatery he had frequented last year before visiting his friend Klimt, who was, at the time, also in custody at the Liesel.

Gross was tight-lipped about his reasons for wanting the interview with Schreier, so Werthen did not press the issue. Instead he enjoyed his meal, hoping they would not be too late in returning home service. Perhaps he should telephone Berthe, but knew how difficult it was to find a public phone.

Gross finished his meal first, daubed his lips with the cotton napkin, counted out some coins — far less than his half of the bill — and was off without a word, leaving Werthen to gulp down the last of his food and take care of financial matters.

This was the Gross Werthen knew and respected. For a time there during this investigation the great criminologist had seemed to be floundering, dithering; now suddenly he had purpose to his stride.

"I am betting he has made his first mistake," Gross said as they entered the vestibule and gave their names to a desk sergeant, who took them back to the cells.

Schreier was in the B block, reserved for murder suspects. There was one other inmate in this cell, a wiry man with a tattoo on his neck. Werthen recognized the design: it was the Indian sign for power and the sun, the swastika, but this criminal had inverted the symbol, changing it from the left-facing wheel of life to the right-facing representation of German nationalism and anti-Semitism. Werthen could only guess at the crime this hoodlum was in custody for, but by the terrified eyes of Shreier, who watched as the man was led from the cell to allow for the privacy of their interview, it must have been bad. Most likely Drechsler had arranged such a pairing as a special inducement to Schreier. After all, a man scared half out of his wits is easier to persuade than one comfortable and secure.

"Dr. Gross," Schreier said in a high, pleading voice once they were alone in the cell. "You've got to save me. I am innocent of any crime. Why have they thrown me in here with this monster? He tells me he strangled his female cousin for having sexual relations with a Jew. He thinks *I* am a Jew."

Werthen could smell the fear exuding from Schreier, a thickset man in his forties with a sallow complexion. Drechsler's plant strategy seemed to be working.

"Calm yourself, Herr Schreier," Gross said. He tapped the man's shoulder and Schreier sat on the edge of his iron bunk. They sat opposite on the other inmate's bunk after Werthen had given the blanket a quick inspection for any movement. Gross made a quick introduction of Werthen, but the prisoner was interested only in Gross.

"You've got to tell them, Dr. Gross," Schreier pleaded. "I've done nothing wrong. He sent for me. It is the lord's honest truth."

"He?" Gross asked.

"Mahler of course. He wrote and said he

wanted to reach an agreement. I knew he would have to come around sooner or later. The singers were adamant. They cannot survive without us. How else would the public know who to clap for unless we initiate such applause?"

"Where is the letter?"

"I burned it, as Mahler instructed."

"I cannot help you if you continue to lie," Gross said evenly. "You are being held for attempted murder, did you know that?"

Schreier shook his head. "Impossible."

"No. Very possible," Gross said. "They are drawing up the charges as we speak and hope to have a confession from you by the end of the weekend. I imagine they will be successful in that endeavor."

Gross said this last bit meaningfully and Schreier obviously understood the connotation.

"They can't beat a confession out of me."

"It has been known to happen. Are you a physically courageous man, Herr Schreier? Can you tolerate pain very well?"

Schreier's eyes grew wider at this comment.

"I thought not," Gross said. "So, it is time you were honest with me. Where is the letter?"

Schreier looked to Werthen for a moment

as if for assistance, but the lawyer maintained a stony appearance.

"The letter, Herr Schreier. I shall not ask again."

Gross rose as if to leave and Schreier crumbled.

"All right, all right. It's at my apartment house. I wrapped it in an oilskin pouch and placed it in the cistern over the *clo* on my floor."

One of the most common places to hide valuables in the criminal class, Werthen knew. In the flush tank over a toilet.

"You hoped to blackmail him, didn't you?"

Schreier said nothing, merely sat hunched over, gazing between his legs.

"Didn't you?" Gross fairly shouted this and the man suddenly jerked himself upright.

"No. It wasn't like that. Mahler's got cheek trying to get rid of the claque. I was going to make sure he never tried again to suppress us. That letter was my insurance."

"It may still be, Herr Schreier," Gross said as he moved to the cell door and called for the warder. "If the letter is there and proves not to be a forgery by you, then you may have saved yourself."

Werthen rose now, too, happy to be leaving the cell and its smell of hopelessness and fear.

As the warder opened the door, Gross turned to Schreier: "I'll see they place that miscreant in some other cell."

"Thank you, Dr. Gross. You are a gentleman. Next time you take a case to trial you just call on me. We'll create the proper atmosphere in the courtroom, just you see."

"I will remember your generous offer, Herr Schreier," Gross said. "And I am sure my colleague will, as well."

FOURTEEN

"I am not sure I care to answer that question, Advokat Werthen."

Justine Mahler had colored from her neck to her forehead. Oh, she knew, he thought. It was written on her face.

"Why do you hector me when the person responsible for Gustl's near death has gone free?"

She was referring to Herr Schreier, who had been released from custody on Saturday after Gross and he fetched the letter purporting to be from Mahler. Close inspection by Gross of the handwriting quickly demonstrated that it was clearly not Mahler's, but neither was it Schreier's, for the criminologist compared writing from Schreier to that in the letter, and found not one similarity in the writing. Added to which, the envelope to the letter bore a postmark from Bad Aussee, near where Mahler was staying for the summer, and

Schreier had been — as numerous witnesses could testify — in Vienna continuously this summer prior to his trip the see Mahler.

"Either I ask these questions," Werthen pressed, "or Detective Inspector Drechsler will."

The door to the sitting room in Mahler's flat suddenly opened and there stood Mahler himself, wrapped ghostlike in a white sheet.

"What in the name of the devil are you about, Werthen?" His voice had lost none of its commanding presence.

"Gustl!" Justine rushed to his side, holding his arm. "You should be in bed."

"I asked you, Werthen, what do you think you are doing?"

Werthen could see Natalie standing behind Mahler. She must have been the messenger, Werthen figured.

"I am asking your sister some questions, Herr Mahler."

"As if she is a common criminal. You want to know, ask me. Yes, she knew about the change of will. I told her. I am a selfish man, I admit. And I regret such a rash action. It will be amended, trust me."

This last he said to his sister, who in turn patted his arm lovingly.

"Back to bed, Gustl," she said. "Don't

trouble yourself with such things. You must only concentrate on getting healthy again."

She led him down the hallway toward his bedroom, entering with him and closing the door behind her. Presumably that was the end of their interview, Werthen realized.

Natalie entered the sitting room now.

"I felt he needed to know," she said.

Werthen nodded.

"She would never hurt him. Justine is devoted to Gustl."

"As are you," Werthen could not help but add.

She paused for a moment. Then, "Yes."

"You have known him for years."

"Since conservatory days." She looked at him with those piercing gray eyes of hers. "I know I must appear ridiculous to the outsider. Something of an old maid hanging about the great composer, hoping that he will finally notice his loyal lapdog. That he might return her love. Does that about sum up your view of me, Advokat?"

He saw no reason not to return candor for candor.

"Yes."

"Well, it is only partially correct. I have no wish that Gustl return my love. Frankly I would not know what to do with it. Nor did I know what to do with my husband's during my marriage. My music and our conversations are quite enough for me. Now that is cleared up, ask away. I have the distinct feeling you wish to tap my font of information about Gustl."

Indeed, Berthe had requested him to do just that. He was taking over her end of the investigation into Mahler's youth as Berthe was in no physical shape to be gallivanting around interviewing people. Gross, he, and Berthe had decided that they would now refocus their efforts. Instead of the larger crime, that is the possible murder of the great composers of Vienna, they would, with this latest and nearly successful attack on Mahler, concentrate on finding the person trying to kill him. Successful in that, they should most likely come up with the perpetrator of other deaths, as well.

"I appreciate your frankness, Frau Bauer-Lechner. Yes, I would, as you suggest, like to ask you a few questions. Specifically about possible enemies Mahler might have made as a young man in Vienna."

"From student days? But it was all so long ago," she said. "We were almost children."

"Some enemies seek revenge over decades, Frau Bauer-Lechner. We have heard of Hugo Wolf, for example."

"But the poor man is in a mental asylum."

"For example, I said. Perhaps there are others. What was the rift between them?"

"Gustl did not think *Der Corregidor* was of sufficient strength to warrant performance at the Hofoper. Quite simple really, and not a matter of spite."

"Before that, I meant. From their time as students together. When I interviewed Wolf he said something about a stolen libretto."

She breathed in deeply. "That old canard."

"Then you know of it?"

"Nonsense. A childish dispute."

"Humor me, Frau Bauer-Lechner."

"Well, if you must. But it really amounted to nothing. In about 1880, I think, Wolf had been digging around in the Hofbibliothek and came across what he thought was the perfect source for a libretto. It was the story of Rübezahl, the famous mountain spirit from German folklore. Wolf was terribly excited about the idea of creating a sort of fairy-tale opera, for it had not been done before. Humperdinck's *Hänsel und Gretel* did not appear until 1893, you recall."

"So how did Mahler steal this?"

"Wolf claimed that he and Mahler discussed the idea of such an opera, Gustl believing that one could only portray such an opera humorously. Wolf, of course, wanted a serious approach. Gustl, after this meeting, decided to work on a libretto. A week later he and Wolf met again, and Gustl asked his friend how his libretto was advancing. Wolf was still researching the subject, gathering more and more stories and had not even begun writing. When Mahler showed him his completed libretto, Wolf became absolutely furious, claiming that he would never write a word of such a tale now that his best friend had stolen the idea from him. Gustl tried to persuade him, telling Wolf he had no intention of actually writing the score to the libretto. It had all been an exercise for him. But from that time on Wolf and Gustl were on the outs. Whenever Wolf saw him, he would pointedly ignore Gustl. Later, after it was apparent Wolf was not going ahead with the project, Gustl did begin writing the full opera. But he gave it up finally, the pressure of work as a conductor claiming too much of his time."

"Hardly seems the stuff of revenge," Werthen said.

"No," she said. "But we musicians are sensitive."

Werthen squinted at her; something further from his interview with Wolf was trying to make it into his mind. Some other comment Wolf had made about the "devil" Mahler.

"Was there anyone else that might harbor such a grudge?" he asked. Then it suddenly struck him. He remembered what Wolf had said; that there was another composer from that time whom Mahler had supposedly stolen from. Someone who had, according to Wolf, ended his days "here." By which he must have meant the asylum.

"Someone else who might have later gone insane?"

Natalie looked at him with a surprised expression. Then she quickly covered this with a grin of near contempt.

"Not all creative people are insane, Advokat."

"I was not suggesting they are. I asked you about someone else from Herr Mahler's past who may have ended up in an asylum. Who may have had a grudge."

"I assumed we were looking for more than a ghost."

She was right, of course. Their perpetrator needed to be among the living. But he persisted, simply because she seemed to be hiding something.

"Of course I could simply ask Hofrath Krafft-Ebing about former patients at his Lower Austrian State Lunatic Asylum."

"All right," she assented. "That won't be necessary. I assume you are referring to

Rott. Hans Rott. He died at the asylum in 1884."

The name was familiar. Both Berthe and Kraus had mentioned the young composer.

"Were they close, Mahler and Rott?" Werthen asked her.

"They were members of the Wagner Society. As was Wolf. I know Gustl had great admiration for Rott's talent. He thought it a tragedy when he died so young, not even twenty-six."

She simply stopped as if there was nothing more to share. But he sensed there was, just as he knew that he was not going to get it from her.

He did, however, have an idea where he could get more information about Herr Rott.

Werthen was seated once again in the office of the editor of *Die Fackel.* His unannounced visit and request for information about Hans Rott seemed to please the journalist, for Kraus was taking obvious delight in looking up the name in the extensive alphabetical files he kept in his office.

"Yes," he said, retrieving a sheaf of notes from a blue file and returning to the desk. "Here he is, 'Rott, Hans.' Born 1858 and

361

died 1884. His father, Karl Matthias was a quite well-known comic actor, in point of fact. Suffered a terrible accident on stage in 1874 and died two years later."

"A stage accident, you say?"

Kraus looked over the lenses of his glasses at Werthen.

"They do happen. I mean, for real."

Werthen was reminded of Schoenberg saying the same about Zemlinsky's recent accident.

Werthen got out his leather notebook and noted that fact.

"Rott was apparently a child prodigy. He began studying at the conservatory when he was sixteen. A scholarship boy. Studied organ with Bruckner, who became a great friend and supporter. Wrote his first symphony by 1876. His next, Symphony in E major was submitted for the Beethoven Prize in 1878. It was there he fell afoul of Brahms, for the old man could not believe this young student was capable of such a composition. He accused him of cheating, of theft. It broke Rott. He was traveling to Germany in 1880, settling for a lower-tier job at Müllhausen, when the incident happened. They took him off the train and he was brought to the psychiatric clinic at the General Hospital. He tried to kill himself there, and was transferred the next year to the Lower Austrian State Insane Asylum."

Kraus looked up from his notes dramatically: "He died there three years later from tuberculosis that he contracted while a patient." He shook his head. "Seems they failed to isolate tubercular patients from other patients."

"And his connection to Mahler?"

"I thought as much. By the way, how is he?"

"Stronger," Werthen said. "It was a close thing."

"Not the food poisoning reported in the *Neue Freie Presse*, then?"

Werthen shook his head.

Kraus all but rubbed his hands, excited by the prospect of insider information regarding such criminal activity.

"So, Mahler and Rott. Yes, I admit to having heard music gossip. One rather shies away from passing on mere gossip, however." Said with a gleeful smile.

"Kraus," Werthen said, shooting him a courtroom look.

"Bear in mind that this is hearsay, Advokat."

"I shall do so. Now out with it."

"They say Mahler was fond of Rott's music. Perhaps overly fond, if you take my meaning. Rott's symphonies and song cycles have mysteriously disappeared since his death. Granted, he destroyed some of them himself, but there were apparently quite a few compositions that have gone missing. There are those who heard the early Rott compositions and who now say there is a striking similarity in his work and Herr Mahler's."

"Plagiarism?"

Kraus shrugged. "I am not a music critic. Nor have I heard Rott's music. But there are those who go so far as to accuse Mahler, yes."

"My God, if that is the case, then there is strong motive."

"Motive, yes," Kraus said, his satisfied cat grin firmly in place. "But opportunity? I hasten to remind you that Rott died fifteen years ago."

Gross was still examining the letter to Schreier when Werthen returned to the flat. The criminologist had turned the sitting room into a chemistry lab, with beakers bubbling over paraffin lamps on the Biedermeier writing desk, a microscope set up by the large street-side windows for extra lighting, and literally dozens of brands of ink and white letter paper spread out over the new leather couch.

"I thought you already ascertained Schreier did not write it," Werthen said by way of greeting.

Gross looked up from the letter he was examining through a handheld magnifying glass.

"To know who did not write the letter is not the same as knowing who did."

He returned unctuously to his examination of the paper.

"That's a fine bit of logic, Gross," he said with rather heavy sarcasm. Werthen felt in high spirits after his morning of work.

But Gross did not take the bait. He made a small "humph" into the paper.

"There is a series of smudges on this paper," he said finally. "Almost at regular intervals. Where have I seen that before?"

"Perhaps on your own journals? It is generally the sign of one who is always correcting his work before the ink has had a chance to dry."

"Yes," Gross said. "Very good, Werthen. And thus gets ink on the edge of his palm thereby smudging the paper intermittently. By the way, your father-in-law is here."

"Herr Meisner." Werthen looked around the room.

"With your lady-wife, man. In her room."

"Why did you not tell me straightaway?"

But Gross had turned his attention back to a close inspection of the Schreier letter, mounted under the lens of the microscope.

Frau Blatschky waved at him as he passed the kitchen on the way to the bedroom.

"I know," he told her. "Gross informed me."

She nodded and he continued on his way to the bedroom, knocking first on his own door and feeling a bit of a fool for doing so.

"Yes?"

Berthe's voice from within.

He opened the door and there was Herr Meisner seated in a chair next to the bed reading from the Talmud. His long, gray beard made the man look like a patriarch. Berthe, lying in bed under the lightweight summer comforter, held a restraining hand up to him, for her father was continuing with the tractate. As far as Werthen could ascertain, he was reading, in Hebraic, from the Third Order of the Mishnah, regarding marriage. He stood at the door, allowing the old gentleman to finish the reading. Strangely, he found comfort in these spoken words, only a few of which he understood. A Talmudic scholar, among other accomplishments, Herr Meisner lived his faith. Berthe seemed to take comfort from the words as well, resting her head on the pillows, and smiling sweetly at Werthen.

As he finished his reading, Herr Meisner carefully placed a length of embroidered silk in the book as a marker, closed it, and laid it on the bedside table next to Berthe's copy of Bertha von Suttner's *Lay Down Your Arms,* which she was reading for the tenth time at least.

Herr Meisner rose and cast Werthen a full smile.

"It is good to see you again," he said, his large hand outstretched to his son-in-law.

They had not seen each other since the wedding in April. Despite Berthe's forebodings, her father had made no argument with their civil marriage. It was, instead, the Werthens who boycotted the proceeding because it was not held under religious auspices. Ironies abound, Werthen thought. Here was a man who held to the old ways in the modern world. A devout Jew, yet he bowed to his daughter's wishes for her marriage. It was his own parents, passionate assimilationists, Protestant converts for convenience's sake, who were so outraged by the decision to hold a civil ceremony that they would not be part of it.

Herr Meisner, a widower for many years, was not a cloying, protective father. He had wide interests. In addition to his successful Linz shoe factory and to his reputation as one of the most noted Talmudic scholars in Austria, he was also an amateur musician of no little talent and a historian of prodigious knowledge.

"Good to see you too, sir."

Their handshake was warm and heartfelt from both sides, but there were no artificial pleadings on Herr Meisner's part to call him by his family name, or worse, his given name. In fact, Werthen did not even know the man's given name.

"Father promises to stay for more than a few days this time," Berthe said, for she knew Werthen was fond of the man.

"Well, I am forced to now, whether I wish to or not."

They had not told Herr Meisner before of Berthe's pregnancy, a precaution until the first delicate months were past and the baby was well on its way. But she had obviously shared the secret with him now and he was not angry. Rather, his comment bespoke his usual gruff irony.

"Especially with this Mahler business afoot," the older man added. "You must bring me up to date on your activities on his behalf. I was at the premiere of his Second Symphony in Berlin in 1895. A gifted composer. Not exactly to my personal taste, but clearly a major talent."

Werthen and Berthe smiled at this, a warm understanding passing between them that it was a comfort to have her father with them once again. Like old times with both Gross and Herr Meisner as houseguests. It was fortunate they had not yet begun redecorating the second guest room as a nursery.

The four of them were gathered around the dinner table and Berthe had convinced Frau Blatschky to cook her old specialties again. The days of bed rest had done her good and the nausea seemed to be in abeyance for the time being.

In deference to Herr Meisner, Frau Blatschky stayed away from pork tonight, opting instead for *beuschel,* a delicate ragout of fine strips of calf lung in a cream sauce served with a tender *knödel.* She paired this with an endive and radicchio salad drizzled with wine vinegar and rapeseed oil.

Gross remained silent through his two helpings of *beuschel.* Berthe contented herself with salad only. Werthen and Herr Meisner made small talk about the latest scandal in Parliament and the rise in strength of Mayor Lueger's Christian Democratic Party: "Neither truly Christian nor democratic in outlook," Herr Meisner pronounced.

Finally, as Gross daubed at his lips with a damask napkin, Herr Meisner brought them around to the subject of Mahler.

"So," he said, "where does the investigation stand?"

For the next half hour Werthen and Gross took turns detailing the progress of their attempts to protect Mahler and to bring the person or persons responsible for the attacks to justice. It had been a long and torturous route, from Alma Schindler's first alert, to the investigation of the deaths of Fräulein Kaspar and Herr Gunther, to the interviews of likely suspects such as Leitner and the stage manager Blauer, as well as hostile critics like Hassler and Hanslick, resentful artists and performers, including Hans Richter, and even the head of the banned claque, Schreier. They also detailed the domestic suspects, the sister Justine who had been disinherited, the faithful Natalie Bauer-Lechner, and Arnold Rosé, suitor of Justine. They described the attempts on Mahler's life, including the cut bicycle brake and most recently the poisoned Turkish delight and the arrest and release of

Schreier.

They went on to explain how their investigation had broadened, spurred on by the reception of an anonymous letter. How they probed the possibility that other famous composers recently dead had been the victims of a serial killer at work. There were Bruckner, Brahms, and Strauss, as well as the young composer Alexander Zemlinsky who had suffered an accident similar to one of Mahler's, falling from his director's podium at the Carl Theater.

"In the case of Brahms, however," Gross intoned, "we have ascertained that his death was, as reported at the time, the result of liver cancer. Strauss, though, is a different matter."

He briefly explained the mysterious summons to the Hofburg that ultimately cost Strauss his life.

"And Bruckner?" Herr Meisner asked.

"We have not yet had the time to investigate that," Werthen said. "Nor have we looked more deeply into the Zemlinsky matter."

"With the latest attack on Mahler we have decided to refocus, returning to our initial investigation," Gross explained. "Your daughter and Werthen have made some intriguing discoveries about Mahler's student days."

Werthen described the most recent information uncovered, about Hans Rott and the gossip that Mahler may have stolen from the dead composer's works.

"You're forgetting the attack on you, Karl," Berthe said, pushing her unfinished salad aside.

Werthen told how his office had been torn apart.

"It was nothing, really," he said, trying to downplay the danger for Berthe's sake.

"Doesn't sound like nothing to me," Herr Meisner said. "What was the intruder looking for?"

"We don't know," Werthen said. "As far as I can tell, nothing is missing."

"And this letter?"

Meaning their anonymous letter, Werthen thought, as the letter to Schreier had not been discovered until after the break-in and assault at the law office.

"It is here. I keep many of the files for my private inquiries at home."

"But the assailant couldn't know that, could he?" Herr Meisner said.

Gross suddenly pounded the table in excitement.

"Exactly. The man was after the letter.

There must be something compromising in it."

"Perhaps the musical score," Berthe offered.

Werthen left the table to fetch the letter. Returning, he spread it out on the dining-room table.

"Ah, yes," Herr Meisner said, viewing the letter and paying close attention to the musical annotation at the bottom of it. "Of course there is little to be learned from the primitive handwriting. But the musical score could be a code. A small hobby of mine, musical codes."

Werthen was reminded of Kraus's tales of how Brahms inserted coded messages into his works.

Gross, who made a study of codes for his book, got up now from his chair and moved next to Herr Meisner.

"I am not so certain about the code," Gross said, "but I do see something new in this letter."

At that, he went into the sitting room and came back with the letter to Schreier and placed it next to the anonymous one.

"There," he said, pointing at several places on each. "You see?"

"The smudges," Werthen said.

"Right. At regular intervals. It seems our

letter writer could not restrain himself from making corrections in the text, thereby staining his hand and smudging the paper. I should say these letters were written by the same person, despite the fact that the handwriting is disguised in both. Find the man who wrote these and we have our killer."

"Then it was most likely this letter your man was after at the law office," Herr Meisner said. "Do you think it safe that you keep it in your home? Come now, Werthen. You have a family to protect."

A sudden and insistent rapping sounded at their apartment door, and everyone froze for an instant.

Finally Gross said, "Rather unlikely the killer would knock."

Nonetheless, he and Werthen went to the door before Frau Blatschky could see to it. Gross made a detour to his room first, and a distinct bulge in the right pocket of his dinner jacket let Werthen know he was now armed.

Gross stood to one side of the door, hand firmly gripping the pistol in his pocket, while Werthen peered through the fish-eye peephole in the door.

"My Lord." He sighed. "What does she want?"

He glanced at Gross. "Put it away. You won't need a gun."

He opened the door to Alma Schindler, looking downcast and almost sheepish, and attired in evening dress as if she had just come from the Hofoper.

"Fräulein Schindler," Werthen said as he ushered the young woman in.

"I am sorry to bother you like this," she said, looking from Werthen to Gross. "But I have felt so awful since our last meeting. I just could not let it go as it did. I was at the opera tonight and I had to leave during the interval. My sister awaits me in a *fiaker* below, so this must be brief. Please accept my apology."

"It is perfectly all right, Fräulein Schindler."

"No, it is not," she said, and stamped a petulant foot. "I was willful and cruel. I want to apologize. I need to apologize."

Berthe and her father had now joined them in the foyer and quick introductions were made all round.

"For pity's sake, Werthen," the older man said. "What kind of host are you? Invite the young lady in for a coffee."

She brightened at this, happy to find an ally.

"No, no. I do not want to interrupt anything. Only to say how sincerely sorry I am for the way I acted."

"Fräulein Schindler," Berthe said. "I am sure we can take care of this tomorrow at the office."

But Herr Meisner again interrupted. "So this is the famous daughter of Schindler. I cannot tell you how much I appreciate your late father's work, young woman. The man was a genius of landscape."

She looked almost adoringly at Herr Meisner. "Do you think so really? So do I, but then I am not impartial. He was such a good man."

"I am sure he was, dear girl. Now do come in and join us for a spot of coffee."

He ushered her into the dining room, a protective arm around her shoulders.

Werthen, Gross, and Berthe were amazed at this, and could only follow. What in the world could the old man be thinking of? Werthen wondered.

Alma allowed herself to be guided into the dining room; so much for her concern for her waiting sister.

In the dining room, Herr Meisner seated the young woman next to him. Upon entering, Gross quickly swept up the letters and put them in his jacket pocket along with his pistol.

"Now exactly what is it you have to apologize for?" Berthe's father asked.

She blushed down to her partly exposed décolletage.

"I can hardly imagine such a charming young lady to be guilty of a major faux pas," Herr Meisner continued.

"Fräulein Schindler made some rather unfortunate remarks while we were visiting Zemlinsky," Werthen said.

She looked up. "Your son-in-law is too generous. The unfortunate comments were of a racial sort. Anti-Semitic, in fact."

The older man let out a sort of guffaw at this. "Well, you would hardly be Austrian without a bit of that in your blood, young lady. Do not lose sleep over it, but I find it commendable that you have come to unburden yourself of this. Bravo for you."

Frau Blatschky appeared in the doorway. "Shall I serve coffee, madam?" she said to Berthe.

"Please, Frau Blatschky," Berthe said.

"And an extra cup for our young visitor," Herr Meisner said.

"Oh, no. Thank you so much, but I really must be going." She reached out and patted Herr Meisner's hand. "I thank you so much, sir. You have made me feel so much better. Perhaps I can actually watch the last act of the opera now."

She was up and made her adieus. No one but Herr Meisner attempted to detain her. She left behind a slight smell of violets in her wake.

"My Lord," Herr Meisner said as the apartment door closed. "What a splendid young woman. Werthen, you do her a disservice to describe her as a spoiled dilettante. She has something, does Fräulein Schindler. A real presence."

"A presence, to be sure," Werthen said, but meant something quite different than did Herr Meisner.

FIFTEEN

The next morning, Werthen left Gross, Herr Meisner, and Berthe huddled over the musical notation on the anonymous letter, attempting to break its possible code. He went to the office, and Tor was already there, working fastidiously on a handwritten copy of a will for the von Tuma family patriarch. Werthen had given Tor a key his second week on the job, so dependable and trustworthy had he proved himself to be.

After this case is over, Werthen thought, I must see to adjusting the man's salary. The law office could not afford to lose someone as valuable as Tor to the competition.

Tor was never a talkative sort; this morning they shared only a brief *guten morgen.*

Once in his inner office, Werthen began sorting paperwork into urgent and less urgent piles, culling those that could be handled by Tor and those that must be seen to himself.

His morning work was disturbed, however, when he heard the outer office door open and then a mumble of voices. Tor knocked and poked his head inside.

"A gentleman to see you, Advokat. From the police." Tor looked almost fearful as he uttered this last word.

He ushered in Detective Inspector Drechsler, who appeared to be in a hurry.

"Advokat," he said by way of greeting.

Tor closed the door slowly behind him.

"What can I do for you, Inspector? I hope it is not about that break-in."

"No, no," Drechsler said importantly. "I was in the neighborhood and thought I might find Doktor Gross with you."

"He's at the apartment. May I be of assistance?" Werthen motioned to a chair, but Drechsler shook his head.

"I just wanted to let you chaps know that our little night watch effort has finally borne fruit."

"Night watch?"

"Herr Gunther's killer, remember? He was seen by one lady of the night leaving the premises, and we had hoped to find another who could provide a better description."

"Right. Sorry. Success, you say?"

"My sergeant finally found another young

woman whose territory is closer to the Hofburg, and she distinctly remembers the man in question."

"How can she be so sure?" Werthen asked. "After all, it was . . . how long ago?"

"About three weeks ago. And she can be sure. It was the very night one customer tipped her five kronen. That stuck in her mind, as did the face of our man."

Werthen felt a frisson of expectation. "She gave a description?"

Drechsler paused a moment. "Well, actually nothing too exact. A bit above medium height, stocky build. It was the eyes she remembered most. Said they looked like they could suck you into the depths. I did not bother to query which depths she might be referring to."

Drechsler chuckled at his attempted quip, but Werthen remained silent.

"At any rate," the policeman continued, "he scared her so much she didn't bother continuing her sales pitch to him. But she says she could identify him if she ever saw him again."

"Did she mention any other characteristics?" Werthen asked. "Facial hair, a beard, mustache. Anything?"

Another pause from Drechsler. "Sorry. I'll have my man interview her again. Mousy little creature. Mitzi Paulus. What men could see in her I don't know. Lives in a miserable little garret in the Kohlmarkt."

"Have you presented her with a rogues' gallery of our suspects? I am sure we can obtain some photographs from the Hofoper."

"We are onto that now, Advokat. However, it is not the easiest thing getting photographs of men who are not known criminals. We're working through the newspapers and the Hofoper. It takes time."

"Bravo to you, Drechsler. I will let Gross know of your information. We are making headway. I feel it."

"Tell that to Meindl. He was outraged we released Schreier. Said he'd have my liver for breakfast. Puffed up little adder he is."

Werthen agreed entirely with this final description. Drechsler then made his adieus and was shown out by Tor, who appeared at the office door just at the appropriate moment.

Werthen made his way later that morning to the Hofoper. It was time to speak with Arnold Rosé and in the interval of rehearsals seemed the most opportune time and place to do it.

Coming onto the opera from the rear, that

is from the Inner City side of the building, he was reminded again of the scandal and tragedies that accompanied the difficult birth of that august institution. The Hofoper was expert at spawning tragedy not only on its stage.

The architects, August von Siccardsburg and Eduard van der Nüll, were both close friends and colleagues, well respected in Vienna before the competition for the opera house. In 1860, when the competition was announced, they submitted their plan, per regulations, anonymously, with only a motto to identify whose it was. In their case, they chose a saying that would later have ominous overtones: *"Fait ce que dois, advienne que pourra,"* "Do what you must, come what may."

Their plan for a monumental new opera house to replace the old one nearby was cheered initially by the press who claimed that the architects *composed* the plans rather than designed them. The planned exterior was imposing enough; the interior with its lavish central stairway, salons and main auditorium decorated with statuary and paintings by some of the finest artists in the empire, would put the Royal Court Opera in a class by itself, the newspapers declared.

This honeymoon was short-lived. As construction began the following year, delays and cost overruns ensued. Worse, the level of the newly created Ringstrasse ended up becoming several meters higher than originally planned. Thus, by the time the Court Opera finally was nearing completion in 1868, its entrance on the Ringstrasse was, in fact, below street level.

The press, eager for headlines, began calling the new building the sunken chest and an "architectural Königgrätz," after the 1866 defeat of Austrian troops by Prussia. When the emperor himself casually remarked to an aide that the entrance was indeed low, tragedy à la Viennois resulted. Unable to bear such criticism, van der Nüll hanged himself in April of 1868; his friend Siccardsburg died two months later, of a "broken heart," the same scurrilous press reported. Neither lived to see completion of the building they had "composed." In the event, the public learned to live with a partially subterranean entrance, and the emperor, chastened by this experience, confined himself from that time on to the polite phrase, "It was very nice; it pleased me very much," whenever asked for his judgment about a public event.

Werthen entered the side doors and made

his way to the auditorium where Richter, filling in for Mahler, was just finishing morning rehearsals for *Tannhäuser*. The third violin chair had, Werthen noticed, been filled. A bearded, middle-aged gentleman had taken the deceased Herr Gunther's position in the orchestra. Rosé, seeing Werthen, nodded, and they sat together in red plush chairs on the main floor as the rest of the orchestra went off for their mid-morning coffee.

"It was good of you to see me. Do you want something to eat or drink as we talk?" Werthen asked.

"I eat sparingly," the tall, elegant violinist said. "I assume you want to talk about these attacks on Gustav."

"Attacks?"

"Please, Advokat Werthen. Justi and I do not have secrets from each other. Not a string of accidents, but a concerted effort to kill Mahler. And to answer your as yet unasked question, no, it is not I. Whether or not Gustav chooses to write his sister out of his will if we marry is of little matter to me."

"And your position in the orchestra?"

"This is not a parallel case to my brother's. Unlike him, I have real power in Vienna's musical world. I have a secure position, one that cannot be taken from me out of domestic spite. Austrian bureaucracy, for all its failings, does at least guarantee one security in his job."

"Actually, I did not come to accuse you or even to vet you," Werthen said. "Rather I want to know more about Herr Mahler's past."

"You think the person who wants to kill him has an old grudge?"

"It is a possibility. What do you know about Hans Rott, for example?"

Rosé showed no surprise at the name. "That he is dead and could not be the one to have attacked Gustav."

"I realize that, as well, Herr Rosé. What I would like to know is something about their relationship."

"Gustav and Rott? There is not much to say. Gustav thought, mistakenly so, I believe, that Rott was the most talented of our generation."

"Do you know his music?"

Rosé cast Werthen a baleful look. "Not all that again."

"All what?"

"That Gustav stole the man's music after he died in the asylum. Nonsense. Utter nonsense."

"How so?"

"You've only to listen to the compositions

of both to hear that."

"Have you?"

Rosé looked suddenly discomfited. "Not in decades. I believe I heard part of one of Rott's early symphonies. So many years ago."

"Then how can you call it nonsense that Herr Mahler might have borrowed from Rott's work?"

"Because it is not in Gustav's nature to cheat. He is, if anything, too pure for this world. He is too hard on himself. And thus on others."

Werthen pushed on. "Were they friends?"

"We were all chums of a sort back then. But those were student days. Rott was not the sort of young man to actually have friends. He had commitments instead. When his father died — his mother had already died years earlier — Rott was only eighteen. Suddenly the weight of the world was cast upon his shoulders. It unhinged him, I am sure."

"What weight? You mean having to make his own way as a teenager?"

Rosé nodded. "And that of his younger brother. He had to make a living for both of them, and had to keep the brother out of trouble, as well."

"What was this brother's name?"

Rosé thought for a moment. "Karl, I think it was. Never met him myself, but from what I heard he only wanted to carouse and play the large man with the ladies. There was some story about him, born on the wrong side of the sheets. There were rumors at the time of a dalliance on the part of the mama with a noble, perhaps even a Habsburg. It escapes me now, but this younger brother couldn't have been more than fifteen, sixteen at the time. As I say, I never met him, not even at Rott's funeral. He was conspicuously absent. Not old Bruckner, though. Wept like a baby for Rott, his star pupil."

There was little more to be learned from Rosé, so Werthen left him to the tuning of his violin. As he was walking up the aisle to the exit, Herr Regierungsrath Leitner joined him.

"I hope you discovered something useful. This business must stop."

"Yes," Werthen said. "And thank you again for arranging the interview."

"Are you any closer to catching the culprit?"

"Close," Werthen said. "And getting closer every day."

Werthen was not sure, but it seemed that this remark, more bluff than truth, caused

Leitner a spasm of concern. The look passed in an instant, though, to be replaced by his usual neutral countenance.

A yipping and barking erupted from the stage, and Werthen was astonished to see the stage manager, Siegfried Blauer, at the helm of a brace of hunting dogs, tugging this way and that on their leather leashes. In his outmoded muttonchops and with these dogs all about him, he suddenly looked like a younger version of Emperor Franz Josef.

"My God, man," Blauer boomed at a red-faced gentleman in lederhosen accompanying him. "I thought you said these animals were trained."

"They are," the other replied. "For hunting, not necessarily for gallivanting about the stage."

"Leitner!" Blauer cried out, shielding his eyes from the stage lights to see into the auditorium. "Are you out there? Do you hear? This is insanity. Seventy hunting dogs for the entrance scene? He must be mad."

Leitner turned to Werthen for a moment. "He means Herr Mahler, I am afraid. It was his wish to have the dogs onstage. He is a great one for theatrical effects."

"Leitner," Blauer called out again in his Ottakring drawl. "We need some beasts who can hold their water onstage."

"Please forgive me, I must see to this."

"Of course," Werthen said. "And thank you once again."

But Leitner was now too engaged in this canine drama to pay him further attention.

"What is the occasion?" Werthen asked that evening upon returning to his flat.

An open bottle of *sekt* — faux champagne — lay in an ice bucket; Gross and Herr Meisner were toasting with long-stemmed glasses. Berthe was joining the toast with what appeared to be mineral water in her glass.

"Ah, Werthen," Gross said jovially. "There you are. Good that you could make it home in time for the festivities."

"In honor of what, might I ask?"

Gross beamed a smile at him. "You are the one who makes private inquiries. Tell *me* what this is about."

"You've done it. You broke the code."

"Not I," Gross said, somewhat sadly. "No. The laurels go to your esteemed father-in-law."

"That's wonderful," Werthen said. "And what did it say?"

Gross waved his glass of *sekt* like a conductor's baton. "Not so quickly. First, you must follow in our footsteps to the discovery."

"Really, Gross," Werthen spluttered. "We hardly have the time for parlor games."

"Karl," Berthe interrupted. "Don't be such a stick. It is really quite fascinating. Papa, please tell Karl how you broke the code."

Herr Meisner was only partly joining in the general gaiety, Werthen could tell, eager to keep his daughter happy.

"It is really no great achievement," he began.

"Nonsense," said Gross. "I personally exhausted all my cipher knowledge in the task. Numerical codes, alphabet codes, everything from Caesar's cipher to the Napoleon I system. I was about to tear my hair out, but of course I have little left to tear. Then our most knowledgeable colleague, Herr Meisner, joined the fray."

Such praise was clearly embarrassing for Herr Meisner, but he managed a bland smile.

"Please, Papa," Berthe urged.

"Well, it was a bit of a puzzler at first, I must admit. As I said, I have made a study of musical codes. Musicians since the time of Bach have played with secret messages encoded in their compositions. Typically, one uses letter names of the notes to spell out a message. Usually these are the names of friends and associates."

"Right," Werthen said. "Brahms had a penchant for such games, I am told."

Herr Meisner cast him a friendly glance. "Indeed. For Bach it was the use of the F–A–B–E in his canons, referring to his fellow composer and friend, J. C. Faber. Over the years, composers got more and more ingenious in developing their alphabet. For example, E-flat stands for the letter *s,* naturally, because in German our name for that note is *Es,* and B-sharp is the equivalent of *Hah,* or *H.* You mention Brahms, but also Schumann delighted in musical jests, inserting names of friends in his work. I am told the Irish composer, John Field, once complimented a dinner hostess with melodies produced by B–E–E–F and C–A–B–B–A–G–E. Just last year the British composer, Edward Elgar, published his *Enigma Variations,* hinting that the various melodies of his variations are based, in fact, on a well-known tune. I have yet, I dare say, to break the code, though I favor *Auld Lang Syne* as the inspiration."

"And this was a simple sort of cipher like those?" Werthen asked.

"Unfortunately, no," Herr Meisner said.

"Musicians have also created codes using an ascending scale of quarter notes, a dozen of them to represent the first twelve letters of the alphabet. Rhythm has also been used in such endeavors, creating a cipher system not unlike Morse code. Additionally, we must also contend with basic letter substitution systems. Here, as the great ninth-century Baghdad cryptographer, Al-Kindi, has shown, one simply develops a system of replacing one letter with another. For example, the letter *A* is always replaced by *B,* or *B* in turn is replaced by *H.* Also, we have the work of Porta, whose secret alphabet was used widely in the early seventeenth century. Which brings me finally to the work of that notable seventeenth-century British clergyman, Bishop John Wilkins."

"Yes, yes," Gross said, unable to control his enthusiasm. "His *Mercury: The Secret and Swift Messenger* was a revelation for me."

"You should also read his work on the construction of an artificial language for the use of diplomats, scientists, and philosophers. It makes inspiring reading."

"Papa," Berthe said, urging him back to the subject at hand.

"Yes. The good bishop wrote his book on cryptography when he was just twenty-seven and I believe it proved quite handy for chaps during the English Civil War. In that book he touches on language as concealed in musical notes. In chapter eighteen, as I remember, he posits an alphabet of descending notes, beginning with A, and leaving out letters *K* and *Q* as their sound may be created by the C. But Wilkins goes on to employ a letter substitution system as well as the use of Latin as base language. Once I recalled that system, the rest was mere secretarial work."

"What was the secret message?" Werthen's curiosity was well and truly piqued by now.

Herr Meisner took a slip of paper out of his vest pocket and, squinting at it, read, "Hans Rott salutes and condemns you from the grave, Mahler."

"You are absolutely certain?"

Herr Meisner nodded his head solemnly.

"But that is marvelous," Werthen said.

Gross clapped Werthen on the back, handing him a glass of *sekt*.

"So now you know the reason to celebrate. Someone who was connected with Rott seeks revenge on Mahler for stealing the man's work. Now we only need to find who that someone might be."

Werthen, however, began to have second thoughts. "But why would this person expose himself so? Why such an overt lead."

"Hardly overt," Gross said. "In point of fact, it took two skilled cryptographers to break the code."

"Still," Werthen said.

"My friend," Gross reassured him, "this message includes several valuable pieces of information. One points to Hans Rott, and another tells us our enemy here thinks he is invincible. His ego is immense; he believes the rest of the world is comprised of idiots. Thus he can create false leads about the murders of famous Viennese composers and at the same time thumb his nose at us with this coded piece of music. This lets us know, via the false leads, that perhaps we were getting too close to him earlier in our investigation. Still a further piece of information we gain is that our culprit has a working knowledge of music and composition. Perhaps he associated with musicians."

"My God, could it be?" Werthen said.

"What is it, Karl?" Berthe took his arm, alarmed at his sudden change.

"Speaking with Arnold Rosé today, I discovered that Rott had a younger brother who was not the best sort of citizen."

Gross clapped his meaty hands together. "Ah, yes, now we are getting somewhere."

Sixteen

Werthen thought it odd that church bells should be ringing this early. It was still before dawn, and as he listened to this faux Angelus, he felt a throbbing at his temples and a dryness in his mouth. One too many celebratory glasses of *sekt* last evening.

By the time he realized it was the phone and not church bells ringing, the sound had ceased, only to be followed a few instants later by an insistent tapping at the bedroom door.

Berthe rolled over groggily. "What is that, Karl? Mice?"

"Nothing, darling. Go back to sleep."

He slipped out of bed, wrapping his silk robe around him as he went to the door.

Gross, looking bleary-eyed and with a tuft of his tonsured fringe askew, spoke quietly but with urgency.

"Get dressed. Our man's been at his dirty work again."

■ ■ ■ ■

She lay on her back in a pool of dried blood.
The gaping wound at her neck had already
attracted flies. Drechsler swatted at them
with his derby.

"I don't like this one little bit," he spat
out. "I tell you the young lady's name and
place of abode, and the next thing I know,
she is dead. Who did you tell?"

"And I do not appreciate your insinua-
tion, Inspector. I told no one. Not even
Gross, here. I forgot. Other matters intervened."

"Werthen," Gross said. "How could you,
man? If I had known of her existence,
perhaps this young woman would still be
alive."

The statement was so preposterous that
not even Drechsler commented on or added
to it.

They were in the garret room of Mitzi
Paulus, of whom Drechsler had indeed apprised Werthen just the day before. An officer had thrown the one window open, but
the fumes over the Kohlmarkt this morning
were not much better than those within: a
combination of cheap perfume, human
sweat, and dried blood. To take his mind off

this, Werthen quickly explained to Gross about the young woman and her supposed ability to identify the man she saw the night Herr Gunther was killed.

Then turning to Drechsler, Werthen said, "I take it your sergeant was unable to talk to her again?"

"You take it correctly," Drechsler said morosely. "But how the hell did he find out we were on to him through this tart?"

Gross sighed. "She was in a dangerous profession. Perhaps this murder is merely a coincidence." But he uttered this with such a lack of conviction that it was clear he did not think so either.

"Think, man," Drechsler persisted. "There must have been someone. Perhaps our conversation was overheard?"

The only thing Werthen could think of was the fact that Herr Tor seemed to arrive at the office door just as Drechsler was leaving. Had he overheard? But that was patently absurd. The mouselike Tor was hardly capable of murder. He mentioned none of this, but instead went on the offensive.

"And why not assume that it was not your own sergeant who told one too many friends about his great success? Or perhaps you yourself spoke about it out of turn and were overheard?"

"I must say, Drechsler," Gross added, "I agree wholeheartedly with Werthen. "Why put the blame on him?"

"Meindl is turning apoplectic."

"That," Gross said, "is Meindl's affair, not ours."

They used their Montenuovo letter to gain access to the K und K Hofarchiv in the Hofburg, presenting the baleful clerk in his white coat with a birth registration request. They were searching for the records for one Karl Rott, born circa 1860. Rosé had told him the younger brother was about two years younger than Hans Rott, who was born in 1858.

The clerk had an ink smudge on his right earlobe, the result of a habit of rubbing his ear with his pen hand, Gross explained once the young man had taken their form and disappeared into a labyrinth of wooden shelving that held a formidable array of bulky, gray file boxes.

Gross had been the one, after Werthen had explained about Rosé believing there to be some question surrounding the propriety of the birth of this second son, who advised a further search for birth records.

As they waited Werthen once again thought of how the information about Mitzi

Paulus could have gotten to the killer. Perhaps, as with Herr Gunther, their man was only tying up loose ends, getting rid of any possible witnesses to his crimes. Thus, he would remember the young woman who had approached him and looked into his empty eyes. He would know her territory, where to find her. But would she actually go with the man? After all, she said she could recognize him. He had frightened her the first time she had seen him. Now she knew that he was wanted by the police, one would assume she would be doubly fearful of him.

Or perhaps, as they had suspected all along, the perpetrator was not working alone. He had someone else he could send to Mitzi Paulus, a stranger, who had bargained with her, trudged up the three flights of creaky stairs behind her to the bedroom garret over the Kohlmarkt and then slashed her throat as she began to disrobe and was defenseless.

Their nemesis was a cur. Not a man, or men, at all. How many had died now in the pursuit of Mahler's death? Three innocent victims.

"Nothing here for a Karl Rott." The clerk had returned, but not empty-handed. "I did find a file for Hans Rott, though. I was at the *R*s, so thought it might be worth a look."

"It is not Hans we are searching for," Gross said with some displeasure.

"I realize that, gentlemen. But seeing's how you've been dispatched by Prince Montenuovo himself, I thought you might appreciate thoroughness."

"Quite right, my boy, "Gross replied, attempting to rein in his monumental impatience. "Do forgive my brusqueness."

"That's fine, sir. Many of our clients pay me no heed, as if I were simply a piece of furniture here. I do appreciate it, though, when my diligence does not go unnoticed."

"Perhaps you could just inform us of what you found, if anything," Gross said.

The clerk clutched the file closer to his breast. "Well, there is mention here of Hans Rott being first born to the actor Karl Matthias Roth, later changed to Rott, and one Maria Rosalia Lutz, a singer. A later addition to the file shows that he had a half brother, legitimized to the name of Rott."

"Legitimized?" Werthen said. "Whose child was it then?"

The young clerk blushed as he spoke. "Well, it says here that the file for this brother is in the imperial house archives. Perhaps Prince Montenuovo can enlighten you."

Which, Werthen realized, meant that the younger brother was most likely the illegitimate child of Maria Lutz and a member of the royal family.

"You believe it to be important?" Prince Montenuovo asked once Gross made the reason for their visit clear.

"Imperative, Prince," Gross said.

"This is hardly the sort of information we like to make public."

"He may by our murderer and the one attempting to kill Mahler," Werthen said. It was hardly the time for decorum.

"Yes," Montenuovo said in an even tone. He leaned back in his chair, looked at a fresco of two putti gamboling on the ceiling over his baroque desk, and then he made a most unprincely clucking sound with his tongue.

"It shall be done. If you could wait outside. My attendant will see to it."

Thus it was that ten minutes later they were presented with the birth certificate of young Wilhelm Karl, born December 20, 1860, later to bear the family name of Rott. But in the document the true father was listed as Archduke Wilhelm, one of Franz Josef's brothers. A bachelor all his life, the prince died in 1894, but, it appeared, his progeny lived on.

Mahler was looking like his old self, working on the score to *Tannhäuser* as Justine showed Werthen into the large sitting room with the Bösendorfer grand. Meanwhile, Gross had gone to check on further leads with Drechsler.

Werthen had often wondered how conductors managed to direct an orchestra of fifty or more and a cast of singers that sometimes reached into the hundreds — especially in Mahler's grandiose performances — through two or three hours of a complex and demanding operatic score. Here was an obvious partial explanation: hard work, attention to detail, and intensive cramming that would make a *matura* candidate, an aspirant for a secondary school degree, blanch. Mahler, who must have conducted the opera a score of times in his career, was pecking out the score with his left hand while making detailed and last-minute notes with his right.

Despite being near death only days earlier, Mahler was going to conduct tonight's special performance of *Tannhäuser,* a tribute to Wagner's widow, Cosima, who was to be in attendance.

"Werthen," he called out once seeing the

lawyer. "Have you caught him?"

"Soon, Herr Mahler."

He nodded at his sister, who was waiting by the door. She shut it behind her as she left.

"I want to make this positively clear to you and your detective friends. I do not want my sister, Natalie, or Herr Rosé any further discomfited by your inquiries. They are not to be treated as common criminals. Is that understood?"

His face suddenly took on a ferocious, predatory look.

But Werthen was having none of his bullying techniques.

"Someone is trying to kill you, Herr Mahler. Someone who has now killed three others in the process."

"Three?"

"Yes. I have just come from the gruesome scene of a crime where a young woman was butchered. She probably had seen our man leaving Herr Gunther's and she paid for it with her life."

"This is terrible," he said.

"Yes, and it is no time for assumptions and societal or familial niceties. You hired me to do a job and I intend to do it."

"Well, where were you then when I needed you? Sent your assistant to do the job when

I had asked for you."

Werthen did not want to say the obvious; that no one can save you from a killer who is determined enough or willing to give his own life in the process.

"Tor is a competent man," Werthen replied.

"For wills and trusts. But I hired you for more than that. Besides, he was late." Mahler raised his eyebrows at this unpardonable sin.

"I am sure you are familiar with the difficult train connections that need to be made. The railway does not always run on time."

"A full day late," Mahler said. "We were expecting him on the Wednesday. In the event, he did not arrive until Thursday, and then had to return to town that very afternoon."

"The police were there. If they weren't able to protect you, I doubt I could have."

"Police." Mahler almost spat the word out.

"But I have not come about any of this. I want to know about Hans Rott."

Mahler looked up from the keyboard.

"I am forgetting my manners. Please take a seat."

He rose from the piano bench and led the way to twin chairs by the daybed. Seated again, he squinted his eyes at Werthen.

"What is it you want to know?"

"Would anybody associated with Rott have cause to do you harm?"

"Maria and Joseph! Is it that old gossip again, following me around like a load of tripe? Enough, I say. I have heard enough of it."

"So there could be reason?"

Mahler looked as if he might explode; a vein bulged at his temple and throbbed at an alarming rate.

"I will say this only once because you are a virtual stranger to me and my household. You do not know the high value I place on honesty and loyalty. Therefore, in answer to your question, no, there could be no reason a sane person would want to avenge any supposed wrong I might have done to Hans Rott. Art is sacred, Werthen, don't you see?"

"I am a mere lawyer. Please explain."

Mahler pursed his lips, not finding the ironic comment at all humorous.

"A man's artistic work, in this case Rott's compositions, are like a communion with the great unknown. With the spirit that animates the universe. To steal that work would be a profound sin. I am not talking now of influences. We are all influenced by those persons who have gone before us. We do praise to that person or persons to demonstrate such influence in our work. But to take a man's notes, to thieve one's themes or melodies . . . It is unthinkable. Can't you see that?"

Werthen said nothing. Mahler's conviction was real enough, though.

"So, no. I can see no reason why anyone connected to Rott would wish to seek revenge upon me. In ways I loved the man. He was the purest of our generation. Perhaps the best composer I have ever known. A simple man, but an artist through and through. I never did him harm. In fact, I was more than generous in my loans to him. He was always short of funds. An orphan you know. And then he had, if I remember correctly, a brother to support."

"Wilhelm Karl," Werthen offered. "Did you know him?"

Mahler shook his head. "Never met the man. But as I recall, he was the younger brother. Do I recall hearing he went to America? Probably one step ahead of the bill collector. Or some irate father."

Werthen considered this.

"Now, dear Advokat. If there is nothing else, I have a performance to prepare for."

"Really, Fräulein Schindler. I could not accept such generosity."

Berthe was amazed at the young woman's cheek. Coming to call once again uninvited and then seemingly disappointed that Karl was not here to greet her. Berthe herself was somewhat unconventional in regard to social etiquette, but even for her this was too much.

"No, no, Frau Werthen —"

"Meisner," Berthe sharply corrected her. "Frau Meisner." She felt somehow that this young woman knew her name, but simply refused to use it. Perhaps to make the older woman seem more conventional.

This reproach, however, did not dampen the young woman's enthusiasm; she was like a puppy with a new bedroom slipper.

"Pardon me," she said cheerily. "Frau Meisner. But as I was about to say, the tickets will go to waste unless you and your husband use them. Herr Moll, my step-father, has come down with a nasty summer cold and Maman refuses to leave his side. Besides, now that she is, well, in a certain way indisposed, I imagine she feels better out of society's curious gaze anyway."

"Indisposed?" Berthe asked, knowing full well what the euphemism meant. But she wanted Fräulein Schindler to actually say the word. Such a misplaced sense of prudery, she thought. As if having a child were something to be ashamed of.

"Well, pregnant, you know," the other said.

And then Fräulein Schindler surprised Berthe by bursting into tears.

"Every last bit of Father will be forgotten now," she moaned between tears.

Whatever Berthe thought of the young woman, it seemed these tears were real enough. And the pent-up emotion behind them. Berthe rose and went to her, sitting beside her on the leather sofa and wrapping a tentative arm around her.

"Now, now," she consoled, about to tell her something idiotic like it was not worth crying over or not to worry. Instead she said, "Have a good cry."

As the tears slowly dried up, Alma Schindler looked frankly at Berthe.

"I am filled with apprehension, Frau Meisner. What if Maman dies in childbirth. She is somewhat old to be having another baby, it can be a dangerous procedure. Then I and my sister should be truly orphaned. First my beloved father and now Maman. Or, and I am not too proud to metion it, with a new baby to care for Maman shall refocus her attention to it. That, too, would be as if I were orphaned. And my stepfather, with this simple act of procreation, will completely supplant my dead father in the affections of Maman. I know I must sound a venal young woman for voicing such fears, but there it is. I should be rejoicing Maman's new baby. Instead, I dread it."

Berthe felt her heart opening to the young woman — suddenly seeming so vulnerable. Was this what her father, Herr Meisner, had seen in her the other night? Is that why his heart, too, had opened to Fräulein Schindler?

"I value your honesty, Fräulein Schindler. We have little control over such fears. And I shall share something with you, as well. You see, I am also pregnant and am filled with both joy and yes, fears. I am fearful that when I am a mother, that is all I shall be allowed to be. That motherhood will become some kind of trap where my role is tightly defined by society. Fearful that my husband will also subscribe to such a role for me."

"You are an ambitious woman, then, Frau Meisner?" Her eyes, still red from crying, sparkled as she said this.

Berthe had never thought of herself in that regard. "Yes," she said. "I suppose I am. I have a persona of my own, if you understand."

Alma Schindler seemed almost to wiggle in delight at this utterance.

"Oh, I do so understand. It is what I too feel. And I live in mortal terror lest I fall in love with some man who wants to quash that persona, that spirit."

"But could you ever love such a man?" Bertha asked, amazed.

"Of course. Every man I have ever been attracted to is a forceful, domineering, creative genius. Such a man wants only one talent in the household."

Berthe thought that in this case there could hardly be a worse choice for Fräulein Schindler than Gustav Mahler. If ever there was a man who wanted to be completely in charge of his career and household, it was Mahler.

"That is me," Fräulein Schindler said brightly. "Full of contradictions. My mind cannot control where my heart leads me."

"Then I might try muzzling that heart of yours." Berthe laughed. "At least for the next few years until you have a chance to be on your own, to become your own woman."

"Please say you will come," Fräulein Schindler said with real sincerity.

"Come where, my dear?" Herr Meisner said as he entered the sitting room, freshly arrived following an after-lunch stroll. "And, might I add, how charming it is to see you once again."

411

"Herr Meisner. Good to see you also."
Like an adolescent, Alma Schindler rose as
the older man came to her.

He gestured her to be seated. "Go where?"
he asked again.

"I was just trying to convince your daughter to join me at the Hofoper this evening. I
have tickets for *Tannhäuser.*"

She quickly explained the sickness in her
family and her mother's reluctance to leave
her husband's bedside.

"A fine idea," Herr Meisner said. "It
would do Berthe a world of good to get out
of the flat for an evening. Silly antediluvian
notion that a lady must lie in at such a
time."

He stopped suddenly, not knowing if he
had misspoken.

"It is all right, Father," Berthe said, and
then added in a joking tone, "I told Fräulein
Schindler of my oh-so-delicate condition."

Herr Meisner smiled at this. "There you
are, and what do you think, Fräulein Schindler? Would it not be fine for Berthe to
breathe the invigorating cultural air of the
Hofoper? Even if it is Wagner."

"But, Herr Meisner, Wagner is the apogee
of art."

"Apogee, as in a distant moon, Fräulein
Schindler?"

She laughed at this. "No, Herr Meisner. You purposely misconstrue my meaning. Apogee, as in apex. And yes, it would be wonderful for Frau Meisner to attend."

"But you mention both your mother and father unable to use their tickets," he said.

"I was hoping to induce Herr Werthen to accompany us," Fräulein Schindler said.

But Herr Meisner merely shook his head at this suggestion.

"Nonsense. Karl is far too busy trying to track this villain down before he makes more mischief. But I, on the other hand, am an old man at loose ends in the great metropolis and only too eager to accompany two young beauties to hear the apogee of music."

"Father!" But Berthe was not as scandalized as she tried to sound.

Fräulein Schindler looked at her mischievously. "Is it settled then, Frau Meisner?"

"Well," Berthe began.

"You know Karl's taste in music goes toward the symphony or chamber music," Herr Meisner said. "I would be doing him a favor going in his stead."

"There you have it, Fräulein Schindler. My father has spoken. We shall be delighted to share your seats."

■ ■ ■ ■

Werthen's mind was in a whirl. He walked
from Mahler's flat to meet Gross at the Café
Frauenhuber, hoping that the mere physical
rhythm of one foot in front of the other
would help him put order to the chaos of
thought pulsing in his head.

The moment he had left Mahler's apartment, a statement the composer had made
came back to him. Tor had not arrived in
Altaussee until last Thursday. At first Werthen did not understand why that should be
significant. Perhaps Tor stopped off to see
friends on the way. Perhaps he had taken a
small, albeit illicit, vacation of a day. He
deserved it; he had only to ask Werthen for
a holiday. What difference could it make,
anyway?

But as he walked on, this small discrep-
ancy nagged at him until he finally realized
its real importance: If Tor had not arrived
in Altaussee until Thursday, that meant that
he could still have been in Vienna last
Wednesday. The day Werthen was attacked
at the office.

Another block of walking made Werthen
see how utterly ridiculous that was. If Tor
had wanted to find some document in the

414

office — say the letter he had sent — then all he had to do was rifle through the drawers when Werthen was not there. There had been ample opportunity for that. No need to call attention to a break-in by turning the office upside down and then assaulting him.

It took a half block more for Werthen to render this argument null. Perhaps Tor *wanted* to call attention to such a break-in, assuming, thereby, that no one would suspect him of it for the very reasons Werthen himself had posited. In other words, Tor had staged a break-in and assaulted Werthen in order to plant a false trail away from himself.

By this time he had reached the Ringstrasse and began navigating the warren of streets toward the café. He recalled now his conversation with Natalie Bauer-Lechner at the train station last Friday night when they had brought Mahler back to Vienna half dead. She, too, confirmed what Mahler said. Werthen had not registered it at the time, but clearly it had been percolating in what the nerve doctors were calling the subconscious.

Natalie Bauer-Lechner had mentioned Tor arriving "yesterday." Which meant Thursday, not Wednesday. He had heard the statement, lodged it, but only processed it now for its true significance.

Gross was already waiting for him at the café, seated in the same place they had occupied the other day while interviewing Herr Hanslick. Otto, the headwaiter, greeted him with his usual good cheer and promptly brought him a mocha without bothering to ask him.

Werthen could not hold back, but blurted out his suspicions regarding Herr Tor.

Gross merely nodded. "I, too, was cogitating along those lines. The discovery of the given name of 'Wilhelm' rather tipped the scales. As with the inversion of the family name, Tor for Rott. Criminals like to keep their aliases as close to their original names as possible to avoid confusing themselves."

Werthen felt excitement growing in him like a palpable presence.

"So Tor could be the long-lost brother of Hans Rott, avenging his brother for what he thinks is Mahler's plagiarism. He is about the right age, and Mahler remembered hearing that this brother might have gone to America. Tor spent time in America, or so he told Berthe. My God, Gross, he had ample opportunity, as well. He was on hand each time in the country when there was an attack on Mahler. Before the bicycle accident and then last week before the poisoning."

He thought for a moment. "But how could he be responsible for the events at the Hofoper itself?"

"This is where our theory of an accomplice must come into play," Gross responded. "Tor, or Rott, has someone on the inside that is aiding him. After all, it is too much to assume that he had access to the backstage and that no one would have noticed this stranger roaming about."

"And what of Gunther and the Paulus woman?"

Gross stirred his coffee. "Either Tor or his accomplice could have done those killings."

"It is difficult to imagine Tor in the role of the killer," Werthen said, remembering the man's shyness, reticence, almost quaking nature.

"A man can change his mannerism and appearance as easily as he can his name," Gross counseled. "Meekness is the perfect disguise for a man with anger enough to kill several times."

Gross had another thought. "Perhaps we should question Frau Ignatz once again," he said. "As I recall, she told me she saw no strangers in the building the day you were attacked. If I interpret that statement literally, it leaves the possibility that she may have seen Herr Tor. After all, he is no stranger to her. If Tor is Rott, that explains something else that was bothering me about your assault."

Werthen was about to ask what that was, but Gross charged ahead.

"The locked door to your office. Thus far we have hypothesized that it was the unusual actions of a burglar, but why couldn't the locked door be the habitual actions of an employee?

"How could I have been so blind?" Werthen suddenly said.

"Do not berate yourself, friend," Gross consoled. "Neither did I see through him. But for now, this is a theory, only. We have no hard proof. However, I know how we might gather some, and without the necessity of interviewing your impertinent *portier* again.

"His writing," Werthen said. "The telltale smudges. We have reams of his hand-written documents at the office."

As they quickly paid and made their way to the door, Herr Otto stopped Werthen for a moment.

"A couple of things you might want to know, Herr Advokat. Last week as you left, I saw a man follow you."

"Following me?"

"Yes. He was standing on the corner. I noticed him because he stood there the entire time you were speaking with Herr Hanslick. He pretended to look at a display in the milliner's shop, but every once in a while he quickly gazed into the windows of this café. Then when you left I saw him carefully hide his face from you, as if you might recognize him. After you had gone half a block, he set off after you, pulling his bowler down tight over his eyes."

"Lord, Herr Otto, you would make a good inquiries man yourself. Can you describe this fellow."

"Oh yes, sir. Larger than average and somewhat thick. A nose that is more round than narrow. He carried himself close, you know. As if he was the humble sort, maybe even shy. But when he started following you, it was clear he was neither. Seemed to me more like a hawk hunting prey, if you take my meaning."

"I do, Herr Otto, very well," Werthen replied. "And thank you."

Herr Otto had just supplied a close description of Wilhelm Tor.

"You mentioned 'a couple' of things," Werthen said before leaving.

Herr Otto nodded. "Right. Last week I

mentioned how Herr Hanslick and his friend Herr Kalbeck were deep in discussion."

" 'Thick as thieves,' I believe was the expression you used."

Herr Otto reddened. "Yes, well, perhaps that was a bit on the melodramatic side. Yesterday I overheard a conversation between them that explained much."

He looked at Werthen sheepishly. "They were talking at a certain volume. I am no snoop."

"Nor was I suggesting you were."

"Well, it seems the two of them had invested a packet of money on a gold mine in South America and had just confirmed it was all a swindle. Lost their money and their self-respect, by the sound of it. They had just got wind of the possible problem last week. So that is presumably what they were discussing."

"Not thieves at all, then," Werthen said. "Rather the victims."

SEVENTEEN

The foul smell struck them like a hammer the instant they opened the door to Werthen's. Just as with skunk spray, the reaction to this stench was automatic and extreme. Werthen threw his hands over his mouth and nose, while Gross dug in his jacket pocket for a handkerchief to cover his face.

Halting in the doorway, they did not see Tor at first, then Werthen noticed a pair of boots sticking out from under the desk.

Wilhelm Tor had not died nicely. His mouth was twisted into a rictus of pain. Green bile and vomit was spread down the front of his vest. From beneath him exuded the noxious odor as a stain of waste spread on the parquet.

Gross, heedless now of the smell and horror of the scene, immediately got down on one knee and put a finger to the man's carotid artery. Then he leaned over, his nose centimeters from the man's gaping mouth and took in large breaths.

"Arsenic poisoning," he said, rising and brushing at his pants. "Unmistakable smell of garlic."

They quickly scanned Tor's desk and saw the edge of a small box under a sheaf of papers. Lifting the papers, Werthen discovered a container of powdered Turkish delight.

"Does this mean what I think it does?" he said.

"It would appear so," Gross replied. "A rather lovely form of irony. Herr Tor managed to poison himself with his own creation. He must have confused the poisoned pieces of candy with the original ones when his sweet tooth got the better of him." Gross sounded almost gleeful at this prospect.

"But this is patently absurd," Werthen said. "All our labors and investigations, and then to have the man do himself in accidentally."

"He was not the greatest strategist," Gross said. "After all, look at all the failed attempts he made on Mahler's life. No, I find this a most fitting conclusion to his miserable career in crime."

Gross bent over the man again, going through his pockets, and extracted a well-worn leather notebook cum money purse.

"And what of his accomplice?" Werthen said, for they both agreed he must have had help on the inside at the Hofoper in the early attempts on Mahler's life. "Perhaps, knowing somehow that we were getting close, this accomplice killed Tor to save himself?"

But Gross was not listening, too busy going through the leather notebook.

"Here's a familiar name," Gross said, handing the notebook to Werthen, his thick forefinger underscoring a name and address.

"Herr Ludwig Redl," Werthen read. The address was in the Twelfth District.

"Wasn't that the stagehand Blauer told you about?" Gross said. "The one he let go for incompetence?"

"It must be the same," Werthen said, making the connection now. "Tor's accomplice?"

"Most probably so," Gross said. "One would assume Tor hired him to do the deeds. To lace Mahler's tea with paint thinner, to drop the fire curtain."

"But Blauer indicated he'd already fired the man before the final attack at the Hofoper, the collapsing podium. He was supposedly off to America and a fresh start."

Gross shrugged this off. "This Redl fellow

423

could have rigged the podium long before he left. A stress fracture that finally gives out. He could have been thousands of miles away when the 'accident' finally happened."

Something did not seem right to Werthen about all this, but Gross's elation was infectious.

"One should not complain simply because we were unable to put the handcuff s on the man, Werthen. Sometimes fate gives the criminalist a hand in such matters. Now, I think it is about time we call Drechsler and apprise him of matters."

Drechsler, after arriving with a brace of policemen and listening to Werthen and Gross's explanation of the real identity of Wilhelm Tor, came to much the same conclusion that Gross had. Death by accidental ingestion of arsenic, which was obviously to be found in the Turkish delight.

"Serves the blighter right," Drechsler added. "Of course we will have to wait for the coroner's report, but it's a certainty the man's ingested a fair amount of the poison. And just as certain this batch was tainted with the poisoned sweets meant for Herr Mahler. This should make Meindl happy for once."

The other officers stood about the room

with noses stuffed into the crook of the elbows, trying to block the hideous stench. They were waiting for the arrival of an ambulance to remove the body to the city morgue in the cellar of the General Hospital.

"And Herr Redl," Gross prompted.

"Yes. To be sure. I'll dispatch some men out to that address immediately. There is always the possibility the man is still around, that he only spread the rumor that he was emigrating to America."

He nodded at the senior officer with him, who presumably went off to coordinate this particular errand.

Drechsler was almost smiling when Werthen looked at him now.

"Well, I imagine our Herr Mahler will breathe more easily now. Thanks to you chaps."

"Thanks more to Tor's own incompetence," Gross said, but one could tell he was proud of this outcome.

"You may still be able to vacation with your family," Werthen said to Drechsler, and the detective inspector nodded hungrily at the idea.

"I'd give my pension for a good night's sleep."

Twenty minutes later, with the ambulance

carrying the remains of Wilhelm Tor away, and after commissioning the *portier,* Frau Ignatz, to get a cleaning crew into the office by morning, Werthen and Gross were on their way back to the Josefstädterstrasse.

The early evening was glorious. The sky over the Josefstadt to the west was turning pink suffused with peach. Gross whistled bits and pieces from Mozart: a portion of an aria from *Cosi fan tutte,* a line or two repeated endlessly from *Eine kleine Nacht-musik.* He was clearly pleased with the outcome, but Werthen felt a slight unease.

Perhaps it was merely the sense of anticlimax and that they had not been allowed to make the arrest. They could not question the man and confirm their suspicions. Instead, they would have to make do with their deductions, to whit, that Tor was in fact actually Wilhelm Karl Rott, younger brother of Hans Rott. He had formed a mania about Mahler, blaming him for everything, not just possible musical plagiarism, but for his brother's slip into insanity and ultimate death as a result of the tuberculosis he had contracted while in the asylum. Older brother Hans's incarceration and death forced Wilhelm to support himself however he could, and thus probably added to his resentment for Mahler. A large quota of sins to avenge.

How long had his hatred festered? There was no telling, but it did seem Wilhelm attempted to carve out a life for himself, for his law degree was genuine. In any event, Werthen now assumed that by early summer Tor had resolved to kill Mahler and had hired Redl, the stagehand at the Hofoper, to help him in this endeavor. How had the two met? Unless Drechsler was able to track the man down, they would never know for certain anything about this collaboration. They did know that such efforts led to the death of the soprano, Fräulein Kaspar. And what of Herr Gunther? He must have seen something from his seated position in the orchestra pit. Perhaps he approached Redl later and threatened him with exposure. Perhaps he could see that the dropping of the fire curtain was no accident at all, but rather the result of malicious intent. Gunther lived a meager existence: perhaps he hoped to better himself financially through his threats.

Whatever the case, Gunther paid for his knowledge with his life. Was it Redl or Rott, alias Wilhelm Tor, who did the deed? That, too, would be an uncertainty. And then came Berthe's fortuitous advertisement for a legal assistant. Fortuitous, for by this time

Rott-Tor must surely have known of Werthen's investigation. Thus, if hired, he would be on the inside of the investigation and also have access to Mahler away from the Hofoper. It must have seemed a heaven-sent opportunity for Tor, for it put him in direct contact with Mahler, enabling him to cut Mahler's bicycle brakes, and, when that failed, to poison him with arsenic-laced Turkish delights.

And what of the anonymous letter announcing the killing of the great composers of Vienna? As a member of the firm, Tor-Rott would be privy to much, Werthen knew. And suddenly a vague memory came to mind, of a day when he was making a list of suspects and Tor came in to deliver some pages to him. Did the man linger overlong by the desk? Had he seen that Werthen added a column of suspects from out of Mahler's youth, that his investigation was about to head in a new and, for Tor, danger-ous direction?

Most likely that was the case. Tor knew that, once the case of Hans Rott was uncov-ered, it would only be a matter of time before suspicion led to the younger brother, to himself, in fact. Thus, he concocted a diversion, a false trail for them to follow, which they happily did for a time, looking for someone who had killed Bruckner, Brahms, and Strauss, and who made an attempt on the life of Zemlinsky. And all the while, Tor was thus free to make further attempts on the life of Mahler. Not one of his or Gross's finer hours, Werthen thought as they walked through the Volksgarten and reached the wide expanse of the Ringstrasse.

And then there was the unfortunate Fräulein Paulus, the prostitute who was butchered in her garret. Clearly Tor had listened in to Drechsler's conversation at the office, and knew he was about to be identified. That final act of extreme brutality was clearly the act of a tortured mind. One could only be pleased that Tor's life had ended, that his string of evil deeds had been brought to an end, no matter by what means.

So why was Werthen still feeling on edge?

"Cheer up, Werthen," Gross said as they let a fast-moving *fiaker* pass by before crossing the Ring. "Your lady-wife is sure to be pleased with your labors. And for my part, I shall delight in sharing with Herr Meisner the final moments of our Wilhelm Tor."

Ten minutes later, reaching the flat in the Josefstädterstrasse, they discovered from Frau Blatschky that Berthe and her father

had left only moments before for the Hofoper.

The frau looked reprovingly at Werthen. "I tried to talk sense into her. A woman in her condition should not be out in public. But that father of hers! And the Schindler girl. Between them they convinced her." She clucked her tongue.

"I am sure it will be fine," Werthen said, disappointed at not seeing his wife.

Gross's disappointment was greater in learning that Frau Blatschky had not pre-pared any dinner.

"We shall dine out then," Werthen an-nounced, assuming a more cheerful air than he felt. "How about it, Gross? What do you say to a schnitzel at the Café Frauenhuber?"

"I would not protest, my friend."

After briefly freshening up and as they were about to leave, the phone rang. Wer-then answered it only to learn from Drechs-ler that Herr Redl was not to be found at the address in the Twelfth District. The landlady noted he had moved out weeks before, telling her he was on his way to Bremerhaven, there to catch a ship for the United States.

"The boys on the street will be happy now," Drechsler added before hanging up. "We can finally cancel the protective force detailed for Mahler and concentrate on crimes that have actually happened."

They took a *fiaker* to the café, and Gross paid the fare. Clearly they were to have a celebration this evening, so Werthen put aside his own odd feelings and enjoyed a glass of the *sekt* Gross ordered from Herr Otto.

The schnitzels, when they arrived, were appropriately large and the kraut salad was tangy, with just the right amount of wine vinegar and caraway.

Werthen was, in fact, beginning to actually feel celebratory when Herr Otto came to their table with a quizzical look on his face.

"Herr Advokat, I finally remember what it was I have been meaning to tell you."

"About Hanslick's South America debacle?" Werthen said merrily.

Otto shook his head. "No, sir. It was about the man who followed you last week."

"Yes," Werthen said. "That little matter seems to have been settled."

"In that case then, I won't bother you gentlemen. I hope you enjoy your meal."

But something in Herr Otto's expression raised Gross's curiosity.

"Do tell, Herr Otto. What is it you remembered?" the criminologist asked.

"Nothing really. Just a bit of physical description I failed to report earlier."

And as Werthen listened, he suddenly stiffened. He looked at Gross, and the criminologist was expressing the same concern.

Eighteen

"Wonderful seats," Berthe said. "Such a treat."

Fräulein Schindler squeezed her hand. "I told you," she said. "You need to get out more, Frau Meisner."

"Please," Berthe said. "Call me Berthe."

This pleased the younger woman so much that she leaned over and gave Berthe a kiss on the cheek.

"And what about the poor old gentleman to your right?" Herr Meisner said, for Alma Schindler was seated between them in the third row of the orchestra.

Alma leaned over and gave him a peck on the cheek, as well.

"Oh, this shall be such great fun," she said delightedly.

The orchestra began to tune up. They were close enough to hear each instrument separately. Berthe looked around the magnificent hall at all the men in their smoking tuxedoes and the women in tiaras and evening gowns, their opera glasses glued to their eyes, eagerly searching the crowd for friends or, better yet, nobility. One had to be quick at this, though, for Mahler's new regulations forbade the house lights to be up during performances. Seeing and being seen was thus relegated to these moments before the opera began.

Berthe felt a sense of lightness and elation. They were right, Alma and her father. She really did need to get out more.

Alma's opera glasses sat in her lap.

"Would you mind?" Berthe said, gesturing toward them.

"Be my guest."

Berthe slowly adjusted the focus to her eye. As faces came into sharp focus, Berthe began tracking the glasses around the great hall, catching intimate glimpses of those in the first and second tiers of boxes. A glittering tiara here, a mouthful of white teeth there. One fresh young man wearing a hussar's mustache and an insouciant grin waved at Berthe as she swung the glasses onto him.

Then suddenly she stopped the arc of the glasses, recognizing someone. The figure bobbed for a moment in the frame, but she held the small binoculars firmly and was able to focus clearly on the man.

Herr Siegfried Blauer. Unmistakable with those anachronistic muttonchop whiskers of his. She took the glasses away from her eyes for a moment, to see exactly where her telescoped gaze had wandered.

Yes, she thought so. He was sitting in the second tier of balconies, in Mahler's special box, quite alone. Putting the opera glasses back to her eyes, she saw him lean forward in his seat, laying his hands on the crimson-cushioned balustrade. Then he began moving his hands quite dexterously, as if playing the piano. It seemed at first a nervous tic, but he continued to move his hands to a silent rhythm, exactly as if at the keyboard.

What an extraordinary man, she thought. And what a chance he is taking sitting so brazenly in Mahler's box. Berthe well remembered that day when Herr Regierungs-rath Leitner had taken her and Karl on a tour of the Hofoper, and he had told her in no uncertain terms about Mahler's proclamation that no one was to use his box. Leitner himself, part of the opera administration, had concealed from Mahler the fact that he had been sitting in that box the day Mahler's podium had crumbled underneath him.

She stared up at the distant form of the

stage manager, Blauer. What was he doing there, anyway? One would think his proper place was backstage, making certain that all was in readiness.

"See somebody?" Alma said.

Berthe smiled at her. "No, not really."

Berthe was about to hand the glasses back, but Alma indicated she was more content to simply stare at the bucolic scene painted in gold relief onto the house curtain, waiting for the first glimpse of her beloved Mahler.

Another brief survey of the house accounted for several more familiar faces. Herr Leitner himself sat in a second-tier box near the stage on the opposite side of the auditorium from Mahler's. He was talking animatedly to a heavyset woman with a low décolletage and a vulgarly large ruby at her throat. His wife? But most men are not quite so animated with their own wives. Then Berthe realized who this was: Mahler's old flame, Anna von Mildenburg, who was, due to a mild cold, not performing tonight. She was, however, healthy enough not to miss this gala evening. The singer sat back in her chair, wearing an expression on her full mouth halfway between a smirk and a smile.

Then, only two boxes away, she caught

sight of Justine Mahler and Natalie Bauer-Lechner, both of them looking rather grim. Not even they were allowed into the sacrosanct precincts of Mahler's private box. Natalie tugged nervously at a garnet broach around her neck.

This was intriguing, Berthe thought.

Fifteen minutes later and the opera had still not begun. Berthe could hear the unmistakable sound of dogs barking from somewhere deep in the stage behind the house curtain.

"I do not know what the matter could be," Alma Schindler said, her voice sounding impatient. "Herr Mahler is usually so punctual."

"More time for us to gawp at all the finery," Herr Meisner said with a laugh.

They looked like ants. Self-important insects all dressed up in their finery, so pleased with themselves to be sitting in the elegant Hofoper, as if a ticket to this spectacle made their inconsequential lives worthwhile.

If they could only know beforehand of the plan, the elegant, final gambit. Those in the first few rows of the orchestra would never know of it. The rest, the survivors, could read about it in tomorrow's papers.

Only minutes to go now, and finally Herr

Gustav Mahler would receive just retribution.

Such a long wait. But it would all be worth it. Minutes left. Just minutes.

"Get those animals assembled on the stage," Mahler demanded, as the dogs strained this way and that. One emptied its bladder on the wooden base of what was supposed to be a marble column, making the gray paint run.

The trainer was called from the wings, trying to calm his dogs while the flustered cast member who was meant to lead the dogs in a triumphal entrance broke into a fierce sweat.

"Control your animals, will you?" Mahler thundered at the trainer, who now, like his operatic counterpart, began perspiring at an amazing rate, feeling the maestro's eyes boring into him like hot drills.

"I am sorry, sir," the red-coated usher said, "but we cannot allow you to enter without a ticket."

"And I am telling you," Werthen said, "that this is a matter of life and death. Prince Montenuovo himself has given us free passage."

This only served to make the usher more

disbelieving and suspicious.

"Fine, and the emperor has given me permission to toss out any rowdies. So now leave, gentlemen, or I will call for assistance."

Unbidden, Gross feigned a fainting spell, distracting the usher and giving Werthen the chance to jump around him and make a dash for the second tier of seating. What they had learned from Herr Otto made niceties such as reasoning with an usher irrelevant.

Werthen knew where he was headed. His initial meeting with Herr Regierungsrath Leitner stuck in his memory, as did the existence of the secret door that Leitner had showed him that day. It led backstage from the second-tier corridor; the one from which Mahler could quickly make his way from his seat to the stage during rehearsals.

Werthen gave no thought to his throbbing right leg as he stormed up the carpet-covered marble stairs, the usher now shouting behind him. Neither did he consider trying to find the administration and stop the performance. There was no time for that. Instinct told him that tonight there would be something conclusive, something dramatic. Something to end it all.

This was really too much; twenty minutes past opening time and still no sign of the conductor. The orchestra had fallen silent, finished with its tuning minutes before.

Berthe, still in possession of Alma's opera glasses, scanned the audience once more, focusing again on Blauer seated in Mahler's box. He was in a nervous state, Berthe could see, his hands continuing to move over the balustrade. The man's mouth was now pinched into an expectant scowl as well.

And then it all became clear to her. It was the mouth that did it, for it focused her attention on that part of the man's face when normally his muttonchop whiskers diverted her attention. Now she saw it, the Habsburg chin, or rather the famous lack of chin and the resulting overbite. Blauer had that pronounced hereditary blemish as surely as if he were a Habsburg himself.

But of course he was, if he were Hans Rott's illegitimate brother. That thought came clear and unbidden into her mind.

Karl had told them about this younger Rott brother, born on the wrong side of the sheets, perhaps the off spring of nobility. That would account for the man's startling resemblance to the Habsburgs.

And the way he moved his hands over the balustrade. Just like a trained pianist, not a stage manager from Ottakring.

What did they know of Blauer? They had not bothered to track down his bona fides, taking his word that he was who he claimed to be.

And seated in Mahler's box. Of course. It was meant as a personal affront. To be so public about it meant that Blauer intended to act tonight, to somehow do away with Mahler here and now at the Hofoper in front of the thousands of gathered devotees of music.

My God, it must be so, Berthe told herself. He had the means and opportunity for the attacks on Mahler here at the opera itself. As to Blauer's presence in Altaussee, they would have to later ascertain his whereabouts during those incidents.

For now, she knew she must act.

Blauer ceased his faux piano playing, suddenly thrusting himself out of his seat and moving out of Mahler's box.

She rose, as well.

"What is it, Berthe?" Alma said.

Berthe handed her the glasses. "Sorry. I must visit the ladies' room."

Her father showed concern and Alma

441

asked, "Would you like me to go with you?"

"No, no. It is fine. I shall be back in a moment."

What to tell them? That she surmised from a chin and nervous fingers that Blauer was the killer? They would only laugh.

The stage manager had met her before. She could at least approach him as an acquaintance. Speak with him. Find out one way or another.

She knew she was making no sense; so be it. Instinct drove her on. But what would she do once she reached the man?

Werthen did not ask himself why the house lights were not yet out. Something had delayed the performance, and whatever it was, he was thankful for it. The delay won him valuable time. What they had learned from Herr Otto still pulsed in his mind. One bit of description Herr Otto had failed to include: the man who followed him from the Café Frauenhuber the day he was attacked wore muttonchop whiskers.

Not Tor, then. Tor had been made to look the guilty party by someone else; someone who was still at liberty and could still do Mahler harm. That someone was clearly Siegfried Blauer, stage manager at the Hofoper.

The death of Tor could mean only one thing: Blauer intended to play his final hand tonight. Werthen was sure of it. Blauer had to be stopped, and by him. The police protection of Mahler had been canceled following the discovery of Tor's body, and neither Drechsler nor Meindl could be reached by phone. One had left for his family in the mountains, and the other was somewhere in attendance at the opera at this very moment.

Werthen quickly made his way along the now abandoned corridor to the second-tier stage door, looking quickly around before trying it.

Opening the door, Werthen found himself on the metal balcony high above the backstage. Below him a swarm of dogs were being cowed to submission by a handler. He thought he saw Mahler for an instant, but the man turned and left the area by a far door.

Then he caught sight of Blauer, just letting himself into the under-stage through a trapdoor in the main stage. Werthen quickly made his way down the metal stairs. A tall, lanky stagehand about the size of Werthen saw him descend, but only tipped his hat to him, thinking that if Werthen knew the existence of the secret door in the corridor, then he must be someone from administration.

"Blauer," Werthen said to the man. "I need to see him."

Werthen's failure to add the "Herr" to the name of the stage manager only confirmed in this man's mind that this interloper belonged.

"Herr Blauer is below stage," the worker glumly told him.

"Yes, I know. If you'll allow me." Werthen made for the trapdoor, but the stagehand stopped him.

"I'm sorry, sir," the man said.

"I need to speak with him urgently."

"No one is allowed down there but the stage manager during performances. The revolving stage is too dangerous."

One dog, its tail docked and ears long and silken, managed to escape its lead and started dashing about the stage.

"Get that dog," shouted the handler.

The stagehand averted his attention from Werthen for a moment to make a lunge for the hunting dog, and Werthen made a dash for the trapdoor.

In the under-stage, Blauer heard the trapdoor open overhead and to his rear before he could reexamine the charge he had earlier set. The delay in the start of the opera had made him skittish; he had to once again assure himself that all was in order. Now, however, he instinctively moved out of the dim light, partly concealing himself behind the massive iron support used to help revolve the stage from one scene to another. The barking of the hunting dogs grew louder as the door opened, and then a tall, slender man began descending the stairs, poorly backlit by the light coming from above.

That meddlesome lawyer again, Blauer thought, for Werthen and his friend Gross were much on his mind. He should be celebrating, Blauer told himself. But if the lawyer had come to the opera, it could mean only one thing. His intricate ruse had failed.

Blauer was suddenly disgusted with himself. He should have killed Werthen that day at the law office. Caved his head in for him properly, not just given him a warning tap. But Blauer had planned it to look like a break-in gone wrong, not a homicide. One further bit of diversion. After all, how could the guilty party be the humble and bumbling Herr Tor if he was in Altaussee when the attack happened?

But then later, when it was discovered that Tor was not in fact in Altaussee on the Wednesday, suspicion would be thrown on him all the more heavily.

Blauer would like to have gloated more over his many intricate maneuvers. Now, however, was not the time. Mahler would die tonight. And this idiotic lawyer was not going to stop him. He leaned over, plucking a razor-sharp dagger out of the sheath in his boot just as the new arrival reached the bottom step and ventured toward the stage-revolving machinery.

Berthe lost her way as she mounted the stairs toward the balcony boxes. By the time she had re orientated herself and found Mahler's box, it was empty.

So Blauer had not returned. Had he left the Hofoper altogether? She doubted it. After all, a stage manager's place was behind the curtains. It was what he did. It had to be where she would find him. She recalled the secret door Leitner had showed her and Karl, and leaving Mahler's box, she headed for the wall at the far end of the corridor.

They had wasted enough time with the dogs. Now it was time to begin.

Mahler pushed his shoulders back and strode through the side door into the auditorium. The lights began to dim as he marched solemnly to the orchestra pit and took his position at the podium, tapping his baton on the top of the music stand.

This would be a performance to be remembered, he told himself.

"Marvelous, isn't he," Alma Schindler whispered in Herr Meisner's ear as Mahler raised his arms, ready to commence the first notes of Wagner's overture.

"He does have the proper bearing," Herr Meisner returned in a whisper. "But poor Berthe. No getting back in now until the second act."

From behind, a florid woman in a sequined gown shushed them.

Blauer let the man pass the iron support behind which he was hiding before he made his move.

"Herr Blauer," the man called out.

Blauer cupped his left hand around the man's mouth and drove the blade upward into his back. There was a satisfying crunching sound as the blade went home. Air escaped the man's mouth and onto Blauer's cupped hand. He withdrew the knife and struck three more times, finally allowing the corpse to collapse to the ground.

There was no stopping him tonight.

■ ■ ■ ■

Werthen paced nervously by the trapdoor,
waiting for the stagehand to return. The fellow had released the loose dog and gripped
Werthen's arm just as he was about to lift
the trapdoor. He'd refused to let Werthen
pass, and was about to raise a stink about
it, perhaps drawing Blauer's attention.

Instead, Werthen had requested the stagehand to go below and fetch Blauer. He told
the astonished worker that Herr Regierungsrath Leitner himself needed to see him
urgently about the closing scene. There was
to be a last-minute change.

"Isn't that just like them," the stagehand
muttered. "Throw a wrench into things at
the last minute and expect us to fix things."

Werthen commiserated with the stagehand, but was firm about him fetching
Blauer.

But the worker had been gone too long
now. Werthen was suspicious. This was not
a good sign.

He heard the first notes of the overture
coming from the orchestra and at the same
time he inched the trapdoor open again.

Berthe opened the secret door to the backstage just as Werthen began descending the stairs under a trapdoor. She paid no attention to the admonitions of a stagehand that admission was restricted. Neither did she pay heed to her own body's warnings, the nausea returning that was a constant reminder of her pregnancy.

Karl might be in danger. That was the only thought on her mind.

Wagner's music filled the under-stage so that Blauer did not hear the trapdoor lifting again. Neither had he bothered to turn the dead man over and discover his mistake.

He saw that his deadly charge was still in place, and smiled. Just one more of those things, like wielding a knife lethally, that one learned from a life on the streets.

Again the white heat of anger rushed through him, thinking how his life had been formed — and ruined — by Mahler. If not for him, then Hans would have been a great musician, perhaps himself the director of the Hofoper, and he, Wilhelm Karl, could have also become a musician of note. Hadn't he shown his composition abilities with his coded note to Werthen and Gross? All these years of work and planning to get even with the man — assuming the persona of Siegfried Blauer and becoming a stage manager, just so he could get close to his quarry — and now he was within minutes of success. Now he must leave this dungeonlike under-stage before the first scene change.

As the music swept around him, Blauer turned to go.

"What are you up to, Blauer?"

Werthen stood facing him and Blauer gave a jump as if seeing a ghost.

Then Werthen glanced down at the still body of the stagehand, sudden rage filling him. "You animal."

Blauer did not say a word, but uttered a snarl, leaping onto Werthen and tumbling them both to the ground.

Werthen tried to roll away from the man, but Blauer had him in a bear hug, squeezing the life out of him. This was no time for gentlemanly behavior: Werthen brought a knee up into the man's testicles and heard him groan in pain. Blauer relaxed his grip for an instant and Werthen moved out of reach, but Blauer kicked his legs out of under him as he was rising. Pain seared through his right knee, but Werthen still tried to stumble to his feet.

In the dim light he caught the flash of a steel blade as Blauer swept his hand up from his boots. Sparks flew as the stage manager swept the knife at him, missed, and struck the iron stage support instead. Werthen quickly took his jacket off and wrapped it around his left arm as the other rose and circled toward him. Blauer feinted to the left and then struck to the right, but Werthen leapt back, out of reach.

Suddenly his backward progress was blocked by the iron support, and Blauer smiled like an insane person.

"That's it for you, Herr Advokat."

He lunged for Werthen, but his head suddenly jerked, and he gaped out of startled eyes. Then he crumpled to the ground.

In the space vacated by Blauer, Werthen now saw Berthe, one of her evening shoes gripped tightly in her right hand, its sharp heel broken from the impact.

"Berthe . . ." He held her in his arms for a moment.

"There's no time for that now," she protested, wriggling from his embrace.

"But how did you know about Blauer?" he asked.

"Nor for that," she said. "Explanations come later. What was he planning?"

Werthen lost no time in securing the unconscious Blauer with the laces from his own boots, hog-tying him securely with the leather laces. Then he made sure the man had no further weapons on him.

Only then did he notice wires leading from a leather bag, one attached with a brad to the underside of the revolving stage, and a second to the immovable stage flooring. The ends of these two wires were joined by a third scrap piece of wiring.

Werthen opened the satchel and discovered ten sticks of dynamite deftly and securely tied around a large dry-cell battery. The battery was connected by two wires to a thin pencil detonator. Wires led from this detonator to one side of a small black box that Werthen immediately recognized from his studies of electricity as a relay. On the other side of the relay the two overhead wires were connected.

Berthe, leaning over him, let out a low sigh.

"Get out of here," he said, rising and turning to her. "Tell someone above stage that there is a bomb set to go off."

The overture gave way to singing overhead, and suddenly the gears of the revolving stage churned into action. Both Werthen and Berthe quickly saw what was about to happen, for the piece of scrap wire connecting the two terminals overhead would stretch and ultimately break as the stage began to slowly move. Werthen realized that

Blauer had rigged the primitive bomb to be set off by the very movement of the revolving stage, employing the same kind of technology that a burglar alarm used. Once the overhead circuit or loop was broken, the relay would switch on to complete the circuit to the detonator, sending electric current into it and triggering a miniature explosion. This would, in turn, set off the sticks of dynamite. Chillingly, frighteningly logical. And very effective, Werthen knew.

"Run," he told her. "Now."

"There's no time," she said.

Indeed, there was no longer even time to get to the lever above to shut off the revolving stage. And Blauer was still unconscious, so he could give no assistance.

Werthen saw that he could not simply pull the overhead wires loose, for that would set off the bomb. Nor could he separate the detonator and battery from the dynamite, for they were strapped too tightly together for quick removal. Instead he would have to disarm the bomb at the load, at the charge itself. He had only seconds to act.

From his youthful days on the Werthen estate and helping the gardener, Stein, to dynamite beaver dams on the streams that flowed through their property, Werthen understood that this was a tricky maneuver.

Cut the wrong wire first, and there would be the same result as with breaking the overhead loop: the detonator would go off.

Two wires led from the battery to the detonator. Which one was it? He needed to cut the positive feed first, for that would stop the flow of electrical current. But it was too dark in the under-stage to make out any signs of positive or negative poles on the battery.

He searched the ground quickly for the knife Blauer had been wielding, found it, and held it to the wires. Sweat broke out on his forehead, dripped from the back of his hairline into his shirt collar. Which was the positive wire?

The stage moved slowly now, tugging at the overhead connection.

Which wire first?

The left one. It had to be blue. He closed his eyes trying to see the gardener Stein's gnarled hands as he worked such detonators.

"Hurry," Berthe urged, glancing upward as the wire connection between the revolving and fixed stage was about to rip apart.

No more time for thought. Werthen crimped a length of the wire and slid the sharp knife up and sliced quickly through it.

454

My God, what had he done? He had cut
the wire on the right. A sudden and instinc-
tual change of mind. No. It was more than
that. A rhyme from his boyhood had come
back to him: *"Links ist nichts, rechts ist am
besten."* A jingle taught to him by Stein to
recognize negative and positive wires: "The
left is nothing, the right is the best."

He let out his breath in one long, slow
exhalation, feeling Berthe's reassuring hand
on his shoulder.

Gross was still talking with the usher when
Werthen returned, the leather pouch con-
taining the dynamite in his hand.

The usher now was more solicitous than
before, having finally been shown Prince
Montenuovo's letter.

"Is everything in order, sir?" he said to
Werthen as he and Berthe came down the
stairs.

Werthen handed the pouch to the bewil-
dered man.

"I believe all is in order, yes," he said.

The usher opened the bag and gasped.

"Don't want to go dropping that," Werthen said. "Nasty stuff, dynamite."

Gross showed no surprise that Werthen
should return with not only high explosives
in hand, but also his wife.

"Looks as though you two had a near miss," Gross said, peering into the bag too.

"We all did," Werthen said. "But let the music play on."

This time when he embraced Berthe, she made no attempt to resist.

EPILOGUE

Several days later they were seated around the Biedermeier dining table in Werthen and Berthe's flat. Their afternoon tea consisted of a rather impressive *guglhupf* and a superbly flaky strudel. Frau Blatschky had outdone herself today, Werthen thought. Gross was regaling them with his interview with Siegfried Blauer earlier in the day at police headquarters.

"The man is clearly delusional," he said. "Blames Mahler for everything that ever went wrong in his life, starting with the death of his older brother Hans. But, as with many twisted personalities, he also possesses genius. And now that the game is up, he has been most cooperative. In fact, he takes great relish in sharing his devious plans."

Gross paused for a moment to enjoy a forkful of pastry.

"First and foremost," Gross announced, "was his disguise as Blauer, a self-educated man from Ottakring who was able to patiently work his way up to stage manager at the Hofoper once Mahler was made the new director. He took his time, did Blauer, relishing his revenge, trying different macabre ways in which to kill Mahler and not draw attention to himself. Then, once you confronted him at the opera, Werthen, he saw you as an adversary. He had to do something, and discovering there was a recent change of personnel in your law office, he went about befriending the hapless Tor. Did you know they had both been in America?"

"Tor told me he had lived there for a time," Berthe said.

"Yes, well," Gross continued, "it appears that Blauer, or Wilhelm Karl Rott, also made a trek across the ocean to find his fortune. In Blauer's case, however, he only found himself a slough of gambling debts and was thrown among the street gangs of New York. To pay off his debts he was forced to become a foot soldier for the East Side Duck Boys, with whom, it seems, he learned his dubious skills with poisons, knife-fighting, and bomb-making. He was only too happy to brag about his career this morning to me. He promises to write his memoirs, in point of fact. I am not sure how much of this is fact and how much fiction, but it does make for an intriguing tale and explains his knowledge of some deadly arts."

"One hopes for some biblical justice here," Herr Meisner said. "An eye for an eye. The man does not deserve to live."

Gross, however, was not to be detoured by a discussion of punishment.

"Blauer arranged a 'chance' meeting with the lonely Tor at a *gasthaus* the lawyer frequented. Tor was starving for friendship, companionship, a kind word from another human. It was easy to make him believe that he, Blauer, was really a true friend being persecuted by the opera administration, and especially by Herr Mahler. He convinced the needy Tor that everyone was against him, that they were trying to involve him in a series of accidents; trying to make it appear the he, Siegfried Blauer, was actually trying to kill Mahler. Blauer took a huge chance with the man, even telling him of the 'coincidence' of his visit to the violinist, Herr Gunther, the night of the man's suicide. And now they were trying to hang that death on him, as well, he had complained to Tor. And Tor had eaten it all up, had believed him and kept him informed of events in the ongoing investigation."

"How could he be so gullible?" asked Berthe. But then she remembered her initial interview with Tor and the self-deprecating manner he presented. Blauer had filled the vacuum Tor felt in himself.

Again, however, Gross was not allowing any digressions. He pushed on with his explanation as if not hearing Berthe.

"Once Blauer had a man on the inside of the investigation, as it were, he could begin to manipulate things. He was particularly elated about what he called his 'great musicians' gambit," Gross said. "As you surmised, Werthen, Tor did see your list of suspects and when he reported this to Blauer, that scoundrel knew it was only a matter of time before an examination of Mahler's youth would lead to Hans Rott and thence to his brother, as in fact it did. Thus his anonymous letter leading us to the false trail of somebody murdering our great musicians."

"So Tor had nothing to do with any of it?" Herr Meisner asked, a puff of powdered sugar on his upper lip.

"Only an unwitting accomplice," Gross said.

"It was fortunate that your Herr Otto remembered the muttonchops," Berthe said to her husband.

"Yes," Werthen allowed. "That was a close thing."

That night before proceeding to the opera, Gross and he had confirmed Tor's innocence by quickly checking Tor's handwritten documents at the office against the letters they had from the killer. None of the documents contained the telltale smudge.

Ignoring these comments, Gross blustered on. "Blauer also used Tor's trips to Altaussee as cover for his own evil doings. During Tor's first visit to Mahler's villa, Blauer himself snuck up at night to tamper with the brakes on the bicycle that clearly belonged to the composer. Later, Blauer even talked Tor into placing the poisoned Turkish delights in Mahler's study without the composer being aware of it. An anonymous gift from a fan, Blauer had told the credulous man. And Tor did not make the connection of Mahler's sudden illness with the presence of those tainted candies, nor did the newspapers report that such was the case."

The criminolgist finished his pastry, took a sip of coffee, and then smiled brightly.

"Blauer was most ingenious, I have to admit. He even implored Tor to stop over in Linz on his way to Altaussee on a wild-goose chase to deliver a supposedly urgent message to an imaginary friend of Blauer's. The stopover cost Tor the better part of Wednesday, and accounted for him arriving on Thursday in Altaussee. And when that was discovered, as Blauer knew it ultimately would be, then suspicion would be planted on Tor as the one who attacked you in the law office, Werthen. The game was up, however, after Tor told Blauer of the conversation between a police inspector and Werthen. Tor subsequently read newspaper reports of the death of the subject of said conversation, Fräulein Paulus, and unwisely confronted Blauer, his confidence and trust shriveled to a raisin of doubt. Blauer immediately knew that he must silence Tor. The man had served his purpose, anyway. All too easy to give him some doctored snuff — Tor's one bad habit — and then, after watching him die in painful convulsions, to simply leave some more poisoned Turkish delight at the scene and let Werthen and me draw our own conclusions.

"Unfortunate man," Berthe said. "Herr Tor, I mean."

"And what of the other loose ends?" Herr Meisner asked. "What, for example, of the alibi you say Blauer had for the day of the death of young Fräulein Kaspar?"

Gross nodded. "Yes, the loose ends. To be

certain, his absence was noted in Leitner's records. However, he was, in fact, there that day, hidden amidst the rigging high overhead. But from his seat in the orchestra Herr Gunther saw Blauer and wanted to blackmail him with such knowledge. With tragic results for Herr Gunther, I might add. The violinist should have stuck to music and left crime to the professionals."

"And what of the death of Strauss and the injury to Zemlinsky?" Herr Meisner further asked. "Those two incidents seemed to give real credence to Blauer's false trail about the deaths of Vienna's great musicians."

"Perhaps we shall never know about Herr Zemlinsky's fall, "Werthen said. "I hesitate to repeat the oft-repeated phrase, but accidents do happen, especially in the theater."

Werthen paused just long enough for Gross to add, "And about the death of Johann Strauss and the mysterious summons from the Hofburg that transformed his chill into pneumonia . . . Well, I have ascertained that Strauss's second wife was in Vienna during that time, visiting friends."

"As you suspected," Werthen said, nodding his head. "The angry ex-wife as culprit?"

"You cannot mean it," Berthe exclaimed. "She must be brought to justice."

Gross and Werthen both understood the impossibility of that suggestion, for any incriminating proof had already been destroyed by Strauss's widow. But neither said anything.

There was silence for a time and then Werthen said, "I feel somehow responsible for Tor. And for the innocent stagehand killed when Blauer mistook him for me."

"Nonsense, Werthen," Gross said. "The guilt is all on that villain Blauer, or Herr Habsburg as he now demands everyone address him. No, Werthen, do not put such blame on yourself. We have done our duty by Herr Mahler."

"*And* Fräulein Schindler," Herr Meisner reminded them. "They will make a splendid couple, I believe."

Herr Meisner was prescient in such a statement. Werthen knew that whatever that young woman sought, she would get.

In the silence which this remark induced Gross suddenly slapped his thigh.

"My apologies, Werthen. In all the tumult, I have forgotten a most important telephone message I took for you early this morning. It seems your parents are coming for a visit."

Werthen could not have been more surprised if Gross had told them the North Pole was melting. Looking at Berthe, he could see she shared his amazement.

Gross smiled at them somewhat sheepishly. "Thought it might be good if the future grandparents were informed of your wife's condition, so I sent them a letter not long ago. I do hope you've no objection."

Berthe answered for them. "None at all, Doktor Gross. None at all."

ABOUT THE AUTHOR

J. Sydney Jones is the author of twelve books, including the nonfiction *Hitler in Vienna, 1907–1913,* the guides *Viennawalks* and *Vienna Inside-Out,* and the Vienna-based suspense novel *Time of the Wolf.* A long-time resident of Vienna, Austria, he now lives in Santa Cruz, California.

The employees of Thorndike Press hope you have enjoyed this Large Print book. All our Thorndike, Wheeler, and Kennebec Large Print titles are designed for easy reading, and all our books are made to last. Other Thorndike Press Large Print books are available at your library, through selected bookstores, or directly from us.

For information about titles, please call:
  (800) 223-1244

or visit our Web site at:
  http://gale.cengage.com/thorndike

To share your comments, please write:
  Publisher
  Thorndike Press
  295 Kennedy Memorial Drive
  Waterville, ME 04901